WITHDRAWN

Mollie On The Shore

Mollie On The Shore

Elizabeth Jeffrey

PIATKUS

Copyright © 2005 by Elizabeth Jeffrey

First published in Great Britain in 2005 by
Piatkus Books Ltd of
5 Windmill Street, London W1T 2JA
email: info@piatkus.co.uk

The moral right of the author has been asserted

A catalogue record for this book is available from the British Library

ISBN 0 7499 0756 8

Set in Times by
Action Publishing Technology Ltd, Gloucester

Printed and bound in Great Britain by
William Clowes Ltd, Beccles, Suffolk

Acknowledgements

My thanks for their invaluable help to: Jane Stanway and the staff at the Local Studies Department, Colchester Public Library; staff at Walton-on-Naze Library; Liz Bruce and Joan Barker at Frinton and Walton Local History Society.

Author's Note

Copperas was a strange, twig-like mineral, with pieces sometimes as thick as a man's thumb. Found in the London clay of the North East Essex coast, it was washed up by the tide or out of the cliffs on to the beach, and was collected every day by the 'mine (short for mineral) pickers' and taken to the Copperas House, where it was steeped and boiled and processed into crystals to be used in dyeing, tanning and ink-making. It was also used as a component of gun-powder. The industry died out with the decline of the cloth trade in the middle of the 18th century.

Bibliographical resources:
The Victoria County History of Essex, Vol II, 'The Copperas Industry'
British Archaeology, Issue 66 – 'The Forgotten Chemical Revolution'
Copperas & The Castle by Geoffrey Pike
Smuggling in East Anglia 1700 – 1840 by Sam Jarvis
The Tankerton Copperas Works & The Copperas Industry in the South of England by Tim Allen & Geoffrey Pike

To my grandchildren,
Rachael, Benjamin, Jessica, Matthew, Katie, James and
Daniel, with my love.

Chapter One

'Ain't you got no 'ome to go to?' Old Sol said grumpily as Mollie tipped the last basket of 'mine' into his tumbrel and marked it off on her tally stick. He rummaged in his voluminous pocket, brought out a dull-looking token and handed it to her. 'The rest o' the pickers left hours ago.'

'Ten minutes, more like.' Mollie spat on the token and put it in her pocket.

'Well, you're the last one.' He gave his old donkey a nudge and began to trudge up the beach for the last time that day, back to the yard known as the Copperas House at the other end of the village, to empty the cart of the copperas 'stones' or 'mine' that the pickers had gathered.

Mollie watched him go, then turned, kicked off her shoes and went down to the water's edge. This was the time she liked best, when the rest of the pickers were gone, having cleaned the beach of the twig-like lumps of copperas that were washed up out of the sea or out of the London clay of the cliffs every day.

The water was warm as it lapped her ankles. She bent and splashed her arms and face, reviving herself after the last four hours spent bent almost double picking up pieces of the dull-brown mineral. The last day of June in the year 1801 had been scorching hot, with a heat haze shimmering over the sand. The picking, which always had to be done between tides, had been when the sun was at its hottest.

1

Mollie had been glad of her faded bonnet with its deep frill at the back to keep the sun off her neck. Her arms were already burned brown.

She lifted the skirt of her old cotton dress higher and sloshed a little deeper into the water, savouring the luxury of five minutes absolute peace. There was not a soul to be seen. Even the Grainger girl from the big house on the cliff, who sometimes wandered about at the very far end of the beach, hunting no doubt for pretty shells, was not there today. She lifted her face to the gentle, cooling breeze that had recently sprung up and closed her eyes blissfully.

Suddenly, a wave higher than the rest rolled in, covering her knees and the hem of her bunched skirt, a reminder that the tide was now rising quite fast. Reluctantly, she turned from the water and made her way up the beach to where she had left her shoes. She wiped the sand off her feet with the hem of her skirt and slipped her feet into them. She was quite proud of her shoes. They had only cost sixpence from the second-hand clothes shop and they almost fitted. She straightened up with a resigned sigh. Time to go home to the cottage beside the Copperas House and Aunt Rose's perpetual nagging and complaining.

Mollie had lived with Aunt Rose, Uncle Sam and cousin Richard ever since she could remember but she had always known that she was not their child. It was no secret that she had been born in Frinton and that when her mother, Jane, who was Uncle Sam's sister, died, not many days after Mollie was born, Uncle Sam had fetched her and brought her to Nazecliffe to live with him and Aunt Rose. Mollie had the distinct impression that Aunt Rose hadn't been consulted over this and had not been well pleased to have an orphaned baby foisted on her, particularly as the child's father had immediately gone away and joined the Navy. Mollie often wondered about her father; what he was like and where he might be on the high seas. Ever since her earliest years she had dreamed of him returning with untold riches and whisking her off to live in some beautiful foreign city with him. It was a dream that hadn't changed in all her sixteen years. Neither had it materialised, for he had never come back, even for a visit.

She took her time walking home from the beach, but as she turned into the narrow, rutted, shop-lined High Street, she felt an arm draped round her shoulders and a familiar voice said, 'Ma says she hopes you've earned enough tokens to buy four hot pies from the pie shop for supper.'

She twisted round and looked up into her cousin Richard's affectionately grinning face. 'An' if I haven't, I'll give you three guesses who'll have to go without,' she said resignedly, rummaging in her pocket and bringing out three tokens with the letters J G stamped on one side and NAZE-CLIFFE on the other. 'I on'y picked six bushels today,' she explained. 'It was so hot on the beach...'

'You reckon you were hot! You shoulda bin shovellin' coal all day in the boiler house, like I have,' Richard said, 'Nearly killed me, it did. Beats me how me Dad manages, workin' in that heat all the time. As soon as I finished work I went down and took a dip in the sea to cool off.'

'I didn't see you,' Mollie said in surprise.

'No, I was up by the old church, well outa sight. Well, come on, are you gonna get these pies? You don't want to be in trouble with Ma again, do you.'

'No. I'll be in trouble enough because I on'y picked six bushels. She don't like it if I don't pick at least eight. I'd like to see her pick eight bushels on a tide. Specially in this heat.' Mollie rubbed her aching back.

'I'd like to see her pick one bushel!' Richard laughed. 'Poor old dear, she's getting so fat she has a job to get out of her chair these days.'

Mollie darted into the pie shop and bought the pies in exchange for two tokens. These the shopkeeper could redeem from the office at the Copperas House at the rate of tuppence a token.

'She doesn't need to,' she said, resuming the conversation where it had left off. 'She jest orders me around to do

3

everything. I even have to tie her boot laces for her. She's lazy, thass her trouble.'

Richard was silent. He didn't like to be too disloyal to his mother but he couldn't deny that what Mollie said was true. He was aware that his mother disliked Mollie, a dislike that seemed to be growing rather than lessening as the years went by. She had resented having Mollie thrust on her after Aunt Jane had died and she had often been cruel to her. Richard couldn't count the number of times he had rescued the poor shivering little girl from the coal shed where she'd been banished for some trifling misdemeanour and cleaned her up before she could be sent back again for getting herself dirty. He had never forgotten and neither had Mollie. Any more than either of them could forget the beatings. Richard never got beaten, it was always Mollie who bore the brunt of Rose's temper, which could be sudden and vicious. When he was little Richard had cried with her, shouting out to his mother to stop hurting Mollie, feeling the pain as keenly as if the stick had beaten his own back. Afterwards he would cuddle her, holding her quaking little body close and wiping away her tears. These experiences had forged a bond between the cousins as close as that of any brother and sister.

Mollie thrust a pie into Richard's hand. 'Thass yours,' she said firmly.

'Why? What's wrong with it?' he asked, turning it over.

'Nothin'. It's the biggest.' She grinned and winked up at him. At eighteen, two years older than Mollie, he was already a head taller. 'You're a growin' lad. Go on, take a bite, then she can't pinch it for herself.' Mollie had learned ways to get the better of her aunt. 'Half a minute. I'd better get a loaf as well.' She disappeared into the baker's.

The purchases made they turned right out of the High Street into Copperas Lane. This was even narrower than the High Street, little more than a rough cart track between two rows of drunk-looking wooden cottages. As they went

4

along a vile, pungent smell, sulphurous and choking, began to fill the air. It came from the Copperas House, a huddle of large black buildings in a yard at the end of the lane, over which a pall of thick smoke hung to add to the stink. The boiler house stood in the middle of the yard and to one side of it was a huge heap of sea coal. A block of wooden stables adjoined a brick-built counting house and there were several long, low sheds beyond which were the pits where the copperas was left to dissolve. Outside the yard on the leeward side, although this really didn't make much difference as far as the stench was concerned, stood a small brick house. This was the house where the 'copperas boiler', the man responsible for every stage of processing the copperas, lived, rent-free.

Mollie was very proud that Uncle Sam was the copperas boiler at Grainger's Copperas House. It was an important job. She idolised her Uncle Sam. He was everything Aunt Rose wasn't, even in appearance. Whereas Aunt Rose had been quite a big woman, even before she ran to fat, he was a small, wiry man yet with the strength of an ox. Where Aunt Rose was bad tempered and intolerant he was mild mannered and peace loving. He was always kind and gentle with Mollie and when he was at home Aunt Rose somehow managed to curb her tongue; if she wasn't exactly friendly she hardly ever shouted at Mollie and never, ever hit her. Mollie had often wished Uncle Sam could stay at home all the time.

They reached the house and went up the three steps to the door, which was standing open. Aunt Rose was sitting just inside, fanning herself.

'Did ye get the pies?' she greeted Mollie.

'Yes. They're still hot.' Mollie opened the bag and showed her.

'On'y three?' Rose's lip curled. 'Lazy little bitch, ye didn't pick enough mine to get four, did ye. Well, ye know who'll go 'ithout, don't ye.'

'I've got the other one, Ma,' Richard said, taking

5

another bite of the pie in his hand. 'I was fair starved so I made Mollie gimme mine straight away.'

'Well, you're a growin' lad.' His mother smiled on him fondly. Then her smile died as she turned to Mollie. 'I don't s'pose you thought to bring a loaf as well, did yer?'

'Yes, I did.' Mollie put it on the table.

'Hmph.' Mildly disappointed, Rose shrugged. 'Go an' find yer uncle. Tell him there's a pie here waitin' for 'im.'

'I can do that, Ma,' Richard said.

'No. You've jest done a hard day's work, boy. She can go.'

'Yes. I don't mind.' Mollie took off her bonnet and laid it on the bench beside the door, then she ran her fingers through her thick, dark hair to free it from the constraints of the bonnet and went across the practically deserted yard to find her uncle. She was quite a tall girl and walked with an easy stride, her head held high. Her looks were striking rather than pretty; her mouth a little too wide, her nose a little too long. But her eyes were quite beautiful; they were large and an unusual tawny brown, fringed by long, dark, curling lashes under finely arched brows. She was looking eagerly for sight of Sam because she savoured what little time she could spend with him out of earshot of Aunt Rose. She passed the shed that held the furnace and the big lead-lined boiler. She had never, ever been allowed in there; it had always been impressed on her that it was far too dangerous. The men who worked in there wore special thick leather aprons and breeches, with gauntlets up to their elbows because of the risk of being splashed by the boiling liquid as they stirred the vats with huge paddles. Sam was at the far end of the yard where it reached almost down to the quayside, standing beside the long, shallow, sloping, chalk-lined pit into which the copperas, collected every day from the beach, was tipped. Two men were raking over the 'stones', while another man poured water on to them.

6

'That'll do for ternight,' he called to the men as he turned away and went to the shallowest end of a second pit, where he stood looking at the dark, evil-smelling, sulphurous liquid that was forming from stones that over time had begun to dissolve. This liquid drained through a wooden trough into a holding cistern. He nodded to himself and then glanced up and smiled as he saw Mollie.

She came over and linked her arm through his, heedless of the filthy leather apron he was wearing. 'There's a pie for you in the house, Uncle,' she said. 'All hot and steamy. I've jest brought 'em home from the pie shop.'

'You're a good gal, Mollie,' he smiled at her affectionately. His gaze softened even further. 'An' with them big brown eyes you're gettin' to be the very image of yer mother. She was a beauty, too.' His tone changed abruptly and he turned away, untying the thick leather apron. 'I'll jest go an' take this clobber off and clean meself up a bit or I shall get it in the neck from yer aunt. Tell 'er I'll be there as soon as I've had a word with Mr Mark. I wanta check the scrap iron's been delivered to put in with termorrer's boil.'

Mollie knew what he was talking about. Scrap iron was added to the liquid from the cistern when it was boiled in the great lead-lined boiler. The boiling could take several days, during which more scrap was added as needed and more 'liquor' as it evaporated. When the boiling was done the resulting liquid would be poured into tanks and left to crystalise. It was a lengthy, time-consuming, dirty, evil-smelling business, but Sam was a conscientious man and loved his work.

Mollie waited a few minutes after he had gone into the counting house, hoping that perhaps Mr Mark would come out with him. Mark Hamilton, or Mr Mark as he was always known, was manager at the Copperas House. He was tall and rangy, with a pleasant, open face, a ready smile and fair hair that he had a habit of running his hands through when he was thinking. Unlike most of the men, he

7

rarely wore a hat. He was related to the Graingers – James Grainger owned the Copperas House although he didn't visit it much – and according to Uncle Sam knew more about running the place than anybody. Sam had great respect for Mr Mark. So had Mollie, because he knew who she was and sometimes smiled at her if he saw her in the yard.

She waited a little longer but when it was apparent that Mr Mark wasn't coming out she went back to the house. Eventually, Sam appeared and the four of them took their places at the table, Richard and Mollie on stools, Sam and Rose at either end in Windsor elbow chairs. Mollie had already cut slices from the loaf and she was about to take a bite of her pie when Rose said in the wheedling tone she used on Mollie when Sam was around, 'I could do with a cuppa tea now, Mollie, love. I'm fair parched.'

Immediately, Mollie got up and poured her a cup. There was never any shortage of tea in the house; Richard saw to that. He and three friends had a small boat that they took fishing. Most of the 'fish' they caught were in the form of tea and tobacco, wrapped in waterproof packets, which had been dropped into the shallows off the coast over the side of boats coming into Harwich from the continent. Not only tea and tobacco but all manner of contraband might find its way to the shore on a good haul, provided the Revenue Cutter and the Riding Officer were busy patrolling another part of the coast.

Richard's somewhat risky method of supplementing his income was accepted with pride by his mother and with reluctance by his father, their silence bought with some of the little luxuries the upper classes took for granted. Rose was fond of a tot of genever and Sam was not averse to a pipe of tobacco or a tot of rum on a cold night.

Mollie worried about Richard's activities but not for the world would she have betrayed him.

She sat down again to her now lukewarm pie but before she could take a bite Rose wanted more bread; then she

8

wanted jam; then another cup of tea, all requested in the same wheedling, apologetic voice. But whatever her tone the result was the same – by the time Mollie ate her pie it was cold and everyone else had finished. It was always like that and if Sam offered even a word of protest Rose would round on him.

'Thass right, man, take her part. You always side with her. She's your little pet. Never mind me. Never mind my sufferin'. You know the pain I'm in all the time; you know what a job I have to walk; yet you expect me to get up and wait on everybody hand and foot while she sits on her backside and does nothin'.'

'It's all right, Uncle. I don't mind,' Mollie said now, as she saw Sam about to argue. 'I'm a lot younger than Aunt Rose.'

'An' not so fat,' Richard murmured under his breath as he got up from the table.

'What did you say?' His mother glared at him.

'Nothin'. I'm off out now.'

'Where to?'

'If you don't ask questions you won't get no lies told you.' He tapped the side of his nose.

A smile spread over Rose's face. 'Yes, boy, we're runnin' a bit short o' tea.'

'Then you'll hev to eke it out. I'm off down the pub.' He picked up his cap and went out. Sam followed him, but only as far as the step, where he sat down and filled his pipe with illicit tobacco. The searing heat of the day had gone but the air was still oppressive and filled with sulphurous fumes and smoke. Sam was so used to the stink that he didn't even notice it and neither did his wife, sitting in her chair in the doorway. Only Mollie, who spent hours every day in the clean, salty atmosphere of the beach, felt stifled by the perpetual stench even though she had lived with it all her life.

She gathered the platters from the table and took them to the shelf under the window where a tin bowl stood. She

9

poured hot water from the kettle on the hearth and a ladle of cold rainwater from the tub under the shelf to wash them up. Then she put them in the cupboard next to the chimney breast. When she had tipped the water out into the yard and made sure that everything in the room was neat and tidy she said goodnight to her aunt and uncle and went up to her room.

Because it was up under the eaves it was quite a large room, covering the space of the two bedrooms below, but the slope of the roof meant that there was only a small area in the middle where she could stand upright. Nevertheless, it was her room, her refuge, where neither Richard nor her uncle would wish to come and invade her privacy and her aunt wasn't able to because the stairs were too steep and narrow. It had always been the one place where she could escape to avoid her aunt's wrath and the stick with which she vented it.

Mollie loved her little room. She had made a patchwork cover for the bed and a rag rug for the floor. There was a chest of drawers under the window and on this were arrayed pretty shells that she had found on the beach when she was picking mine. In pride of place was a piece of greyish stone that was shaped rather like a snail that she had found in the cliff one day. She had sometimes searched for another one but she had never found one. She had an old wicker chair in the corner opposite the stairs and she had made a patchwork cushion for it so the hole in the seat was covered.

She opened the window to let a little air in and leaned her elbows on the sill. Beyond the Copperas House she could see the busy quayside where the sea coal for the furnace and the scrap iron for the boiler was unloaded from barges before the river snaked off into the distance between green fields and hedges. She often marvelled how the river came in from the sea and curled round on itself, turning the tall cliffs at the far end of the town into a peninsular with the sea on one side and the river

10

on the other. She sighed. It must be wonderful to live high up on top of those cliffs, like the Graingers did, far away from the smoke and stink that was making their fortune for them.

Chapter Two

The hot days of summer cooled into autumn and autumn froze into winter. Nothing else changed. Every day except Sunday the women, mostly from the cottages in Copperas Lane, were out gathering the stones that had been washed up on the shore or out of the cliff. After a high, stormy tide the pickings were good, especially if the sea had lashed the cliff, undermining it and bringing chunks of it sliding down on to the beach. But that didn't happen often.

Mollie was out each day between tides with the rest of the pickers, most of them, like her, wearing red, hooded cloaks – in varying states of disrepair – as protection against the biting wind or driving rain. When the picking was finished for the day she would hurry home to soak her chilblain-swollen hands in warm water to get some life back into them. But even Aunt Rose agreed, albeit grudgingly, that sometimes the weather was too bad for working on the beach.

There was one thing to be said for Aunt Rose, she kept a good fire. In fact, the living room was often warm to the point of stifling, because there was no shortage of sea coal to keep it going. Sam Barnes, being the all-important boiler man, was allowed to take as much as he needed from the great heap beside the boiler house for his own use.

Compared with the amount the great furnace under the boiler took this was very little. Richard filled the box on wheels that served as a coal scuttle every morning but on a really cold day Mollie would be sent to replenish it at least once. She hated this. She felt humiliated walking through the yard pulling the coal box and shovelling coal into it while the men were at work, and more than anything she dreaded that Mr Mark might see her, although she wasn't quite sure why it mattered. For the most part the men ignored her because they didn't quite know how to treat her. She belonged to Sam Barnes and he was in a class of his own, neither one of the labourers nor part of the management. Yet it didn't seem right that a young girl like her should be heaving coal and now and again one of them would say sheepishly as he passed her, 'Here, give us the shovel. I'll do that for yer,' and be rewarded with a grateful smile.

One of the reasons Rose Barnes enjoyed a good fire was that when nobody was about – except Mollie, of course and she didn't count – she would lift her ample skirts to warm her knees, with the result that her shins, which nobody saw so it didn't matter, were mottled purple. Most of her day was spent warming her knees and drinking tea and woe betide Mollie if she didn't keep the kettle filled from the tap in the yard.

Now that she was older and Aunt Rose less mobile Mollie received the lashings from Aunt Rose's tongue rather than her stick. Rose had given up the stick when her niece's agility began to exceed her own, but whereas lashings from the stick were only painful for a short while, the continual carping and complaining went on and on until sometimes Mollie was ready to scream.

'When did you last polish my brass? You know I like my brass to look nice. When I could do it myself I could see my face in it all the time. Look at it now! I'd be ashamed for anybody to walk in the door and see it.'

'I'll do it when I've finished the ironing, Aunt Rose.' Mollie picked up the second flat iron from the hearth, spat on it to make sure it was hot enough and went back to the

13

heap of ironing on the table. Privately, she thought it wouldn't hurt Aunt Rose to polish her own brass. She could do it sitting in the chair. But wisely she said nothing as she ran the iron expertly over her uncle's shirt.

'No, you won't. You know very well you've got to go and get meat from the butcher's for tonight's stew. An' then it'll be time to go pickin' and you hevn't even got the vegetables ready. High tide was an hour ago and there'll be good pickins today after last night's storm.' Rose lifted her skirts a bit higher and rubbed her knees. 'Oh, I know you, missy. You'll dawdle about and dawdle about till it's too late to find anything on the beach, you lazy little toad.'

Mollie bit her tongue against a sharp rejoinder. She was tired because last night the howling gale and the rain beating on the roof of her attic room had kept her awake, but she managed with difficulty to keep her voice level as she asked, 'Which shall I do first, finish the ironing, prepare the vegetables or fetch the meat, Aunt?'

'Finish that shirt, then go and get the meat. And mind and make sure he doesn't fob you off with gristle. You'll hev to take it back if he does. I'm not payin' for rubbish.'

An hour later, with the stew bubbling over the fire, the coal box replenished and dumplings all ready for Aunt Rose to drop into the pan, Mollie shrugged on her red cloak and thick shoes and headed thankfully for the beach.

High tide had been at midday and it was now just past two o'clock. As she left behind the stink that hung perpetually over Copperas Lane and hurried down the High Street towards the beach Mollie sniffed the air, which was clear and sharp and sweet smelling. She lifted her head towards the sun, shining now in a brilliant blue sky as if to make amends for the gales and rain of the previous night. She took a deep breath. It was the last day of March and even though it was still bitingly cold, it was good to be alive. It was also her birthday, although of course nobody had thought to mention the fact. Nobody ever did, in case it set

14

Aunt Rose off on one of her hard-done-by monologues, aimed partially at her husband; how she'd been forced into bringing up *his* sister's child, as if she hadn't enough to do bringing up her own. Mollie sighed. She'd heard it so many times she could recite it off by heart.

The fact that her birthday was never recognised hadn't stopped Mollie keeping a careful tally over the years and she knew that today, 31 March 1802, she was seventeen years old. Seventeen and quite ready to fall in love. If only she could find someone to fall in love with. Preferably someone whose life didn't revolve round that stinking hole of a Copperas House, she thought bitterly, pulling her cloak more closely round her.

She could hear the waves pounding long before she reached the beach. It always took a long time for the sea to settle down after a gale had whipped it into a heaving, frothing frenzy. After last night's lashing the sand on the beach was flattened and littered with great mounds of brown seaweed and piles of shingle that had been hurled up from the sea bed. Copperas in all shapes was plentiful and the pickers were already out, calling to each other and complaining about the cold. Most of them Mollie recognised from the cottages and they gave her a smile and a nod of recognition. At the gap in the cliff at the end of the beach Old Sol and his donkey were waiting patiently for the full baskets to be emptied into his tumbrel, Old Sol stamping his feet and flapping his arms across his chest in an effort to keep the worst of the cold out.

Mollie took up her basket and began picking up lumps of the brownish-coloured mineral. It was generously strewn along the beach so it wasn't long before she had a basketful and she began to drag it back to where Old Sol was waiting.

'Thass a bit heavy for you. I'll carry it for you, if you like,' a man's voice said from behind her.

She straightened up and turned to see a pleasant-looking

15

young man of about Richard's age in a thick fisherman's guernsey and a battered sou'wester coming across the beach towards her.

Seeing her surprise he grinned, his teeth showing white in his weatherbeaten face. 'Well, I know how heavy a full basket of this stuff is,' he said, picking it up as if it was no weight at all. 'I used to come and help my ma to pick mine when I was a young shaver. That was afore I started fishin' with me dad.' He nodded towards the dark, angry-looking sea, where white horses could be seen on the tops of the waves almost to the horizon. 'Too rough to take the smack out in this weather. Dad an' me always say, if you're caught out in it you hev to make the best of it but there's no sense in askin' for trouble.'

He emptied the basket into Sol's cart and waited while Mollie made the mark on her tally stick, then he walked back along the beach with her.

'Hev I seen you afore?' he said as they began filling the basket again.

She shrugged. 'Dunno. I don't reckernise you.'

He shook his head. 'No, I don't come this way as a rule. I live further along the coast road towards Frinton.' He stole a glance at her and his face cleared. 'I know who you are,' he said with a note of triumph, 'You live with my mate, Dick Barnes. You're his sister.'

'No, I'm not Richard's sister, I'm his cousin,' Mollie corrected him, faintly irritated. 'But you're right, I live with him and my uncle and aunt.'

'Well, thass near enough for me. I knew you was suthin' to do with Dick. I seen you with him a time or two. My name's Joe Trayler.'

Her face cleared. 'Ah, yes. I seem to recall him mentionin' your name. Mine's Mollie. Mollie Barnes.'

He grinned at her. 'Pleased to meet you, Mollie Barnes.'

As they talked he helped her to fill the basket again and again. Soon she had eight tokens in her pocket.

'I'd better not collect any more today,' she said with a

16

laugh. 'Aunt Rose'll expect me to work at this rate all the time.'

'Well, we'll do a bit more, then you can keep a couple o' tokens in your pocket ready for when you don't hev such a good day,' he advised, smiling at her.

'I never thought of that,' she admitted as they began to fill the old basket again.

'Did you know there was another cliff fall round by the old church last night?' he said as they worked. 'It's right on the edge now. Look, you can see it from here.'

She straightened up and shaded her eyes with her hand. 'Good heavens! It looks as if it'll topple in the water any minute.'

'When we've finished here we'll go an' take a closer look.'

'I don't know whether I should,' she said doubtfully.

He looked surprised. 'Why not?'

'Well, I don't know you, do I.'

'I've told you, I'm Dick's mate.' He shrugged. 'But if you don't want to...'

She hesitated, then she nodded. 'Yes, yes, I do. I'd like to come.'

'Thass good. It's not that far, so it won't take long.' He picked up the basket and took it to Old Sol, then she stowed it with a heap of others on the shore and they set out to walk to the old church.

The beach had been partially sheltered from the wind but out on top of the cliff it howled and buffeted as if it was angry that it hadn't done more damage in last night's storm. Mollie pulled her red cloak more closely round her and shivered.

'Cold?' he said. 'You dunno what cold is. You oughta be out there fishin' for cod when it's like this, then you'd know what cold is. There's bin times we've had to chip the ice orf the riggin' so the weight of it don't turn the boat over.'

'No thanks,' she said, shivering again.

17

When they had walked for nearly half a mile the cliff path suddenly ended. It was as if a giant had taken a huge bite out of the cliff, leaving the path on one side of the yawning gap and the church teetering on the edge of the other. In between, down on the beach, was a huge jumble of gravel with lumps of masonry sticking through it.

'We'll go round the other side, but better keep away from the edge in case more of it crumbles away,' Joe said. 'Look, can you see them two coffins sticking out o' the cliff? Thass where another bit o' the churchyard has gone.'

'Ugh!' Mollie shuddered.

'Oh, thass nothin' new. Sometimes bits o' coffin are washed up on the beach from previous cliff falls,' he said nonchalently. 'People take 'em home an' build rabbit hutches.'

'What about the bodies?' Mollie whispered.

'Oh, they're long gone. Either crumbled into dust or washed away. Sometimes one'll fetch up in Pennyhole Bay round by the point, but not often. Watch your step, here, it's a bit crumbly.' He took her arm to guide her. 'Shall we go and look in the church?'

'Might as well, now we're here. I've never been in this church.'

'No, it ain't bin used for a long time now. It's not safe.'

'I wonder they hevn't put a fence round it to keep people out.'

He shrugged. 'Reckon they don't think it's worth it. Time they've done it the whole lot'll be in the sea.'

They reached the church porch and he pushed open the door with some difficulty. As it creaked open there was a squawking and a rush of wings as a flock of seagulls, disturbed from their perches on every available ledge, flew out of a hole in the gable over the east window. The whole of the stone wall had a jagged diagonal split from top to bottom and the stained glass in the window was gone. There was a split in the north wall as well and it looked as if it wouldn't take much for the entire corner to fall. There

18

was an overpowering smell of damp stone and seagulls' droppings.

'I don't think we should stay. It doesn't seem very safe,' Mollie whispered, looking up into the arched span of the nave and noticing that one of the pillars supporting the arch was badly cracked.

'It's all right as long as we stay down this end,' he said, putting his arm round her.

'But we're right under the tower, here. Supposing it was to topple. . .' She looked up and could see the bell in the belfry, white with more seagulls' droppings. 'I don't like it, Joe,' she whispered. 'I think we should go.'

'All right,' he said carelessly. 'I jest thought you'd like to see it, thass all. You won't be able to come here much longer, 'cause it'll be under the sea.' He dropped his voice to a sepulchral whisper, 'an' all you'll hear is the bell tollin' under the sea from drownded sailors.'

'Oh, don't Joe.' She huddled nervously under her cloak 'Look, I'm glad I came. But I'd really like to go now, if you don't mind.'

As she spoke the ground under them gave a lurch and then settled. A lump of stone fell from somewhere up in the eaves.

'Aye. You're probably right.' Joe said. He led the way back outside.

She followed him but pulled up short as they reached the door. 'Gracious, it's almost dark. I didn't realise we'd been in there such a long time. Oh, I shall be in real trouble when I get home. I'm never out as late as this when I go pickin' mine. I'd better run.' She gathered up her skirts and set off. 'Thanks for your help on the beach, Joe,' she called over her shoulder.

'Wait a minute. I was gonna walk you back,' he called back.

'No. Better not. Goodbye.'

She ran until she got a stitch in her side, then she stopped and rubbed it and ran on again. It was quite dark by the time she got back to the house.

19

Uncle Sam and Richard were both sitting at the table, each with a large plate of stew in front of them. Aunt Rose was standing by the stove ladling a plate for herself. She laid it carefully at her place on the table and fixed Mollie with a steely look. 'An' where might *you* have been?' she asked, her tone icy.

'I've been pickin'. You know I've been pickin'.' Mollie put eight tokens on the table. 'I did well today. There was plenty on the beach.'

'You had help, too, from what I've heard,' Aunt Rose said. 'Madge White from the cottages was pretty quick to come an' tell me you'd gone off with some man.'

'I dunno about "some man", Aunt.' Mollie turned to Richard. 'It was your mate, Joe Trayler, Dick. He came an' gave me a hand because he couldn't go out fishin' with his dad. He said he reckernised me because he's seen me with you.'

'I 'spect you went off with 'im to pay 'im for 'is help,' Rose remarked, tight-lipped.

Mollie frowned. 'What do you mean?'

'What do I mean?' Rose mimicked. 'You know very well what I mean. Madge saw you both goin' off along the cliff.'

'Yes. He took me to see the old church,' Mollie said eagerly. 'There's been a cliff fall and the church is nearly toppling off the edge. We went inside. There's a great crack down one end...'

'An' did you lift yer skirts for 'im while you were there?' Aunt Rose demanded.

Mollie flushed and Sam said, 'Now, Rosie, that's enough o' that talk.'

Rose rounded on him. 'Enough o' that talk, you say? Don't you think thass what I've been watchin' for ever since we took 'er in? Like mother, like daughter, thass what I say. She'll turn out a jest as big a slut as your precious sister was. Well, I've had one bastard foisted on me, I'll make damn sure I don't hev another.' She turned on Mollie. 'I don't doubt it's in the blood, but I'm tellin'

20

you now, if you think you can play fast an' loose like your mother did and expect me to give you house room, you can think again. This is a respectable house and we're a respectable family.' She turned back to her husband. 'Thanks to you we were forced to cover up one sin but I'll see to it we don't cover up another. She can sleep in the hedge and beg in the gutter before I'll hev another bastard under my roof.' She sat down heavily, unused to standing up for so long, her face red with temper.

'Calm down, Ma, you'll do yourself a mischief,' Richard said, trying to smooth things over. 'Mollie on'y said she'd been to see the old church with Joe. He's my mate. He's a decent enough chap.'

'*He* might be. What about *her*? There's bad blood in her, I know it and he knows it.' She nodded towards Sam, who was looking at Mollie, completely stricken.

'What does she mean, Uncle Sam?' Mollie asked, near to tears.

'We'll hev a talk later,' Sam said gently. 'Come an' hev some stew, dearie, it'll warm the cockles o' your heart.'

She shook her head. 'I don't think I want any, thank you.' She took off her cloak and hung it up, then she went upstairs to her room, the happy mood of the afternoon completely shattered. And all because of something she didn't understand.

Chapter Three

It was cold in her room after the warmth of the kitchen downstairs. Mollie took the shawl that she used as an extra coverlet from her bed and wrapped herself in it. Then she sat huddled in her old wicker chair, staring into the darkness.

What could Aunt Rose have meant? Why had she called her that dreadful word? Everybody knew what it meant, but it couldn't be true in her case because she knew exactly who her parents were. Her mother was Uncle Sam's sister, Jane, who was married to Alfred Jones. And it was common knowledge that Jane had died when Mollie was born and that Alfred had gone to sea because he was too upset to remain in Frinton without her and that Uncle Sam and Aunt Rose had taken Mollie in and given her their name, so that she became Mollie Barnes instead of Mollie Jones. Those were the facts. There was no mystery about them. So why had Aunt Rose said those dreadful things? And even worse, why hadn't Uncle Sam denied them?

While these questions were going round and round in her head she could hear raised voices from the kitchen, two floors down. This in itself was unusual because Uncle Sam never, ever raised his voice. Although he was a small man he was very definitely head of the house and his word, softly spoken but firm, was law. Even Aunt Rose knew better than to oppose him as a rule but it seemed that tonight she had overstepped the mark and was receiving the brunt of his displeasure.

Mollie huddled further into her shawl. It was all her fault for walking along to the old church with Richard's friend, Joe, even though it had been a perfectly harmless expedition. She gave a sniff. It was all her fault for being born in the first place. She wished her father would come home from wherever he was and take her away from Nazecliffe, away from Aunt Rose, who hated her, and away from the stink of copperas. She would miss Uncle Sam and Richard, of course, but that was all. She looked up at the square of grey that was the window and once again, as she had done countless times before, prayed for her father's return.

She had no idea how long she had been sitting there when she heard a step on the narrow stair and saw the flickering light of a candle approaching.

'Thass me, Mollie. Do you mind if I come up?' It was Uncle Sam. Now she knew it was something really serious because he never came to her room, insisting that it was her private place.

'No, I don't mind,' she said in a small voice, watching as his balding grey head appeared. He put the candle down on the chest of drawers and sat down on the edge of the bed. He was in his shirtsleeves and waistcoat and the thick-set trousers he changed into when he came home from work.

'Thass comfy up here,' he said, looking round, 'but not very warm.' Mollie knew he felt the cold because he worked in such heat all day.

'You can wrap yourself in my patchwork quilt if you like, Uncle,' she said.

'No, I'm all right.' He stroked his moustache for several minutes, then he said, 'I 'spect you wonder what Aunt Rose was talkin' about downstairs.'

She nodded. 'I know she was mad at me because I went to the old church with Richard's mate.' She frowned. 'I

23

dunno why she should be. We on'y walked there an' had a look.'

'I know, dearie.' Uncle Sam stroked his moustache some more.

'But I don't understand ... why did Aunt Rose call me that awful name, Uncle Sam?'

He started to stroke his moustache again, then changed his mind and rubbed both hands over his balding head. 'There's somethin' I've never told you, Mollie,' he said at last. 'I should've told you years ago and I've been meanin' to but somehow the time has never seemed quite right.' He paused uncomfortably.

Mollie stared at him. Whatever could he mean? Before she could open her mouth to ask he went on, 'You see, thass not quite true that Jane and Alfred were your parents.' He shook his head. 'In fact, thass not true at all. The truth is, your mother was my youngest sister, Mary.'

Mollie licked her lips. 'And my father?'

He took a deep breath. 'Ah, now, thass a different kettle o' fish.' He pulled out his pipe, tamped down the tobacco and lit it. When he had got it going to his satisfaction he relaxed visibly. 'Thass high time you knew the whole story,' he said with a sigh. He patted the counterpane. 'Come an' sit here an' I'll tell you.'

Puzzled, she did as he asked. He put his arm round her. 'Your mother was a pretty girl and bright with it,' he began. 'Jest like you, on'y her hair was fair where yours is dark. She didn't fancy pickin' mine so she managed to get herself a place in a big house and went into service. She was there for about two years, I s'pose. Then one night she came to us, me an' Rose. It was a cold, foggy night, as I remember, six or seven weeks before Christmas. She told us she'd been turned out because they'd found out she was in the fam'ly way.' He gave a sigh. 'Well, that was a facer! I didn't know what to do with her. We couldn't keep her here. Richard was not much above a twelve month old, as I recall an' he was more than a handful for Rose – she's never been all that strong – so we did what we thought best and I took her over to Frinton, to my other sister, Jane.'

'Jane an' Alfred didn't hev any children?' Mollie asked. For some reason her mouth had gone dry and she was having difficulty in swallowing.

'No, nor ever likely to. Jane was ill an' like to die, although I didn't know that when I took Mary there. But it was the best thing, as it turned out. Mary was happy to nurse Jane an' they agreed that after the baby was born she would stay on to look after her.'

'So what happened?'

He shook his head. 'The worst possible thing. We all knew Jane was dying; we'd prepared ourselves for it. But we none of us had ever thought that it would be Mary that went first. But she did; she died jest three days after you were born. Well, Jane was too ill to look after a baby so there was only one thing for it – I had to bring you back here for Rose to look after. An' this is where you've been ever since.'

Mollie frowned. 'But why wasn't I told all this right from the start, Uncle? Why was I always led to believe Jane and Alfred were my parents? And who was my father? Does anybody know?'

He nodded. 'Oh, yes. Mary told me what had happened, poor girl. Nobody else knows, not even Aunt Rose, but it's right that you should be told. The master of the house had –' he turned his head away '– he'd had his way with her. He'd used her, night after night, threatenin' to hev her turned out if she didn't do as he said. Of course, before long she found she was in the fam'ly way. She hid it for as long as she could, then the cook tumbled to why she was puttin' on weight round the waist and she was dismissed. 'Course, the master was never blamed; they said she'd most likely bin tumbled in the stable loft with one of the stable lads.'

'Poor Mary,' Mollie said sadly. She looked up. 'But I still don't see why there should've bin all the secrecy in the family. . .'

His mouth took a bitter twist. 'Because the big house was Cliff House, up on the cliff, and the man that took advantage of my sister Mary was Mr James Grainger, owner of the Copperas House.'

She stared at him in amazement. 'Don't you hate him?'

'After what he did to my sister? How it killed her? What do you think? Of course I hate him.' He turned away so that she shouldn't see his face working.

'I don't understand. Why are you still here, workin' for him, after what he did?'

He sniffed. 'In the first place I don't see much of him. He doesn't often show his face in the place where his money is earned for him; he might get his hands dirty. And in the second place, if I left here I wouldn't on'y lose my job I'd lose the roof over our heads. I can't afford to do that, this is a nice comfortable little place an' I'd hev a job to find us a better one. And thirdly, I'd have to tell your aunt why we were leavin'. I've never told her Mary's secret an' I don't intend to.'

Mollie digested this, her mind in a whirl. After some time she said, 'Did Jane die?'

He nodded. 'Yes, she lasted about a year after Mary died.'

'What about Alfred?'

'He got a woman in to look after Jane and when she died he married her. We've lost touch but I b'lieve they've got a fam'ly now.'

She gave a crooked little smile. 'So all my prayers that my father would come home from sea and take me away to some beautiful foreign land were wasted because...' suddenly, her eyes widened as the truth hit her. 'James Grainger? Mr Grainger at Cliff House is my father?'

Sam gave a mirthless little laugh. 'For what it's worth, yes. Not that it'll ever do you any good, dearie. He's not likely to welcome you with open arms as his long-lost daughter now, is he? If you've got any sense you'll forget all about that side of it. Truth be told the countryside is probably littered with his bye-blows, the randy old...' He broke off, suddenly remembering where he was. Embarrassed, he patted her knee and got up from his seat beside her. 'There, now I've told you the whole story. Nobody else knows it, but you were entitled to be told. Now you can forget it. Your home is here, Mollie, for as long as you want it. Your aunt won't ever speak to you again like she did tonight, I've seen to that. I think you should come downstairs now an' hev some o' that nice stew.'

'Thank you, Uncle, but I'm really not hungry,' she said. 'You can tell Aunt Rose I'm sorry if I upset her but I'd rather stay here and think about what you've told me tonight.' She looked up at him, a sad, wounded look in her brown eyes. 'Don't you see, I'm not who I thought I was. For seventeen years I thought I knew exactly where I came from, who my parents were; now I find it was all a lie. Don't you see? I've got to get used to being somebody else.'

He pulled her to her feet and put his arms round her. 'You're not somebody else, Mollie, my girl. You're still my little girl. Remember, I've always known who you really are.'

She put her head on his shoulder and wept. 'But I haven't, Uncle. It feels as if my past has all been scrubbed out and I don't know what to put in its place.'

'I'm sorry, child. I see now I should have told you before.' He let her cry, holding her close. After some time, he said, 'Now, thass enough, sweetheart. You get yourself undressed and into bed an' I'll bring you a nice mug o' hot milk. That'll help you to sleep.'

He went off down the stairs and ten minutes later came up again with the milk.

'Now, what you've got to remember,' he said, as he handed it to her, 'is that nothin' has changed as far as anybody else is concerned. You're still the Mollie Barnes you always were. An' I'll tell you this, an' all. Your Aunt

Rose is more fond of you than she'll ever let on. She's a funny old bundle but her heart's in the right place.' He dropped a kiss on her forehead. 'Goodnight, Mollie, my girl. I'll leave the candle for you.'

'Goodnight, Uncle.'

After Sam had gone she sat up in bed still wrapped in her shawl, her hands round the mug of milk, warming them. She surveyed her room by the flickering candle. She was lucky, she realised that. She had a good home with Uncle Sam and Aunt Rose, even if she and her aunt didn't always see eye to eye, and she had this room all to herself. It wasn't until tonight, when she feared she might lose it all that she had begun to value the security of her life.

And now she knew the whole story she could appreciate Aunt Rose's point of view, too. It couldn't have been easy for her to take on her sister-in-law's bastard, especially one as wayward as Mollie had been as a child. She recognised in this hour of absolute honesty that although some of the beatings she had received had been undeserved, a good many had been justified and the hostility between her and her aunt had been fostered as much on her side as Rose's. She decided that from now on she would show a bit more appreciation for her home and a bit less resentment for the part she was expected to play in running it.

She drained the last of her milk and blew out the candle. She was just drifting off to sleep when a sudden thought hit her like a hammer blow.

James Grainger was the man responsible for her mother's misery and ultimate death. James Grainger, the owner of the Copperas House. James Grainger, who lived at the big house on top of the cliff. That meant that James Grainger was her FATHER. She stared up into the darkness, digesting this and trying to come to terms with the fact that she had Grainger blood flowing in her veins. The thought gave her no joy; rather it filled her with fury that such a man could take his pleasure with no care for the misery it might cause.

28

'One day,' she whispered vindictively, 'One day, I don't know how, but I am determined that I shall sit at that man's table. He may not know I am his daughter, but *I* shall know. And I shall laugh at him for his ignorance.'

With that, she turned over and slept soundly till the morning.

But when she woke the vow she had made to herself seemed hollow in the cold light of day. How could she ever hope to sit at the table of such a rich and powerful man as James Grainger, even though he was . . . she could hardly believe it . . . *her father*?

Could it be true? She went over in her mind what her uncle had told her of her birth the previous night. Her mother had been a servant at Cliff House and the master of the house had raped her? Seduced her? Whichever it was the end result had been the birth of a child. And she, Mollie, was that child. That was what Uncle Sam had said. And Uncle Sam never lied.

She got dressed and went downstairs. Aunt Rose was already there, moving stiffly about the kitchen.

'Come along, girl, you're late today. Get the porridge on the stove quick, your uncle and Richard'll be in for their breakfast shortly,' she said, but gave Mollie a brief smile as she spoke, the usual edge to her tone missing.

Mollie put the pan on the stove and left Rose to stir it while she laid the table. She could see how painful it was for her aunt to walk and she realised, with a new, heightened awareness, that it was the pain in her legs that caused Rose to spend most of her life sitting in her chair, but that sitting in her chair all day meant that she had grown fatter and fatter, and the added weight made it more and more painful to walk. It was a vicious circle from which there was no escape. For the first time she felt sorry for her aunt.

Richard and Sam came home for a quick breakfast.

'Mustn't be away too long,' Sam said, blowing on his porridge. 'Mr Mark says the Master's likely to pay a visit

29

today so we've got to make sure everything's ship-shape.' He took a noisy spoonful and swallowed it. 'Not that he'll stay long. He's too busy gamblin' his money away to bother much about the people who earn it for 'im.'

'You're right enough there, Pa,' Richard said, helping himself to more porridge. 'Last time he came he on'y stayed long enough to look at the books. Said the stink made him gag. Never mind the men who hev to work in it.'

'If you work in it long enough you don't notice it, thass what they say,' Sam said. 'I've never found the truth of it, meself, although you do get used to it.' He got up from his chair. 'Better be getting' back. Come on, boy.'

'Don't forget to fill the coal box up before you go back, Richard,' Rose said. 'You know Mollie don't like that job, but I do like to keep a good fire.'

'Yes, all right, Ma.' He winked at Mollie as he reached for a last piece of bread and jam to take with him. 'I could leave it for you, Moll, if you like. It'd give you an excuse to come over while the Master is there. He might...'

Mollie felt herself flushing. 'I don't want to come over while he's there, thank you very much.'

'No, it's your job to keep the coal box filled,' Sam said. 'That yard is no place for a young girl. There's always accidents happenin'. On'y yesterday young Parrott got acid spilled over him. Wasn't wearin' his leather trousers and got his leg burnt bad. Might even lose it and if he don't he'll be scarred for life.'

'I was on'y teasin' her, Pa,' Richard said. 'I'll fill it up, don't worry.'

'Well, you'd better get on with it. Time we was gettin' back.'

After the two men had gone Mollie cleared the table and washed up while Rose enjoyed another cup of tea.

'Seems to me Mr Mark is left to run that place,' Rose said, pouring her tea into her saucer and slurping it noisily. 'Thass a lot of responsibility for a young man. An' he's

30

on'y a nephew o' Mr Grainger, from what I can make out. Good job your uncle's there to keep a eye on things.'

'Mr Grainger's son is there as well,' Mollie said.

'Some o' the time. Accordin' to Sam he's not very reliable. Bit like his father, I reckon. Pour me another cup, Mollie, will you?'

Mollie did as she was asked, then emptied the teapot out into the backyard. Like his father. Was she, too like her father? Resolutely, she put the thought from her and went back indoors.

She spent the morning cleaning the house. She tried not to keep an eye on the yard of the Copperas House, but her gaze kept straying to the window in case she might catch a glimpse of James Grainger making one of his infrequent visits. Of course, she had seen him before, many times, but today she had an almost morbid desire to look at him and see him for what he was.

He didn't arrive until she was getting ready to go down to the beach for the daily collection of the all-important copperas twigs. Suddenly, there was extra activity about the yard and she saw a portly, black-clad figure in a tall hat striding about with Mr Mark, the young, fair-haired manager. As she watched Uncle Sam came out of the boiler house and began to speak to the two men. Mr Mark nodded his head as he listened but James Grainger took out his pocket watch, looked at it and then snapped it shut impatiently before turning on his heel and striding over to where his horse was tethered. He climbed on it with the help of a passing lad to give him a leg up and cantered off without a second glance. Uncle Sam finished what he was saying and went back into the boiler house. Mr Mark followed him.

Mollie had watched all this. In fact, James Grainger had passed within inches of her as he cantered away. She had seen his florid face with the large, fleshy nose and bristling whiskers. She had seen the old-fashioned, slightly grubby

31

grey wig under his tall hat. He of course, hadn't noticed her. She was beneath his notice.

But she had watched him and seen him for what he was, an arrogant, self-important man. There was even arrogance in the way he sat his horse. In those few seconds she saw a man who held those he considered beneath him – even those who kept him where he was – in contempt. It was plain that anyone who overstepped the boundary between master and servant would be given short shrift from James Grainger.

The boundary between servant and master was a different matter, of course, she thought cynically.

Late now, she hurried along to the beach with the rest of the women pickers, her jaw set. Last night she had made a vow that she would sit at that man's table. This morning she had realised that this was impossible. But now she had seen him at close quarters, and her determination was renewed. Somehow, she would one day take her rightful place at his board.

Chapter Four

As the days went by Mollie realised the wisdom of her uncle's words. It was true, nothing had changed as far as the rest of the world was concerned. If anybody bothered to think about it – and most people didn't – she was still what she had always been, the daughter of Sam Barnes's dead sister from Frinton. Even Aunt Rose soon reverted to her old nagging ways.

But things had changed for Mollie. The mythical father who would whisk her off to exotic foreign lands no longer existed for her; she knew that she was the illegitimate daughter of a servant and that her destiny lay in her own hands and in quite a different direction. At Cliff House. But how and when she would be able to bring this to pass she couldn't imagine; in fact when she thought about it rationally she realised that the whole idea was ludicrous. Yet it persisted. And it wouldn't go away.

Spring came and with it the stunted daffodils she had planted round the back door of the cottage. It was a measure of her determination that she had done this. She knew that flowers didn't flourish in the vicinity of the Copperas House; the scrappy little gardens in front of the cottages in Copperas Lane bore testimony to that. Only the odd splash of red from a brave geranium or two as the summer wore on gave a touch of brightness to the otherwise baked earth.

Throughout the summer as she gathered mine from the beach Mollie's gaze would turn towards Cliff House, the imposing white building that dominated the cliff top and she would invent increasingly outlandish schemes for gaining entry there, always ending in the revelation of her true identity and a grovelling apology from the hitherto haughty master. Even she herself found some of her ideas laughable and in her more rational moments she realised that the only way she was going to get a foothold in Cliff House was to secure a place as a scullery maid and with any luck to work her way up to be parlourmaid. The only problem with that was that parlourmaids didn't, and never would, sit at the family table.

She was thinking along these lines late one afternoon – her daydreams, fanciful as they were, helped to alleviate the boredom of picking mine. It had been a pleasant, warm afternoon in early August, but with calm and tranquil seas the pickings were few and far between. Hardly realising what she was doing she had wandered further and further along the beach in her search, dragging her basket with her. There was nobody else about; most people preferred to stay as near as possible to Old Sol and his donkey so they didn't have far to go to empty their baskets. Time spent dragging heavy baskets long distances was time wasted. But now everybody, including Sol, had gone home to tea, disgusted with the day's meagre pickings.

Mollie was so deep in her own thoughts that she hadn't noticed how far the sun had moved to the west. She had also committed the unforgivable sin of failing to keep an eye on the tide. When at last she turned to retrace her steps she was surprised to find how far the shadow thrown by the cliff had lengthened across the beach. Worse, the water had risen so far that in places it had already reached the foot of the cliff, almost cutting off her retreat. Annoyed with herself for being so stupid, she took off her shoes and tied the laces together and hung them round her neck. She realised that if she wasn't very quick she would find herself completely stranded, so she left her basket, which was barely half full, and ran across to where the cliff jagged out across the beach and stepped into the water, clinging on to the rocky surface and climbing above the waterline where she could. Once she slipped and found that the water came nearly up to her waist and was rising quite quickly. Alarmed now, she managed to struggle round the point, but instead of the wide expanse of beach she had expected, she found herself in a little sandy bay.

With her dress clinging wetly to her legs and her cotton bonnet askew she took stock of where she was. She remembered now, this was a small, secluded bay where nobody came because there were rarely any pickings to be had. And also, it got cut off at high tide by a jagged finger of cliff. Sizing up the possibilities, she cursed herself for a fool for not remembering this when she passed it before. She knew she wouldn't be able to clamber over the jagged outcrop but with luck she might still be able to wade round it, even if the water came up to her neck. She wished now she had learned to swim, but there had never been time and in any case, girls in her position didn't. She gathered up her sodden skirts and began to run across the sand.

'Oh, thank God. You down there, I need help.'

Mollie hesitated. If she didn't get round that point in the next few minutes she would be completely cut off and very likely drowned.

'You down there. Help me. Please.'

It was the 'please' that did it. Mollie looked up and saw a girl of about her own age waving her arm some 15 feet above her on the cliff face. She was half sitting, half lying on a ledge of scrubby grass and hanging on to a bush of wild broom.

'Don't just stand there! Go and get help! I can't move. I've hurt my ankle.' The girl – Mollie recognised her as the Grainger girl from Cliff House – waved towards the point.

Mollie ran across the sand and into the water but it was up to her waist before she had gone many steps.

35

'Thass too late,' she called. 'I can't get round the point. The tide's cut me off.'

'Can't you swim?'

'No, I've never learned.'

'Well, crawl over the rocks.'

'I can't. They're slippery with seaweed. I might fall in an' drown.' Mollie was beginning to panic.

The girl was silent for a moment. Then she said, 'You'd better come up here with me, then, if you can't get across. The sand down there will be completely covered within the next hour.'

Mollie looked up at her and then at the sea, crawling relentlessly up over the sand. The girl was right; in less than an hour the place where she was standing would be under at least three feet of water.

Charlotte Grainger leaned over. 'Quickly, now. Look, you can get a foothold there, where the cliff has crumbled, then if you move to your right, there's another foothold.' She pointed. 'That's it, just there. Now you can climb up by those tussocky hummocks, but mind the gorse, it's very prickly.' She watched Mollie's progress for a minute or two. 'That's the way I came up. It's quite easy to climb the cliff in the places where there's been a landslip, as long as you're careful.' She leaned down and a shower of pebbles cascaded on to Mollie. 'Watch out. There's a hole just there. That's where I twisted my ankle. Why haven't you got any shoes on? Oh, they're tied round your neck. It was a bit silly not to put them on to climb the cliff, you'll cut your feet to ribbons. Here, give me your hand, I'll help you up this last bit.'

'No, better not, Miss,' Mollie said breathlessly. 'I might pull the pair of us down. I can manage, thank you.'

With an effort she hauled herself over the edge to where Charlotte was sitting and sat beside her. Above them the cliff hung straight and sheer.

'What's your name?' the girl asked.

'Mollie. Mollie Barnes, Miss.' Now they were at close

36

quarters Mollie felt a little in awe of the girl she had always thought of as 'the Grainger girl'. She was a very pretty girl, with fair curls and very blue eyes and a pert, tip-tilted nose; a picture of soft femininity that was belied by the stubborn set of her jaw. She was wearing a green and white striped dress – streaked liberally with clay from the cliff – with a white fichu. In her straw bonnet with matching green ribbons she looked more suitably dressed for a gentle ride in the country than climbing the cliff.

'I expect you're wondering what I was doing, to get myself stuck halfway up this cliff,' Charlotte said with a sigh.

'Thass not my place to ask questions, Miss,' Mollie answered primly.

Charlotte let out a peal of laughter. 'Maybe not. But don't tell me you aren't curious.'

'Well, Miss. . .'

'I was looking for fossils. I collect fossils and you can find all sorts of interesting things on the beach and also buried in the cliff. Look, I carry a little bag to put my findings in. It's got these in it, too.' She pulled out a small trowel and a little knife. 'They're for prising things out of the cliff.'

'Fancy that.' So it was not just pretty shells that Mollie had seen her searching for on the beach.

Charlotte put them back in the bag and pulled the drawstring. 'You never know what you might find, you know. About thirty years ago there was such a violent storm that all the sand was washed away from the beach and they found all sorts of bones of huge animals that had been buried in the mud. They even found the tusks and teeth of what they thought were elephants and rhinoceros too.'

Mollie's eyes widened. 'What did they do with them?'

'I don't know. Gave them to the Zoological Society, I suppose,' she said with a shrug. 'I've never found anything big, but I often find quite interesting things buried in the cliff. I'm afraid I climbed a bit higher than I'd intended today and then caught my foot in that hole.' She pulled up her dress a little to reveal her ankle, badly swollen over a green shoe that was, again, totally unsuitable for cliff climbing. 'It's very painful,' she added thoughtfully.

'If you was to take your shoe off I could wrap your ankle in my dress to cool it a bit, Miss. Thass still wringin' wet where I waded in the water so it'd be nice and cold.'

'That's a very good idea. Can you get it off for me? No, not your dress, silly, my shoe. It's a bit tight now my ankle has swollen. That's it. Now, if I put my foot in your lap you can wrap your skirt round it. Ah, that's really nice.' She wriggled herself into a more comfortable position. Then she said, 'What were you doing, down there on the beach?'

'I was pickin' mine, Miss. For the Copperas House. Like I do every day.' She shrugged. 'There wasn't much about today and I went further along the beach than I intended. Thass how I got caught by the tide.'

'Good thing you did. At least now I've got some company. I suppose we shall have to stay here now till the tide turns and you can go and get help.'

'I could try and climb to the top of the cliff,' Mollie said doubtfully, looking up at its sheer face.

'Indeed you could not! It's far too dangerous. There are steps to get up the cliff on the other side of that headland so once the tide's gone down enough to get round it you'll be able to go up to the house and get help.'

'That won't be for an hour or two, Miss. The tide's still on the make.'

'Well, it won't come up this far so we're quite safe.'

They sat in silence for a while, listening to the waves on the shore. Then Mollie said, 'I collect things off the beach, too, Miss. I've got some very pretty shells and several bits of brownish stuff that looks like glass.'

'I guess that's amber,' Charlotte said. 'You can polish it up and make it into jewellery.'

'Oh, I never thought of that. I've got a thing like a stone snail shell, too. Thass quite pretty – I mean, it's grey but it's got lines on it and it's all curled round and round.' She demonstrated with her finger in the palm of her hand. She looked up. 'I found it in the cliff one day.'

Charlotte's face lit up. 'That's an ammonite. I'm sure it's an ammonite. I've been looking for one of those for *ages*. I've got a piece of shark's tooth and several stones with the imprint of small creatures but I've never found an ammonite. You're lucky to have found one.'

Mollie shrugged. 'I jest happened to see it so I picked it out an' took it home.'

'Where's home?'

'The boiler man's cottage in Copperas Lane. My uncle is boiler man at the Copperas House.' She spoke with pride.

Charlotte digested this. She had never been down Copperas Lane. She knew that it was a lane, little more than an alleyway, really, off the High Street, which she had to pass on the way to Miss Robert's Haberdashery store, but she had always been led to believe that it was a dirty, smelly place and that rough people lived there. But Mollie didn't seem rough, although her dress was faded and torn in places and stained with wet sand. Her funny little cloth bonnet didn't match her dress, either. And those shoes! Almost as heavy as the gardener's.

'My father owns that place,' Charlotte said thoughtfully, 'but I've never been sure what happens there. What do they do?'

'Well, the women collect the bits of copperas off the beach. Then it's stored and boiled an' that. Then it turns into crystals an' they put it in barrels.' Mollie gave a rough explanation based on her own sketchy knowledge.

'But what's it *used* for? That's what I want to know.' Charlotte wriggled her foot into a more comfortable position.

Mollie frowned. 'They use it in dyein', to make black things blacker and dark things darker, I believe. Thass used

39

for ink, too. There's a shed where the ink is made. I ain't allowed there. If you fall in the ink vat you die, Uncle Sam says.'

'Oh, I see.'

They both sat staring down into the sea, digesting what Mollie had said, as the tide slowly and insidiously crept up the cliff face.

Presently, Charlotte gave a little shiver. 'I'm glad you're here, Mollie. It's beginning to get chilly and if I was here alone I'd be worrying about Old Boney.'

'Old Boney?' Mollie echoed.

'Napoleon. I'd be watching for his ships on the horizon, coming to invade us.'

'I don't know nothin' about that,' Mollie said flatly.

'Well, my father says the peace with the French won't hold much longer. He's convinced they're building flat-bottomed boats in preparation for an invasion. And if they do invade he's sure they'll come here.'

'What, to Nazecliffe?' Mollie was not impressed.

'Quite likely. To the Essex coast, anyway. Papa would like Mama and me to go and stay with friends in Cambridge, out of danger, but Mama won't hear of it.' She hunched her shoulders gleefully. 'And I don't want to go and miss all the fun. Especially if they send soldiers from the garrison in Colchester to defend us.'

Mollie looked at her doubtfully. 'Do you think they'll do that? Send soldiers here, I mean?'

'Oh, yes. There's no doubt if there's an invasion we shall be prepared for it. My brother says they're already thinking of sending troops to camp on the cliffs just down the coast from here.'

Mollie listened, spellbound. In Copperas Lane all the people were too busy trying to make enough money to feed their families to concern themselves with much else. Few people could read so what was reported in the newspapers went unnoticed; in fact, as far as the workers were concerned the only sign of potential conflict was an increas-

40

ing order from the gunpowder factory further up the river for the components to make into gunpowder. Yet another use for copperas.

After a while Mollie leaned forward and pointed. 'Looks as if the tide's turned, Miss,' she said. 'See? The water's gradually leavin' the high-tide mark.'

'Ah, yes, so it is. That's good. I'm getting hungry.'

'I'm afraid it'll be another hour or more before we can get round the point,' Mollie said. 'How does your ankle feel now, Miss?' She unwrapped it from the folds of her now practically dry dress. 'Ah, the swelling's gone down a lot.'

'It still aches. I don't know whether I shall be able to walk on it,' Charlotte said doubtfully.

'Well, if you can't you'll have to sit here till I can fetch help. It might be dark by then,' Mollie told her. 'Might be getting chilly, too.' She glanced at Charlotte. 'Won't your mam be wonderin' where you are?'

'No, she's out calling.'

'Callin' what?' Mollie frowned.

'Calling. Visiting. Or leaving calling cards. That's what she does in the afternoon. Unless she's what's known as "at home". Then people come and call on her.'

'What for?'

'What do you mean, what for?'

'What do they all go round callin' on each other for?'

'They drink tea and eat small cakes and sandwiches and exchange the latest gossip.'

'Oh. Is that what you do, too, Miss?'

'No, I do not,' Charlotte said emphatically. 'I've got far better things to do with my time.' A sudden thought struck her. 'Won't your people be wondering where you are?'

Mollie nodded. 'Yes,' she said, remembering the last time she had been late home and the row that had ensued. 'I'll probably get a right rollickin' from Aunt Rose. She'll never believe me when I tell her where I've been.'

'Do you tell her lies?'

41

'No, I don't. But she don't always believe me, even when I tell her the truth.'

Suddenly, a man's voice called from the top of the cliff. 'Miss Charlotte. What are you doing down there? I've been sent to search for you. Nannie's nearly out of her mind with worry.'

Both girls looked up and saw an elderly man with a red face and a shock of grey hair looking down at them over the edge of the cliff. 'Oh, it's all right, Perkins,' Charlotte called. 'I twisted my ankle when I was climbing on the cliff. Mollie, here, has been keeping me company. We're perfectly all right.' She turned to Mollie. 'It's only Perkins, our groom.' She turned back to Perkins. 'Perhaps when the tide goes down a bit more you could send someone to help me. I'm not sure I can walk very far.'

'I'll fetch Sid, Miss Charlotte. He'll be the best one.' Perkins's head disappeared.

'I think I should be goin', Miss, now they know where you are and someone's comin' to fetch you,' Mollie said.

'No, stay.' Charlotte put her hand on Mollie's arm. 'You can come back and have tea with me.'

'No, I don't think I should do that, Miss, thank you.' The mere thought of it made Mollie's stomach churn. All this talk of calling cards and people being 'at home', having nannies and grooms, brought home just how far apart their lives were. It was misfortune that had brought them together on the cliff and she had liked Miss Charlotte very much, but it was a friendship that could never extend into everyday life and Mollie knew it.

Anxiously, she scanned the point, watching for the appearance of a rescuer, both for Charlotte and for herself. Suddenly, she saw him.

'Ah, look, Miss, here's a young man come to get you, so I'll be off. Good day, Miss. And thank you.' Not far short of panic-stricken and before Charlotte could stop her, Mollie began to scramble down the cliff. She tore her dress and her knee in an effort to escape with all possible speed

42

and she passed a young, dark-haired man in grubby breeches and heavy gardening boots, who had sloshed his way through the receding water at the bottom of the cliff with apparent ease, at a run.

'Thank you, Mollie.' She heard Charlotte's voice on the wind and she raised her hand in acknowledgment. Then she rounded the point, clambering over boulders where the water was still too deep to wade through, as if afraid someone would chase her and haul her back. She didn't stop running till she reached Copperas Lane and realised she had left her shoes on the ledge with Charlotte Grainger.

Chapter Five

Lying in bed that night and thinking about it Mollie could hardly believe that she had spent several hours stranded by the tide with Miss Charlotte Grainger from the big house on top of the cliff; talking to her just as easily as she would talk to Richard, or one of the girls up the lane. She smiled ruefully up into the darkness as she recalled that Aunt Rose had had difficulty in believing it, too.

'Of all the cock an' bull tales I've heard in my life, that about beats all,' she'd said, pursing her lips disapprovingly.

'But it's true, Aunt Rose,' Mollie had insisted with a toss of her head. '*An'* she wanted me to go back an' hev tea with her.'

'A likely story,' Aunt Rose had sneered. 'An' I s'pose you left her your shoes 'cause she hadn't got any.'

'No.' Her voice had dropped because she'd been ashamed to admit her cowardice. 'I ran off in a hurry 'cause I was scared about goin' there to tea.'

But for once she'd met with Aunt Rose's approval. 'An' so you should be. The likes of us don't take tea with the likes o' them. I'm glad you know your place. So what about your shoes?'

'I left 'em on a ledge. I know where they are. I'll fetch 'em tomorrow.'

'Then why didn't you say so, instead o' makin' up all that rubbish about talkin' to the gentry.'

44

But the following day, when Uncle Sam came home for his midday meal he was carrying a package.

'Mr Mark asked me to give you this from Miss Grainger,' he said. 'I reckon it must be your shoes.'

Mollie undid the string and found that it was indeed her old shoes, but they didn't look quite so scuffed and broken any longer; they had been polished to a high shine. She flushed with embarrassment to think that somebody at Cliff House had been given the task of cleaning such old, worn-out shoes. She hoped no-one would know who they belonged to.

'Well, fancy that,' Aunt Rose said, which was as near to an apology for doubting Mollie's word that she could manage. She bent her head and pointed under the table. 'What's that white thing on the floor? It must've come outa the parcel.'

Mollie picked it up. It was an envelope on which she could make out a large M because that was the first letter of her name, but that was as far as her reading skills went. She slit open the envelope carefully and found a letter inside. She took it out and smoothed it flat on the table. Then she sat and looked at it uncomprehendingly.

Uncle Sam cleared his throat and got up. 'Time I went back to work. You, too, Richard.' He picked up his coat and left, unwilling to join in the humiliation of being unable to read Mollie's letter.

Richard, less concerned, stood up and bent over it. 'Can you make anything out, Moll?' he asked.

Mollie pointed to several Ms. 'I reckon that's my name,' she said. 'But thass all.' She picked it up and put it to her nose. 'I reckon it's from Miss Grainger. It smells all nice and scented. I wonder what she says in it.'

'Dear Mollie, Thank you for keeping me company on the cliff. Come and hev tea on Friday. Love from Miss Grainger,' Richard improvised, pointing to various words.

'Oh, get away. Don't tease,' Mollie said, laughing and giving him a push. 'Go back to work or you'll get your pay docked. Then you won't hev any money to spend at the pub.'

Richard gave her hair a friendly tug and went off, whistling.

'Do you reckon thass right, what Richard said?' Aunt Rose said, after he'd gone. 'The letter, I mean.'

Mollie looked at it again. 'No, 'course not. He made it up. He can't understand writin' any more than you or me.' She looked at it again. 'I wonder what it does say.'

'Let me see.' Rose held out her hand. She looked at it for several minutes. 'No, I can't make no sense of it, neither.' She looked up at the pendulum clock on the wall. 'You'd better get your shoes on an' get down to the beach. Thass pickin' time. You can clear the table when you get back.' She handed back the letter.

Mollie ran up to her room and put the letter safely away. Then she put her shoes on. They looked too good now to wear collecting mine from the beach but they were all she had so she had no choice. She wished she knew what was in that letter. Supposing it needed an answer! Miss Grainger would think her rude for not replying. But there was nobody she could ask.

When Sam Barnes left the house and went back to the yard he called first at the office, a small brick building just inside the gate, to see Mr Mark. He got on well with Mark Hamilton, the nephew of James Grainger's wife. He was a serious-minded, sensible young man. For all he was only in his early twenties, he more or less ran the Copperas House since James Grainger rarely put in an appearance and Sebastian, James's son, who might have been expected to show some interest in his inheritance, was almost as elusive.

Mark was sitting at his desk, a not unhandsome man, with deep-set hazel eyes that missed very little, a long, straight nose and a cleft chin. Before him was a mug of beer and a lump of bread and cheese from which he was

46

taking alternate gulps and bites as he pored over a set of figures. He looked up, surprised, as Sam entered.

'Sam?' he said. 'Is something wrong?' The boiler man rarely came to the office without invitation.

'No, sir.' Sam snatched off his cap. 'I've jest come to say thank you for bringin' my Mollie's shoes an' for the letter from. . . ' he hesitated and cleared his throat because he wasn't absolutely sure who the letter had come from.

'The letter from my cousin Charlotte? Yes, well, she was very grateful to your niece for keeping her company while she was stranded.' Mark took a draught of beer. It was a measure of his knowledge of the men who worked at the Copperas House that he was aware of Mollie's relationship to Sam. Neither James nor his son Sebastian even knew the names of the men who worked for them, let alone their families.

'Is the young lady's. . . ' Sam hesitated. It was hardly the thing for the likes of him to mention Miss Grainger's foot. 'Is the young lady's injury mended?'

'Oh, yes. She's able to walk on it quite normally now, thank you.'

'Thass good. Would you be so kind as to tell the young lady that Mollie asked after her and said thank you for the letter.'

'Yes, Sam, I'll do that.' Mark nodded.

Sam left the office. He'd done what he could. Miss Grainger would know Mollie had received the letter and had asked after her so she wouldn't expect a written reply. Satisfied, he made his way to the cooling tanks, where the processing of this batch of copperas was nearing its end. The liquid from the pits where the raw copperas was left to liquefy had been pumped into the big boiler and boiled, together with several hundred pounds of scrap iron, for nearly three weeks, more liquid being added as evaporation took place. The resulting concentrate had been tapped off into one of the cooling tanks, where it had remained for the past two weeks.

47

Richard was there, in thick leather breeches, apron and heavy leather gauntlets, draining off the liquid that was left now the processing was complete so that it could be used again. Sam walked the length of the walkway beside the tank that was being emptied, which was some 30 feet long and 6 feet wide. Inside it, bunches of twigs had been hung at intervals and the liquid had crystallised on to them and on to the bottom and sides of the tank, in some places to a depth of 4 or 5 inches. Sam had never ceased to marvel at the transformation of stinking liquid acid into these shining crystals. When Richard had finished draining off the excess liquid, which would be boiled up again, he would shovel up the crystals and spread them on boards in the drying house before they were packed into barrels and sold.

Sam watched his son for several minutes without speaking, then he said, 'I'll tell young Ned you're ready for 'im to barrer the stuff to the dryin' house.'

Richard looked up, wiping his gauntleted forearm across his forehead and knocking his cap askew. 'He should be here. I told 'im I was ready for 'im.'

'I'll fetch 'im over.' Sam turned and went back to the boiler house, calling to young Ned to 'Look slippy with that barrer or I'll give yer what-for,' as he went.

As the days went by and she thought more and more about it, Mollie realised what an opportunity she had missed. Of course, at the time she had been overawed by the fact that she was in Miss Grainger's company and had completely forgotten Uncle Sam's revelation about her birth and the vow she had made to sit at James Grainger's table. Now she was annoyed with herself because when she had been given a golden opportunity to do just that she had fled like a scared rabbit, terrified at the mere thought of it.

She felt a little ashamed, as if she had somehow betrayed the mother she had never known but who had suffered so much for her sake, and she made up her mind that if ever an opportunity like that arose again she wouldn't let it slip past her. Not that it was likely to; chances like that were once in a lifetime.

She still worried, too, about whether Miss Grainger's letter should have been answered. She had not seen her on the beach since that day but that was not surprising; by the time her foot was better the tides wouldn't have been right for her. Afternoon low tides were when she could usually be seen looking for fossils. Nevertheless, Mollie slipped what she had always called her 'stone snail' – an ammonite was the name Miss Grainger had given it – into the pocket of her skirt. If she ever got the opportunity she would show it to her, perhaps even give it to her if she wanted it.

It was a warm autumn afternoon towards the end of September before Mollie once again noticed the figure of Charlotte Grainger wandering about at the far end of the beach. The tide was at its lowest ebb so the large expanse of sand that would later be covered by the sea had been patterned into tiny ridges by the movement of the receding waves. The sea was calm and blue, except where darkened patches and streaks of brownish yellow could be seen, some stretching far out towards the horizon. These were the sandbanks, barely covered by the water at low tide, that made this coast treacherous; some of them even dried out enough to walk on at very low tides. Mollie had never done this, for Uncle Sam had warned her too many times of the danger of being cut off when the tide turned. She finished filling her basket and straightened up, rubbing her back. Then she dragged it over to Old Sol to be emptied.

'Thass me lot for today, Sol,' she said as he handed her the token. 'Me back hurts so I'm finishin' early.'

'Rose won't be very pleased.' He grinned at her, showing toothless gums. He lived with his wife in one of the cottages in Copperas Lane so he was well aware of Rose Barnes's temper.

'I'll make it up tomorrer,' she said with a shrug and went

off along the beach with no more than a quick word to the other women, who were still bent nearly double, their eyes raking the pebbles and shells and heaps of seaweed left by the tide, looking for the heavy brown copperas twigs with which to fill their baskets.

But her step slowed as she left the women behind and came closer to Charlotte Grainger, unsure how to approach her without appearing forward, or rude.

Then Charlotte saw her and waved. 'Mollie,' she called. 'Come and see this pretty shell.' She held it out for Mollie to look at. 'The trouble is,' she said, putting her head on one side, 'I've got so many pretty shells. I can't resist them. I'm supposed to be collecting fossils, not just pretty shells.'

'That one's quite unusual, though, Miss,' Mollie said. 'You don't usually find them with that bluish tinge.'

'That's true.' Impulsively, Charlotte handed it to her. 'You have it. You told me you collected shells. Add it to your collection.'

'Oh, thank you, Miss.' As Mollie put it in her pocket she felt the ammonite. 'I've brought somethin' for you, too. To thank you for sendin' my old shoes back. An' to thank you for your letter,' she added, blushing. 'I didn't answer...'

'Oh, no, it didn't need an answer.' Charlotte said hurriedly. She, too, was slightly embarrassed. It hadn't occurred to her when she dashed off those few lines thanking Mollie for her help and her company that the girl wouldn't be able to read them. It was only afterwards that she had realised how thoughtless she had been. 'I just wanted to thank you for your help and company that afternoon.'

Mollie relaxed visibly. She pulled her hand out of her pocket. 'I thought you might like this to add to your collection,' she said shyly.

'Oh, yes, I remember! You told me you'd found an ammonite!' Charlotte took it and examined it carefully. 'It's perfect. And you found it on the cliff?'

'Yes. Back there.' Mollie waved her arm.

'Are you sure you don't want it?'

'Thass not that I don't want it. I'd like you to hev it,' Mollie said honestly.

'Oh, you are a dear.' Charlotte smiled at her and a little dimple appeared at the corner of her mouth. She put her head on one side. 'I should like to show you my collection, Mollie. Will you come back with me now?'

Mollie took a step backwards. 'Oh, Miss. I dunno,' she said, completely forgetting her resolve now that she was faced with it.

Charlotte caught her hand. 'We'll go in the side door and up the back stairs if you're nervous. Not that there's any reason to be because there's never anybody about at this time in the afternoon. Mama's either resting or entertaining, Pa's probably out hunting or dozing in his study and the servants are busy in the kitchen. Come on. It won't take five minutes.' By this time she was pulling Mollie towards the steps cut into the cliff leading up to Cliff House.

As they reached the top of the cliff Mollie realised that Cliff House was even bigger and more imposing than it appeared from the beach. It was built in white stone, which had taken on an almost pinkish glow in the late afternoon sunshine. Long windows opening on to the terrace looked out over smooth green lawns and rose beds to the sea beyond. Symmetrically placed above them were two more rows of smaller windows.

'The main door is just round the corner to the left,' Charlotte explained, 'but we won't go that way. We'll go in by the little door round the other side.' She turned and smiled at Mollie. 'Not that you have any reason to be afraid. You're my guest, Mollie.'

Mollie smiled back nervously. 'It's nice of you to say so, Miss.'

The side door opened into a stone-flagged boot room. A row of boots and outdoor shoes were ranged along one wall with coats and cloaks hanging above them. The rest of the

51

room was given over to cupboards and shelves. There were two doors at one end, one of which Charlotte explained led to the kitchens. She opened the other on to a plain wooden staircase.

'Come along,' she said as she began to mount the stairs. 'My room is just up here.'

'Just up here' meant to Mollie a bewildering journey along corridors covered with thick blue-patterned carpet that seemed to turn innumerable corners, past more doors than she could count, with long mirrors at intervals that reflected the way they had come, making the corridors seem twice as long and confusing her even further.

As they hurried along she caught sight of herself, a tallish, rather untidy-looking girl, with dark hair tumbling down round her shoulders, her hat dangling down her back by its ribbons, her old blue dress faded and torn at the hem and her shoes – now the shine had gone they looked what they were, old and worn out. Beside her, Miss Grainger, possibly a year or two older although much the same height, looked very neat and trim, her fair curls caught up at the back under a little yellow hat that tipped forward over her brow, and a pretty dress of flowered cotton with a wide yellow sash. Even her slippers were yellow. The contrast made Mollie feel more awkward and uncomfortable than ever.

But Miss Grainger didn't appear to notice. She flung open the door on to a big, airy room that was flooded with sunshine. It was the most beautiful room Mollie had ever seen. The walls were covered with creamy wallpaper patterned with garlands of pink and blue roses. The curtains at the window were pale blue velvet and the bed was draped from a central boss in the ceiling to each corner with muslin of the same colour. A pure white counterpane covered the bed.

Wide-eyed, Mollie slipped off her old shoes before entering the room and treading on the pale creamy carpet.

'You can sit down, if you like,' Charlotte said, indicating a chair covered with the same blue velvet as the curtains.

'No, it's all right, thank you, Miss,' Mollie said, licking her lips and remaining just inside the door.

'Well, do come in. You can't see my collection from there,' Charlotte said with an encouraging smile. 'It's all in this cabinet. Come and see.' She opened the doors of a small black lacquered cabinet, revealing rows of tiny shelves. 'There. You can look for yourself. Most of the shelves are empty, of course, but I'm adding to my collection every day.' She pulled the ammonite out of her pocket. 'This is my prize possession, thanks to you, Mollie. I think I'll put it on a shelf of its own. But look, I've got razor shells, cockle shells, sharks' teeth; I've even found a trilobite – well, not exactly the animal, but a piece of rock with the shape of it imprinted on it.'

Mollie was fascinated. 'I've got one o' them, an' one o' them,' she pointed to one thing after another. 'I hevn't got one o' them. Thass a pretty shape.' She was so interested in what she was looking at that she didn't notice that Charlotte had tugged the bell pull and ordered tea to be brought up until she heard the rattle of china. Then she looked round and saw a young girl in a flowered dress and long white apron, a white frilly cap on her head, setting out the tea things on a small table by the window.

'Oh, I'd better be goin',' she said quickly. 'Thass your tea-time.'

'No, indeed. You're having tea with me,' Charlotte said firmly. 'Look, Kitty's brought muffins.' She lifted up the lid of the chafing dish, releasing a delicious, spicy smell. 'And fruit cake.' She turned to the maid. 'Thank you, Kitty, that will be all. I'll ring if we need anything further.' She patted the window seat beside her. 'Come and sit down, Mollie, and tell me about yourself.'

'Not much to tell, Miss.' Nevertheless, as she ate delicious muffins, the butter dripping down her chin to be wiped away by the thick damask napkin she had been given, and drank tea from cups she could nearly see through, she found herself relaxing and, prompted by Charlotte Grainger's gentle probing, telling her how she had been born at Frinton and brought up by her uncle and aunt after her mother died giving her birth. As she recounted the story she realised how clever Uncle Sam had been in constructing her past, because nothing she said was a lie, yet it hid the real, terrible truth. A truth that she could never reveal, least of all to Miss Grainger. Her half-sister.

Chapter Six

Mollie pondered on the words 'half-sister'. Could it be possible? Charlotte's hair was fair and curly whereas hers was dark and straight; Charlotte had blue eyes whilst her were brown; and Charlotte was neatly pretty, which she was not. Mollie always thought of herself as lanky and plain, never even realising that her creamy skin and regular features could make her strikingly attractive, especially when she smiled. She dragged her attention back to the girl beside her, the girl who must never, ever suspect.

'Do you and your friends go down to the beach collecting copperas every day, Mollie?' she was asking, handing her the muffin dish.

Mollie shrugged and took another one. They really were delicious. 'Most of the women from Copperas Lane collect it, except when the tides are too awkward, but I wouldn't say they was my friends. I don't really hev friends. I know a lot o' people, if thass what you mean, but not to say they was friends.'

Charlotte helped herself to a third muffin. 'It's the same with me. I know a lot of girls my age but all they think about is what the next fashion will be.' She pointed to a fashion magazine on her dressing table. 'I've looked through that one, but I couldn't spend hours poring over it. I'm really not interested in whether gingham or muslin is *de rigeur*. I'd rather pore over my book of fossils.' She indicated a slim book bound in red leather. 'But nobody else seems to be interested in that sort of thing,' she said sadly.

'I am,' Mollie said quickly, then bit her lip. 'Sorry, Miss, I shouldn't hev spoke out o' turn like that.'

Charlotte laughed delightedly. 'You didn't speak out of turn. I was glad to hear you say it.' She reached for the fossil book. 'Would you like to look at this?' Then, seeing Mollie's look, 'There are a lot of pictures. More pictures than writing.'

Carefully, Mollie licked her fingers and then wiped the remains of the grease from her muffin off on to her napkin before she took the book and opened it. She had never seen, let alone held, a book like this before. The endpapers were marbled in reds and blues of all shades and the pages were thick and stiff. Between each page there was a sheet of tissue paper to protect the pictures, which were carefully executed and beautifully coloured paintings of rocks and shells and fossils. Slowly and carefully, she turned each page, enthralled by what was there, the shapes, the colours, the intricate designs.

Then, with something approaching reverence, she closed the book and handed it back to Charlotte.

'Oh, thank you for lettin' me look, Miss. I shall never forget.'

Charlotte smiled delightedly. 'That's good, because now when you find things on the beach or in the cliff you'll know whether they're worth keeping. And if they are you can bring them and we'll put them in my collection.'

'Yes, Miss.' But Mollie didn't think she would; in fact, she doubted if she would ever speak to Miss Grainger again, even though the young lady's words seemed to include her in the making of the collection. She got to her feet. 'I think I better be goin' now, Miss. Aunt Rose'll be wonderin' where I am.'

'Oh, yes, of course. I wasn't thinking.' Charlotte stood

up, too. 'I do hope you'll come and take tea with me again, Mollie. I've really enjoyed showing you my treasures.' She gave a sigh. 'Nobody else seems interested in them.'

'Well, I've enjoyed lookin' at them,' Mollie said. 'Thank you for showin' 'em to me.'

Charlotte led the way back through the endless corridors and down the back stairs. As they went Mollie saw the heavy wooden doors with their highly polished brass knobs and finger plates, the wide, thickly carpeted main staircase leading down to the big black and white tiled entrance hall, and the heavily flocked wallpaper, things she had been too awestricken to notice as she had come in.

At the bottom of the stairs Charlotte pushed open the door into the boot room.

'Seb! You startled me. I didn't expect to find you here.'

'And where else would I take off my boots but in the boot room?' A young, dark-haired man with grey eyes and a face that was just a little too long and square-jawed to be handsome, but was yet very pleasant-looking, especially when he smiled, as he did now, looked up. 'Oh, hullo! Who have we here?' He stood up in his stockinged feet and gave a little mocking bow. 'Sebastian Grainger,' he introduced himself with a flourish.

'This is my friend, Mollie Barnes,' Charlotte said quickly. 'She collects copperas from the beach for the Copperas House. I took her up to my room to show her my collection of fossils.'

'Oh, your beach combings,' Sebastian said, slightly disparagingly.

'You needn't say it like that. Mollie's very interested in fossils,' Charlotte said. She turned to Mollie. 'Aren't you, Mollie?'

'Yes, Miss.' It was all Mollie could manage. She wished Miss Grainger hadn't told this young man that she was a mine picker.

Charlotte saw her discomfort and took her arm. 'Oh, don't take any notice of my brother, he's quite harmless,' she said. 'Come on, I'll walk to the cliff steps with you.'

'I'll come with you,' Sebastian said, to Mollie's obvious consternation.

'No, you won't. You've already taken your boots off.' Charlotte ushered Mollie out of the door. 'I've really enjoyed showing you my treasures, Mollie,' she said as they walked to the top of the cliff. 'I do hope you'll come and take tea with me again.'

'Thass nice of you to say so, Miss,' Mollie said cautiously. 'I enjoyed it, too. But I don't think I can come again. Not like I did today. It wouldn't be right, me bein' who I am an' you bein' who you are.'

They reached the cliff top. Charlotte stood with her head on one side. 'I understand what you're saying, Mollie, and I respect your views, although I'm not sure I agree with them.' She smiled at her, showing the roguish little dimple at the corner of her mouth. 'But don't worry. I shall think of something.'

Mollie looked back, frowning as she started down the cliff steps. 'What do you mean, Miss?'

Charlotte waved. 'Watch where you're going. You don't want to fall down the cliff,' was her only answer.

Mollie walked back along the beach, keeping a careful eye on the incoming tide. She liked Miss Grainger very much and she had enjoyed the time she had spent with her but she was realistic enough to know that it couldn't happen again. She wasn't even sure that she wanted it to. The way things were at Cliff House was so different, so far above anything she had ever known, that she knew she could never feel at ease there. Miss Grainger's enormous bedroom, with the pretty drapes over that huge bed, the heavy silver tea service, the dainty china cups that you could almost see through, the delicious spicy muffins on that silver dish all spoke of a way of life that was totally beyond anything she could have imagined, not to mention the carpets that your feet sank into and the heavy oak stair-case leading down to the hall. It made her realise the impossibility – the stupidity – of the vow she had made that she would sit at James Grainger's table; having been inside his house she realised that could never happen. But she had been to his house and taken tea with his daughter so perhaps she could console herself that the vow was at least partially fulfilled. With that she was content. More than content. The thought of actually fulfilling that vow filled her with nothing short of terror.

She reached the place where the cliff dipped and the huddle of houses built in the gap had grown over the years into a small town, with shops either side of the High Street and roads and lanes branching from it. Outside the Crown and Anchor at the corner of Copperas Lane Richard was deep in conversation with Joe Trayler, the man who had taken her to see the old church on the cliff.

'That'll be about four days, I reckon,' Mollie heard Joe say as she approached. He tipped his cap to her. 'Arternoon, Miss. I reckon you'll be int'rested to know the corner of the church on the cliff fell in last week,' he said, 'You remember there was a great crack down behind the altar when we was there? Well, that broke away an' fell in the sea. Jest like that.'

'But we haven't had any gales to bring the tide up in the past few weeks,' Mollie said. 'At least, not that I remember.'

'No, there weren't even a strong wind the night it happened.' Joe shook his head. 'Wouldn't do to go inside the place now. 'T'aint safe.' He leaned towards her and said softly. 'How would you fancy a nice bit of Brussels lace, Mollie?'

Richard gave him a playful punch on the shoulder. 'Stop tryin' to get round my cousin, Joe Trayler. You don't think she's got time for the likes o' you, do you?'

Joe looked offended. 'She could do worse.'

'She could do better, 'n all.' He dropped his voice. 'Specially if you get caught by the Revenue men an' get sentenced to hard labour. Or get transported.'

Joe leaned towards him and whispered. 'Then it's up to you to see that I don't, Dick Barnes. 'Cause as sure as eggs is baby chickens, if I get caught you'll go down with me.'

Mollie looked from one to the other, shocked at their words, but they were both grinning from ear to ear as if the whole thing was a huge joke.

'You won't get caught, I'll see to that,' Richard said, tapping the side of his nose. 'I'll make sure the Ridin' Officer is well outa the way when you're due in.'

Joe winked at Mollie. 'A coupla yards o' Brussels lace, you said? I shan't forget, Mollie.' He tipped his cap again and walked off, whistling.

Mollie opened her mouth. 'I never . . .' But he had gone.

'Don't worry, he's on'y pullin' your leg,' Richard said. 'Come on, time we was home. My belly's flappin' against my backbone I'm that hungry. What about you?'

'No, I'm not hungry,' Mollie said. She gave him a sideways glance, debating whether or not to tell him where she'd been. In the end she couldn't resist it. 'I'm not hungry 'cause I've had tea with Miss Grainger up at Cliff House,' she said, trying to sound nonchalant.

He swung round. 'You've *what?* I don't believe you.'

'Please yourself,' she said with a shrug. 'But I'm tellin' you, I had tea there, lovely spicy muffins drippin' with butter and tea outa cups that thin they could hardly hold the tea in.'

'Get away!' He believed her now and his look was both incredulous and admiring. 'How did you manage that?'

'She collects things so I gave her my stone snail to add to her collection. She said it was a ammo . . . ammo somethin' or other. Quite rare. So she took me to see the things she's dug outa the cliff. She told me that years ago there was a lot o' animal bones dug up outa the sand. Huge animals, elephants and sechlike. She ain't found anything very big but she's found shark's teeth.' She paused. 'An' then I stayed to tea,' she finished, trying – and failing – to sound offhand, as if it was a commonplace occurrence.

60

'Well, I never.' He nodded. 'I hev heard tell about big bones bein' found on the beach.' He looked at her with admiration. 'Well, thass no wonder you're not hungry.' He patted his belly. 'But I am. What's for supper?'

She put her hand to her mouth. 'Oh, Lor, I forgot! I was supposed to get meat pies.' She delved in her pocket and brought out three tokens. 'Oh, good, I've got plenty. I'd better run back an' get them. Tell Aunt Rose I shan't be long.'

By the time she got home Richard had told his mother and father where Mollie had been. Their reaction was predictable.

'Tryin' to get above yerself,' Aunt Rose said with a sneer. 'The likes of us not good enough for yer.'

'It wasn't like that,' Mollie protested. 'I didn't want to go in the first place, but she made me. You can't defy the Quality now, can you?' She looked at the faces round the table and took in the thick china and the mugs of dark tea. This was where she belonged. This was where she felt comfortable. But it had been lovely to get a taste of how the rich people lived. Just for an hour or two.

'No, Mollie, you can't defy the Quality. But it would hev bin better if you hadn't got acquainted in the first place,' Uncle Sam said in his mild but firm tone.

'That wasn't my fault, neither,' Mollie said hotly. 'I couldn't leave her stuck halfway up the cliff that day, with nobody knowin' where she was, could I? She coulda died, an' it woulda bin my fault.'

Uncle Sam sighed. 'No, you couldn't refuse to do a charitable act,' he admitted.

Richard nudged her foot under the table. 'Don't you go getting' ideas above yer station, girl. You stick to Joe Trayler. He's got his eye on you an' you could do worse. Him an' his father make a good livin' from the fishin'.' He winked at her. 'You'll never go short on a cuppa tea if you marry Joe.'

'Oh, stop it. I don't wanta marry Joe Trayler. I don't

61

wanta marry *anybody*, not for years an' years.'

'Hm. I hope you will. I don't want you under my feet for too much longer,' Aunt Rose said cruelly.

'Now, Rose.' Uncle Sam said quietly. 'You've been very glad of Mollie's help over these past years and don't you forget it.' He turned to Mollie. 'Your home is here for as long as ever you want it, Mollie, my dear.' He looked at her and said firmly, 'This is where you belong, Mollie, not up at Cliff House.'

'I know, Uncle Sam. An' this where I wanta be,' she said, knowing exactly what he was telling her, but not entirely sure that she was answering him truthfully.

'All right. Now, we'll hev no more of this kinda talk. Is there another cuppa tea in the pot?'

A week later, when Mollie came downstairs to riddle the fire and put the kettle on, Richard was sitting at the table looking grey with exhaustion. On the table was a large, oiled-silk package.

'Thass my share,' he said, grinning at her. 'I couldn't find out where Old Beaky, the Ridin' Officer was goin' to be so I had to tip Joe the wink and he had to drop his load over the side o' the boat in the shallows an' mark it with a buoy. Then we both rowed out and fetched it when I knew the coast was clear.'

'You'll get yourselves into serious trouble,' Mollie said, worry making her voice sharp.

'Nah. We've bin in this game long enough to know what's what.' Richard yawned widely. 'Make us a cuppa tea, an' put me a bit o' bacon between a coupla bits o' bread, Moll. I gotta get to work.'

'You wanta watch out you don't fall asleep at work. You could fall in the boiler an' be killed. Or you could spill acid all over yerself an' be scarred for life . . . '

'Oh, leave off,' he said irritably, 'I know what could happen if I'm not careful. I've seen too many men . . . ' He broke off. 'Is my bacon ready yet?' As he was speaking he slit open the package on the table and a large packet of tea, and a slightly smaller one of tobacco fell out. Under the oiled silk they had been wrapped in were two yards of Brussels lace.

Mollie's jaw dropped as he held it up. 'I never ... '

'Well, there y'are. Joe said it was a present for you,' He grinned at her. 'I told you he'd taken a shine to you, Moll.'

'Well, I hevn't taken a shine to him an' I don't want him gettin' ideas,' Mollie said firmly. 'You'd better take it back to him.'

'Don't be daft. What would Joe Trayler want with Brussels lace? Nah, you keep it now he's brought it over for you. It'll go on your weddin' dress.' He laughed and ducked as she made to box his ears.

While she was busy with his breakfast Richard picked up his jacket and felt in the pocket. 'Mustn't forget to take this out.' He pulled out a flask. 'Dad likes his tot o' rum even if he don't care for the way it gets here.' He yawned again. 'Come on, Moll, you got my breakfast ready yet?'

Mollie put it on a plate and pushed it over to him. 'I don't like this business you're in, Richard,' she said, her face creased with worry. 'What if you get caught?'

'Don't fret. I'll make sure I don't,' he said, taking a large bite. He chewed it for several minutes, then he said, 'Mollie, don't you realise there are more owlers on this coast than owls in the night sky.' Owlers was the local name for smugglers. 'Thass how a good many people round here make their livin'. Stands to reason the Ridin' Officer on the land an' the Revenue Cutter on the water can't cover everywhere at once. With all the creeks and inlets, the miles of lonely marsh an' all the beaches up an' down this coast, they don't stand a chance, poor buggers, specially when they get a tip-off where stuff is gonna be landed an' it's miles away from where the real business is happenin'. I'd feel sorry for 'em if I wasn't enjoyin' runnin' rings round 'em. They're on a hidin' to nothin' and thass what us owlers take advantage of.'

63

'They won't feel sorry for you if they catch you,' Mollie said, banging his mug of tea down in front of him.

'Then I must make sure they don't.' He raised his mug to her and took a draught of tea. 'I'll say this for you, Mollie-O. You make a real good cuppa tea.' He grinned. 'I must remember to tell Joe Trayler that.'

Mollie leaned across the table to him. 'An' while you're at it you can warn 'im not to set his cap at me or he might get it thrown back in his face,' she said.

Chapter Seven

Mollie didn't see Charlotte Grainger for several weeks. As autumn began to slip into winter, with days when the fog oozed silently in, rolling the sea flat as it came, or when gales whipped the waves into furious mountains of froth-covered broth that crashed on to the shore, smashing everything in its way and undermining already weakened stretches of cliff, she felt confident that the young lady from the big house would be snugly ensconced by the fire and unlikely to venture on to a bleak, windswept beach.

Not that the beach was a place where Mollie, along with the rest of the mine pickers, was eager to linger in such weather. Wrapped in their red flannel cloaks, nobody stayed longer than was necessary to earn enough tokens for their needs. Even Old Sol, stamping his feet and flapping his arms, was wont to shout, 'Aint you got nearly enough? My owd donkey here's fair froze.' It was fortunate for everybody that the rougher the weather the more prolific the pickings.

But there was the occasional day when the sun shone, the air was clear and the sea had an icy, though not inviting, sparkle.

It was on such a day, in early November, that Mollie wandered along the beach after finishing her day's picking, simply enjoying the bright winter sunshine and the rhythmic sound of the waves crashing on to the sand, reluctant to return home to the sulphurous atmosphere of Copperas Lane. As she went, her old red cloak pulled tightly round her to keep out the cold, she picked up a pretty shell, or a lump of what she now knew to be amber, or a stone worn smooth by the action of the sea. Ambling along, her thoughts turned to Joe Trayler.

Encouraged by Richard, Joe had turned out to be quite a persistent suitor and in desperation she had taken a walk along the cliff top with him on two or three occasions. Aunt Rose approved of this now, but somehow Mollie couldn't see herself married to Joe. She liked him well enough, but not enough to want to bear his children, nor to spend the rest of her life ministering to his needs in a pokey little cottage. Not, to be fair to Joe, that he would provide her with nothing better than a pokey cottage. According to Richard, and indeed to Joe himself, he was a man of means. Or at least he soon would be. If he wasn't caught by the Revenue men first, she had scathingly replied.

The trouble was, he was becoming rather possessive and she didn't know how to discourage him without upsetting Richard, who was very keen to see her married to his friend. It was quite a dilemma.

She turned back the way she had come and kicked a lump of seaweed to uncover what treasures might lie underneath. Disappointingly, there was nothing but a razor shell and a few cockle shells. She straightened up and walked on a little way.

Suddenly, above the sound of the waves she was sure she heard her name called. She glanced over her shoulder, thinking she must have imagined it since a moment ago the beach had been deserted, but there was Charlotte Grainger, her blue cloak flying out behind her to reveal its pale silk lining, its hood fallen back so that the wind tumbled her fair curls, running over the sand, frantically waving and calling to her.

'Mollie! Mollie! Oh, I'm so glad I've found you, I've

been wanting to see you for days. I've got some wonderful news,' she called breathlessly, 'You're to ... ' The rest of her words were lost as a large wave crashed on to the beach. 'What do you think of that?' she finished as she reached Mollie's side.

'What do I think of what?' Mollie asked suspiciously. 'I'm sorry, Miss. I never heard what you said.'

'Oh, dear,' Charlotte put her hand to her heaving breast. 'Let me get my breath back and I'll tell you.' She stood panting for a moment or two. 'Let's go over there, under the cliff where it's a bit sheltered.'

Puzzled, Mollie followed her and sat down beside her on a lump of driftwood that had been thrown up by the last tide. They both automatically pulled their cloaks closer, Mollie's of faded and shabby red flannel, Charlotte's of best quality wool.

'Now,' Charlotte said importantly. 'How would you like to come and live at Cliff House?'

Mollie gaped, a thousand unlikely thoughts flitting through her mind so quickly that they were gone before they had properly formed. Had they discovered ...? No, they couldn't have. But what if ...? Supposing ...? The only thought that stuck was one of horror.

'Oh, I couldn't ... I mean, no, ...I mean, it wouldn't be ...Oh, no, I'm not ... ' She was shaking her head vehemently as she spoke.

Charlotte put her hand over Mollie's. 'I'm sorry, Mollie. I was so excited it's all come out wrong and I've frightened you. Let me start again.' She smiled at Mollie and was rewarded by a somewhat sickly smile in return.

'Now, it's like this,' she began, turning Mollie's rough, work-worn hand over and holding it in her own, which was protected by a soft kid glove. 'Nannie's quite old. She's looked after me since I was a baby, although as I grew up she became more of a maid to me than a nurse; you know, looking after my clothes, brushing my hair, lacing my stays, keeping my room tidy, that sort of thing.'

Mollie nodded, although she didn't know. She couldn't imagine anybody helping her with her stays, even if she'd worn any. And as for anyone else keeping her room tidy or looking after her clothes, she could just imagine Aunt Rose's reaction to that idea!

'Well,' Charlotte was speaking again. 'Nannie's sister is ill and she's had to go to look after her and she says she's not coming back. She says she's getting too old to be a lady's maid and I ought to have somebody who's younger to look after me.' She sighed. 'I shall miss her. I love Nannie, she's a dear, although she has become a bit fumble-fisted and stiff of late. Anyway, Mama agreed with her, although of course she didn't want to let her go.' She spread her hands. 'So now I am without a maid.'

Mollie nodded slowly. 'I see.' She did see. In fact she was several jumps ahead and her heart was beginning to flutter but whether it was with anticipation or fear she wasn't at all sure.

'Mama said we should advertise for somebody but I said there was no need because I knew just the person I should like.' She squeezed Mollie's hand. 'So, you are to come and see Mama and if she thinks you're suitable, and I'm sure she will, you are to come and live at Cliff House and be my personal maid. What do you think of that?'

Mollie chewed her top lip for a minute, frowning. Then she said honestly, 'I think I might quite like it, Miss, but the trouble is, I don't know anything about bein' a personal maid. I don't know about anything except pickin' mine.'

Charlotte put her head on one side. 'Can't you sew?'

'Oh, yes. I can sew,' Mollie answered with a shrug. 'I always hev to alter the clothes I get from the second-hand shop. An' I do all the darnin' cause Aunt Rose says I'm better at it than she is. But that might be because she don't like darnin',' she added thoughtfully.

But Charlotte wasn't listening. 'That's all right, then. Can you iron?' She began ticking off her fingers.

''Course I can.'

68

'Can you clean and tidy a room?'

'Reckon so. I've had to keep our house clean ever since I can remember.'

'Who brushes your hair?'

Mollie looked at her in surprise. 'Why, I do, o'course.'

'Then if you're able to look after your own hair you'll be able to look after mine.' She leaned towards Mollie and said, 'I've never trained a maid before so I'll train you to look after me and you can train me in the right way to treat a maid.'

'I dunno if I can do that, Miss. I ain't never bin anybody's maid,' Mollie said gloomily.

'Well, you can start with me,' Charlotte said. She stood up, suddenly businesslike. 'That is, if Mama approves, and I'm sure she will. You're to come and see her. Will tomorrow morning suit you?'

Mollie opened her mouth and then shut it again, blowing through her lips. 'I . . . er, yes. What time?'

'Oh, half past eleven, I should think. That's when she's usually in the morning room seeing to household things. Come to the back door and ask for Ellis, she's Mama's personal maid. She'll be told to expect you and she'll take you to Mama.' She hunched her shoulders gleefully. 'I'll see you when Mama's finished with you. And don't look so worried, Mollie, everything will be all right, I promise you. I must go now or I shall be late for tea.'

Without giving Mollie a chance to speak she got up and left, hurrying back along the beach, turning to wave as she went up the cliff path. Mollie remained sitting where Charlotte left her, too stunned for the moment to move.

'I dunno as thass such a wunnerful good idea, you goin' to work up at Cliff House, Mollie,' Uncle Sam said quietly, chewing over her news with the tough meat of his mutton stew that night. 'I don't think thass the place for you. Not at all, I don't.'

'No more do I,' Aunt Rose agreed firmly, although for

quite a different reason. 'Who's gonna help me if you're livin' the life of a lady up there on the cliff? Hev you thought o' that?'

'An' what about Joe? You've bin stringin' him along these past weeks. You can't jest drop 'im like a hot coal,' Richard said.

Mollie looked at the faces round the table by the light of the oil lamp. Uncle Sam looked worried but she knew it was because of her mother's fate and her own unspoken relationship to James Grainger. The other two were only concerned with their own interests.

'I'm not droppin' Joe like a hot coal, Richard, 'cause I never picked 'im up in the first place,' Mollie said. 'You kept all on at me to go out with him so in the end I went to keep you quiet, not because I wanted to.'

'He brought you that lace,' Richard reminded her.

'An' I said he could hev it back. He still can. I've got no use for it. The likes o' me don't deck theirselves in Brussels lace.'

'P'raps your lady up at the big house 'ud like it,' Aunt Rose said sarcastically.

'P'raps she would. But thass not my place to offer it to her.' Mollie speared a piece of potato although her appetite had deserted her. 'Anyway, I might not suit. I've got to see Miss Grainger's mama tomorrer.'

'Miss Grainger's mama,' Richard mimicked.

Under the table Mollie kicked his shin.

'Ouch!' He glared at her. Then a sudden thought struck him and his glare turned to a smile. 'Yes, Moll, that'd be very good for you to go up to Cliff House to work,' he said. 'You'd like that. An' you'll better yerself. Yes, thass a very good idea. An' you can always see Joe on your afternoon off.'

'I don't want to see Joe on my afternoon off or at any other time,' Mollie said firmly. As she spoke she frowned at him, wondering what had brought about such a sudden change of heart. But he merely continued to smile at her.

'You'll make a very good lady's maid,' he said mysteriously.

'A lot you'd know about *that*!' his mother said, her voice scathing. 'Clear the table, Mollie.'

After she had cleared the table and washed up, Mollie took a bowl upstairs to her room. Then she came down and got a kettle of hot water and a jug of cold water from the tap outside and took these up the two flights of stairs. Then she came down again because she had forgotten the soap and towel. All this activity was watched by Aunt Rose, sitting tight-lipped on one side of the fire and Uncle Sam, inscrutable behind a cloud of smoke from his pipe on the other. Richard had gone to meet Joe at the pub.

In her room Mollie washed every inch of her body, carefully scrubbing the ingrained dirt from her finger and toenails. Then she washed her hair. When she had finished she tipped the dirty water out of the window. Then she put on a clean shift and got into bed.

But it was a long time before she slept and, when she did, she dreamed she was getting lost down long, thickly carpeted corridors that turned and twisted and led nowhere and all the while a voice was shouting, 'You're late!' She woke up trembling and lay watching the shape of her window gradually emerging out of the blackness and turning from dark to light grey. Then it was time to get up and begin the day's tasks.

At half past ten, the floor swept and the room tidied, she went up to her room and put on her best dress, the one she always wore when she went to church with Uncle Sam on Sundays. It was a kind of muddy brown – not a colour she would have chosen – but it had been the best she could find at Mrs Tattersall's second-hand shop for the money Uncle Sam had given her. She had altered it to fit and worn with a white neckerchief, which she was always careful to keep spotlessly clean, it looked quite presentable unless inspected too closely, when the darns under the arms and the mend in the skirt became apparent.

71

She brushed her hair till it shone, then tied it back with a piece of ribbon she had taken out of an old shift. There was not much she could do about her shoes except rub them as hard as she could with a piece of rag.

At eleven o'clock she went downstairs and took her red cloak from behind the door. Aunt Rose, warming her knees by the fire, watched as she tied it under her chin.

'Are you goin' pickin' when you've bin up to Cliff House?' she asked.

'No, I'm not. I've got my best dress on an' anyway, the tide won't be right.' Mollie answered indignantly.

'Well, you'll hev to pick twice as much termorrer.' Aunt Rose turned back to the fire and gave her knees an affectionate rub. Clearly, she thought the expedition to the big house was a waste of time.

Mollie walked the length of Copperas Lane without encountering anybody. They were all on the beach, where Aunt Rose considered she ought to be. At the end of the High Street she turned left and took the road that led to the top of the cliff. The slope was gentle at first, with cottages dotted at intervals on either side, but as it became steeper the cottages thinned out until the last quarter mile or so was little more than a track, just wide enough for a carriage to pass, through gorse-covered scrubland. From this vantage point the sea stretched to the horizon on her right and to the left the river curled back on itself from the estuary, flowing past the quay at the Copperas House – which was hidden by the town at this point – and on through green fields bordered by hedges on the way to Kirby. At the top of the hill the track ended with iron gates proclaiming the entrance to Cliff House. Beside them was a little kissing gate which Mollie slipped through and crunched her way up the gravel drive. In front of her was the tall, ivy-covered house with a large oak front door behind a porch supported by stone pillars. Either side of the porch were big, square-paned windows, with smaller ones above. It looked even more grand than when she had viewed it from the seaward side yet it still managed to retain a warm, welcoming look.

Welcoming or not, by this time Mollie's mouth was dry, her hands were shaking and she wished with all her heart that she had never agreed to come. Yet a tiny part of her, almost buried under her nervousness, was excited at the prospect of a chance to live in this lovely old house, and a small voice kept hinting that this was where she rightfully belonged. She tried not to listen to that small voice, realising, as Uncle Sam had told her before he left that morning, that it would do no good and it would be best to forget it.

She squared her shoulders and marched purposefully round to the back of the house. The best thing to do was to pretend she wasn't nervous, then perhaps she wouldn't be.

She knocked on the door and asked in her best voice if Miss Ellis was there.

'She's expectin' me,' she added primly.

'Oh, is she indeed!' the scrubbing woman who had answered the door said. 'Well, you'd better step inside. No, not too far. Jest there.' She indicated a large doormat just inside the kitchen door.

Mollie waited, twisting her hands together under her cloak, watching a plump woman in a large white apron, obviously the cook, standing at the table and expertly covering a pie with pastry and fluting the edge. Then she opened the door of a huge oven at the end of the room and put the pie inside. An enormous dresser ran the length of the kitchen, filled with matching china. On the top shelf copper jelly moulds shone. Mollie had never seen such a big kitchen. Nobody had to edge round this table like they did at home, and the ceiling was high, with hooks for the big hams that hung from it.

After a few minutes Ellis came into the kitchen. 'Ah, you're here,' she said briskly when she saw Mollie. 'Good. You're on time. The Missus will see you now. Follow me.'

The journey was reminiscent of the one Mollie had made with Charlotte, only this time she was following a tall, rather thin woman in a purple dress that rustled as she walked. Over it she was wearing a large apron that fastened with a button at the neck and another at the waist. Mollie kept her eye on the buttons as they went up the back stairs and along carpeted corridors, until Ellis knocked and opened the door to a big, airy room. The first thing Mollie noticed was that the floor was covered with the most beautiful carpet, patterned in pink and gold. Carpets seemed to be the thing she noticed about this house, she realised, probably because they didn't have any at home. Then she saw a lady in a dove-grey morning gown sitting at a desk between two windows at the far end of the room.

She turned her head. 'All right, Ellis, that will be all,' she said with a slight nod. She held her hand out. 'Come over here, Mollie. I want to look at you. My daughter seems to think you're a paragon of all the virtues. Is it true?' She smiled as she spoke.

'I dunno about that, Ma'am.' Mollie wasn't even sure what the words meant. She walked gingerly across the carpet towards the lady, who had the kindest face she had ever seen.

Chapter Eight

The journey over the pink and gold carpet seemed to last for ever and Mollie was very conscious of her shabby shoes, revealed by the drab, not-quite-long-enough brown dress. But at last she was standing in front of Mrs Grainger, who, to her surprise, was actually smiling at her.

'What a very pretty girl you are. And your dress brings out the colour of your lovely dark-brown eyes.'

Such kind words and said with such sincerity that Mollie felt tears welling in her eyes. Nobody had ever called her pretty before. She dipped an awkward curtsey. 'Thank you, Ma'am. This is my best dress. I've never liked the colour much,' she added honestly.

Beatrice Grainger smiled again, noting the darns and the mended tear. 'Well, now. Do you think you would like to come here and be my daughter's maid?'

Mollie nodded cautiously. 'If you please, Ma'am. I think I should like it very much, if I'm suitable.'

'Well, we'll see.' Beatrice leaned forward. 'Tell me about yourself, Mollie.'

Mollie repeated the well-rehearsed version of her birth and upbringing. She had known, from the moment she set eyes on this lovely lady with the startlingly blue eyes, that she could never bring heartache and sorrow to her by divulging the real truth of her birth. Uncle Sam had been right. It was a secret only he and she shared and never to be told to another living soul. In her heart she knew that she should never have come here and that the best thing she could do would be to go away from this house and never come back, for if the truth were ever to come out ... oh, it didn't bear thinking about. But neither did a life spent picking mine, or worse, married to Joe Trayler. Not after the chance she was being offered here.

'... an' I've bin with Uncle Sam and Aunt Rose ever since,' she finished.

'I see,' Beatrice said when she had finished. She frowned slightly. 'Sam Barnes? He's your uncle? I seem to have heard that name before.'

'Thass right, Ma'am. He's boiler man at the Copperas House.'

Her face cleared and she nodded. 'Ah, yes. That's where I've heard the name. I've heard my nephew Mark speak very highly of him to my husband.' She regarded Mollie for several minutes, looking her up and down. Mollie stood quietly, hoping she couldn't see the way her heart was thumping in her breast. At last Beatrice spoke again.

'Are you honest, Mollie? Are you to be trusted? If you came into this room when it was empty and found a florin on the floor what would you do with it?'

Mollie frowned, puzzled. 'But I wouldn't come in here if the room was empty, would I. It wouldn't be my place, Ma'am,' she said.

'But supposing you did, for some reason,' Beatrice persisted. 'The florin. What would you do with it?'

Mollie shook her head, still puzzled. 'I wouldn't do nothin' with it, Ma'am.'

'Wouldn't you pick it up?'

Mollie flushed. 'No, indeed I wouldn't. If I picked it up somebody might come in an' think I was tryin' to steal it an' I'd never steal. My Uncle Sam has always told me never to take anything that didn't belong to me an' I never have. Well,' she added, trying to be completely honest,

'I've picked up shells an' things off the beach but they don't belong to nobody, do they.'

'Anybody,' Beatrice corrected absently. 'They don't belong to anybody.'

'No, so that don't count.'

'No, that doesn't count,' Beatrice agreed, making a mental note that the girl's speech would have to be attended to. She nodded briskly. 'Now, my daughter tells me you've never had any experience of being in service.' It was a statement but sounded like a question so Mollie answered it.

'No, Ma'am. But I'm willin' to learn. An' I can sew, an' iron an' keep a room clean ... ' she tried to think what other things Charlotte had listed yesterday on the beach.

Beatrice laughed. It was an infectious, throaty chuckle and Mollie smiled with her although she didn't know what she had said that was so funny.

'Oh, I don't think you'll be required to clean rooms, Mollie. Tidy them, perhaps, but we have maids to do the cleaning and dusting.' Beatrice looked at her, a long and searching look. Mollie returned her gaze without fear.

'I think sixpence a week to begin with, as you've no experience. Of course, you'll be provided with your clothing and your keep. Will that suit? We'll put it up to ninepence after a month and a shilling after three months, if everything is satisfactory.' Beatrice smiled at her encouragingly.

Mollie's eyes widened. 'You mean, I can come here? I can be Miss Grainger's personal maid?'

'That's exactly what I mean. But you must learn to call her Miss Charlotte, not Miss Grainger. Now, when would you like to start work? Tomorrow? Or do you need longer to go home and consult your aunt and uncle and collect your belongings?'

'No, Ma'am. Tomorrow will be jest right.'

'Good. Would you like me to send the gardner's boy to carry your trunk?'

77

Mollie blushed. 'I don't hev a trunk, Ma'am, thank you all the same.'

'Ah, no, of course.' Beatrice cursed herself for her lack of tact. She smiled at the girl. 'Very well, Mollie. I hope you'll enjoy working here at Cliff House. Be here tomorrow at nine-thirty sharp and Ellis will find you something suitable to wear. I think I agree with you, the dress you're wearing is not a particularly good colour, even though it does make your eyes look darker.' The conspiratorial way she smiled took any offence out of her words. 'Now, I'll ring for Ellis to see you out.'

The door burst open and Charlotte nearly fell into the room. 'No need, Mama, I'll see Mollie out.'

'Charlotte! You naughty girl. You've been listening at the door,' her mother admonished sternly.

'I know. But it was only because I was so desperate.' Charlotte ran up to her mother and smothered her with kisses. 'Oh, thank you, darling Mama. But I knew you'd like Mollie. How could anybody not like her!'

Charlotte's words came back to Mollie as she listened to Aunt Rose's tirade about her ingratitude at leaving Copperas Lane just at the time when she was needed and when she was becoming useful. 'After all I've done for you over the years, slavin' and scrapin', workin' my fingers to the bone to give you a good home. You're a selfish, ungrateful little bitch. Trying to get above yerself. Well, no good will come of it. You mark my words.' With that Aunt Rose refused to speak another word to her.

Uncle Sam was his usual kindly self. 'We shall miss you, Mollie,' he said, after his wife had taken herself off to bed. 'But you've got the chance to better yourself an' I don't blame you for takin' it. But jest remember what I said, no good can come of ... you know ... rakin' up the past, so best forget I ever told you.' He reached in his waistcoat pocket and pulled out a shilling. 'There, buy yerself somethin' pretty to take with you to remind you of your Uncle Sam.'

Her eyes filled with tears. 'Oh, Uncle. I shall come back an' see you. I don't need a present to remind me.'

He closed her fingers over the shilling. 'Buy yerself somethin', all the same.'

She didn't even see Richard.

The next morning, clad once again in the hated brown dress, Mollie put her collection of shells, her patchwork quilt and cushion and a clean shift and stockings into a bundle and set off for Cliff House, smiling a little at Mrs Grainger's notion that she night need help with her trunk. She had said her goodbyes to Uncle Sam the night before and Aunt Rose was sitting by the fire with her back to her, ignoring her farewell.

When she reached the High Street she called in at the pawn shop, where there were often unredeemed things for sale, and after a good deal of thought spent Uncle Sam's shilling on a pretty little filigree gold brooch with an amethyst stone. She pinned this carefully inside her bundle and continued on her way.

Once again she took the cliff path, pulling her red cloak round her against the brisk north-east wind. The tide was just on the turn; fanned by the wind it was still hurling itself against the base of the cliffs in a fury of white foam, sending up showers of spray before being dragged back to be replaced by the next angry onslaught. She stood for several minutes, watching the green, heaving sea and listening to its relentless rhythm as it crashed against the cliffs. There would be good pickings when the tide went out, but that never need concern her again, she thought happily.

She bent her head against the wind, hitched her bundle a little higher and continued on her way.

Ellis was already in the kitchen when she arrived at Cliff House, drinking a cup of tea with Cook.

'She looks as if she could do with a cup, an' all,' Cook said, nodding towards Mollie.

Ellis put her cup down on its saucer. 'She can have hers when she's changed her clothes,' she said briskly. 'Come along Mollie. This way.'

Once again Mollie found herself following the buttons on Ellis's overall, but this time it was only along the passage from the kitchen to the sitting room Ellis shared with Cook. Here, draped over the horsehair sofa, were two purple striped dresses and two overalls similar to the one Ellis was wearing, an assortment of underclothes and several small white aprons with lace edging. A row of soft black shoes, some of them barely worn at all, were ranged under the window.

'I think you'll find these things will fit you,' Ellis said, looking her up and down. 'You look about the same size as Maud. She left last year because she thought she could do better at Beaumont Hall, although from what I've heard she's not so happy there. However . . . ' She held one of the dresses against Mollie. 'Yes, that looks about right. Can you alter it to fit if necessary?'

Mollie nodded eagerly. 'Oh, yes, Miss, thank you, Miss. I'm quite good with my needle.'

Ellis's stern features softened slightly. 'Ellis will do, Mollie, when you address me. Now,' she pointed to the shoes. 'Try and find a pair that fit reasonably well because you'll be on your feet for a good part of the day. But they're all quite soft so they'll soon mould to your feet.' She went to the door. 'I'll leave you to change. When you're ready come back to the kitchen and you can have a cup of tea and one of Cook's morning buns before you begin work. Don't be long, now. Miss Charlotte is out riding but there's quite a lot for you to do before she gets back.' Her tone, though brisk, was not unkind.

Mollie tried to hurry but she had never seen such fine linen shifts before and it was impossible not to finger them just a little before putting one on. And she had never worn stays before so they were difficult to fasten. But the petticoats were easier. First she tied on a thin cambric one followed by one made of fine flannel before slipping one of the purple striped dresses over her head.

She was still struggling with the buttons when Ellis returned.

'Ah, good, it looks as if everything fits. As I thought.' As she spoke she was deftly fastening the buttons down Mollie's back. 'What about the shoes?'

Mollie held out her foot. In truth she hardly felt she was wearing shoes at all, these slippers were so soft and light.

'Are they comfortable? Do they pinch at all?'

'No, they're quite comfortable.'

Ellis slipped her into the large white overall and fastened the buttons. 'Now, brush your hair and tie it up under this cap and you'll be ready.' She handed Mollie a hair brush. 'I'll have the rest of your things taken up to your room later.' She pinched her lip. 'Oh, and I must find you an afternoon dress, because these will be your morning clothes. That dress you came in is hardly suitable. Did you bring another?'

Mollie flushed. 'No, thass the on'y one I've got.'

'Well, never mind. I'm sure we can find you something.' She looked disparagingly at Mollie's bundle, left on the floor just inside the door. 'So this is all you've brought with you?'

Mollie nodded, suddenly ashamed. Then she saw the glint from the little amethyst brooch pinned on the bundle. 'Do you think I might wear my little brooch? It was a present from my Uncle Sam.' She unpinned it and showed it to Ellis.

'It's not usual for servants to deck themselves in trinkets,' Ellis said, then, seeing Mollie's crestfallen face she smiled. 'But I don't see why not, just for today, as long as you keep it hidden under your collar.'

'Thank you, Miss ... thank you, Ellis,' Mollie said, managing a shy smile for the first time since she arrived.

81

'Well, now, come and have your tea and then I'll take you and show you your room.'

Back in the kitchen a place was laid at one end with a morning bun on a plate that had rosebuds round the rim. Cook poured a cup of tea from a large teapot standing at the side of the stove into a matching cup and saucer.

'There you are. You look as if you could do with fattening up a bit,' she said cheerfully.

'Thank you.' Slowly, Mollie ate the delicious bun and drank her tea, watching Cook deftly kneading dough. 'Did you make this?' She held up what was left of the bun.

Cook's smile faded. 'Yes. What's wrong with it?'

'Oh, nothin'. Nothin' at all. I was goin' to say thass the best bun I've ever tasted.' It was quite true. It also taught her that Cook, kind as she was, was not open to criticism.

Five minutes later Ellis came back.

'You'd better look to her hands, Ellis,' Cook said, pointing to Mollie's chapped and chilblained fingers. 'They'll need a good soak and a dose of olive oil and caster sugar before she's let loose on Miss Charlotte's fine things.'

'Ah, yes. You're right. I knew there was something else I needed to do.' Ellis was pouring hot water at the sink as she spoke. 'Come here, Mollie. Now wash your hands carefully and then soak them in the water for a few minutes.'

Mollie did as she was told, savouring the warm, silky water. Then Ellis poured a little olive oil into her palm together with a good sprinkling of caster sugar. 'Now, rub it well in,' she instructed.

Again Mollie did as she was told, amazed at how soft her hands became.

Ellis inspected them. 'Good, now you must keep them well creamed. I'll give you a little pot of cream and you must use it every night before you go to sleep. It's important to keep your hands soft and smooth or they'll snag the fine fabric you'll be handling. Now, follow me and I'll take you to your room.'

The room was on the second floor with a view out over the sea. It held a single bed, a chair and a chest of drawers, over which hung a painted mirror. There was a rag rug on the floor. Although it was not as big as Mollie's room at home it looked bigger because the ceiling didn't slope.

'I've brought my patchwork quilt with me,' she said shyly. 'I made it myself. May I be allowed to put it on my bed?'

'This is your room. You can put what you like in it, within reason,' Ellis told her. 'If you're cold there's an extra blanket in the bottom drawer of the chest there.'

She looked at the fob watch pinned on her overall. 'It's nearly eleven. Time I took you to Miss Charlotte's room. Will you be able to find your way back up here tonight? Remember, your room is the third door from the top of the stairs. The first door is where Kitty, the kitchen maid sleeps. She has the room at the head of the stairs so that she doesn't disturb us when she gets up to light the fires. The next one is Tilda's; she's the housemaid. Then it's your room. Mine is the one at the end of the corridor because it's bigger.' There was a note of pride in her voice as she imparted this piece of information.

'Who sleeps in there?' Mollie asked, pointing to the two rooms between the one she had been given and Ellis's.

'Nobody. They're mainly used for storing unwanted furniture. If there's anything from there you would like in your room you only have to ask.'

'Oh, no. I'm sure my room is very nice as it is, thank you,' Mollie said quickly. She followed Ellis to the stairs, being careful not to tread on her new dress as she went. 'Are there any more servants?'

'Oh, yes. Cook, of course, you've met. She has her rooms downstairs. Then we have a scrubbing woman and a laundry woman but they live in the village. The groom and the gardener both have rooms over the stables. Arthur is the butler and he also looks after Mr Grainger and Mr

Sebastian, but naturally, his room is in another part of the house.'

'I see.'

'You'll be given your own candle from the kitchen when you come to bed. The master and mistress are not mean over candles but of course they don't like waste.' She was now speaking over her shoulder as they made their way back down the stairs.

'I see.' Mollie didn't know what else to say.

'Are there any questions?'

'I don't think so.' There were hundreds, but Mollie didn't know where to begin.

'Ah, yes, I forgot. You will, of course, eat in the kitchen with us. Mealtimes are set but if Miss Charlotte's requirements make you late then your meal will be kept for you.' They reached the bottom of the first flight of stairs and Ellis paused. 'Naturally, these are the stairs you will always use. Only in exceptional circumstances do the servants use the front stairs.' She pushed open a heavy door leading to the main part of the house. 'This way,' she said, her voice dropping to a respectful quietness.

Mollie tried to memorise the way to Miss Charlotte's room. Six steps along from the door along the beautiful blue carpet, turn to the right; one, two, three, doors along, tap at the door and walk in.

Charlotte's room, the same room Mollie had taken tea in, was a shambles, with clothes draped on chairs, strewn on the floor, flung carelessly on the bed, hairpins spilled over the dressing table and cold washing water still left in the bowl on the washstand.

'You can see Miss Charlotte is without a maid,' Ellis said, tight-lipped. 'I've been doing what I can but I can't be everywhere at once. Perhaps you'd like to make a start before she gets back. I'm afraid she's not the tidiest of creatures.' With that she left.

The next half hour was one of the happiest of Mollie's life as she straightened Charlotte's room, putting things

84

away, hanging dresses in the long cupboard in the chimney recess, emptying slops and bringing up more coal. She was just finishing making the bed, smoothing her hands lovingly over the soft linen sheets and straightening the pale-blue muslin drapes round it, when Charlotte burst in.

'Oh, Mollie, you're here! That's wonderful.' She took off the jaunty little green hat she had worn for riding and flung it on the bed. 'Help me out of these things,' she said. 'Tuppence went through a huge puddle and splashed water all over my skirt. Mind you, it was a good day for a ride; there's a good fresh wind to blow the cobwebs away.' She glanced round the room. 'I'm afraid I left rather a muddle, didn't I. I'm not very good at putting things away, but I see you've done it for me.'

'I might not hev put them all away in the right place, Miss Charlotte.'

'Oh, that doesn't matter. You'll know where they are when I want them.'

Charlotte chattered all the time as Mollie helped her to change out of her riding habit and into a warm, rose-pink, velvet dress. Then Mollie brushed her hair and between them they managed to pin it up into some kind of order.

'Ouch. That went straight in!' Charlotte squealed as a hairpin went straight into her head.

'I'm sorry, Miss Charlotte, but I ain't never done this sort of thing before.'

'You'll learn. Don't worry. Yes, that looks all right.' Charlotte scrabbled in a drawer and pulled out a narrow pink ribbon. 'Tie this round, it'll hold it all together. Yes, that's lovely.' She put her head on one side, giggling. 'Now we'll go and sort out my fossils. I've been dying to show you the new ones I found halfway up the cliff. I think they're teeth from some kind of animal, but I can't imagine what. You wouldn't expect to find teeth halfway up a cliff, would you? Come and see.'

'I don't think I should. Not now, Miss Charlotte. I'm supposed to be workin'. I'm supposed to be lookin' after

85

you,' Mollie reminded her. 'I b'lieve you usually hev a cup of chocolate when you come in from your ride. Shall I get it for you?'

'Oh, yes. I'd quite forgotten.' She giggled again. 'It's just that I'm so excited to think you're here, Mollie.' She became serious, putting her head on one side. 'I should like to think we can become friends as well as mistress and maid, you know.'

'Thank you, Miss Charlotte. Thass very kind of you to say so,' Mollie answered, but she found herself superstitiously crossing her fingers behind her back as she spoke.

Chapter Nine

Working at Cliff House opened up a whole new world to Mollie. She had never imagined anyone could own as many clothes as she saw in Charlotte's wardrobe. There were gowns of silk and muslin, dimity and velvet, satin and lace and often combinations of various materials – many of which she couldn't even put a name to – in a single garment. Then there were shifts and petticoats to match, plus drawers full of stockings and gloves and little lace caps and a whole shelf of hats, not to mention the racks of shoes. No wonder she needed a personal maid, Mollie decided. It would take all one person's time to look after all these beautiful things, never mind running around after a delightful but rather spoiled mistress.

There was the kitchen hierarchy to be learned, too. It was Cook's domain and her word was law, even over Ellis and Arthur. At mealtimes Cook sat at the head of the table, with Ellis on her right and Tilda, the housemaid on her left. Mollie was assigned the place next to Ellis, opposite Kitty, the kitchen maid. At the other end of the table Arthur presided, with Perkins the groom on one side and Bragg the gardener on the other, with Sid, gardener's boy and general helper, at his side. A strategically placed empty chair halfway down the table on each side effectively divided the men from the women.

Thursday was Mollie's designated afternoon off but she

often didn't take it because she had nowhere much to go. Uncle Sam was at work so she couldn't see him and Aunt Rose did nothing but taunt her with 'getting above her station' so there was no pleasure in visiting Copperas Lane. Added to that she was not anxious to run across Richard and his friend Joe Trayler.

In any case, to Mollie work was one long holiday. She thoroughly enjoyed looking after Charlotte's clothes and running her errands. She didn't feel at all put upon running down to the kitchen last thing at night for a hot brick when she had already carefully warmed her mistress's bed with the warming pan; nor did she mind fetching a book from the library or a forgotten shawl from the drawing room, even though she might be busy at the time mending a torn ruffle or hem.

As for Charlotte, although she ordered Mollie around with little thought, she seemed to regard her more as a friend than a servant and on rainy winter afternoons spent endless hours and earned Mollie's eternal gratitude by teaching her to read and write.

'Well, when we can't go out walking or looking for fossils on the beach we might as well occupy ourselves usefully,' she said airily when Mollie attempted to thank her. 'In any case, I'm looking forward to the time when you can read aloud to me. I like being read to.' She put her head on one side, watching Mollie struggle with the book she was trying to read, pointing to every word and mouthing it silently. 'But I don't think you're quite ready for that yet.'

Mollie looked up, frowning. 'I'm tryin' very hard, Miss Charlotte. But thass difficult,'

'I know.' Charlotte smiled sympathetically. 'And try and remember to say *it's* difficult, not *thass* difficult, Mollie. And trying has got a g on the end, -ing, trying.'

'I'm trying very hard,' Mollie repeated carefully. 'But it's very difficult.'

'Capital!' Charlotte said, clapping her hands. 'Now, put

that book down and let's go and look for fossils on the beach. It's stopped raining, the sun's come out and it's ages since I added anything to my collection. Ah . . .' She paused in mid clap. 'What's the state of the tide? We don't want to get caught out like I did once before.'

Gratefully, Mollie closed her book. Although she was determined to master this reading business it wasn't easy and sometimes the words seemed to dance mockingly on the page, defying her to make sense of them. She glanced at the clock, although it was hardly necessary since she had an almost built-in knowledge of the tides, born of years of picking mine on the beach. 'Thass about half-tide. We've got an hour or two before the beach is covered.' Then she remembered herself as she got to her feet and said carefully, emulating her young mistress's way of speaking, 'I'll go and fetch your riding boots from the boot room. It will be very wet underfoot.'

'What about you, Mollie?' Charlotte said, in an uncharacteristic burst of concern. 'You haven't got riding boots.'

'Oh, I can wear my clogs. Thass – that's what I always wear when it's wet.'

The scrubbing woman had been working in the boot room and the boots weren't in their usual place. It took Mollie several minutes to find them, on top of the bench, half hidden by a waterproof cape.

As she turned to go back up the stairs the outside door opened, letting in a blast of cold air together with Sebastian.

'Ah, hullo! It's the elusive Mollie, my sister's bosom companion, if my eyes don't deceive me. Usually, I don't get more than a glimpse of a pretty ankle and the tails of an apron as you whisk out of sight round a corner.' Taking off his coat he had placed himself between her and the door to the back stairs.

She bobbed a sketchy curtsey. 'I came to get Miss Charlotte's boots, sir,' she said, holding them up and carefully not meeting his eyes. 'Miss Charlotte thought it would be nice to go and look for fossils on the beach, now that the rain has stopped and the sun has come out.'

'Good idea. I'm damned if I don't accompany you.' He pulled out his pocket watch. 'Oh, hang it, I can't. I promised Pater I'd go and give Mark a hand down at the Works.' He looked up and grinned. 'Never mind, I'm already late so another half hour won't make much difference, will it.' He shrugged his coat back on. 'I'll wait for you on the cliff steps. What do you say to that, Mollie?' He smiled at her, his grey eyes dancing.

'I'll tell Miss Charlotte. I'm sure she'll think it very nice that you want to come.' She bobbed another curtsey.

'Oh, I'm sure my sister won't care one way or the other. But what do you say, Mollie?' He raised one eyebrow.

'I'll be happy with whatever Miss Charlotte wants, sir,' she answered, making her voice deliberately wooden. She knew he was trying to flirt with her and although she was flattered, she valued her position too much to encourage him. But he was still standing with his back to the door she must pass through to get to the stairs.

She took a deep breath. 'Please, sir, if I might pass? Miss Charlotte is waiting for her boots and she'll be cross if I keep her waiting.'

'Does she get cross with you, Mollie?'

'No, sir. Not often.' Mollie was holding on to her temper with difficulty. She wished he would move or that there was some way she could get past him. 'Please, sir, will you let me pass. It would go badly for me if I was to be found here alone with you.'

He nodded. 'Yes, you're quite right. I shouldn't have delayed you,' he said. 'It was quite wrong of me. Please forgive me.' He picked up her free hand and kissed the back of it, then stepped aside and opened the door for her. 'Tell Charlotte I'll see you both on the cliff steps in five minutes.'

Thankful that he couldn't see her flaming face Mollie hurried back up the stairs.

'I'm sorry I was so long, Miss Charlotte, but the scrubbing woman had moved the boots and I couldn't find them,' she said breathlessly, though whether it was from hurrying up the stairs or from her encounter with Sebastian she couldn't be sure. 'And then Mr Sebastian came in and asked what I was doing and I had to tell him. He said he'd like to come too and he'll meet us ... you ... on the cliff steps in five minutes.'

'What's got into him, I wonder? He's never shown any interest in looking for fossils before,' Charlotte remarked as she held out her foot for Mollie to pull on her boot.

A few minutes later – Charlotte in her warm blue cloak and Mollie in a green one Charlotte had tired of – they hurried across the lawn to where Sebastian was waiting for them at the top of the cliff steps. Now that the rain had stopped, everywhere looked bright and fresh in the early December sunlight. Raindrops jewelled the bare black branches of the trees, making them glisten in the slight breeze that had sprung up, and holly berries glowed red amongst their prickly green leaves. Below them, the sea heaved gently in the rising tide, spangled all over by points of sunlight.

'It's a long time since I've been beachcombing,' Sebastian said, picking up a broken shell and handing it to Charlotte.

She handed it back to him. 'That's not the kind of thing we're looking for. We're looking for fossils; I've got all the shells I need.'

'Here's a nice piece of amber, Miss Charlotte,' Mollie called from a little distance away. She had seen the army of mine pickers in their shabby red cloaks at the far end of the beach and was anxious to keep as far away from them as possible, knowing the kind of jibes she could expect if they noticed her.

Sebastian immediately bounded over to where she stood. 'Let me see.'

She held out her mittened hand to show him.

He put his hand under hers to hold it steady. 'It doesn't

91

look much,' he said, 'Just a piece of coloured glass. I don't think it's amber at all.' He smiled into her eyes. 'Were you just saying that to get me to come over here, Miss Mollie?' he asked, with exaggerated politeness.

'Indeed, I was not, Sir,' she answered, pulling her hand away from his. 'I'm quite sure this is a piece of amber.' She wetted her finger and rubbed the surface. 'And look, do you see? There's a little insect, I think it might be an ant, trapped inside. We'll be able to see better when it's polished properly. Look, Miss Charlotte.' She held it out to Charlotte, who had just wandered along to join them.

'Oh, it's not fair that you should not only have found a piece of amber but a piece with an insect trapped inside it. That's really quite rare,' Charlotte said petulantly, peering at it lying in Mollie's palm. 'I haven't found *anything* yet.'

'Well, I've spent a good many years on this beach so I've got a good eye for looking, Miss Charlotte.' She held it out. 'It's another piece for your collection.'

'Yes, so it is.' Charlotte put out her hand but before she could take it Sebastian had whisked it out of Mollie's hand.

'Oh, no you don't, Charley. I'm going to take it and have it polished and made up into a brooch, since you say it's such a find,' he said firmly.

'Oh, what a good idea. I'd never thought of that,' Charlotte said. 'Thank you, Seb.'

Sebastian put his head on one side. 'I don't recall saying I was going to have it done for you, Charley,' he said, half-laughing. 'I could have another fair bosom in mind.' As he spoke he looked at Mollie and gave her a broad wink.

She turned away quickly, and glanced up at the sky, saying. 'I don't think we should stay down here much longer, Miss Charlotte. I think it's going to rain again.'

Charlotte gave a cursory look at the gathering clouds. 'Oh, it won't rain for ages yet. Let's go and see if we can find anything in the cliff. Did you bring the bag with my little pick-hammer and notebook, Mollie?'

'Yes, I've got them here.' Mollie glanced again at the

approaching cloud. Twenty minutes, she gave it, and coming from the north-east it probably held snow, not rain, unless she was much mistaken. It was certainly cold enough. However she had no choice but to follow Charlotte to the cliff face, where she was busily showing her brother the most likely places to find fossils.

'Oh, you're so much taller than me, you can reach without having to climb,' she was saying. 'Can you see anything, Seb?'

'No, only this hard, mud-like stuff,' he said, stepping back and wiping his hands together. 'It's filthy. I don't know why on earth you spend your time digging around in it.'

'Because you never know what you might find,' she said, digging around with her little pick. 'And it's not fair. Mollie's found a piece of amber today and I don't want to go back without finding something too. You just need to look a bit harder, Seb.'

Tired of being under his sister's supervision Sebastian pulled out his watch. 'I've got to go. I'm supposed to be at the Works, giving Mark a hand and I'm already late,' he said.

'Oh, that's a shame. But never mind. Off you go, then! Mollie, you're a bit taller than me. You come and look. I'm sure there's something just up there. Look.'

'My sister is very persistent,' Sebastian said as he passed Mollie. 'I can't imagine how she can get so much pleasure from poking about on a filthy cliff face. I can think of much more congenial ways to pass my time, can't you, Mollie?' The way he smiled at her made Mollie blush to the roots of her hair, although when she came to think of it he had said nothing in the least out of place.

'I think we should go back, Miss Charlotte,' Mollie said, after a further twenty minutes of fruitless searching. 'The tide's coming in fast now and it's beginning to rain. In fact, I think it's not rain, it's snow.'

Charlotte looked up and saw the heavy black cloud overhead and a snowflake fell on her face. 'Oh, Mollie, you're right, it is snowing! What fun! But I suppose we should be getting back. We don't want to get trapped by the tide like we did once before. We might die of exposure.'

Mollie gathered up the little pick-hammer, put it in the bag and they hurried along the beach to the cliff steps. By the time they reached the top of the steps the snow was swirling round them like feathers from a hastily plucked goose and Charlotte was complaining, with what breath she had left that Mollie should have warned her earlier. Mollie said nothing but vented her irritation by making Charlotte run too fast across the lawn to the house.

Later, Charlotte sat wrapped in a shawl and shivering in front of a large fire in her room, her rather bedraggled gown draped sadly over the end of the bed and her cloak, together with Mollie's, left downstairs in the boot room to dry, along with the boots.

'I don't know what your mama would say if she could see you, I'm sure, Miss Charlotte,' Mollie said, stirring the mixture of warm milk and brandy she had fetched from the kitchen before handing it to her.

'Well, she doesn't need to know we got caught in a snowstorm.' Charlotte curled her fingers round the mug and looked up. 'Aren't you cold, too, Mollie?' she asked, deliberately changing the subject.

'Me? Nah. I don't feel the cold. I've been out in worse'n that a good many times pickin' mine. I mean, picking mine,' she corrected herself.

'Well, I'm cold. Right through to my bones.' Charlotte shivered again. 'I hope I shan't die of pneumonia. It really was too bad of you not to warn me, Mollie.'

Mollie bit her lip against a sharp retort and tried to concentrate on all the good things about her young mistress.

Later that same night, after Mollie had gone to bed with a hot brick wrapped in flannel at her feet, the bell that connected her room with Charlotte's bedroom rang. She sat up. So much for going to bed early. What could the wretched girl want now, she thought uncharitably. Reluctantly, she left her nice warm nest and putting on a pink quilted wrap – another of Charlotte's cast-offs – she re-lit her candle and padded down the cold back stairs and along the carpeted corridor to her mistress's room.

Charlotte was sitting up in bed swathed in a fur shawl. 'Oh, Mollie, I think I'm dying,' she croaked. 'My throat feels as if I've swallowed pins. And I've got such a headache.'

Mollie put her hand on Charlotte's forehead. It was burning. 'You're not dying. You've got a bit of a chill, Miss Charlotte, that's all,' she said cheerfully. 'I'll just go down to the kitchen and fetch you a powder and make you some hot lemon. I shan't be long.' She looked down at the pink wrap. 'Oh, I s'pose I'd better go and put some clothes on first.'

'Oh, don't bother with that. Just get me the powder and a drink. The only person likely to be in the kitchen is Cook and she's probably gone to bed, anyway.' She gave an apologetic smile. 'I'm sorry to drag you out of bed,' she said in a small voice, 'but I do feel so very, very ill.'

Mollie smiled back at her. It wasn't often Charlotte apologised. 'That's all right. I forgive you, Miss Charlotte. I wasn't asleep,' she said. 'All the same, I think I'd better make myself respectable before I go wandering about the house.'

'Well, don't be long.' Charlotte said crisply.

She wasn't too ill to give orders, Mollie thought as she made her way back up to her room and pulled on her dress.

With a last look at her nice warm bed Mollie made her way down to the kitchen, holding her candle high and shivering in the cold night air. She knew that the kitchen would be warm because the big range was never allowed to go out but she was surprised to find that the oil lamps were still alight. Then she saw that there was somebody sitting at the long scrubbed table. It was Mr Mark. He was eating the steak and kidney pie that Cook had apparently kept hot for him over a saucepan. He looked grey with tiredness.

Mollie stopped short in the doorway. This was the first time she had seen Mr Mark since coming to work at Cliff House and she had never in her life been as close to him as this.

'Oh, I do beg your pardon, Sir. I didn't know you were here. I just came down to get Miss Charlotte something for her sore throat. But I can get it later.' She turned to leave.

'No, no, come in. It's Mollie, isn't it? Mollie Barnes.' He smiled at her; the nice smile she remembered from the Copperas House.

She nodded, then because she couldn't help herself, blurted out, 'You're very late tonight, Sir. Is there anything wrong at the Works?'

He shook his head. 'No, there's nothing wrong. Just some figures that I couldn't get right. Worried about your Uncle Sam?'

'Yes, Sir. I thought p'raps there'd bin an accident ... seein' as how you're so late.'

'No, no. Everything's fine. Sam's fine. He's a good man, your uncle.'

'I think that, too, Sir. He's been like a father to me ever since I can remember.' She was still standing in the doorway.

He waved her in. 'Don't mind me. Come in and do what you've come to do, Mollie,' he said, then, a trifle impatiently, 'And please don't call me "sir"; the name's Mark. I'm employed by Mr Grainger, even though he is my uncle.'

'I see. Very well, S ... Mr Mark.' She busied herself with lemons and the lemon squeezer at the end of the long table. Glancing up she found herself being studied by a pair of deep-set hazel eyes. Disconcerted, she looked away and said quickly, 'Miss Charlotte was out in the snow and she's caught a chill so I'm making her some hot lemon.'

'What about you? Weren't you out in the snow, too?'

She laughed. 'Oh, yes, but when you've spent years out in all weathers picking mine you don't catch chills easily.'

'No, I guess not. Picking mine is not for the faint-hearted.' He finished his meal and pushed the plate away. Then he sat massaging his temples.

'Have you got a headache, S... Mr Mark?' she asked.

'What? Oh, yes, I have. I expect I've been poring over ledgers for too long.' He ran his fingers through his over long fair hair, making it look even more untidy.

'I shall be making Miss Charlotte a powder in a minute. I could make one for you as well, if you like,' she offered shyly.

'That's very kind of you.' He smiled again and she noticed that his smile reached his eyes, crinkling them at the corners and breaking up his otherwise rather stern features.

She turned away quickly to hide a sudden, unexpected blush. She had not really been in Mark's company before and had hardly ever spoken much to him, but he looked so tired, somehow so vulnerable, sitting at the table in his rather grubby white shirt, with his cravat hanging from his collar, just as he had loosened it when he sat down to his meal, that she had an inexplicable urge to go over and put her arms round him and cradle his head against her breast.

She couldn't understand it.

Chapter Ten

'You've been a long time,' Charlotte said petulantly when Mollie arrived back with the hot lemon drink.

'Well, I had to squeeze the lemons, Miss Charlotte,' Mollie answered, handing it to her. 'I got quite a surprise when I got to the kitchen. Your cousin Mark was there, eating his supper. He said he'd worked late so Cook had kept it hot for him.'

'Dear old Mark. He works very hard.' Charlotte sipped the lemon, thoughtfully. She lifted her head and looked at Mollie. 'He's in love with me, you know.'

'Oh.' Mollie was taken aback. Charlotte had never mentioned this before. 'I didn't realise that.' A picture of the tired, work-stained man she had just seen sitting alone at the kitchen table somehow didn't seem to fit with the fun-loving, spoiled daughter of the house.

'Of course, he hasn't told me so,' she said complacently. 'He's far too shy.'

'Then how can you be so sure?'

'Because I am. I can tell. I know the signs. Not that I'll ever marry him, although it's not against the law for cousins to marry.' She looked up. 'His mother and mine were sisters. Did you know that?' She didn't wait for a reply but went on, 'It's always been thought that Aunt Alice married beneath her, although I always liked Uncle Jack, even though he was only a ploughman. Anyway, they're both dead now.'

'Is that why Mr Mark came to live here?' Mollie asked. 'Because his parents died?'

'Yes. Well, no, not exactly. Being a poor relation, Papa gave him work at the Copperas House and it seemed more convenient for him to live here with us, so that's what he does.'

'How long has he been here, Miss Charlotte?'

Charlotte hunched her shoulders. 'Two? Three years? Something like that. Long enough for him to have learned more about the business than Sebastian ever would. Mind you, that's not difficult. Seb only pays lip service to working there; he's not in the least interested in copperas.' She handed her empty mug back to Mollie and lay back on her pillows. 'That was nice. My throat feels better already.' She gave a sigh. 'I think Papa would be quite pleased if I married Mark because that would mean he would always stay and run the business.' She yawned. 'But I'm not quite ready to marry and settle down yet. I want to have some fun first.'

'I'm glad to hear it, Miss Charlotte. Now, if there's nothing else you want perhaps you wouldn't mind if I went back to bed. It's getting late and I'm a bit cold.' Mollie knew her voice sounded wooden. For some reason she felt quite irritated by her mistress's confidences. It was probably because she was tired.

Charlotte was immediately contrite. 'Oh, yes, I'm sorry, Mollie. Of course you must go back to bed. It was thoughtless of me to keep you here listening to my prattle just because I'm feeling so much better. Off you go, now. I'll see you in the morning. Oh, just plump up my pillows before you go, will you?'

Mollie went back upstairs, undressed for the second time that night and climbed back into her nice warm bed. But she didn't sleep. Every time she closed her eyes she saw Mark sitting alone at the kitchen table. Somehow, try as she might, she couldn't see him married to Charlotte.

*

The next day Charlotte was her old self, the sore throat forgotten. The snow too was melting fast in bright winter sunshine.

'Oh, good. We'll be able to go looking for fossils again today,' she said, clapping her hands.

'I don't think so, Miss Charlotte,' Mollie answered as she helped her into her favourite figured muslin petticoat and sarcenet bedgown. 'The cliff steps will be far too muddy. They were bad enough yesterday. And with all the melting snow they'll be even worse today.'

'Oh, but ...'

She turned her head as the door opened and Beatrice came in. She was warmly wrapped in a paisley shawl against the cold. A lace cap was perched on her fair, greying curls.

'Good morning, Charlotte. How are you today?' she said in a kind, but no-nonsense voice. 'Much better, I hope.'

'Good morning, Mama. Yes, I'm quite recovered, thank you.'

'That's good. Because I'd like you to come visiting with me today. I have several calls to make.'

'Oh, Mama!' She waited impatiently as Mollie adjusted her neckerchief, then held up her curls so that she could fasten a black velvet ribbon round her neck, twisting this way and that to see the effect in the mirror. 'Do you like my new neckerchief, Mama? I bought it the last time I was in Colchester.'

'Yes, it's very nice. The pink edging matches your dress particularly well,' Beatrice said, a trifle impatiently, 'But don't change the subject. I wish you to come visiting with me and there's an end of it.'

Charlotte sighed. 'Very well, Mama. But I hope the carriage won't get stuck in a rut,' she added wickedly. 'Mollie says it will be very muddy out today.'

Beatrice raised her eyebrows in Mollie's direction.

'With the snow meltin', an' that, Ma'am,' Mollie said, nervousness making her forget how Charlotte had taught her to speak.

100

Beatrice smiled at her. 'How very thoughtful, Mollie. But I daresay Perkins will manage the horses very well. He usually does.' She turned back to her daughter. 'Be ready at two, Charlotte. I shall be waiting.'

'Very well, Mama.'

With a rustle of silk Beatrice reached the door, where she turned back. 'It's Thursday. Your afternoon off, Mollie, I believe?'

Mollie dipped a brief curtsey. 'That's right, Ma'am.'

'Ask Cook to fill a basket for you to take home to your aunt and uncle. Tell her ... no, I'll tell her when she comes to talk over the day's menus.' She smiled. 'Have a pleasant afternoon, Mollie, and there's no need to hurry back. I'm sure Charlotte can do without you for a few hours.'

Charlotte's eyebrows shot up. 'Oh, Mama!'

But Mama had gone.

'Well, I hope you'll enjoy your visit more than I expect to enjoy visiting my mother's friends,' Charlotte said later as Mollie was helping her to dress for the afternoon's visiting.

'My aunt isn't usually very pleased to see me,' Mollie admitted. 'She says I'm getting airs and graces above my station.'

Charlotte looked at her in surprise, then burst out laughing. 'Oh, how very funny. And are you getting airs and graces, Mollie? *I* don't think you are.'

Mollie thought for a bit, then she said, 'Well, I suppose it depends who I'm talking to, Miss Charlotte. I reckon the women I used to go mine picking with might think I am, but it doesn't feel like it when I'm with you.' She handed Charlotte her muff. 'There you are, Miss Charlotte. All ready. You mustn't keep your mama waiting.'

Charlotte made a face. 'Indeed no. That would never do.'

Mollie received the welcome she expected from Aunt Rose.

'You hevn't bin high nor by for a month or more,' was her greeting. 'I thought you was s'posed to hev every

101

Thursday afternoon off. There's a pile of ironin' over there waitin'. You know I can't do it. Not with my legs.'

'All right, Aunt. If you'll just let me take off my cloak I'll get on with it. Or would you like me to make you a cup of tea first?' She took off her cloak, warm green with a scarlet silk lining, that Charlotte had tired of, and laid it carefully over a chair.

'Yes. I'm fair parched.' Rose watched her suspiciously. 'An' don't bring your high an' mighty ways home here, Miss Hoity Toity.'

Mollie ignored that remark and began to empty the basket she had brought with her. 'Cook sent a nice wedge of her pork pie for you. She makes delicious pork pies. And here are some slices of ham, too.' She looked up. 'We could have the ham tonight and save the pork pie for you to have tomorrow.'

'Yes. Well . . . ' Aunt Rose was mollified against her will. 'When you've put them things away you'd better sit an' hev a cup o' tea before you start on the ironin'. I've had terrible trouble with me legs an' feet in this cold weather. An' my stummick's bin playin' up somethin' cruel . . . '

To the accompaniment of Aunt Rose's list of ailments Mollie drank her tea, disposed of the ironing, swept and dusted the living room and set a pan of potatoes on the stove to cook. By the end of the afternoon Aunt Rose, warming her knees in front of a roaring fire, looked almost affable as she gazed round the room, transformed now that the dust-laden clutter had been tidied away.

'You oughta come home more often, Mollie, girl. You know we're always pleased to see ye,' she said, biting into yet another of the cakes Cook had put in the basket.

'I come when I can, Aunt.' Mollie glanced up from laying the table and pushed a strand of hair back under her cap. 'Ah, here come Uncle and Richard. I'll take them a pan of hot water so that they can clean themselves up before they come in.'

'They usually fetch it theirselves. They can't expect to be

waited on hand and foot.' Aunt Rose's voice followed her as she went down the steps to the back yard. As soon as Uncle Sam saw her his face lit up with pleasure and even Richard seemed pleased to see her.

Later, as they all sat round the table eating the ham Mollie had brought and the potatoes she had cooked Richard repeated his mother's words.

'You should come home more often, Mollie. This ham is a real treat,' he said, helping himself to another slice.

'An' there's pork pie on the slab for termorrer,' Aunt Rose said smugly.

'Thass really lovely to see you, Mollie,' Uncle Sam said, apparently the only one more interested in her presence than the contents of her basket. 'You're certainly lookin' very well.' He looked at her intently. 'Do they treat you right, my girl?'

'Oh, yes, Uncle. I'm treated very well. Miss Charlotte is very kind to me. She's even teaching me to read and write.'

'Well, I never!' He beamed at her admiringly. Then his face changed. 'Do you see much of . . . ' he hesitated and jerked his head in the direction of the Copperas House, then began again, trying to make his voice sound offhand. 'Do you see much of . . . the others? The Master and Mistress, I mean?' He chased a last bit of potato round his plate as he spoke.

'Yes, I often see the mistress, when she comes into Miss Charlotte's room. She's a very nice lady. And very kind to me. But I hardly ever see the master. I'm not supposed to. The servants are told that they must get out of the way if they see the master or mistress coming. I've talked to Mr Sebastian, though, Miss Charlotte's brother. He came looking for fossils with us only yesterday.'

'You want to watch out,' Richard said with his mouth full. 'From what I've heard he's quite a one . . . '

'We don't need to know what you've heard, Richard,' his father said sharply.

'I was only goin' to say . . . '

'Well, don't.' Uncle Sam turned back to Mollie. 'Mr Mark told me he'd spoke to you the other night, Mollie. If ever you was in any need I'm sure he'd bring me a message.'

'Yes, I'm sure he would, Uncle.' She laughed. 'But I don't think I'm ever likely to be in need. Not while I'm in Miss Charlotte's service.' She looked at the clock on the wall and got up from her chair. 'I must be getting back. Miss Charlotte will be wanting me to help her change for supper. She's been out paying calls with her mother this afternoon.'

'I'll walk back with you,' Richard said, cramming the last piece of ham into his mouth.

'There's no need. I know the way.'

'Thass dark. You never know who's about.'

'I've never known you worry about me before.' She was fastening her cloak as she spoke.

'Let the boy walk with you, Mollie. That cliff road is a lonely place on a dark night,' Uncle Sam said. 'And there's rumours about the French again. We can always tell when there's an invasion scare because o' the extra sulphur we hev to supply to the gunpowder factory. An' that must be serious this time because I've heard they're campin' troops on the cliffs down the coast towards Clacton. They reckon if Old Boney should come in his flat-bottom boats, he'll likely land on this coast. I've even heard tell that they're talkin' of puttin' troops in the lookout tower at the end of the naze to keep watch for 'im; I dunno how true it is. Anyways, you shouldn't be out there in the dark on your own, my girl.' Uncle Sam's tone brooked no argument. 'Richard, take a lantern to light the way.'

Mollie kissed her uncle warmly and her aunt with less enthusiasm, and followed Richard out of the house.

'Joe Trayler's right upset that you spurned him to go an' work up at Cliff House,' he began before they were halfway up Copperas Lane. 'He was all ready to speak to

Dad about you an' him getting' married.'

'Oh, if you're going to start all that you can go home and leave me to find my own way back,' Mollie said irritably. 'You know very well I never had any intention of marrying Joe Trayler.'

'You walked out with him.'

'Only a few times. And that was only to keep you quiet, because you kept all on at me.'

'Thass not what Joe thought.'

'Then Joe thought wrong.' She stopped and faced him. 'I don't want to marry Joe Trayler. I never wanted to marry him and I never shall want to marry him. Have you got that into your thick skull?'

'I was on'y sayin' ...'

'I don't care what you were only saying. I don't want to hear any more about it.'

'My stars, you've turned very uppity with your posh voice an' niminy-piminy ways, Miss.'

'I don't know what you're talking about.'

They walked on in silence to the end of Copperas Lane and into the High Street. 'You don't need to come any further if all you wanted to do was to carry on about Joe Trayler,' she said when they reached the cliff path.

'Oh, come on, Mollie. You know that wasn't all I came for. You know I wouldn't like to think of you walkin' along here all alone in the dark,' he said, taking her arm. 'There's no tellin' who you might meet. You heard what me dad said. This is a lonely road an' there's some funny people about.'

'Most of them are shady friends of yours, I don't doubt,' she said, but there was a hint of laughter in her voice because she could never be angry with Richard for long.

'My friends ain't shady,' he protested, then sensing her change of mood, 'but there is somethin' you could do for me, Moll.'

'Oh, yes? Do you know, I thought there might be. Somehow, I didn't think you were coming all this way with me for the benefit of my health.'

'Don't be like that, Moll. You know I wouldn't want to see you come to no harm. Anyway,' his voice dropped to a mutter. 'What I want you to do won't be no trouble to you.' His voice rose again as he changed the subject. 'What's it like at Cliff House? Do you hev a room to yerself?'

'I've got my own bedroom, yes. Why do you want to know?'

He shrugged. 'I jest wondered. Sometimes maids hev to share a room, don't they?'

'Maybe. But I don't. I've got a nice little room all to myself up on the top floor. It's got a chest of drawers and a washstand as well as a chair and a comfortable bed.' She warmed to her subject. 'And there's a pretty shaped mirror over the chest.'

'What about the winder?'

She looked blank. Then her face cleared. 'Oh, the window. Well, it is a bit high up because my room's in the attic, but if I stand on my chair I can see out. Not that I bother much because all I can see is the sea. I can't even see the beach to know whether the tide's in or out.'

Richard nodded approvingly. 'I'm glad you've got a nice little room.' He stopped and handed her the lantern while he took out his pipe and lit it. Then he retrieved the lantern and they walked on.

'So, what was all that about? And what is it you want me to do, Dick?' Mollie asked. 'You'd better be quick and tell me. We're nearly there and I'm not going to stand about talking to you in this icy wind.' She pulled her cloak more tightly round her as she spoke.

'All I want is for you to put a light in your winder when I tell you to,' he said.

She stopped and stared up at him. 'Why should I do that?' Then understanding dawned. 'If it's to do with your smu ...'

'Ssh.' He put a finger smelling of tobacco over her lips.

'You don't need to know what thass all about. All I'm askin' is that you put a light in your winder now an' again so's to let certain people know the coast is clear.'

'No. I'm not going to.' She shook her head vehemently. 'I don't want anything to do with your ... whatever it is that I don't need to know about but can very easily guess.'

'Yes, you will, Moll.' His tone was wheedling. 'Don't forget you owe me for how I looked after you when we was little. I saved you from Mum's slipper a good many times, didn't I? Remember how I used to clean you up when you'd bin shut in the coal hole? I always looked out for you, Mollie, you know that. Well, now it's your turn to look out for me.'

'You'll need more looking out for than I can do if you and your friends get caught by old Boney's ships,' Mollie said crisply. 'You heard what Uncle Sam said. There's very likely going to be an invasion. The French are coming.'

'Yes. I heard. But that'll never come to anything. The French are too busy fightin' in other places to worry about invadin' this coast. In any case, they'd never dare try it, not with all the sea defences being built at Harwich and Felixtowe.'

'How can you be so sure they won't?'

'Because my mates are back and forth across the channel. They know what's goin' on. An' they know how to avoid trouble over there when they pick the stuff up. It's landin' the stuff this end where the problem is. An' thass where you come in. I need to be able to let 'em know we've made sure the Ridin' Officers are busy elsewhere, as you might say, so the coast will be clear for them to do what they hev to do.'

'That's all very well; the Riding Officer is on horseback, so you can keep track of him, but what about the Revenue Cutter, out on the water? How will you know where that is?'

'Because it can't be in two places at once. An' if it gets

tipped off that there'll be a drop on Tollesbury marshes, that's where it'll be.'

'How will I know when you want the light put up?'

'When Sid, the gardener's boy says to you, "Dick sends his love", thass the night you put up the light.'

'How will . . . ?'

'Don't ask so many blamed questions, mawther.' Richard was becoming impatient. 'But if you must know, Sid's father is one of our gang. Now, I'm not sayin' another word.'

She heaved a sigh. 'I don't like it.'

'You don't hev to like it. All you hev to do is *do it*. Remember, Moll, you owe me. You wouldn't want to see your ole cousin landed in prison, jest because you wouldn't lend a hand, would you? Not after all we went through together as kids?' He blew the lantern out. 'Now, here y'are. Stick this under your cloak, but mind you don't burn yerself, thass still a bit hot from the candle. Now, remember, all you hev to do is put it on your winder sill and light it when I say. Thass not much to ask, now, is it?'

'I s'pose not.'

'Good gal.' He dropped a kiss on her forehead and turned to leave her.

'You will be careful, Dick, won't you?' she whispered into the night.

The only reply she received was a faint chuckle.

Chapter Eleven

Putting the lantern in her window worked. At least, as far as Mollie could tell, it worked. She didn't doubt that she would have heard some harsh words from Richard if it hadn't. Once every three or perhaps four weeks – once it was nearly two months – Sid the gardener's boy would sidle up to her and say, 'Dick sends his love, Mollie.' Then, he would look at her with his head on one side and say, 'He's werry lovin', that bruvver o' yourn, ain't he? Are you sure he'm your bruvver an' not your sweet'art?'

'We've always been very close,' she would reply enigmatically and move out of his way before he could question her further. She didn't enlighten him that they were only cousins and not brother and sister; he was suspicious enough as it was.

But she hated it when the message arrived. She was always fearful that something would go wrong, that she would be found out, that somebody from the house would see the beacon in her window and ask what it was there for; worse, that the lantern would somehow catch fire and burn the house down. But as time went on and nothing unpleasant happened she realised that her fears were unjustified and life moved very smoothly and pleasantly at Cliff House.

Christmas passed and the New Year came in with a flurry

of balls and parties for Charlotte. Mollie was kept busy altering and re-trimming gowns and petticoats, adding new robings, stitching fresh lace on to neckerchiefs, dyeing feathers a different colour; anything to make it look as if her young mistress was always wearing something different, without going to too much expense. Sometimes, when she was kept stitching far into the night, Mollie had the feeling that perhaps the Graingers weren't quite as wealthy as they liked people to believe. They liked to move in affluent circles but there was great deal of fuss and anxiety when, at the end of January, the turn of Cliff House to do the entertaining arrived. Cook complained because she had to make do with brisket when she needed sirloin for the roast; half a dozen eggs wasn't nearly enough for the soufflé, and as if she didn't have enough to do, the hothouse strawberries were too squashy to be served as fresh fruit and had to be turned into strawberry shortcake.

Beatrice, anxious that there should appear to be no shortage of servants, even called in Mollie and her own personal maid, Ellis, to wait on table. Mollie enjoyed this, even though she had only been given the sketchiest of training by Tilda, the housemaid, who waited on table every day and was used to it. She enjoyed seeing the table decked with the family silver, which only rarely saw the light of day, especially the two heavily embossed five-branched candelabra, which Arthur had spent a whole afternoon polishing and then placed lovingly at an exact distance from each end. She loved seeing the ladies in their beautiful, brightly coloured dresses, with their fans and feathers and their jewels sparkling in the light from the chandeliers. And the men – the older ones bewigged and powdered, the younger ones more fashionably preferring their own hair – who almost outshone the ladies in their elaborately embroidered silk waistcoats and blue, mulberry or green coats. But she had never imagined people could eat so much at a single sitting and as she moved between guests with tureens of vegetables well past their best but expertly disguised by

110

Cook to make them appear fresh she was amazed at the gluttony of the so-called gentry.

Mr Grainger, at the head of the table, expansively urged his guests to drink the wine that had been discreetly watered a little by Arthur, doubling as butler for the evening. In the intervals when the guests were fully occupied with laden plates, the servants stood back in the shadows, waiting, ready to pass condiments, replenish plates or mop up spills, their eyes discreetly averted – Mollie had yet to discover how she could avert her eyes yet still be alert to the needs of the guests, but she managed to watch James Grainger out of the corner of her eye. It was the first time she had really had the opportunity to take a good look at him, albeit covertly, and she didn't much like what she was seeing. Wearing a yellow coat upon which Arthur had worked hard but with limited success to remove the stains, he was a gross, ill-mannered man, shovelling food into his mouth and drinking steadily, his face becoming ruddier with each glass. Now and again he surreptitiously slipped his fork under his wig and scratched behind his ear. It gave her no pleasure at all to think that this overweight, overbearing, loud-voiced man had fathered her; that here was the man who had forced himself on the mother she had never known, resulting in her shame and ultimate death. She gave a tiny shudder of disgust to think that this man's blood flowed through her veins. James Grainger might like to think of himself as one of the gentry but Uncle Sam, her beloved, upright Uncle Sam, was more of a gentleman than this oafish man would ever know how to be.

She turned her attention to Beatrice, at the other end of the table. She looked quite regal in crimson satin, her fair, greying hair piled high on her head and topped by an arrangement of matching crimson feathers. Now and again, at the sound of a loud guffaw from her husband's end of the table, she glanced up with an expression of distaste that was gone almost before it formed. But Mollie saw it and felt a stab of pity for her.

111

Her thoughts were interrupted as Sebastian raised his hand and beckoned her. He was looking remarkably handsome in a peacock blue coat with large covered buttons, with his dark hair left to fall naturally into a curl. He was sitting between two ladies Mollie didn't recognise, both young and attractive, but inclined to simper and giggle at everything he said. She couldn't help wondering briefly if his father had been as handsome before he coarsened and ran to seed.

'More grapes for Miss Evans, Mollie,' he said as she approached.

She fetched them from further down the table, where Mark, in a coat of a similar cut but in a darker shade of blue, was listening with apparent interest to an elderly lady's reminiscences.

'Ah, now the grape scissors are missing,' Sebastian said, looking up at her. 'Where can they be?'

'Just by your elbow, Sir.' She kept her eyes downcast as she'd been told.

'Now, would you pass me a peach, Mollie.' As she handed him the bowl of peaches he made sure that his hand brushed hers, causing her to glance at him in surprise. He smiled at her as he took one. 'Thank you, Mollie. A remarkably smooth skin, don't you think?'

She blushed and moved quickly back to her station in the shadows.

At the appropriate time, Beatrice got to her feet as a signal for the ladies to leave the gentlemen to their port and cigars. Arthur would stay in the dining room in case he was needed, but the other servants would leave; ribald jokes and racy tales from gentlemen in their cups were not for female ears, not even those belonging to servants.

Mollie went back to the kitchen with the others for a much-needed cup of tea and to help with the clearing up.

Ellis returned from taking the tea tray into the drawing room for the ladies and grabbed a left-over chicken leg. 'I hope to goodness this doesn't happen too often,' she said,

112

flopping into a chair and putting her feet up. 'After running around all day getting milady ready and then having to wait on table while they all gorged themselves, I'm just about worn out.'

Cook passed Mollie a sandwich. 'Eat that, then you can help with the washing-up,' she said. 'I hope it won't be too long before Arthur lets us know the men have left the table and gone to the billiard room with their whisky, then we can finish clearing up.'

'Yes, I've got to lay the table for breakfast before I go to bed,' Tilda said, yawning. 'Not that anybody'll be up very early to eat it.'

Mollie said nothing. She couldn't go to bed until she had helped Charlotte out of the pale green silk dress with the spotted organdie petticoat that she had spent the last three days altering. But it had been well worth the effort because her young mistress had looked dazzlingly pretty tonight, the pink ribbons twisted in among her curls and hanging down behind adding the finishing touch. Mollie hoped Mark hadn't been jealous at the outrageous way Charlotte had flirted with the curate.

Three days later Mollie paid a visit to Copperas Lane, a basket with the last few remaining remnants of the supper on her arm. It didn't amount to much, a slice of pork galantine, a wedge of brawn on the point of going off and two bruised and slightly mouldy peaches. The supper had been costed very carefully to ensure there was no waste and most of what little was left had been eaten in the following days by the family.

At first Aunt Rose was suspicious of the peaches, saying she'd never seen the like. But when Mollie cut a slice for her she changed her mind and ate the good bits from both of them before the men returned from work.

Over the meal, which Mollie had augmented on her way there with pies from the pie shop, she told them about the supper at Cliff House, making even Aunt Rose laugh as she

113

described the way one dowager lady made her way to the drawing room after the meal, having had rather more wine than was good for her.

'She was a bit like a ship in full sail with the wind gusting from the wrong direction,' Mollie said, laughing so much she had difficulty in telling her tale. 'And every now and again she would lurch to one side and say, "Oops, I must have caught my foot in my skirt," or "Oops, who left that sideboard in my way?" and all the time trying to look dignified even though the huge feather decoration on her head had become dislodged and slipped to one side. It was better than a circus but of course we daren't laugh because we weren't supposed to notice.' Mollie wiped the tears of laughter from her eyes. 'She had to make three attempts to get through the door from the dining room to the drawing room. In the end Arthur had to guide her. He pretended she was losing her fan and gave her a sharp shove in the right direction. Oh, you should have seen Ellis mimicking her in the kitchen afterwards! We laughed till we cried.'

'You really like it at Cliff House, don't you, Mollie, my girl,' Uncle Sam said a little later when the hilarity had died down.

'Yes, Uncle, I do,' Mollie said, nodding seriously. 'I like being Miss Charlotte's maid and I think Mrs Grainger is a lovely lady. But I don't like the look of Mr Grainger at all. I'm glad I don't see him very often.' She noticed the look of relief that passed over her uncle's face and was glad she had spoken.

'We don't see 'im very often, either, do we, Dad,' Richard said cheerfully. He made a face. 'Ugh. I think this brawn's off.'

'Then don't eat it,' his mother said. 'Give it to me. I can't see anything wrong with it. Smells a bit strong, thass all.' She put it between two slices of bread and took a bite. 'Yes, 'tis a bit ripe,' she agreed, after a couple of mouthfuls. 'P'raps you're right. I'll give it to the cat.'

'No, we don't see much of 'im,' Uncle Sam said, return-

114

ing to Richard's words. 'We don't see much o' Master Sebastian, neither. 'E's s'posed to do the orderin' but if it was left to 'im we'd always be short o' sea coal an' we'd always be runnin' out o' scrap iron for the boiler. I don't know how the place 'ud keep goin' if it wasn't for Mr Mark. He's the one who keep an eye on things.'

'Yes, he looked after Jim Stokes today when 'e got splashed with liquor,' Richard said, his mouth full of pie. ''E was that gentle with him, 'e oughta bin a doctor.'

'What happened, then?' Mollie asked.

'Jim was pumpin' the liquor out the pits into the boiler an' the pipe sprung a leak and shot acid all over 'is leg. Burnt 'is trousers through and took the flesh off 'is leg,' Sam explained. 'That was jest a good job it wasn't his face. 'E'd 've bin scarred for life. As it is 'e won't walk for a week or two.'

'The trouble is, the pipe's old. Needs renewin', like everything else in the place,' Richard said. 'We bodge things up all the time to make 'em last longer an' this is the sort o' thing that happens. An' all because the management won't pay for new. I'll be glad to get out o' the place.'

'Are you leaving, then, Dick?' Mollie asked.

He tapped the side of his nose in a gesture of secrecy. 'Not jest yet,' he said, winking at her. 'But I'm workin' on it. Which reminds me, I've got somethin' to give you before you leave, Mollie.'

She frowned. 'Oh, and what's that?'

'You'll see.' It was a length of Brussels lace, inside which was a large piece of candle. ''Cause the lantern must be runnin' low by now,' he whispered, closing the door behind them as he slipped it into her basket.

'Is this from. . .?' she began, pointing to the lace.

'No, thass not from Joe Trayler, thass from me,' he said quickly. He dropped his voice. 'For services rendered, you might say.'

'I'd rather go without the lace and not render the services,' she whispered back fiercely.

115

'You're a lovely girl, Mollie, one o' the best.' He gave her a big, smacking kiss.

'And you're full of cupboard love, Richard Barnes,' she said, but she was smiling. 'And I notice you're not worried about me walking back to Cliff House on my own in the dark tonight.'

'Ah, no, well, I gotta see a man about a ...'

'... Pint of porter. I know.' She went off up the lane, laughing. She had never been afraid of the dark and the prospect of walking back to Cliff House alone along the cliff path didn't worry her in the slightest, in spite of the continued rumours of an invasion by the French.

She went along Copperas Lane, where dim candles threw patches of greyish yellow light across the path from the windows of the cottages, and into the High Street. Having lived away from the Copperas House for several months she had almost reached the end of the High Street and was going towards the cliff path before the stench of it left her nostrils. The longer she was away from it the worse it seemed when she returned; a sickening, throat-catching stink that seemed to thicken the air and make it difficult to breathe. She could hardly believe she had lived with it all those years without being troubled by it.

This evening a cold wind was blowing in from the sea so she stopped for a few minutes and gratefully held up her head to gulp the fresh, salt-laden air into her lungs. She could hear from the sound of the sea crashing below that the tide was full, and now and again, even up on the cliff path, she could feel the spray as an extra large wave hurled itself against the cliff.

She pulled up her hood and hurried on, thinking about the visit she had just paid to her uncle's house. Uncle Sam never changed; he was still as loving and anxious about her welfare as ever, and Aunt Rose – well, Mollie liked to think it was not just the goodies she always took home with her that made her aunt more affable towards her these days. Suddenly, her thoughts were interrupted by the sound of

116

footsteps behind her. She cocked her ear and listened, thinking she must be mistaken because there was rarely anybody on this path on a winter evening. It was different in summer, when lovers strolled here, away from prying eyes. She quickened her pace a little, wishing that Richard had offered to come with her after all, but the footsteps were moving faster, gaining on her. She caught her breath. Cliff House was still nearly half a mile away; she had passed the last of the cottages with their comforting lights so there was nothing but the black bulk of trees and bushes to one side of the lane and a sheer drop to the beach on the other. She began to run, haunted by visions of being captured by French soldiers.

She ran until she was out of breath and then stopped, hiding behind a bramble and listening. The footsteps seemed to have faded. Relieved, she walked on more slowly, rubbing the stitch in her side. It was pitch black now, the sickle moon and stars reflecting mere pinpoints of light in the black water pounding below to her right. She could hear her own ragged breathing almost keeping time with her footsteps on the frosty path as she hurried gratefully towards the lights of Cliff House that were still much too far off.

She didn't know what it was that she tripped over, whether it was a bramble, an exposed root, or a large stone, but suddenly she found herself falling headlong on to the path. For a moment in the darkness she thought she was falling over the cliff as she heard her basket go clattering down among a shower of stones and she clutched at a clump of grass, afraid to move for a moment, in case she went the same way. After a minute she stretched out her arm to see if she could feel where the edge of the cliff was, then edged well away from it and sat up.

Suddenly, she was dragged roughly to her feet. 'You little chump. I thought you'd gone over the cliff!' It was Joe Trayler's voice.

'So it was you following me!' Mollie said, clinging to

him out of fear. Then, she realised what she was doing and pulled away. 'You frightened me half to death,' she said angrily. 'What were you doing, following me like that?'

'Dick told me you was on your way back along the cliff path so I thought I'd come an' keep you company. See you didn't come to no harm.' He took her arm.

She shook him off. 'I suppose the two of you cooked up the idea between you. No wonder Richard didn't offer to walk me back. I thought it was a bit odd,' she said, still angry. 'Well, get this into your thick head, Joe Trayler. I don't want your company. I'd rather walk back on my own. How many times do I have to tell you that?'

'Oh, you'll change your mind when you git turned outa the big house.' He nodded towards Cliff House. 'An' I'll be there, waitin' for you. I'm a patient man, Mollie, don't worry.'

'Then you'll wait for ever. I like it at Cliff House. I don't intend to be turned out, as you put it.' Her voice rose. 'And if I was turned out I wouldn't come to you. Not if you were the last man on earth.'

'Ah, you don't mean that, Mollie. You're jest playin' hard to get. Come on, give us a kiss.' He grabbed her and she felt his rough, whiskery face and smelt the beer on his breath before she could turn her head away. 'Get off me!' she shouted, trying to push him away.

'Mollie? It is Mollie, isn't it?' It was Mark's voice coming through the darkness. 'Are you in trouble?'

'Yes, yes. I'm ...'

But before she could say more Joe said, 'We was jest hevin' a bit of a kiss an' a cuddle, thass all, Sir. Well, I'll be getting' back, Mollie. The gentleman'll see you the rest o' the way, I'm sure. Goo'night, darlin'.' And he went off, whistling in the darkness.

'I'm sorry, Mollie. I didn't mean to interrupt ... I mean ...' Mark was clearly as embarrassed as she was.

'You didn't interrupt anything, Mr Mark. Really, you didn't. I'm glad you arrived when you did,' she said,

118

wiping her mouth on the back of her hand. 'It wasn't . . . it wasn't what you might think. I knew I was being followed and I got frightened and ran. Then I tripped over and Joe Trayler caught up with me. He seems to think . . . well, he's got the idea that I like him,' she finished lamely.

'And you don't?'

'Not the way he'd like me to. Just because he's Richard's friend, he . . . oh, dear.' Suddenly, she burst into tears. 'I'm sorry, Mr Mark. It's just that I was so frightened. When I fell over I lost my basket over the edge of the cliff and I thought I was going over with it. And it was so dark . . . and I knew there was someone following me . . . and then he came along and tried . . .'

Mark pulled out a handkerchief that smelled of copperas and gave it to her. 'It's all right, Mollie. Come on, dry your eyes and I'll walk the rest of the way with you,' he said gently. 'It's not far now. You can take my arm if it would make you feel happier.'

'Thank you, Mr Mark.' Gratefully, she slipped her hand into the crook of his arm. It felt warm and safe and the darkness was no longer menacing.

'If you let me know when you are going to visit your uncle I can always walk back with you,' he offered. 'I don't usually leave work till fairly late, so it wouldn't be difficult to arrange.'

'That's very kind of you. It would be nice to have company on a dark night.'

But even as she said the words she knew she could never ask him. In any case, spring would soon be on its way and with it the light evenings when there would be no need to. And by next winter he would probably have forgotten he ever suggested it.

All too soon they reached Cliff House.

Chapter Twelve

It was several days before Mollie had the chance to go and look for the basket that had fallen over the cliff the night she fell on her way home in the dark. During this time she had been kept busy stitching yet another set of frills and robings, inserts and ribbons on to Charlotte's peacock blue taffeta gown, this time in pale blue, which, with a yellow figured petticoat, would effectively disguise the fact that she had already worn it to several functions already. As she stitched, Mollie let her mind wander back to that evening and the encounter with Joe Trayler and then Mark. She hoped she hadn't given Mark the wrong idea about her and Joe Trayler. Even now she was still confused in her mind as to what exactly was said. She remembered how frightened she had been, and then, when she realised who had been following her, furious with Joe. But had she made it plain to Mark that Joe meant nothing – less than nothing – to her? She couldn't remember. But she could remember walking back to Cliff House holding Mark's arm and him saying he would be happy to walk back from Uncle Sam's with her if she was nervous, so perhaps he had understood. Her needle flew as she day-dreamed about walking all the way from Copperas Lane to Cliff House with Mark, especially on a dark night.

'Have you nearly finished stitching on those ribbons, Mollie?' Charlotte's voice interrupted her thoughts.

Mollie put in the last stitch and bit off the cotton. 'There, it's done.' She shook it out. 'Look, nobody would guess you've already worn this gown twice, Miss Charlotte.'

'Thank goodness for that.' Charlotte sighed. 'My friends will *all* have a new gown for the Spring Ball tonight. I don't know why Papa wouldn't let me have one. I think it's very mean of him. After all, he knows how important it is to me.'

'Well, you'll look very pretty in this one, Miss Charlotte. This colour blue suits you; it brings out the blue of your eyes.' Mollie glanced at the little enamel clock on the mantelpiece. 'But it will match the blue circles *under* your eyes if you don't lie on your bed and rest for an hour. You want to look your best tonight, don't you. Where is it you're going?'

'To Beaumont Hall. It's going to be quite a big affair, you know. The officers from the army camp at Weeley have all been invited. Not, of course, that I'm interested in army officers, but I do wonder if that new young Riding Officer will be there. What was his name? I met him at the Saunders last month. Charles, that was it. Charles Doe. He was nice.' As she prattled on she allowed Mollie to help her off with her gown and slippers and tuck her under the covers. Soon her eyelids drooped and she slept.

Mollie quickly tidied the room. Now Charlotte was asleep she could take the opportunity to slip out and look for the lost basket. Putting on the brown pelisse that Charlotte had given her only that morning she hurried out, across the lawn and down the cliff steps. She knew she hadn't got much time because the tide was coming in and the spot where the basket had fallen over the edge of the cliff was some distance away, not far, in fact, from where the women and children were spread across the beach, bending over their task of mine picking. She smiled a little to herself as she saw Old Sol, standing as patiently as ever with his equally patient old donkey, waiting for them to empty their baskets into his tumbrel. It seemed a lifetime

121

since she was one of their number, searching for lumps of copperas on the beach every day. Every night when she said her prayers, as Uncle Sam had taught her to do, she thanked the Lord for her good fortune in coming to live at Cliff House.

She hurried along the beach, scanning the cliff face for any sign of the basket as she went. She doubted she would find the contents, but the basket belonged to Cook and it wouldn't be long before she missed it and began asking where it was. She was beginning to think it had gone, blown into the sea by the wind, or stolen by some athletic and beady-eyed beachcomber, when she spotted it, halfway up the cliff, lodged firmly against a gorse bush. Her heart sank. She was wearing a rather fetching gown of russet taminy, one of Charlotte's cast-offs, under the brown pelisse; neither of these garments were at all suitable for clambering about on the cliff. Cursing her stupidity in rushing out without waiting to change she walked up and down, with one eye on the encroaching tide, looking for an easy way up. Here and there, where there had been an old cliff fall, the ascent was often quite easy, but there was no easy way at this point, although there was plenty of scrub and gorse to hold on to.

She felt a tug at her skirt. 'Is that your basket up there, Miss? Do you want me to fetch it down for yer?'

She turned and saw a boy of about ten years old, in a grubby shirt and torn breeches. 'Hullo. Yes, it is my basket and I would be glad if you could get it down for me.' She smiled at him. 'You're Alfie Stokes, aren't you?'

He flushed with surprise and seemed to grow several inches in his pride at being recognised by such a grand lady. 'Thass right, Miss. Fancy you knowin' my name.'

She smiled at him again. 'I know a lot of things, Alfie Stokes. How is your father? He had an accident with some acid the other day, I believe.'

Alfie's eyes widened. 'Cor, yes, Miss, he did. Fancy you knowin' that, too. 'E can't work at the minute so me an'

122

my bruvver hev to pick extra mine to 'elp Mum feed us.'

'Then I mustn't keep you. But if you could fetch the basket down for me I'd be grateful.'

'Right away, Miss. I'll hev it down in a jiffy.' He scrambled up the cliff like a monkey and was back down beside her, basket over his arm, in less than a minute. Miraculously, the piece of lace wrapped round the candle that Richard had given her was still lying, a trifle soggy, in the bottom of the basket.

'Thank you, Alfie,' she said as she took it. She felt in her pocket and pulled out tuppence, all she had. 'There. That'll help to make up for the picking time you've lost.'

He looked at it, spat on it and put it in his pocket. 'Cor, thank yer, Miss, you're a real lady, you are.' Then he ran off to give his mother his unexpected earnings.

Mollie watched him go. He clearly hadn't recognised that she had been among the army of pickers herself less than six months ago. Sometimes she could hardly believe it herself. She turned and hurried back the way she had come, reaching the cliff steps only minutes ahead of the tide.

Later that evening, having cleared up the room after the pandemonium of getting Charlotte ready for the ball, Mollie sat dozing by the fire, glad of a few hours peace before her young mistress returned. As she sat there she mulled over what Alfie had said when he rescued her basket, 'You're a real lady, you are.' She gave a little laugh. Little did Alfie know that she wouldn't be sitting here half asleep waiting for Miss Charlotte to come back if she was a real lady; she would be with her, enjoying herself at Beaumont Hall.

She glanced at the clock on the mantelpiece and poked the fire back into life. They were late tonight. She strained her ears, listening for the carriage on the gravel drive, but the only sounds to be heard were the hoot of an owl and the distant murmur of the sea. She settled herself back in the chair and closed her eyes.

123

She must have dropped off to sleep because it seemed like only moments later that the door burst open and Charlotte came into the room, her face flushed and her blue eyes sparkling with a mixture of champagne and excitement.

'Oh, Mollie, Mollie, you'll never guess! I'm in love! Madly, ecstatically, everlastingly in love.' She hauled a bewildered Mollie to her feet and danced her round the room. 'I've met the most handsome and adorable man tonight. His name is Captain Pilkington and he's with the Royal Artillery. We danced and danced and then he took me in to supper and after that we just sat in the conservatory and talked. Until the last waltz, of course. Oh, that was wonderful. He held me really close, like this, which, of course, the gentleman isn't supposed to do. People are so old-fashioned, Mollie, tut-tutting when a man puts his arm round a lady's waist. After all, it's only a dance. Ah, but *what* a dance!' She closed her eyes, savouring the memory. Then they flew open again as she said, 'And what do you think? You know the tall tower at the end of the naze? Seb aired his knowledge by telling us that it was built by Trinity House as a landmark nearly a hundred years ago.' She waved her arm dismissively. 'Anyway, soldiers from the camp at Weeley are going to be stationed there because it's a good vantage point to watch for enemy ships on the horizon. Then beacons can be lit along the coast. Not that Arnold ... Captain Pilkington thinks it will ever come to that, of course. He thinks all this talk of invasion is just scaremongering.'

'I hope he's right,' Mollie said with a shudder. 'I don't like the thought of being murdered in my bed by all those Frenchies.'

'Oh, don't be silly, it won't come to that, Mollie. The important thing is –' her eyes sparkled with excitement '– Arnold tells me he is one of the officers who will be with the lookout party quite often, so we shall be able to meet whenever we like. Well, almost whenever we like.' She

124

released Mollie and flopped down into the chair, her legs stretched out and her arms hanging over the sides in a most unladylike manner.

'Very nice too, Miss Charlotte, I'm sure,' Mollie said, straightening her cap and stifling a yawn. She had heard these extravagant claims of undying love from Charlotte before, many times. They tended to last three days at the most. 'I'm glad you've had a good time tonight. Shall I help you get ready for bed now?'

'Oh, I don't think I'll ever sleep again, Mollie. I'm just so excited. Have you ever been in love, Mollie? No, of course you haven't. Oh –' she threw her head back '– it's the most wonderful feeling in the world.'

'I'm sure it is, Miss Charlotte. But it's very late. Perhaps if I was to fetch you some warm milk it would help you to settle down,' Mollie said, with just a trace of impatience. 'You need to get your beauty sleep, you know. You wouldn't like your young man to see you all bleary eyed and tired looking, would you.'

'Oh, I expect I'll sleep late in the morning. I've had such a wonderful evening.' She held up her hair for Mollie to unfasten the buttons at the back of her gown. 'But, yes. Some hot milk would be nice.' She stood reasonably still while Mollie undressed her and slipped her nightgown over her head. Then she slid between crisp white linen sheets and lay waiting while Mollie plodded wearily along the empty corridors and down darkened stairways to the kitchen to heat up the milk.

By the time she returned Charlotte was fast asleep, her golden hair tumbled round her on the pillow and a contented smile on her face.

With a sigh of exasperation Mollie took the milk up to her own room and allowed herself the luxury of drinking it in bed. Not that she needed anything to make her sleep; at half past one in the morning she was nearly dead on her feet.

But her last thoughts, before falling into a deep and

dreamless sleep, were not for Charlotte but for Mark. What would he do if he discovered that the woman he loved, and who everyone expected him to marry, had fallen in love with someone else? Unlikely though it might seem, supposing that this was a real and genuine thing on Charlotte's part, how would he bear continuing to live in the same house? Perhaps he wouldn't. Perhaps he would go right away. The thought that he might possibly leave Cliff House gave Mollie a jolt in the pit of her stomach. She couldn't imagine the place without him. Even when she didn't see him for days on end it was comforting to know that he was there, that she might come upon him in the corridor as she was hurrying to do Miss Charlotte's bidding, or even in the kitchen as she had that night just before Christmas. It was a treasured memory that was only allowed to surface in the privacy of her own little room. Sometimes, in less rational moments, she wondered if she might possibly be falling in love with him, but she squashed the thought. Mark Hamilton might only be the nephew of James Grainger, but he was far above the likes of Mollie Barnes. In any case, he was in love with Miss Charlotte – and they were destined to marry, once she had got over imagining she was in love with every handsome young man she danced with, and had grown up a bit.

The next day it rained and Charlotte was fretful, partly because she couldn't take the walk she'd planned and partly because she was exhausted after the excitement of the ball. Mollie's patience was tried to the utmost; nothing she did was right, nothing she suggested was listened to. All Charlotte wanted to do was look out of the window and complain about the rain.

Mollie was relieved when there was a knock at the door and Sebastian came in. He was looking very handsome in buckskin breeches and a maroon waistcoat, freshly washed and shaved, with no hint in his appearance that he had spent half the night dancing and drinking

'Your sister is like a bear with a sore head, Sir,' she whispered as she let him in. 'I hope you'll be able to cheer her up a bit.'

Charlotte turned away from the window towards him. 'Hullo, Seb. You're looking very spry, which is more than I feel.' She laid a hand on her aching forehead. 'If you've come to tell me you're cross because you didn't have a single dance with me last night, all I can say is, you should have asked me for my card earlier, before it got filled up.' She turned back to the window.

'I haven't come for that,' he said, raising a quizzical eyebrow in Mollie's direction. 'In fact, there were so many delightful young ladies there that I was far too busy dancing with them to even think of dancing with you, Sis.'

Charlotte's head shot round. 'Oh, you horrible man! Are you insinuating that I'm not delightful, or pretty, or whatever it was you said?'

'I was insinuating nothing of the kind,' Sebastian said with a theatrical sigh. 'The fact was, with all those dashing army officers there, I knew you wouldn't have time to spare for me.' He turned to Mollie. 'You're right, Mollie, she's in a terrible mood. I don't think I'll show her what I've got here. I'll come back another time.' He went towards the door.

'What is it? What have you brought? Wait. Show me.' Charlotte got up from the window seat and went over to him. 'What is it? Is it something for me?'

'No, it's just something I thought you might like to see.' He came back into the room and sat down, steepling his fingers. 'You remember the day I came with you to look for fossils, a few months back?'

Charlotte frowned, pretending to have forgotten.

'I'll wager you remember, Mollie?' he said.

'I believe I do, Sir,' Mollie answered. 'It's not often Miss Charlotte has the pleasure of your company when she's looking for fossils.'

'Oh, I think I do remember you coming, now you come

127

to speak of it,' Charlotte said with a yawn. 'We found that piece of amber with an ant or something fossilised in it, didn't we.'

'Not *we,* Charley. I believe it was Mollie's sharp eyes that picked it up,' Sebastian said, smiling at Mollie.

'Well, one of us found it.' Charlotte waved her hand dismissively.

'It was Mollie. Am I not right, Mollie?'

Mollie shrugged uncomfortably. 'It might have been, Sir. I spent so many years picking up copperas that I'm used to spotting things on the beach. But it doesn't matter.'

'Oh, but it does. Findings keepings, that's what I've always been told.' He put his hand in his pocket and pulled out a small jeweller's box. 'So, you found it, Mollie, so you keep it.' He handed it to her.

She took it, puzzled, glancing at Charlotte as she did so.

'Well, go on, open it,' Charlotte said irritably. 'I really don't know what all the fuss is about. After all, it was only a piece of amber and there's plenty of it lying around on the beach.'

'Ah, yes. But not with an insect fossilised inside it.' Sebastian smiled at Mollie. 'Aren't you going to do as Charlotte suggests and open it?'

Puzzled, Mollie opened the little box and there, lying on a bed of dark blue velvet, was the piece of amber, polished so that the insect inside was clearly visible and set into a gold, butterfly-shaped brooch. She looked up, startled. 'Oh, I couldn't ... I mean, it's really pretty ... but ...' She glanced at him, her eyes suddenly flashing anger. 'You shouldn't play games, Sir. Not with the likes of me. It's not fair.' She handed the box to Charlotte. 'There you are Miss Charlotte ...'

Sebastian intercepted it and handed it back to her. 'No, Mollie. I wasn't playing games. I had it made into a brooch for you because you found it.'

Mollie put her hands behind her back. 'Thass ... it's very kind of you, Sir, but I can't accept it. It wouldn't be

128

right, thank you all the same.'

'She's right, Seb,' Charlotte said. 'You can't go round giving servants expensive presents.'

He gave a crooked little smile. 'Funny. I never think of Mollie as a servant.'

'No, most of the time, neither do I,' Charlotte said honestly. 'Mollie's my friend, that's how I think of her, although I do order her about at times, I admit. But it doesn't give you leave to shower her with expensive gifts.'

'Oh, come now, it wasn't that expensive,' Sebastian protested. 'I just thought it was a jolly thing to do, to have it mounted and give it to her as she was the one who found it.'

'Well, it's very kind of you, Sir, but it wouldn't do,' Mollie said firmly. 'For one thing, if anybody saw it they might think I'd stolen it, then I'd be dismissed because nobody would believe I would never take anything that didn't belong to me, which, indeed, I wouldn't. I'd never be able to face my Uncle Sam again.'

'Oh, really!' Sebastian snapped the lid of the box shut and shoved it unceremoniously into his pocket. 'Such a fuss over a stupid trinket. I wish I'd never had it done. Well, that's the last time, I can tell you.'

'Don't be like that, Seb.' Charlotte went over to him and put her arm through his, her bad temper forgotten. 'You can always give it to me.'

'I shan't give it to anybody!' he said and left, shutting the door with what was not quite a slam.

'Oh, dear, poor old Seb,' Charlotte said. 'He means well, you know.'

But Mollie wasn't so sure. She had a horrible feeling that the brooch, had she accepted it, might have been advance payment for services she would later be called upon to render.

Chapter Thirteen

Two weeks later Sid, the gardener's boy sidled up to her with the now familiar message, 'Dick sends 'is love,' accompanied by a cheeky wink. Mollie's heart sank. Apart from the ever-present fear that Richard would get caught by the Riding Officer or the Revenue Cutter – one day something would go wrong with his plans, she was sure – she was always fearful that someone from the house would see the bright light in her window and ask awkward questions, or that the lantern would fall over and set the house alight. This last was impossible, she knew that. The window sill was wide and the base of the lantern quite heavy. But it didn't stop her worrying, especially as she had to stand on a chair to put it in place. A further worry on this particular night was that there was to be a small dinner party at Cliff House. Suppose the master took his guests for a stroll in the garden, which was quite likely on a warm, late spring evening, and saw a bright light shining out from an attic window? Awkward questions would be asked and she would lose her place at Cliff House, that was for certain. Every time she thought about it her stomach churned and she felt sick.

But there was worse to come. Arthur came into the kitchen as Mollie was sitting with her feet up drinking a cup of tea while Charlotte was having her rest. Ellis was drinking tea, too, although she had originally come down to fetch the goffering iron to press the lace frills on Beatrice's gown.

'Ah, Ellis. Mollie,' he said, giving them each a supercilious nod. 'I'm afraid your services won't be required in the dining room tonight since there will only be a few guests.'

'They know that. I've already told them,' Cook said. 'But who's coming?'

'I haven't seen the final list,' Arthur said huffily. He was obviously annoyed that Cook had stolen his thunder, yet he couldn't resist imparting his superior knowledge. 'Sir Harcourt Grieves and his wife, Mr and Mrs Henry Mason and Mr Charles Doe will be there, that I do know.'

Mollie's stomach turned over. Charles Doe was the Riding Officer. His job was to catch smugglers. If he saw the light in her window he would know exactly what it was there for and Richard and his men would be playing right into his hands. What could Richard have been thinking of to ask for the light, tonight of all nights?

'I don't care who's coming and who isn't, do you, Mollie?' Ellis was saying. 'I'm just glad we won't have to run around like headless chickens trying to impress all and sundry, like we did at the "do" after Christmas.' She peered at her. 'Are you all right, Mollie? You look a bit peaky.'

Mollie nodded and managed to grin at Cook. 'Yes, I think I must have eaten too many of Cook's suet dumplings.'

'Well, this dinner will be quite informal. Just family and a few of Mr James's business friends.' Arthur brushed a speck of dust from his coat sleeve. 'I shall manage perfectly adequately on my own.'

'Probably better,' Ellis remarked with a touch of spite, 'because you won't be trying to keep an eye on us in case we spill soup down somebody's neck.'

He gave her a smile that was almost a sneer. 'Exactly.'

There was no love lost between Arthur and Ellis.

'P'raps they're hopin' for a match between Miss Charlotte and the Riding Officer,' Cook remarked archly, dredging a flan with icing sugar. 'He's very handsome, from what I've heard.'

Arthur paused on his way to the butler's pantry to count wine bottles. 'Of course, my lips are sealed,' he said, looking down his long nose, 'But I rather think the master has other ideas for Miss Charlotte.'

'I hope he's consulted Miss Charlotte, then,' Mollie said without looking at him.

'By which you mean?' He raised thick, bushy eyebrows, making himself look even more pompous.

Mollie shrugged, remembering Charlotte capering round the room declaring she was in love. 'Nothing. Except Miss Charlotte might have other ideas.'

Arthur snorted. 'Miss Charlotte will do exactly what her father wishes. Make no mistake about that.'

Mollie looked up at the clock and sighed. 'Well, I'd better go and wake her up, I suppose. It'll take me from now till dinner time to get her ready for whatever it is her father has in mind for her.'

Arthur frowned and stared after her as she left the kitchen. She was a bit uppity, that one. He was never quite sure how to take her seemingly innocent remarks.

As Mollie had predicted, it took some time to prepare Charlotte for the 'informal' dinner. Bath water had to be lugged up from the scullery by Kitty and then she had to be dressed in her pale-green muslin gown, revamped out of all recognition with yellow robings and frills. She wore this with a new yellow cambric petticoat with green spots. With green ribbons and tiny yellow feathers in her hair, which had been laboriously frizzed by Mollie, and soft yellow slippers on her feet, she was ready.

'I hope you'll have a lovely evening, Miss Charlotte,' Mollie said, practically pushing her out of the door.

'Some hopes,' Charlotte said over her shoulder. 'Have you seen the guest list?'

As soon as she was out of sight Mollie hurried up to her room. All the time she had been dressing Charlotte she had been agonising over what to do. The message from Richard had been very plain; he wanted the lantern lit tonight. But it was far too risky with the Riding Officer dining in the room below. Yet Richard always said he knew where the Riding Officer and the Revenue men were; and that the lantern meant they were safely out of the way. So what had gone wrong? Or why did he want the lantern lit if he knew Charles Doe would be at Cliff House?

She took out the candle, which was hidden under her spare chemise and the piece of Brussels lace in the drawer and examined it carefully. Unlike the lace, which looked decidedly off-colour, it looked none the worse for having been left out in all weathers and halfway up the cliff for nearly a week. She placed it carefully in the lantern, which she kept hidden under her bed, and then stood on her chair to place it on the window sill. This was always tricky because of its weight, so not until it was safely in place did she risk lighting the candle. This was no problem, she had her own tinder box to light her bedside candle and Richard had given her some sulphur matches he had made at work, where there was no shortage of sulphur, but she didn't trust these at all; they smelled bad and she was afraid they might flare up and catch her clothes alight. Before long the candle spluttered into life and soon the flame glowed strongly. She climbed down from the chair and sat on the bed, her hands clasped together. Had she done the right thing? Or was she leading Richard into a trap? A trap that would land him in prison and would surely lose her her job.

She couldn't take the risk. Quickly, she climbed back up on the chair and blew out the candle, hoping and praying that the men out at sea who were looking for the sign hadn't seen it. She put the lantern on the floor, climbed back on

133

to the chair and leaned her elbows on the sill, peering out into the darkness.

The long dining-room windows that led onto the terrace had been opened to the warmth of the evening and the garden was bathed in the light spilling from them. Mollie strained her eyes to try and look beyond the garden but she could see nothing but blackness and the only sound was of the waves pounding on the beach. Then, far away at sea a pinpoint of light glimmered, then died. Was that a sign? A message? Or nothing at all? She watched and waited for a long time but the light didn't appear again.

Much later, several figures emerged from the house and walked to the end of the garden and stood looking out over the sea, the tips of their cigars glowing in the darkness. Whether they were watching for something or had simply come outside to enjoy a smoke in the warm night air she had no way of knowing but after a while, as they turned and went back into the house, she could hear the murmur of conversation on the night air.

Cramped and cold she got down from her vantage point. Richard couldn't have known Charles Doe would be at Cliff House or he would never have planned a landing tonight. Somebody must have fed him false information. But there was nothing more she could do; Richard had told her if the light didn't show they would know it wasn't safe to land the contraband and it certainly wouldn't be safe tonight. Satisfied she had done the right thing, she straightened her dress, smoothed her hair and went downstairs to wait for Miss Charlotte to return to her room.

It was not late when she came back but she was not in a very good mood.

'I don't like Mr Charles Doe,' she said petulantly, holding up her arms for Mollie to remove her petticoat. 'He's dreadfully rude, you know.'

'Indeed? Now, hold still, Miss Charlotte, your hair is tangled up in a button. There, that's better.'

'He hardly spoke to me the entire evening, although I did my best to be nice to him.' She yawned and stretched widely as Mollie undid her stays. 'I think he was more interested in watching the moths flying into the light from the window. He hardly took his eyes off the garden. I found it quite insulting, to tell you the truth.'

'Well, it is a very beautiful garden,' Mollie said absently, her mind on something else entirely.

The following morning, her good humour regained, Charlotte announced that they would be taking a walk, as it was such a bright, sunny day.

'Are we going to collect fossils, Miss Charlotte?' Mollie asking, picking up the bag that held the little pick and the tiny spade Charlotte used for digging interesting objects out of the cliff.

'No, I thought it might be a change to walk along to the naze,' Charlotte said, deliberately keeping her voice casual.

'Ah, I see,' Mollie said with a nod.

Charlotte swung round. 'What do you mean, "Ah, I see"?'

'I don't mean anything, Miss Charlotte,' Mollie said innocently. 'Shall you wear your chip hat or your new bonnet?'

'My new bonnet, I think,' Charlotte said, after pretending to deliberate. 'The ribbons go well with this blue gown, don't you think?'

'I do indeed.' Mollie fetched Charlotte's pelisse and her own and five minutes later they were walking briskly along the top of the cliff towards spit of land jutting out into the sea. It was known as the naze, some said, because it was shaped like a nose. In the near distance the windows of the tall lookout tower glinted in the sunshine and beyond it the tall masts of the men o'war lying to anchor just off Harwich were visible in the clear air.

As they neared the tower Mollie could see several soldiers, their red coats open as they lounged in the sunlight on a bench by the open door. A few of them were playing cards, one was polishing his boots, another was propped against the wall, half asleep. Much to Mollie's relief, Charlotte kept to the cliff path, which was bordered on both sides by gorse bushes, giving the tower itself a fairly wide berth.

'They take it in turns to be on watch at the top of the tower,' Charlotte said a little breathlessly as they passed. 'Arn ... Captain Pilkington told me. There are two on lookout, and two on guard at the foot of the tower.'

'What about those others?' Mollie whispered, nodding her head in their direction. 'What are they supposed to be doing?'

'*I* don't know, do I,' Charlotte said a trifle tetchily. 'I suppose they've got other duties.'

'Doesn't look like it to me,' Mollie remarked.

'Well, they'd be pretty busy if Napoleon's troops suddenly appeared, I'm sure of that,' Charlotte snapped. 'Don't you realise they're there to defend us?' She stopped and pointed out to sea. 'And that's where the invasion would come from. The soldiers on lookout would be the first to see the ships coming over the horizon.'

'Do you think they will come, Miss Charlotte?' Mollie asked. 'Richard, my cousin, doesn't seem to think it's very likely.'

'And what does he know about such things?' Charlotte said derisively. 'I thought you said he worked at the Copperas House.'

'Yes, he does. But he has friends ... '

'What sort of friends?'

Mollie shrugged. 'Fishermen. Men he meets in pubs.'

'Well, how would they know?'

Mollie shrugged again but said nothing. She could hardly tell Charlotte that they picked up their news along with the rum and tea and genever they smuggled.

'Why, Miss Grainger. How nice to see you.' Both girls turned quickly at the sound of a man's deep voice.

'Captain Pilkington! What a surprise,' Charlotte said, blushing, although it was plainly no surprise at all.

'May I walk with you?' he asked, falling into step beside her and forcing Mollie to drop behind.

'Indeed, I should be delighted.' She gave a little tinkling laugh. 'You can wait for me here, Mollie,' she called over her shoulder. 'I'm sure Captain Pilkington will see that I come to no harm, won't you, Captain.'

'I shall guard you with my life, dear lady.'

They went off, laughing. Mollie stood by the path watching them go. Captain Pilkington was a tall, dark-haired, dark-eyed young man, handsome enough to turn any young lady's head. Mollie could quite see why her mistress was so enchanted by him as she watched him bend his head to give Charlotte his full attention. Indeed, they made a charming couple. But Mollie couldn't help wondering what James Grainger might think of his only daughter wanting to marry an army officer. She gave herself a mental shake. Charlotte was not yet twenty-one and very immature. It would be some time before she was ready for marriage to anybody.

She turned and looked out over the sea. Charlotte had said to wait for her but there was no telling how long she would be and it was not in Mollie's nature to simply stand and do nothing so she began to look for a way down to the beach where she could search for shells or fossils to pass the time. But at this point the cliff was sheer and there was no safe way down so she gave up and found herself a sheltered spot where she could simply sit and watch the sea and the gulls wheeling above it, half-enjoying, half-irritated by the unaccustomed inactivity.

'Mollie! What you doin' here?'

She turned, surprised to hear Richard's voice. 'I could say the same to you,' she retorted. 'Aren't you s'posed to be at work?'

'I'm on me way to fetch some stuff for Mr Mark,' he said. He sat down beside her. 'What happened last night?' he whispered fiercely, gripping her arm. 'Didn't you get my message? I've had to come all the way up here with a barrel o' rum to pay them – ' he jerked his head towards the tower '– for turnin' a blind eye to somethin' that never happened.'

She shook him off. 'Yes, I got your message,' she said. 'But I thought you didn't take risks.'

'What d'you mean?'

'You told me you always knew where the Riding Officer and the Revenue men were. You told me you only asked me to put the light up when the coast was clear.'

'Yes. Well?'

'Where was Charles Doe last night?'

'He'd gone out to dinner. Somewhere in Wrabness.'

'And who told you that?'

'My spy.' He rounded on her. 'Why are you askin' me all these questions? What I wanta know is, why didn't you put the light up last night?'

'Because Charles Doe was at dinner at Cliff House. That's why.' She turned to him tight-lipped. 'Seems to me you need to look to your spy, Richard. Whoever told you he was at Wrabness either made a mistake or wanted to land us all in trouble. Me included.'

'Christ!' Richard let out a breath and mopped his brow with his forearm. 'That was a close call, then. We was bringin' a lot o' stuff in, too.'

'So what's happened to it, then? All the stuff you were supposed to be bringing in?'

He looked at her thoughtfully. 'I reckon most of it's lyin' in the shallows out there,' he said, nodding out to sea. 'Marked by a buoy, an' waitin' for us to go an' pick it up.'

She frowned. 'Won't it spoil?'

'Nah. The barrels are watertight and anythin' else will be well wrapped up in oiled silk. They've done it before. But we can't leave it there for long. We'll have to row out an' collect it tonight. Is there anywhere at Cliff House where we can stow it, Moll, just for a few hours, till we can get it out o' the way?'

'Oh, Dick, don't I take enough risks for you?'

'I ain't askin' you to risk anything, Mollie. All I'm askin' is for you to tell me the lie o' the land. I'll do the rest.'

She stared out to sea for a long time. He picked a blade of grass and began to chew it. 'I was good to you when we was little, Mollie. I looked out for you, didn' I. Now thass your turn.'

'You're blackmailing me, Dick.'

'I can get you some pretty silk. Thass all lyin' out there in the shallows,' he said persuasively. 'You see, thass all a matter o' time. We've gotta get the stuff ashore and stowed while the tide is right and afore the moon is up. Then we'll be away an' you'll never know we've bin near.'

'There's a cellar behind the potting shed,' she said at last. 'I've never known anybody go anywhere near it. You might have to take a crowbar to it to open it.'

'Behind the pottin' shed, you say?'

'That's right. It's well away from the house, by the wall at the end of the kitchen garden.'

'Couldn't be better.' He gave her a smacking kiss. 'You're a good gal, Mollie-O.'

'I wish I could say you were a good boy,' she said gloomily. 'But you're a rogue, Richard Barnes. There's no two ways about it, you're a rogue.'

'Ah, but you love me all the same,' he said with a grin as he got to his feet.

He leaned down. 'Thanks for savin' our bacon last night, Moll. I realise now we'd all hev bin behind bars by now if it hadn't bin for you.' He winked. 'There'll be a little present waitin' for you when you next come home.'

Mollie watched him go, wracked with love for the boy she had grown up with and anxiety for the man he had become. She got to her feet, frowning. Talking to Richard she hadn't realised how far the sun had moved round. Surely, Miss Charlotte should have been back by now, unless she had been so busy talking to Richard that she had missed her. She began to walk slowly along the path in the direction Charlotte had taken with Captain Pilkington, hoping to catch sight of her. She had not gone far when to her relief she saw them coming towards her. As soon as they saw Mollie they moved decorously apart, but not before Mollie had seen Charlotte, her bonnet swinging from her hand, hanging on to the Captain's arm as he gently removed the little bits of grass that were clinging to her curls.

Chapter Fourteen

The next morning Mollie was hurrying along the corridor with Charlotte's early morning chocolate when she saw Sebastian approaching from the other direction. She always smiled to herself at the term 'early morning' because by now the household staff had been up for at least three hours, cleaning and tidying the rooms, burnishing the hearths, and lighting fires so that the rooms would be ready when the family appeared for breakfast.

She had hoped to slip inside Charlotte's door unnoticed but he quickened his step and reached it first. He stopped, barring her way. She saw that he was dressed for hunting rather than a day at the Copperas House, even though it was a working day.

'Why, Mollie,' he said, beaming, 'what a wonderful start to my day, seeing your lovely face.'

Flushing with embarrassment she bobbed a brief curtsey and made to pass him but he side-stepped and blocked her way yet again.

'Ah, no. You don't get away that easily,' he said with a laugh. He bent his head towards hers. 'I still have that little brooch, you know. It's yours, because it was you that found the piece of amber. I had it made specially for you.'

'It was very kind of you, Sir, but you shouldn't have done that and I couldn't possibly accept it,' she said primly. 'In any case, I already have a brooch, thank you.' She turned up her collar to reveal the little brooch she had bought with the money Uncle Sam had given her. She kept it hidden but she always wore it; it was her most treasured possession.

'Oh, Mollie!' his expression was just short of disparaging.

'You needn't think that because it didn't cost a lot of money I don't value it,' she said hotly. 'My Uncle Sam gave me money to buy something nice and this is what I bought. I always wear it and I wouldn't part with it for all the world. Sir,' she added as an afterthought.

He held up his hand defensively. 'All right, all right,' he said, grinning. He sighed theatrically and put his head on one side. 'I just wish I could persuade you to value my brooch as much. Why won't you let me give it to you, Mollie?' He put a finger under her chin and tilted up her face, so that she was forced to look into his grey eyes. 'With my love,' he said softly.

'I don't think you should make fun of me, Sir,' she said, annoyed with herself that he could make her pulse race.

He shook his head. 'Believe me, Mollie, I'm not making fun of you,' he said with a sigh. Then he took a step back as a door opened further along the corridor and his father came out.

'Ah, Seb. Are you going to the Works today?' James called as he strode towards them. Mollie noticed that, like Sebastian, he was dressed for hunting. She noticed, too, that with his paunch and coarse features his hunting pink sat less well on him than on his handsome son.

Sebastian took a step away from her. 'Yes. I intend to look in later, Sir,' he said, trying to sound businesslike.

'That's good, because I want you to get Mark to ... '

Mollie didn't hear any more as she escaped and slipped thankfully into Charlotte's room.

'You're looking a bit red in the face,' her young mistress remarked as Mollie arranged her pillows and handed her the chocolate.

142

'I've been hurrying,' Mollie said briefly. She felt annoyed that Sebastian and his father should take the running of the Copperas House so lightly, leaving the bulk of the work to Mark whilst they did little except spend the profits from it, although she knew it was nothing whatever to do with her.

'There's no need to snap at me, Mollie. I'll thank you to keep a civil tongue in your head.' Charlotte's voice was sharp. She sipped her chocolate, frowning. 'What's the matter with this chocolate? It's half cold.'

'I'm sorry, Miss Charlotte, I got delayed. That's why I had to hurry.' Mollie said. It was almost the truth.

But it didn't matter because Charlotte wasn't listening. She sat in bed looking like the cat that had stolen the cream. 'I think we'll take a walk again this afternoon,' she said. 'And I shall wear my cream muslin. It will look well with my little hat with the russet roses, don't you think?'

'Very well, Miss Charlotte.' Mollie busied herself tidying the room.

Charlotte giggled, her annoyance with Mollie forgotten. 'You don't approve, do you, Mollie. I can see that by your expression.'

'It's not for me to approve or disapprove, Miss Charlotte,' Mollie said, careful to keep her voice level. 'But since you ask, I must say I think you're a little unwise to take walks alone with the Captain. After all, you haven't known him very long, have you.'

'Don't be silly, Mollie. The Captain is a perfect gentleman. In any case, you're never far away, so I could always call for help if I needed to.' She glanced at Mollie. 'Not that it would ever be necessary, of course,' she added hastily.

'No, of course not.' Mollie went about the room folding clothes and putting them away, tight-lipped.

Charlotte finished her chocolate and waited for Mollie to take the tray. 'You don't understand, Mollie,' she said irritably, 'You've never been in love.' She leaned back against

143

her pillows with a sigh. 'I read once, it may have been in a book by Mrs Radcliff, I don't really remember, that time spent away from one's beloved is time wasted. And it's true; when I'm not with Arnold I count the hours until I shall see him again.'

'I think that's a bit of an exaggeration, Miss Charlotte,' Mollie remarked, allowing herself a smile.

Charlotte giggled again, glad to see that Mollie's good humour was restored. 'Yes, you're right, it is. But I know you won't begrudge me meeting him again today because this will be his last day at the tower for a whole two weeks. There's always a detachment on guard duty, or whatever it is they call it, but it's a week at the tower and then two weeks back at base, Arnold said.' She nodded to herself. 'I suppose that's because it's quite onerous, standing guard and watching for the enemy day and night.'

Mollie sniffed but didn't reply. What the soldiers at the base of the tower had been doing when she'd seen them hadn't looked very onerous to her, but she wisely said nothing.

The afternoon walk followed the same pattern as the previous day, except that while Charlotte was gone Mollie was bored without Richard there to talk to. She walked up and down, keeping well out of sight of the tower, uncomfortably aware of the soldiers who were there, fearful that they might see her and try to engage her in conversation. She had heard plenty of kitchen talk about the goings-on of soldiers with unsuspecting girls and with girls who were, to coin a phrase, 'no better than they should be' and she wanted no part of that. She would never be able to face Uncle Sam again if he thought she had been associating with soldiers.

In the end she found a rough path down the cliff that the soldiers had fashioned to reach the beach. She scrambled down it and spent an hour walking on the beach looking for shells and fossils.

144

She was engrossed in her own thoughts, remembering the day Sebastian had been with her and Charlotte as they searched and thinking how much less complicated it would have been if Charlotte had found the piece of amber with the insect trapped inside it, because then Sebastian could have given his sister the brooch instead of trying to make her, Mollie, accept it. She was beginning to feel she knew exactly how that little insect felt.

Suddenly, she heard Charlotte's voice from the top of the cliff. 'Oh, you're down there. I've been looking for you for ages. What are you doing?'

She looked up and saw Charlotte looking down at her, flushed and happy, her hat tipped at a slightly rakish angle.

She gave a sigh of relief. 'Just a minute, Miss Charlotte, I'll come up.'

'But what are you doing down there? Looking for fossils?'

'Yes. I found a way down just over there so I thought I would see if I could find anything.'

'And did you?'

'No. But it helped to pass the time.' Mollie toiled back up the path, which was nothing more than a steep, zig-zag track between scrubby bushes.

'I'm sorry I was gone for so long,' Charlotte said as Mollie reached the top. 'But you see, I shan't be able to meet Arnold for a whole fortnight. Oh, Mollie –' she clasped her hands together '– sometimes I think I shall die of love for him. And to think I won't see him for a whole two weeks! Except at the ball at Thorpe Hall, of course,' she added in a more normal voice. 'The officers of his regiment have been invited to that and naturally I shall be going with Mama and Papa so I shall see him there.' She stood aside as Mollie brushed the dust off her skirt. 'I think I'll wear my lilac for the ball. With lime green feathers in my hair. What do you think, Mollie?'

'The lilac's very nice, Miss Charlotte.' At that moment Mollie would have agreed that sackcloth was very nice

145

because she was so tired of being kept waiting whilst Charlotte and her young man whispered sweet nothings in each other's ears.

Sometimes, over the course of the following summer, Mollie felt as if she was carrying the weight of the world on her shoulders. If it wasn't Richard wanting the lantern lit, making her a party to his smuggling activities, it was Charlotte, calling Mollie her chaperone but then going off and getting up to heaven knew what with her soldier sweetheart. Mollie didn't like Captain Pilkington, although she had to admit she hardly knew him since Charlotte often ran ahead to meet him and they were always late back from their 'walks' so their goodbyes were brief. But what she had seen she didn't much care for. He was just a bit too handsome, too dashing, too eager to whisk Charlotte off. Sometimes Mollie was tempted to follow them and once or twice she did follow them along the path that led through scrubby undergrowth out on to the lonely headland, but something – a fear of what she might see or discover, an innate aversion to what would amount to playing Peeping Tom? – prevented her from following them too far and she turned back, leaving her young mistress laughing coquettishly as the captain's arm stole round her waist.

In any case, what could she *do*? She could hardly burst on them and tell them to stop what they were doing; in truth she hadn't seen them do anything except walk rather too closely together. So she contented herself with warning her young mistress when they got home of the dire consequences of letting young men 'take liberties'.

'What *can* you mean, Mollie?' Charlotte joked, her eyes sparkling, although Mollie saw the blush that spread over her cheeks.

'I think you know very well what I mean, Miss Charlotte,' Mollie answered, her face serious.

'I assure you I do not,' Charlotte insisted. 'Now, are you going to help me trim my new hat? I think perhaps we should walk into the town for some new ribbons.' She gave Mollie a sly grin. 'After all, there's no telling who we might see on the way there.'

Mollie sighed. 'Very well, Miss Charlotte.' She wished with all her heart that the regiment – and Captain Pilkington with it – would be moved to the other end of the country.

It was a wish that was granted as the last hot days of August gave way to a cool September. Charlotte returned from a meeting with the captain very quiet and subdued, and Mollie's spirits rose, hoping the cooler weather was cooling their ardour a little. But as Mollie was helping her to get ready for bed Charlotte burst into tears.

'He's going away. Arnold's going away,' she sobbed. 'His regiment is being moved out and another one is to take its place.'

'Oh, really? Do you know where they're going?' Mollie asked, trying to keep the relief out of her voice.

'No. Arnold said he didn't know.'

'Never mind. I expect he'll write and tell you when he finds out,' Mollie suggested, trying to sound more sympathetic than she felt.

Charlotte shook her head. 'No. He won't. He said it would be best to make a clean break.' She began to sob even harder. 'You see, something he'd never told me before ...'

Mollie closed her eyes. She knew exactly what was coming. 'Yes?' she prompted.

Charlotte stared at her accusingly through her tears. 'You know, don't you? You know he's already got a wife.'

'No, I didn't know. But I'm not surprised,' Mollie said.

'Then why didn't you warn me?' Charlotte cried, venting all her misery and disappointment on Mollie.

'Because you wouldn't have listened. And anyway, it was only a guess. I didn't know for sure.'

Charlotte turned and thumped her pillow. 'I *hate* him. I *hate* him.' Then she buried her head. 'No, I don't. I love

147

him. I shall always love him. I shall never love anyone the way I loved Arnold.'

Mollie sat on the side of the bed and stroked her hair. 'That's what you think now, Miss Charlotte, but in time you'll find someone else to love.'

Charlotte lifted her head. 'You're wrong. You've never been in love. How would you know?'

Mollie shrugged. 'Well, that's what I think will happen. I seem to remember my Uncle Sam had a saying, "There's as good fish in the sea as ever came out of it" and I reckon that must be what he meant. Right now, you think you'll never love anybody else, but one day someone will come along who you'll like a whole lot better and you'll see Captain Pilkington for the rotter that he is.'

Charlotte sat bolt upright. 'Don't speak of Arnold like that. He's not a rotter. He couldn't help falling in love with me, could he?'

'Yes, he could,' Mollie said stubbornly. 'He was already married. But he didn't tell you that, did he?'

Charlotte hung her head. 'No, he didn't. He talked about marrying me.'

'So he's a liar as well as a rotter.' Mollie got up from the side of the bed. 'Now, dry your eyes, Miss Charlotte and I'll fetch you some warm milk. Things won't look nearly so bad in the morning.'

Thoughtfully, Mollie went down to the kitchen. Once Charlotte recovered from her infatuation with Captain Pilkington she would realise what a good man Mark was. She knew he was in love with her, she had told Mollie so. And her father wanted the match so there was nothing to stop their engagement being announced. The idea of this lay like lead in Mollie's breast.

Mollie was right. It didn't take long for Charlotte to recover from her love affair and regain her usual high spirits. There were parties to go to and friends to meet, and she renewed her interest in collecting fossils. Nothing was said about an engagement to Mark and as far as Mollie could see they spent very little time together. It was all very puzzling.

But soon there were other things to worry about.

It was early in October when her young mistress first refused her morning chocolate, saying it made her feel sick.

Mollie pursed her lips. 'Your monthly flowers are very late, too, Miss Charlotte. It's weeks since . . . '

'Yes. I know. I expect I've caught a chill and that's why I feel so sick all the time.' Charlotte spoke impatiently.

Mollie began to lay out her mistress's clothes for the day. 'I hope you're right, Miss Charlotte.'

'What do you mean?'

'I think you know very well what I mean, Miss Charlotte.' She turned and looked at her. 'Miss Charlotte, have you and Captain Pilkington . . . ?'

Charlotte flushed angrily. 'Don't be impertinent, Mollie. I can't see it's any of your business.'

Mollie sighed. 'No. Like you say, it's none of my business, but if you're in trouble I know who's going to get the blame.' She sat down on a chair. 'Miss Charlotte, do you know where babies come from?'

Charlotte frowned. 'What's that got to do with it? Of course I know. Mama told me when my baby brother died. The doctor came with his black bag . . . '

Mollie put her head in her hands. 'Oh, God, you've no idea, have you.'

'No idea about what? I don't know what you're talking about. Oh, Mollie, I think I'm going to be sick . . . '

Later, when Mollie had dealt with her and she was lying back on her pillows she said wanly, 'You're talking in riddles, Mollie. What's all this talk of babies got to do with me feeling so ill?'

'Because babies don't arrive in doctor's black bags, they grow inside their mothers' bellies. Didn't you know that?'

Charlotte shook her head, her eyes wide. She licked her lips. 'What's that got to do with me?'

149

'Because if you got up to things you shouldn't with Captain Pilkington, and I suspect you did, then that's what's wrong with you. You've got a baby growing inside you. Now, tell me the truth. Did he ...?' She couldn't bring herself to say the words.

Charlotte hung her head. 'I didn't think it was right. I said no, but he kept on.' She put her hands over her face. 'And I liked it,' she said, her voice muffled.

'When was this?' Mollie asked.

'The first time was at the ball at Thorpe Hall. '

'How did you manage that?' Mollie interrupted.

'In the summer house down by the lake. You see, we'd had quite a lot of champagne and we started kissing and then ... well, it just happened.'

'Just the once? At the ball at Thorpe Hall?'

Charlotte hung her head. 'Well, no. That was the first time. But then we found this old barn, half-hidden in the undergrowth by the naze. We used to ...' her voice trailed off. 'It was wrong, wasn't it. I should never have ... but he was so ...' her voice dropped to a whisper. 'And I liked it.'

Mollie buried her face in her hands. 'Oh, God. What a mess.'

Charlotte stared at Mollie, her face ashen. 'What am I going to do, Mollie?' she whispered. 'I didn't think ... I didn't realise ...'

'I told you not to let him take liberties,' Mollie said brutally.

'I-I didn't know what you meant.'

'Well, you might have guessed. You might have known it wasn't right to let a young man put his hand up your skirt, never mind everything else you let him do.' Mollie felt as old as Methuselah, lecturing Charlotte on a subject about which she herself was so ignorant.

'No, I knew I shouldn't let him. But it was *nice*. I liked it.'

'That didn't make it right.'

150

'What am I going to do, Mollie?' she repeated in a small voice.

Mollie put her head in her hands. 'I don't know. I really don't know.'

Charlotte put out her hand. 'You'll think of something, Mollie, won't you. You're my friend. I know I can rely on you.'

Chapter Fifteen

'You'll think of something, Mollie. You're my friend. I know I can rely on you.' For three long, sleepless nights the words went round and round in Mollie's brain. The trouble was, she couldn't think of anything. Her mind seemed to be stuck on the fact that she would be blamed for what had happened. Oh, yes, she would get the blame for allowing Charlotte to be left alone with that dreadful man when she was supposed to have been chaperoning her. She would be dismissed, that much was certain. She would have to leave this life she had grown to love; the nice clothes, the little luxuries, the life of comparative ease. And what would happen to her? Aunt Rose was glad enough to see her on her days off provided she was bearing gifts, but Mollie doubted she would be welcomed back to her house permanently. Of course, Uncle Sam would insist on it, dear Uncle Sam, which would only increase Aunt Rose's antagonism. In any case, she couldn't bear the thought of returning to the back-aching drudgery of picking mine in all weathers, with rough and cracked fingers and chilblained toes. And with the winter coming ... she tossed and turned in her narrow but very comfortable bed and tried to dismiss her own problems and concentrate on Charlotte.

Because she knew that if only she could solve Charlotte's problem her own would disappear. Instead of which, she got up each morning more tired than when she went to bed and had to deal with Charlotte's morning sickness, which seemed to last all day, and try to keep Beatrice from fussing and wanting to call Doctor Evans to give her something for the stomach upset that seemed to be lasting rather a long time.

'What are we going to do, Mollie?' Charlotte asked fifty times each day, lying in bed and plucking at the sheet. 'Have you thought of anything yet?'

Mollie slumped down in the chair and put her head in her hands. Then she looked up. 'Have you got any money? Perhaps we could go away somewhere where nobody knows us until ...'

'Then what? What will we do with the ...' she pointed eloquently at her mercifully still flat stomach.

'Oh, I don't know. I really don't know.'

Charlotte leaned up on one elbow. 'You look nearly as bad as I feel, Mollie. Are you all right?'

Mollie gave a kind of snort as her temper snapped. 'Oh, yes. Apart from the fact that I don't sleep a wink at night because I'm worried half out of my mind over you and the fact that I shall soon lose my place here, I'm perfectly well.'

'Why should you lose your place here?' Charlotte asked, genuinely puzzled. 'Mama knows I can't manage without you.'

'Oh, Charlotte. Who do you think is going to be blamed for your predicament?' Mollie pointed to herself. 'I shall be told it's all my fault because I shouldn't have ... Oh, what's the use. It's happened now.'

'Well, if it's your fault I'm like this then you'd better find a way to get me out of it,' Charlotte said unkindly. Then she put out her hand. 'Oh, Mollie, I'm sorry. I shouldn't have said that. Of course it wasn't your fault. You kept warning me, only I wouldn't listen. I shall tell Mama so.'

'I think your mama will have things that will concern her far more than what happens to me when she finds out about

153

you,' Mollie said wearily. 'She won't care that I'll have to go back to picking mine for a few coppers each day in all weathers.'

She closed her eyes, picturing the women in their red cloaks who spent their lives on the beach. Women like Lily Stokes, who augmented her meagre earnings by 'helping' the other women when their monthly flowers were late and they couldn't afford another mouth to feed.

She sat bolt upright in her chair. Lily Stokes! That was it! That was why her mind had kept returning to the mine pickers. Because that was where the solution to Charlotte's problem lay. She stood up, pressing her fingers to her temples. 'Listen to me, Miss Charlotte, it's my afternoon off today ... '

'Oh, you can't leave me, Mollie. Not when I'm feeling so dreadful.' Charlotte held out her hand to detain her.

'Don't be such a ninny.' Worry was making her sharp. 'In any case, you don't feel quite so bad in the afternoons. You'll be perfectly all right while I'm gone.'

'Where are you going, then? Why can't you just stay here with me? I might want ... '

'Because I've thought of a way out of all this. I think I can get you something that will ...'

'That will what?' Charlotte's eyes were wide.

Mollie shook her head impatiently. 'I know somebody. The women who pick mine go to her when they find they're in the family way again and can't afford another mouth to feed. She tells them what to do or gives them something ... '

'What is it?'

'How should I know? I've never had the need of it.' Mollie's voice was still sharp. 'Anyway, it usually seems to work so I'll go and see her and ask her what to do.'

'Oh, thank you Mollie, I don't know what I'd do without you.'

'I haven't done anything yet,' Mollie reminded her. 'Of course, she might not be willing to tell me.'

*

154

Mollie took the usual basket of leftovers from the kitchen but instead of taking the cliff path as she usually did she went down the steps and walked along the beach. It was a lovely autumn day. The tide was coming in quite fast, each wave leaving a lace of froth on the sand to be obliterated by the one that came after. The pickers, in faded skirts and bodices, their chip hats tied under the chin with bits of colourful rag, were emptying their last basketfuls into Old Sol's tumbrel and making their way home, rubbing their aching backs as they went. Mollie followed along behind until she caught up with the last of the stragglers, a very pregnant Betty Knowels.

'Findin' it a bit hard to bend down now, Bet?' Mollie asked, carefully modifying her speech so that Betty shouldn't think she was 'stuck up'.

Betty grinned. 'Yeh. My Fred says I shouldn't come pickin' now but I don't wanta stop if I can help it. We need what few coppers I can earn, 'specially with the baby, an' that. We got that place at the end o' Copp'ras Lane, where Ole Lady Bellman lived. She was turned out after her ole man died because them cottages is for men who work at the Copp'ras House.'

Mollie frowned. She knew this but she felt it was cruel to turn an old lady out of the home she had lived in all her married life. 'Where did she go?'

'I think 'er son took 'er in, although 'is wife didn't think much of it,' Betty said with a shrug. 'Anyways, we got the place because my Fred's a stoker there.' She looked Mollie up and down. 'You've done all right for yerself, ain't yer, up at Cliff House. I wonder you stoop to talk to the likes o' me.'

'Why shouldn't I? I picked mine with yer long enough. You don't forget these things.'

Betty nodded. 'I 'spect you're orf to see your Aunt Rose now.'

'Thass right. I try to come see her and Uncle Sam most weeks.'

'Yer, I know. I seen yer.'

There was a lull in the conversation, then Mollie said casually, 'How's Jim Stokes, now? I've heard his leg still plays him up. Is it worse? I didn't see Lily among the pickers today.'

'Oh, she was here, but she hev to pick as much as she can as quick as she can to get back home. Jim's leg never healed properly so some days 'e can't work an' that makes 'im bad tempered. She don't like to leave the children with 'im for too long when 'e's like that.'

'P'raps I'll call an' see them.' Mollie tried to sound casual but she noticed the quick flick of Betty's eyes towards her stomach and she realised that nothing happened in this close-knit community without everyone's knowledge. 'I've got some brawn from the kitchen at Cliff House. I usually bring something a bit tasty for Aunt Rose but she won't mind if I give it to the Stokes for once, I'm sure.'

By this time they had reached the Stokes's cottage. Two small children were playing on the step and Jim was sitting on a chair just inside the door. Lily came to the door when she heard Mollie's voice.

'You'd better come in,' she said, jerking her head towards her husband. ''E's ain't worth talkin' to, today, 'cause 'is leg's bad again.'

'Has he seen a doctor?' Mollie asked. It wasn't likely, she thought, glancing round the sparsely furnished room.

'Don't be daft. Anyways, I can do 'im more good meself – an' cheaper – with my remedies.' She looked Mollie up and down and said bluntly, 'Is that what you've come for? One o' my remedies? Thass good you've come early. I don't give anything once that begin to show.'

'No. No. I don't need . . . at least, yes, I do, that is what I've come for, but it's not for me,' Mollie said quickly.

'Ah, thass for one o' the maids up there, I 'spect.' Lily jerked her thumb in the general direction of Cliff House and grinned. 'They all say that, the ones that ain't married.

Thass not for me, Lily, they say. But I know different. I can tell by the look.'

Mollie closed her eyes briefly. Oh, what did it matter what Lily thought as long as she gave her what she needed. She smiled. 'Nobody pulls the wool over your eyes, do they, Lily,' she said. 'But I'm still telling you this isn't for me.'

'I believe yer; thousands wouldn't,' Lily said carelessly. 'Well, what d'you want an' how far gone are yer ... I mean, how far gone is she?'

Mollie frowned. 'I'm not sure...'

'How many times hev she missed?'

'Only once. Well, maybe twice.'

'Make up yer mind, girl. Well, never mind, thass not too late. Pennyroyal should do the trick. Or rue.' She went to a cupboard by the fireplace and took out a small bottle. 'Here y'are. I crush it and make it up into a dose. If you ... er, if she can scrounge a drop o' genever to put with it that'll help.' She gave it to Mollie. 'You ... she might need two doses.'

Mollie didn't bother to correct her again. Thankfully, she took the bottle and put it in her basket, removing the parcel of brawn. 'I expect Jim will enjoy a bit of brawn,' she said, 'and this will buy something for the children.' She pressed a sovereign into Lily's hand.

Lily looked at it, then spat on it. 'They pay well up at Cliff House, I see,' she said with a smirk. 'You wouldn't wanta lose your place there, now, would you?'

'No, Lily, I wouldn't,' Mollie replied quietly. 'So I'll thank you to keep quiet about my visit.'

She left and carried on to Aunt Rose's cottage. She found she was trembling, but whether it was with fury at Lily's assumption that the remedy was for her, or with relief to think she had got the answer to Charlotte's predicament in her basket, she wasn't sure.

She didn't stay long with Aunt Rose because she was anxious to get back to Cliff House, where she went straight

157

to Charlotte's room after ordering hot water for a bath to be brought.

Charlotte was asleep. Mollie woke her up. 'Come on, up you get,' she said without ceremony. She dragged the hip bath out of the cupboard. 'I've ordered hot water to be brought up.' She turned at the tap at the door. 'Come in, Kitty. That's it, pour it in the bath. Poor Miss Charlotte has sweated so much during her illness that she needs to be sponged down.' She turned back to Charlotte. 'Come along, Miss Charlotte, we'll soon have you feeling a lot better.'

It was true. After a long, painful, night that both she and Mollie preferred to forget, Charlotte, looking decidedly pale and wan, managed to eat two slices of toast and marmalade for breakfast.

'Oh, I'm so glad you're feeling better, my dear,' Beatrice said when she paid her daily visit to the bedroom that Mollie had made sure held no trace of the night's frantic activities. 'I really thought we should have to call in Doctor Evans if you hadn't made some improvement by today.'

'No, really, Mama, I'm feeling much better. A little weak, that's all.' By this time Charlotte had begun on the second piece of toast.

'I can see your appetite has returned. That's always a good sign. You've eaten hardly anything for the past two weeks.' Beatrice turned to Mollie. 'You're looking very tired, too, Mollie. Clearly, it's been quite a strain for you, looking after Charlotte. I know my daughter is not a good patient.' She stroked her chin. 'Maybe what you need is a little holiday.'

'That's very kind of you, Ma'am, but I'd rather stay here, if you don't mind,' Mollie said bobbing a slight curtsey. 'You see, I haven't got anywhere to go except back to my uncle's house and I really don't want to go back there.'

158

'Anyway, I can't spare her,' Charlotte said petulantly. 'She's my friend. I need her with me.'

'Just make sure you don't make her work too hard for the next few days, then, Charlotte. She looks quite worn out.' Beatrice patted her daughter's hand and got up to go. 'I'm sure we'll think of something,' she said to Mollie. 'Perhaps . . . '

'I've already thought of something, Mama,' Charlotte said, wiping her fingers on her napkin.

Beatrice turned and waited, her eyebrows raised.

'Like I said, Mama, Mollie is my friend, my *special* friend, so she should be treated like one of the family. I think she should take her meals with us and not down in the kitchen with the servants.' Charlotte lifted her chin triumphantly as she waited for her mother's verdict.

Beatrice had very mobile eyebrows. They quickly turned down into a frown. 'Oh, I don't know about that, Charlotte . . . ' she said.

Charlotte heard the uncertainty in her mother's voice and pressed home her advantage. 'But you said yourself how well Mollie had nursed me, mama. You said yourself we must repay her. Well, I can't think of a better way than making her a member of the family, can you? After all, that's what Papa did for Mark.'

'But Mark *is* a member of our family, Charlotte. He's my nephew.'

Charlotte shrugged. 'That hardly counts. It wouldn't stop us marrying, would it? If we wanted to, that is.'

'No,' Beatrice agreed. 'It would be no barrier to your marrying. But that is not the point at issue . . . '

'No. We're talking about Mollie, who has been so good to me and has saved you endless worry and anxiety, Mama.'

More than you could ever know; the thought sped silently through Mollie's mind as she gazed out of the window.

Still Beatrice hesitated. She looked at Mollie standing by

159

the window. She was an attractive girl and had a quiet dignity about her in spite of her position as a servant in the house. She would be no disgrace to any dinner table, yet for some reason she couldn't explain even to herself, because she had taken a real liking to the girl, Beatrice was reluctant to give in to Charlotte's request. In any case, it was unheard of to offer a servant a seat at the family board. What would the other servants think? What would happen when there were guests? Would Mollie still join the family or would she be banned? Beatrice foresaw endless difficulties and took the easy way out, saying, – 'Very well. I shall speak to your father. Naturally, we must respect his decision,' confident that James would refuse Charlotte's request.

'Naturally, Mama.' Charlotte was equally sure he would uphold it. She knew her father had an insatiable eye for a pretty girl.

Charlotte was proved right and it was agreed that when she was strong enough to rejoin the family meal table Mollie should be by her side.

Mollie was not sure how she felt about this. On the one hand she knew she was only taking up her rightful place as James Grainger's daughter; she remembered how she had vowed to sit at his table when Uncle Sam told her of her true parentage. But since she had become Charlotte's maid she had been so happy at Cliff House and so contented with her lot that she had all but forgotten not only her vow but also that she was, in fact, Charlotte's half-sister.

It was ironic that now she had been offered the place at the family table she had so coveted, it no longer mattered to her. The important thing was that she would be there as Charlotte's special friend. She valued that more than anything.

It was over a week before Charlotte was strong enough to go downstairs. In that time she insisted that she and Mollie took their meals together in her room and they read and sewed together, the awful secret they shared strengthening the bond that had already formed between them.

Mollie was to join Charlotte at dinner with the family for the first time on Sunday. She viewed this with some apprehension because she knew that this was the one meal in the week when the whole family was guaranteed to be present.

It was a relief to find that she had been placed between Charlotte and her mother, who sat at the end of the table. Sebastian – who had contrived to sit opposite to her – was next to Mark. James, who appeared after everyone else was seated, sat down in front of a large joint of pork at the head of the table.

He said Grace and then began to carve.

'Ah,' he said, looking down the length of the table in some surprise, 'I see we have a fresh face with us today. I don't remember being told ...'

'I did speak to you about Mollie joining us, James,' Beatrice said quickly. 'I think you must have forgotten.' Or weren't listening, she said, under her breath.

'Ah, yes.' James put down the carving knife and smiled – a smile that bordered on a leer – at Mollie. 'A slightly unusual situation, I daresay, but I have no objection to us being joined by Charlotte's maid.'

'I don't regard Mollie as a maid; she is my companion and my very dear friend, Papa,' Charlotte cut in. 'Nobody could have cared for me better than she did during my –' she hesitated for the briefest of pauses '– illness. She is like a sister to me and I refuse to have her treated like one of the servants any longer.'

James opened his mouth but before he could speak Sebastian clapped his hands. 'Well said, Sis. I must say, the lovely Mollie would be an asset to anybody's table.' He gave her an admiring wink, which sent the colour flooding to her cheeks.

'Please continue carving, James,' Beatrice said icily.

161

'We are all waiting and the vegetables are getting cold.' Fond though she was of Mollie, she was not altogether happy at the new arrangement, for what she knew were purely selfish reasons and nothing whatever to do with Mollie herself.

James carved in silence and the plates were handed round. 'Do you take fat, my dear?' he asked when it came to Mollie's turn.

Mollie was used to eating whatever she was given but she had noticed that both Beatrice and Charlotte had asked for the fat to be removed so she said, 'I would prefer lean meat, if you please, Sir.'

He raised his head and his eyebrows at her well-modulated voice; he clearly hadn't expected it. He continued to stare at her as the plate was passed down to her, gratified at what he saw. Charlotte's maid she might be but on closer inspection she was a damn fine looking filly, no doubt about that. Those big brown eyes and that pert little nose did a man's heart good to see, although the frock was a trifle high in the bosom. It would be better without that scarf thing she had tucked round her shoulders; it hid the best of her charms. He cleared his throat at the direction his thoughts were moving in. It really hadn't been a bad idea on Charlotte's part to suggest she should join the family table. It might liven things up a bit, especially when there were guests. He gave her what he hoped was an encouraging smile.

But Mollie was far too nervous to smile back at him. She was too busy making sure she behaved correctly and used the right knife and fork. She was thankful Uncle Sam had always insisted on good table manners; far better, in fact, than James Grainger himself was displaying, sitting at the table picking his teeth, and belching loudly as the mood took him and looking her over as if she was some kind of prize cow.

By the time she was handed a bowl of treacle pudding she had decided that the more she saw of James Grainger

162

the less she liked him. In fact, the knowledge that she actually had his blood flowing through her veins made her shudder with distaste.

Chapter Sixteen

Mollie noticed that Mark said very little during the meal. Now and again when she glanced up she found his eyes resting on her with an enigmatic look and he would give her a brief smile, but then his uncle would question him about the Copperas House and he would be forced to turn to him and answer. More perceptive than his uncle he could see that Beatrice disapproved of this as a subject for mealtime conversation and he made his answers as short as he could.

In the end Beatrice threw down her napkin and snapped, 'James, your office is the proper place for discussion about work matters. It would be a kindness if you kept it from the meal table.' At any other time she would have said nothing but she was still annoyed with him over the question of Mollie.

It was not, she told herself, that she objected to the girl sitting at table with the family; she was quiet, well-mannered, unassuming and not at all likely to take advantage of her elevated position. In any case, having suffered several miscarriages herself during her long married life, she suspected that she had rather more to be grateful to Mollie for than simply nursing Charlotte through a case of food poisoning, although of course she would never voice her suspicions. But she had always feared that Charlotte had more of her father in her than she, Beatrice,

164

would have liked. Which was, of course, the real reason for her reluctance. God knew, she'd had enough trouble with him and attractive servants in the past, and although he kept his dalliances further from home now, it was tempting fate to parade Mollie's attractive face in front of his eyes every mealtime.

But this was not a reason she could give for denying the girl a place at the family board.

She pushed her misgivings aside and turned to Charlotte. 'And what are you two girls going to do this afternoon?' she asked, making the effort to include Mollie since what was done was done so she might as well make the best of it. She smiled at them both as she waited for an answer.

'We thought we might take a short walk on the beach since it will be low water and the sun is shining. That's right, isn't it, Mollie?' Charlotte turned to Mollie for agreement.

'Yes, that's right,' Mollie answered with a nod. 'Charlotte says she feels strong enough for a walk now, Mrs Grainger. But I shall make sure she wraps up warmly and doesn't walk too far.'

'I'm sure you'll look after her, Mollie. I have no worries about that,' Beatrice said. And meant it.

'I say, that's a good idea. A walk on the beach,' Sebastian joined in the conversation, rubbing his hands together. 'Or are you both intending to poke about looking for stones and shells and things.'

'No, Seb,' Charlotte said sadly. 'I'm afraid I don't feel quite up to clambering about on the cliffs yet.'

'That's good, because if you're just going for a gentle stroll I might come with you. What about you, Mark? Do you fancy stretching your legs?'

'Yes, if the ladies don't object I think I should like that very much.' Mark said, his eyes resting on Mollie before turning to smile at Charlotte.

'Oh, we don't object, do we, Mollie. The more the merrier. What about you, Mama? Will you come, too?'

165

'Oh. No, indeed.' Beatrice held up her hand. 'I like to rest after a good meal.'

Mollie noticed that nobody thought to extend the invitation to James.

The two girls fetched warm cloaks and boots and fur hats, and the four of them went down the cliff steps to the beach, Charlotte clinging possessively to Mark's arm as they went. The tide was at its lowest ebb, far out in the distance the sea lapped lazily and the sand was sculpted into ripples by the movement of the water. It was a pleasant late November day; cold and still, with a faint mist that blurred the distant horizon so that it was impossible to see where the sea ended and the sky began.

When they reached the beach Charlotte was still clinging to Mark's arm, so Mollie was forced to walk with Sebastian, although she had tried to stay by Charlotte's side and avoid this.

'Won't you take my arm?' he asked. 'I notice my sister is glad of Mark's assistance. The sand is very uneven where the cliff has eroded.'

'Your sister has been ill, she's still a little weak, Mr ... Sir ...' she paused, uncertain how to address him in her new, elevated position.

'Sebastian will do,' he said, grinning down at her. 'In fact, if you'd like to be really friendly you can call me Seb.'

She flushed. 'Thank you, but I grew up used to walking on the beach, often barefoot, so the unevenness doesn't trouble me at all.'

'Pity,' he said, grinning at her again.

She bent down and picked up a shell to avoid answering him.

'I thought we had come for a walk, not to search for shells and such,' he said, taking it from her. He stopped to examine it. 'Nothing very significant. Merely a whelk shell,' he said in a mock studious manner as he tossed it away. 'Now this one is much more interesting.' He picked

166

up a tiny pink stone. 'Do you know what this is, Mollie?'

She glanced at it impatiently. 'It's a pink stone. There are hundreds of them strewn around.' She nodded towards Charlotte and Mark. 'I think we should walk on, Sebastian. The others are quite a long way ahead now.'

'That's good.' He picked up her hand and tucked it into the crook of his arm. 'It means we can talk to each other without distraction. And I dare say Mark feels the same.' He gazed at the couple walking ahead. 'They look quite the loving couple, don't they? I dare say it won't be long before their engagement is announced.'

He was probably right, Mollie thought gloomily, especially now that the faithless Captain Pilkington had left the scene. Charlotte had learned her lesson the hard way, now she would doubtless be all to happy too settle down to a quiet life with a loving husband – Mark – in the fullness of time. At that thought a lump of lead seemed to settle in the pit of Mollie's stomach.

Suddenly, Sebastian reached in his pocket and brought out a small box. Mollie recognised it at once as the box that held the amber brooch.

'You see, I still have it,' he said opening the lid. 'As I told you before, it's yours, Mollie. I had it made for you so I'll never give it to anyone else. Why won't you accept it?'

Mollie looked ahead to where Charlotte was clinging to Mark's arm and laughing up at him in her flirtatious manner. She was such a lovely girl it was small wonder that Mark was in love with her. He was not to know she was 'soiled goods'. Mollie squashed that thought almost before it had formed and turned to Sebastian, holding out her hand.

'Won't you let me pin it on?' he asked as he gave her the box.

She took the box and studied the small creature trapped in its amber prison. If Sebastian thought a present like this was the way to her bed he was very much mistaken. She

167

closed the lid with a snap and handed it back to him. 'I think you should keep it to give to the girl you intend to marry,' she said lightly.

He took her hand. 'That's exactly what I'm trying to do, Mollie' he said, his eyes boring into hers.

She pulled her hand away, shocked. 'Oh, no, Sebastian, you can't be serious,' she said, horrified. 'You know that could never be. I know Charlotte calls me her friend and insists that I take my meals with the family now, but you surely haven't forgotten who I am, where I come from. For most of my life I've nearly broken my back picking mine in all weathers on this very beach, lugging heavy baskets of the stuff to where Old Sol and his donkey waited to take it ...'

'I don't care, Mollie. I love you.'

'... to your father's Copperas House, that stinking place I've lived my life next door to, breathing in its noxious fumes ...'

'I still don't care, Mollie. I love you.' He tried to take her in his arms. 'Surely, you have some feeling for me?'

She twisted away from him. 'I've never thought of you as anything other than Charlotte's brother, Sebastian,' she said honestly. 'I realised you liked to flirt with me but I never thought it was anything more than that.'

'But you could if you tried,' he insisted.

'I don't think it would be of much value to you or to me if I had to *try* to love you,' she said slowly. 'I think you love because you can't help it.' A picture of Mark's face flitted through her mind. 'Whether that love is returned or not,' she added sadly.

He pocketed the box. 'I've obviously spoken too soon,' he said. 'It's true we don't know each other very well, although I believe I fell in love with you almost the first time I laid eyes on you. But you need time to get to know me better and when you do I shall ask you again. Because I know you are the girl I want to marry. We're meant for each other, Mollie. I can feel it in my bones. A kind of

168

affinity . . . ' He tried to take both her hands but she pulled away as if he'd scalded her.

'No! I could never, ever marry you, Sebastian. Please believe that,' she said, something akin to panic in her voice.

'But why? Surely, you must have a reason?'

Oh, yes, I have a very good reason, she thought wearily, but not one I can speak of. Instead she said, 'Our backgrounds are too far apart for me ever to bring you happiness, Sebastian. I should never be accepted as an equal in the circles you move in. It would make your life a misery once the first flush of . . . infatuation had worn off.'

'I think you are very cruel to take my love so lightly,' he said, offended. 'I assure you it is not infatuation on my part.'

She laid a hand on his arm. 'Believe me, I am flattered that you should have some regard for me, Sebastian. I assure you I don't take it lightly. But marriage between us could never, ever be. I'm sorry.'

'I don't understand you,' he said, still offended.

She shook her head. 'No, I don't suppose you do. But if you knew me better you would realise the truth of what I'm saying. Please believe me and put the idea of marriage between us out of your mind.'

'I don't give up that easily, Mollie,' he said, stepping forward to kiss the tip of her nose.

But she sidestepped him and nodded towards Charlotte and Mark, walking towards them. 'It looks as if Charlotte has walked far enough. It's time to go back,' she said, putting an end to the conversation.

Lying in bed that night, the lantern once again lit to beam its message to Richard's smuggling cronies, an action with which she still felt uncomfortable, Mollie assessed her position at Cliff House. Things hadn't worked out at all the way she had expected. In her anger at the way he had treated her mother, she had vowed to eat at James Grainger's table.

169

What she had hoped to gain from this was not clear, even to herself. Because it had never been her intention to reveal her true identity; all she had wanted was to sit in her rightful place as his daughter, just once, to vindicate her poor, ill-used mother.

It really seemed that Fate had played into her hands when she met Charlotte and it had been almost too good to be true when Charlotte chose her to be her personal maid. But now things had spun out of control. She had never expected to become so fond of Charlotte, nor that Charlotte would become so attached to her. Neither had she expected to feel a pang of what she recognised as jealousy when she saw Charlotte laughing up at Mark. Indeed, she had no right to feel jealous; Mark belonged to Charlotte and in any case he was never likely to look twice at Charlotte's maid, or companion as Charlotte liked to call her now. But worse than all of that, she had never, ever imagined that Sebastian, the son of the house, the man who was her natural half-brother, would declare himself in love with her.

She lay on her back and gazed at the candle, flickering in the lantern. What was she to do? The obvious answer was to leave Cliff House. But she loved it here, she was happy; the thought of going back to Copperas Lane to live, where Aunt Rose would work her ever harder and jeer at her for not keeping her job was not even to be contemplated. And the alternative to that, marriage to Joe Trayler and a life with too many children, and a husband she didn't love, filled her with horror.

She hardly slept for three nights and when she took Charlotte's morning chocolate in on the fourth morning Charlotte took one look at her and said, 'Oh, Mollie! You look terrible! Are you ill? Was the strain of looking after me when I was poorly too much for you?'

Mollie shook her head. 'No, it's not that, Charlotte. I've not been sleeping well lately, that's all.'

170

'Why not? Are you worried about anything? I'm sure Mama could pay you a little more if that's what concerns you.'

'Good gracious, no. I never think about that.' She managed a little laugh. 'I have more than enough for my needs.'

'Well, what is it then?'

Mollie put her fingers to her temples. 'It's nothing, I tell you. Just leave me alone, will you.' She lifted her head. 'Oh, I'm sorry, Charlotte. I shouldn't have snapped at you like that.'

'It's all right, dear.' Charlotte leaned forward and patted her hand. 'I'm your friend and friends are allowed to snap occasionally.'

At that Mollie burst into tears. 'Oh, I should hate to leave you,' she sobbed.

'But you won't have to leave me,' Charlotte soothed, scrambling out of bed and giving her a hug. 'I couldn't do without you, Mollie, you know that.'

Mollie sniffed and dried her eyes on the back of her hand. 'Yes, of course. I'm being silly,' she said.

Charlotte looked searchingly at her. 'You would tell me if you were in any kind of trouble, wouldn't you, Mollie? I mean ... you looked after me ...'

Mollie gave her a watery smile. 'Oh, it's nothing like that, I assure you, Charlotte.' She gave another sniff and took a deep breath to pull herself together. 'In fact, it's nothing at all. It's been rather cold at night, even with an extra blanket, that's all. That's what's kept me awake, I expect.'

Charlotte nodded. 'I'm sure it must be cold up there under the eaves. I think I shall ask Mama if you can be moved to the room next to mine, just along the passage. It would be cooler in the summer and warmer in the winter. And a good deal larger, too.'

'No, you mustn't do that, Charlotte. Your mother will think ...'

171

'Nonsense.' Charlotte cut her off. 'It's a very good idea. I'm glad I thought of it. I shall speak to Mama today. Now, what shall I wear? The pink muslin?'

She was so kind, such a wonderful friend and companion that Mollie knew she could never leave her. Her natural optimism reasserted itself. There really wasn't any need to worry. Sebastian would get over his infatuation and marry some suitable girl from Colchester or Ipswich, in which case the circumstances of her own birth would never need to be revealed. She fetched the pink muslin from the closet and they began to plan their day together.

But Mollie's troubles were not quite over.

The following Saturday afternoon she was standing with Charlotte in the room that Beatrice had agreed could be Mollie's. They were excitedly making plans about what needed to be moved and what should stay where it was when there was a knock at the door.

Mollie opened it and saw Kitty standing there. The girl was so agitated that she dropped her a curtsey. 'Oh, Ma'am, I mean Miss, there's a man downstairs askin' for you,' she said, her eyes wide with something akin to fright. 'He won't take no for a answer an' he said if I didn't fetch you he'll come an' find you hisself.'

Mollie turned to Charlotte, frowning.

'Oh, who can it be?' Charlotte said, her eyes sparkling. 'Have you got a beau, Mollie?'

'Me? Don't be silly, of course I haven't,' Mollie answered. She shook her head. 'I can't think who it might be.'

Charlotte flapped her hand. 'Well, don't just stand there. Go and see. Don't keep the poor man waiting.'

Puzzled and a little apprehensive, Mollie followed Kitty down the stairs. She had an awful feeling it might be Richard, come to complain that she hadn't lit the lamp when she should have done; yet she was sure she hadn't missed a message – unless Sid, the gardener's boy, had

172

forgotten to tell her, in which case she could hardly be blamed.

She reached the kitchen. To her amazement it was Uncle Sam standing just inside the door, dressed in his Sunday best, twisting his hat in his hands and looking very uncomfortable.

She hurried across to him. 'Uncle Sam! Is something wrong? Aunt Rose isn't ... ?'

'No, your aunt is very well, thank 'ee, Mollie.' He looked round the kitchen, where four pairs of eyes were watching. 'P'raps it would be better if we jest stepped outside a minute.'

Mollie followed him. 'Shall we walk down to the beach, Uncle?' she asked as they reached the lawn.

'No, there's no need for that. What I've got to say won't take more'n a minute.' His face was stern as he turned to look at her. 'I want you to go inside an' pack your bag, Mollie. You're comin' home with me.'

When she heard her uncle's words Mollie's jaw dropped. 'But I can't do that, Uncle. I can't just pack my bag and leave. Miss Charlotte ...'

'I can't help about Miss Charlotte.' Sam's jaw was set. 'I want you outa this place.'

'But why, Uncle? For what reason?' She stared at him. This hard-faced stranger was not the gentle Uncle Sam she knew and loved.

His expression softened slightly as he turned to face her. 'Because you've let me down, Mollie,' he said sadly. 'As you well know, I didn't want you to come here in the first place because I was afraid you might suffer the same fate as your mother. I warned you as plain as I could to be careful. Yet what do I hear?'

Mollie frowned. 'I don't know. What have you heard? I've done nothing to be ashamed of, Uncle.'

'Don't lie to me, girl.' His tone was harsh. 'You've bin to see Lily Stokes. An' that can on'y mean one thing. The very thing I warned you against.' He gave a great sigh.

173

'I'm not sayin' I'm angry with you, Mollie. But I'm disappointed. Disappointed you didn't take more care to guard against ... what happened.' He sniffed. 'So I'm takin' you home with me where you'll be safe an' I can look after you.'

She took a step towards him. 'But Uncle ...'

He held up his hand. 'I don't want no arguments an' excuses. Least said, soonest mended. Jest do as I say. Go an' pack your bag. I shall be waitin' here. An' if you're not back here within ten minutes I shall come an' fetch you.' He placed his feet apart and folded his arms.

'It's not what you're thinking, Uncle,' she said desperately. 'Really, it isn't.'

He swung round. 'No? Are you tryin' to tell me you didn't go to see Lily Stokes? Because I know different.'

'No, I'm not trying to tell you that. I did go to see Lily. I made no secret of the fact. I took some brawn for Jim.'

'And left a gold sovereign, so I'm told.'

'Well, times are hard for them now Jim can't work so much.' She sighed.

'And ...?'

She nodded. 'Yes, Lily did give me one of her remedies.'

'See? I knew it!' It was almost a shout.

She raised her own voice. 'But it was not for *me*, Uncle, and that I'll swear on the Bible.'

'I'd prefer it if you didn't bring the Good Book into this sorry business,' he said.

'Well, how else can I get you to believe me,' she said, near to tears.

He stared at her. 'All right, then. But if it wasn't for you, then who was it for?'

'I can't tell you that, Uncle. In any case, what difference does it make, as long as it wasn't for me?'

'It makes a lotta difference, because if you won't tell me who you got it for then I can only think you're not tellin' me the truth.' His face was like granite.

174

'I *am* telling you the truth, Uncle. I . . . '

He waved her away. 'We've talked long enough. Go an' pack your bag. I'm not hevin' you stay a minute longer in this den of iniquity. The Lord in His mercy knows I never wanted you to come here in the first place. Now, you're comin' home with me.' When she didn't move, he gave her a push. 'An' don't be long!'

Chapter Seventeen

Mollie stumbled back into the house rubbing her hand across her brow. This couldn't be happening; tiredness and worry had made her imagination run riot. Then she glanced back to where Uncle Sam stood like a black statue in the middle of the lawn and knew what had happened was all too real. She dragged herself up the back stairs with a heavy heart. She knew she would have to obey Uncle Sam but she couldn't just leave without a word of explanation to Charlotte. Yet what could she say to her?

She brushed the tears away with the heel of her hand as she went along the corridor. Charlotte was just coming out of the room that, only minutes ago, was to have been hers. She smiled happily when she saw Mollie.

'Well, well, are you going to tell me who your mysterious visitor was . . . ' Her face changed. 'Mollie! What's the matter? Oh, my dear, has somebody died?'

Mollie shook her head without looking up. 'No. Nobody's died. But I've got to leave here. It's my Uncle Sam. He's come to fetch me home,' she muttered. 'He says I can't say at Cliff House any longer.'

Charlotte took a step towards her. 'Why? What's happened? Is your aunt ill?'

Mollie shook her head again. 'No, it's nothing like that. I . . . I can't explain . . . I've just got to go. He's told me to come and get my things. I'm sorry, Charlotte. I didn't

176

want it to be like this. But I have to do as Uncle Sam says.'

'But why, Mollie?' Charlotte's eyes widened. 'What's gone wrong? I thought you were happy here.'

'Oh, I am. You know I am.' The tears were running freely down her cheeks now. 'I've never been so happy in all my life. I hate the thought of having to leave Cliff House and go back to Copperas Lane, that stinking hole where I was brought up. But Uncle Sam says I've got to go with him and I can't go against him. He's always been so good to me.'

'He must have a reason for taking you away,' Charlotte said, frowning. 'Are you sure it's got nothing to do with money? As I told you, I'm sure Mama ... '

'It's got nothing to do with money,' Mollie said quickly.

'Then what is it? Surely, you can tell me.' Charlotte caught her hand. 'I'm your friend, Mollie. I thought we had no secrets from each other.'

Mollie's mouth clamped shut. 'I'm sorry. I can't tell you.'

Charlotte went back into the room that was to have been Mollie's and looked out of the window. Mollie's uncle was standing in the middle of the lawn with his back to her, his legs apart, his arms folded. There was stubbornness in his stance even from this distance. Yet Mollie had always spoken of him as a mild-mannered man; a man she looked up to and respected. A God-fearing man she always called him. It was beyond Charlotte's understanding that he should have turned out to be so stern and unfeeling. She sighed. 'Well, since there seems to be no alternative, I suppose you'd better go and pack your bag, Mollie,' she said quietly, without turning round.

Feeling even more miserable at Charlotte's cool acceptance of her plight, Mollie went up to her old room, a room that already bore signs of being vacated, although she had been in a much happier frame of mind when she had begun clearing it. She sat down on the bed and tried ineffectually to dry her eyes but the tears continued to fall as thoughts

177

tumbled over themselves in her mind. It was bad enough that Uncle Sam believed the worst of her but Charlotte's last words to her had been like a stinging slap in the face. Mollie had expected that she would at least shed a few tears at losing her but she clearly didn't care. Yet only a few days ago she had been insisting that Mollie was not her maid but her companion and friend, and claiming a place for her at the family board. Now, it seemed, she was willing to let her go without a second thought.

It was the casual way in which Charlotte had told her to go and pack her bag that really hurt. After all, if it hadn't been for her stupidity in allowing herself to be led astray by horrible Captain snake-in-the-grass Pilkington Mollie would never have had to resort to Lily Stokes in the first place. Charlotte could have had no idea what courage it had taken for Mollie to go and ask for her 'remedy', with the fear – amply justified, it now turned out – that Uncle Sam might somehow discover that she had been there.

Blindly, she began stuffing her possessions into her wicker case.

Downstairs, Charlotte stood where Mollie had left her, staring out of the window for a few minutes more, then she picked up her skirts and hurried from the room, down the stairs and across the lawn.

'Good girl. You hevn't bin long.' Sam Barnes turned to look at his niece approvingly, then his jaw dropped and he snatched off his well-worn hat. 'I beg yer pardon, Ma'am, I mean Miss, I thought you was my niece.'

'No, my name is Charlotte Grainger and I've come to enquire why it is that Mollie is being taken away from my service.' Charlotte's voice was almost peremptory in her desire to get this over before Mollie returned. 'What has she done that is so terrible that she can no longer stay here at Cliff House, Mr Barnes?'

Sam cleared his throat. This was embarrassing; a matter between him and his niece and not something he wanted to discuss with the likes of this young lady. He took a deep

178

breath. 'Beggin' your pardon, Miss, but I hev reason to suppose that my niece has bin behavin' in a – in a unsuitable manner.'

'I've no idea what you're talking about,' Charlotte said, with an impatient gesture. 'Mollie is hardly ever out of my sight and I can assure you she has done nothing to be ashamed of in my presence. Perhaps you could speak a little more plainly, Mr Barnes. What exactly are you accusing Mollie of doing?'

Sam licked his lips. He didn't like this. He didn't like it at all. 'It's come to my knowledge that she's visited a certain person,' he said uncomfortably, looking anywhere but at Charlotte. 'A person who supplied her with things a decent, unmarried girl had no business to need.' His voice began to rise. 'That bein' so, I'm takin' her home, outa harm's way. My Mollie is a decent, well-brought-up girl an' I ain't hevin' her used ... well, I'm takin' her home an' thass that.'

'Did Mollie admit she'd done wrong?' Charlotte asked carefully.

'No. She told me some cock-an'-bull story about fetchin' the stuff for somebody else. But she wouldn't say who.'

'So you didn't believe her.'

'Well, 'taint likely she'd admit it was for herself. Not after I'd warned her ... ' Sam broke off and kicked a tuft of grass. He didn't like being questioned like this, it undermined his authority.

'You're telling me Mollie would lie herself out of trouble?'

'No. I ain't sayin' that at all.'

'I think you are, Mr Barnes, if you didn't believe what she told you.' Charlotte laid a hand on his arm. 'You should have believed her, Mr Barnes. You've clearly brought her up to be truthful and honest, so why doubt her now?' She paused. 'In fact, I know Mollie was telling you the truth. She acted as she did to help someone, someone who I like to think is a very dear friend, out of trouble.

179

Someone who is extremely grateful to her. You should be proud of your niece, not condemn her, Mr Barnes, because it's quite obvious she would rather lose her position here than betray that friend.' She turned away so that he shouldn't see the tears in her eyes.

He was silent while he digested this. 'You're tellin' me I've misjudged her,' he said at last.

'Totally, Mr Barnes. Mollie is the girl you've brought her up to be, honest and loyal.' She gave him a tremulous smile. 'Please don't take her away from me, Mr Barnes. I know it would make her very unhappy to leave here, especially under such a cloud, and for my own part, I should be lost without her. She has become more like a sister to me than a maid.' Without waiting for his answer she turned and hurried back into the house.

In her little room under the eaves Mollie threw the rest of her things into her case, closed the lid and fastened it. Then she carried it down the back stairs and out through the boot room, her eyes too blurred with tears to notice and her heart too heavy to care whether anybody saw her leaving or not.

Uncle Sam was not standing where she had left him. She brushed the tears from her eyes and looked round for him. It was a minute before she saw him. He had moved to the end of the lawn by the fence overlooking the cliff. Slowly, her feet dragging with reluctance, she went across to him.

'I'm ready, Uncle,' she said dully when she reached him.

He turned and looked at her and in that moment he saw what a wrench it was for her to obey him and leave this place where she was so happy. He put his arms round her and kissed her. 'Oh, Mollie. I'm truly sorry, my girl. I've done you a terrible wrong,' he said, his face working in his effort to keep back the tears.

She screwed up her face. 'What do you mean, Uncle? I don't understand.'

He sniffed and shook his head. 'I should never hev doubted you. I mighta known you'd never lie to me.'

180

'No, Uncle. I've never lied to you,' she said. 'I told you I was telling the truth, but you didn't believe me.'

'No, God forgive me, I didn't believe you.' He held up his hand as she opened her mouth to speak. 'But I shoulda done. I should hev realised you'd never break a confidence. That you'd give up your place here rather than do that.' He looked at her, waiting for an answer. When none came, he went on, 'I respect you for that, my girl. I respect you more'n I can say.' He took a deep breath. 'I think the best thing for you to do is to forget I ever came here today, Mollie. I reckon I've made meself look a right fool.' He nodded towards her wicker case. 'You'd better go an' get that unpacked before somebody sees you with it an' get the wrong idea. I'm real sorry I ever doubted you, my girl.' He turned to go, then came back, took off his hat and gave her a quick peck on the cheek. 'Your mother, God Rest her Soul, would be proud of you, Mollie. An' so am I.' He put his hat back on his head, adjusted it for comfort, and went off, his back straight. He didn't look back.

Fingering the spot where his whiskers had brushed her cheek Mollie watched him until he was out of sight, puzzled at what could have caused such a sudden change of heart. She looked round. There was nobody that he could have spoken to while she was gone so she could only think he had had time to reflect and to realise. Realise what? That he had made a mistake? But he wouldn't have come if he had been in any doubt. She simply didn't understand.

But it didn't matter. She could stay at Cliff House, that was the important thing. She took a deep breath and almost danced back into the house and up the stairs to tell Charlotte the good news.

Charlotte was still standing looking out of the window of the room that was to be Mollie's. She turned as Mollie came in.

'Well?' she said, with a funny little smile.

Mollie shook her head, still bewildered at the turn of events. 'I haven't got to go. Uncle Sam says he made a mistake and I can stay, after all.' She leaned back against the wall, still reeling with surprise. Then a thought struck her and she glanced at Charlotte. 'That is, if you still want me, of course. You didn't seem at all concerned that I'd got to leave when you told me to go and pack, so perhaps ...'

Charlotte came over and hugged her. 'Oh, Mollie, you little goose, of course I want you. You know perfectly well I couldn't do without you.' She sat down on the bed. 'Oh, this has been quite an afternoon. Ring for Tilda to bring us some tea, will you, there's a dear. Look, the bell pull is by the bed. Yes –' seeing Mollie's surprise '– you'll have your own bell now.'

It was not until Tilda had been summoned and had returned with tea and crumpets which they ate sitting on the window seat that Charlotte remarked, 'Your uncle. He's not a man to gossip, is he?'

Mollie shook her head. 'No. Never,' she said firmly. 'Why?'

'I think perhaps I may have revealed a little more than I intended when I spoke to him,' Charlotte said thoughtfully, biting into a second crumpet.

'When you spoke to him? When did you speak to him?' Mollie asked, astonished.

'Why, whilst you were busy packing your bag, of course. You didn't think I was going to let you leave me without finding out what all the fuss was about, did you?'

Mollie's eyes widened. 'You went down and spoke to Uncle Sam? Oh, Charlotte. Thank you. I don't know what you said, but thank you.'

Charlotte licked her fingers. 'That's the trouble. I'm not sure exactly what I said, either.' She smiled at Mollie. 'But I do remember telling him that I couldn't do without you because you were more like a sister to me than a maid. He seemed to like that.' She leaned forward and gave her another hug. 'And so do I.' She got up and went over to the bell pull. 'Now, I'll ring for Tilda to take these tea

182

things and then she can come back and make up the bed for you ...'

'No, don't ring. I'll take the tray down myself,' Mollie said quickly.

Charlotte turned, raising her eyebrows and Mollie flushed.

'I wouldn't want the rest of the servants to think I'm getting above myself,' she explained.' She went over and laid a hand on Charlotte's arm. 'Please don't think I'm not grateful to you, Charlotte, for giving me this room and treating me as your friend,' she said earnestly, 'But you must appreciate that it's put me in a slightly awkward situation with Cook and Tilda and Ellis and the others. It wouldn't do for me to allow them to wait on me. So, I shall take the tray down to the kitchen and then I shall fetch the sheets from the linen cupboard and make up the bed here.'

Charlotte patted her hand. 'Very well, dear, if that's what you want, although I think it's quite unnecessary.' She yawned. 'Oh, dear, I really feel quite tired after all this excitement. I think I shall go and lie down for a while.'

When she had settled Charlotte, Mollie took the tray back to the kitchen and spent a few minutes with Cook and Ellis, who together with Tilda were enjoying a cup of tea with their feet up as they usually did at this quiet time in the afternoon.

'Bin given a new room downstairs, then, hev we,' Ellis, who was inclined to be sour at times, remarked with a smirk. 'Tilda told us when you rang for her to bring tea.' She laid heavy emphasis on the last words. 'I suppose you'll be wantin' one of us to fetch your things down and clean out the room for you, next.'

'That'll do, Ellis,' Cook warned.

'Well, who does she think she is,' Ellis muttered jealously.

'I don't mind giving you a hand, Mollie,' Tilda said. She held up the teapot. 'Do you want a cup?'

Mollie sat down. 'Yes, please, I'd love one,' she

answered, smiling at Tilda and ignoring Ellis's jibes. 'There's nothing quite like kitchen tea, is there.' She put her feet up on another chair. 'I've got a few more bits to fetch from my old room and the bed to make up but I can spare a few minutes while Miss Charlotte is having her rest.' She was careful to call her *Miss* Charlotte. 'And as for cleaning the room, Ellis, you know as well as I do that Tilda makes sure all the rooms are dusted every day, whether or not they are in use.' She took several sips of her tea and turned to Tilda. 'But you won't need to worry about the blue room any more, Tilda, because I'll do it myself.'

'Are you quite sure, Mollie?' Tilda asked uncertainly.

'Oh, yes. I couldn't possibly leave it for you to do.' She grinned at Tilda over the rim of her cup. 'I'm still the same Mollie, Tilda. I still know how to clean a room, even if I do eat with the family and have been given a bigger room downstairs.'

'Except that you'll soon be full of airs and graces,' Ellis said with a sneer. 'No doubt we'll soon be callin' you *Miss* Mollie.'

'Oh, I don't think so, Ellis,' Mollie said cheerfully, determined not to let the other woman rattle her.

'Mollie isn't the kind of girl to get above herself, Ellis,' Cook said quietly. 'So there's no need for you to carry on like that. Let's hear no more about it. More tea, Mollie?'

'No, thanks, I'd better be getting back.'

Mollie made her way back to her room deep in thought. As she reached the bend in the stairs she found her way blocked. Startled, her eyes travelled up from well-worn black boots, past cream buckskin breeches, green waistcoat, white shirt undone at the neck to Mark's rather stern features.

'Oh, I'm sorry.' She made to step out of his way.

He gave her a small, slightly lopsided smile. 'No need to apologise, Mollie. Welcome to no-man's-land.' He sat down on the stairs and patted the tread for her to join him.

184

'This is where we belong, you and I. Neither upstairs nor downstairs. Isn't that right?'

She sat down, careful to keep her distance. 'I wouldn't have thought that was your position, Sir ...'

'Mark.'

'Mark. After all, you're a member of the family.'

'Oh, yes. I'm a relative. A poor relation, to be exact. Hasn't it occurred to you that I'm treated as little more than a servant here?' He sounded quite bitter.

'No, I don't see it like that at all,' she said slowly. 'And I know from what Uncle Sam has told me that the men at the Copperas House think very highly of you. It's you they turn to when there are problems. It's you who knows everything about ... well, everything. They don't ask Mr Grainger, do they?' She turned to look at him and blushed to find his eyes on her. 'I'm sorry.' She mumbled. 'I spoke out of turn.'

He shook his head. 'No, not at all.' He ran his hands through his hair. 'I hadn't really looked at it like that. I've just always been aware that I was taken in because I had nowhere else to go after my parents died. I was given a home and set to work. I started at the bottom and worked my way up. I believe both my uncle and my cousin Sebastian were only too glad when I showed myself capable of running things because it left them free to ...' He ran his hands through his hair again. 'Well, it left them free.'

'I'm sure they're very grateful to know their business is in such capable hands,' Mollie said.

'Yes, I'm sure they are.' He stood up. 'I'm sorry, I'm afraid I'm not very good company this afternoon. I've just been having a few harsh words with my uncle. We don't see eye to eye about how things should be run. In fact, there are quite a number of things we don't see eye to eye over.' He took two steps down, then turned. 'How is my cousin Charlotte? Quite recovered from her indisposition?'

Mollie got to her feet. 'Yes, she's quite recovered, thank

you.' She watched him as he continued down the stairs and wondered whether Charlotte was one of the things Mark and his uncle were in disagreement over.

Chapter Eighteen

Mollie was thrilled with her new room, the more so since only a few hours ago she had been so perilously close to losing it and her whole lifestyle here. As she lay in the wide bed and gazed up at the pale-blue silk draped to each bedpost from a central boss, and savoured the feel of the cool linen sheets, she had to keep pinching herself to make sure she was not dreaming. She had never before known or expected to know such luxury. And it didn't end there. She had her own washstand in the corner, with a cream china bowl and ewer lavishly decorated with pale-blue swags of flowers, a matching soap dish, even a matching chamber pot. She had her own large wardrobe, even if it was filled with dresses that had previously belonged to Charlotte. But that was unimportant because Mollie had become expert in altering the style and trimmings of Charlotte's gowns so it was no problem to alter them yet again to suit her own taste. There was a long cheval mirror, too, in which she could check the results of her labours, and in the corner next to the dressing table stood a chair covered in blue velvet to match the cushion on the window seat. Oh, it was all just perfect.

Then a thought struck her and she froze. The lantern! It was still upstairs under the bed in her old room together with a few odd bits and pieces she hadn't yet collected. But what was she going to do with it? And what was she going to do when she next had a message from Richard that he wanted a light placed in the window? She could never place it in the window of her new room; being on a lower floor she couldn't place it high enough to be visible out at sea and even if it were possible it would be far too dangerous next to those beautiful long velvet drapes. But it would be a risky business leaving it unattended all night in the window of her old room.

She turned over and thumped her pillow. Why was it that for every good thing that happened to her there was something awful to spoil it! She turned back again and tried to relax, telling herself that it was no use worrying about the lantern tonight, because there was nothing to be done about it. In any case it was only a few nights since the last message from Richard so there would be plenty of time to decide what was to be done before she heard from him again. And there was always the chance that he would make other arrangements when she explained the situation to him. For now she would continue to savour the luxury of her new room.

She blew out the candle and wriggled her shoulders into the comfort of the feather mattress, savouring the soft, wide bed and the lavender-scented sheets, and not forgetting to offer up a quick prayer of thankfulness at her good fortune as Uncle Sam had taught her.

She was just dropping off to sleep when she was woken by a sound in the corridor. She listened for a moment, telling herself that she was in a different room now so the sounds of the night were bound to be different. But there it was again, a kind of stealthy, shuffling noise. She sat up in bed and looked towards the door, her ears straining, wondering if she should go and investigate. Then, as she watched, in a shaft of light from the moon she saw the brass door knob turn and the door slowly being pushed open.

Stifling a scream, she sprang out of bed and rushed over, slammed it shut and leaned against it, without waiting to discover who was on the other side. Not that it needed

188

much imagination to guess who was there when she heard his muttered expletive as he caught his finger in the door as she slammed it.

Feeling distinctly shaky she turned the key in the lock and jammed a chair against the door as an added precaution. Not that she had any fear that Sebastian would try his luck again that night but she was disgusted and not a little disappointed that he should have attempted it on her first night in her new room. He couldn't even wait until she was properly settled in. Not that it would have made any difference, of course. Tonight, next week or next month, her reaction would be exactly the same. She climbed back into bed, certain now that she had been right to refuse his gift of the amber brooch. Nevertheless, it was a long time before she slept.

She was woken next morning by a knock on her door and she had to scramble out of bed quickly to unlock it and remove the chair so that Kitty could come in with a jug of hot water. 'Cook said it was all right for me to bring it for you, since I was bringin' it to everybody else,' she said. She gazed rapturously round the room. 'Cor, thass nice in here, init!'

'Yes, Kitty. I reckon I'm very lucky. But I really don't think you should wait on me like this,' Mollie said, sitting on the edge of the bed. 'I don't mind washing in cold water. I'm quite used to it. After all, you don't wait on Ellis, do you?'

'Well, 'smatter o' fact, I do,' Kitty said, dropping her voice, 'but she don't like the rest o' the servants to know. Thass why I thought it would be all right to treat you the same.'

Mollie smiled at her. 'Well, as long as it doesn't get you into trouble, Kitty.'

After Kitty had gone, Mollie washed and dressed and combed her hair, all the while wondering if she should take the little kitchen maid into her confidence over the lighting of Richard's lantern. After all, Kitty slept just along the passage from Mollie's old room, so it wouldn't take a minute for her to slip in and light it when she went to bed and then to extinguish it in the morning. She adjusted the wide velvet band that held her hair in place and smiled at her image in the mirror over the dressing table, glad to have found such an easy solution to the problem.

Then another thought struck her. Supposing Richard got caught? Supposing his smuggling activities were discovered and with them the part that the lantern played? It wouldn't be right to implicate Kitty; neither Richard nor any of his cronies meant anything to her. She didn't even derive any benefit from their illicit trading. No, it would be quite wrong to draw Kitty into the web. She would have to think of something else. With a sigh she gave a final check to her appearance in the cheval mirror and put the problem out of her mind as she went in to greet Charlotte.

'Did you sleep well?' Charlotte asked immediately.

'Extremely well, thank you.' Mollie drew back the curtains as she spoke. She didn't mention the would-be intruder. She was still annoyed with Sebastian but she preferred to deal with him in her own way, without interference from Charlotte. 'If you're properly awake I'll go down and fetch your hot chocolate.'

'Thank you, dear. And bring some for yourself. And some toast. And a couple of lightly boiled eggs, I think. We'll have a cosy breakfast, just the two of us, while we decided what to do with the day.'

Mollie smiled to herself as she went out into the corridor. Not so long ago there would have been no 'deciding' what to do with the day as far as she was concerned because it would all have been mapped out according to the tide and the back-breaking business of picking mine.

She had almost reached the head of the stairs when she saw Sebastian. He was looking dishevelled and distinctly the worse for wear; unshaven, heavy-eyed, his brocade morning gown carelessly tied and gaping open and his neck bands hanging loose. His brutus hairstyle looked even more unkempt than usual.

He half turned when he saw her. 'Oh, Mollie. I've got this excruciating headache. Be an angel. If you're going down to the kitchen bring me up a powder or something, will you?' He was propping himself up on the banister as he spoke.

'And why should I do that?' she asked icily, looking him up and down.

His jaw dropped. 'What do you mean? I only asked ... Oh, God, I feel awful.'

'You didn't feel awful when you tried to get into my room last night, did you?' she said, her voice still cold.

He peered at her, screwing up his eyes in pain. 'Look, I don't know what you're talking about. I just want something for this splitting headache. I've got the father and mother of all hangovers, Mollie, if you want to know.'

'But you came to my room ...'

'I didn't come near your room last night, Mollie, much as I might have liked to have done. I was incapable. Ask Arthur. He put me to bed.' He put his hands up to his head and sank down on the top step. 'Oh, God, I'm never going to go out drinking again as long as I live.'

'Are you sure?' She looked at his fingers, splayed across his forehead. They bore no sign of having been jammed in a door.

'Too damn right, I'm sure. At this moment I'm ready to sign the pledge. God, I feel terrible.'

She looked at him doubtfully. 'No, I mean, are you sure you didn't try to get into my room?'

'What?' He peered up at her. 'No, of course I didn't. In fact, if you'd invited me I couldn't have made it last night, believe me. Oh,' he put his head on his knees. 'For God's sake get me something and bring it to my room before I die, Mollie.'

'I'll ask Arthur to bring you some hot lemon. That

191

should help. And a rag soaked in vinegar to lay on your head.'

'Thanks, Mollie. Will you come back and sit with me and hold my hand?'

'I will not. I've far better things to do with my time.'

'Oh, Mollie. This is no way to treat a dying man. How can you be so hard-hearted?' He dragged himself to his feet and staggered back along the corridor the way he had come.

Mollie watched him go and then continued on her way to the kitchen, puzzled. She didn't doubt that Sebastian was telling the truth. From the state of him this morning he would have been far too drunk to even think about seducing her last night. So who was it that tried to get into her room? She was completely mystified.

After she and Charlotte had eaten a leisurely breakfast together and Charlotte had gone out riding, Mollie took the opportunity to go up to her old room to finish clearing out her belongings and clean it up; she didn't want to be accused of not leaving it neat and tidy. She had just finished stripping the bed when Charlotte walked in, still in her riding habit.

'You've not been gone long,' Mollie said in surprise.

'No, Tuppence got lame so I had to come back. I thought I'd come and see what you were doing.' She sat down on the rush-seated chair under the window. 'This is quite a tiny little room, isn't it.'

'Big enough for a young girl who's spent her life sleeping four in a bed with her brothers and sisters to think she's in heaven,' Mollie said with a grim smile.

'But you didn't have to share with your brothers and sisters. You don't have any brothers and sisters,' Charlotte reminded her.

'I know that. I was lucky. I've always had a room of my own.' Mollie bundled up the bed linen. 'There. I think that's everything,' she said, going to the door. The lantern would have to wait a bit longer.

Charlotte stood up. 'The window's a bit high, isn't it. Can you see the sea from here?'

'Yes. But only if you stand on the chair. Come on, Charlotte. You wanted to walk down into the town to get some ribbons, so you'll need to change.'

'Don't be so impatient, Mollie. Help me up. I want to see for myself.'

'Not now. You might fall, then where should we be?'

'I shan't fall if you give me your hand.' She was already bunching up her velvet skirts with one hand and holding out her other to Mollie.

'I've got my hands full with all this bedding.'

'Then put it down, for goodness sake! Come on, help me on to the chair. I want to see the sea.'

'You can see it much better from your own room.'

'I want to see it from here.' Charlotte began to climb on to the chair, but she was hampered by her trailing skirt, so Mollie had no choice but to help her. 'Oh, what's this?' She reached across the wide window ledge and pulled over the lantern. 'It's very heavy. What is it, Mollie?'

'It's a lantern,' Mollie mumbled. 'Can't you see?'

'Oh, yes, so it is. Is it yours? Didn't Ellis give you a candle to light you to bed?' She kept hold of it as Mollie helped her down from the chair. 'Oh, yes. There's your candlestick, on the chest. So what's this heavy old thing for?'

'I was looking after it for my cousin, Richard,' Mollie said uncomfortably, sticking as near as she could to the truth. 'He gave it to me to light my way home ...'

'When?'

'Oh, ages ago. In the summer.' She realised as soon as the words were out that she'd said the wrong thing.

'In the summer! You wouldn't need a lantern to light your way back from your uncle's house in the summer!' Charlotte said with a laugh. 'Especially, a heavy old lantern like this. Anyway, I would have thought your cousin might need it himself now winter's come.'

'Yes. I'm going to give it back to him,' Mollie said desperately. 'Next time I see him. That's why I left it on the window sill.'

'Funny place to put it. Why didn't you leave it on the floor since it's so heavy?' Charlotte sat down on the bed and studied the lantern, the tip of her tongue poking between her lips. Then she looked up at the window before turning to Mollie.

'That nice lace you trimmed my lilac gown with, Mollie. Where did it come from?' she asked, apparently changing the subject.

Mollie shrugged. 'It was just a bit of cheap lace I found,' she said vaguely.

Charlotte shook her head. 'I don't think so, Mollie. I think I can recognise Brussels lace when I see it,' she said.

Mollie shrugged again but said nothing.

'I wondered at the time how you might have come by it,' Charlotte went on, thoughtfully. 'But now I think I understand.' She looked up at Mollie. 'It was Brussels lace that had been smuggled over from the continent, wasn't it. And your cousin is part of the smuggling gang. Furthermore, I suspect this lantern is used as some kind of signal, probably to say the coast is clear for goods to be landed. Am I right?'

Mollie gave a nervous laugh. 'I think you've been reading too many novels, Charlotte,' she said, biting her lip. In truth, she didn't know what else to say that wouldn't further incriminate her, and Richard with her. Her one thought now was how to let him know that their scheme had been discovered before Charlotte informed the Revenue men.

'Don't be silly.' She waved her hand dismissively. 'I'm right, aren't I? This lantern is used for signalling.'

Mollie stretched out her hand for the hated lantern; the signal that she had never wanted to be involved with in the first place. 'I'm giving it back to him,' she said firmly. 'That's what I came up here for. I shall take it back next time I go home ... I mean, to Uncle Sam's.'

But Charlotte wasn't listening. She was staring at the

lantern in her hand. Suddenly, a smile spread across her face. 'How exciting!' she said, looking up. 'How often do you have to signal, Mollie? And how do you know when to put the lantern up? And what happens to the goods when they're brought ashore?'

Mollie's lips were a thin straight line. 'I'm sorry, Charlotte, I can't tell you anything. I'm taking the lantern back and that's that. I'll be grateful if you never mention you've seen it.'

Charlotte looked at her in surprise. 'You think I'm going to tell the Revenue men, don't you?'

'Well, aren't you?' Mollie asked, equally surprised. 'Isn't that why you keep asking all these questions?'

She threw back her head and pealed with laughter. 'No, no, you've got it all wrong. I'd never do that. I want to help!' Her laugh turned to a frown. 'Oh, dear. We shall have to be careful now that this is no longer your room, but I'm sure we can manage.'

Mollie's jaw dropped. 'You mean you're really not going to report us?'

'Of course I'm not.' Her tone was impatient. She stroked her chin. 'And there must be other ways we can help. Places we can help them to store the stuff till they can get it away.'

'They already use the cellar at the back of the potting shed,' Mollie mumbled unhappily.

Charlotte clapped her hands delightedly. 'Oh, Mollie, you are a dark horse! How long has this been going on?'

'Quite a long time. When there was a consignment due Richard used to give the soldiers on lookout at the tower a keg of brandy to look the other way. Of course they're not there so much now the invasion scare is over so he doesn't always have to do that any more.'

'Well, you can tell your cousin that from now on we shall do all we can to help. It must take ages, even after they get the stuff ashore, to stow it safely. It has to come up the steps and across the lawn ... ' She frowned. 'I'm surprised nobody's ever heard them.'

'They don't exactly advertise what they're doing,' Mollie said dryly. 'And they may not be very keen for two women to get in their way, either.'

'We're not going to get in their way, we're going to help. And I've just had an idea! I'll show you, later,' she said mysteriously.

In spite of herself Mollie was curious as to how Charlotte thought she could be of any possible assistance to the 'owlers' and it was with a certain amount of scepticism that she followed her out of the house later that afternoon.

'This way.' Charlotte led the way across the lawn and then doubled back through the shrubbery. Hidden among the overgrown shrubs was a small door, with peeling paint and rusty hinges.

'The coal used to be brought here when my great-grandfather lived here because they didn't want it delivered too near the house,' she explained, scrabbling among the dead leaves.

'The door's locked,' Mollie said with relief as she tried it.

'Of course it's locked, stupid. Ah, here it is.' Triumphantly Charlotte produced a key that was as rusty as the lock on the door. 'I've brought some grease. That should help.' She smothered both key and lock with grease and pushed the key in. It creaked a bit but it turned, enabling them to push open the door.

'Be careful,' Charlotte warned. 'Let me go first. I've brought a lamp.'

'You think of everything, don't you,' Mollie said, impressed against her will.

'I try. Now, there are several steps down. I know, because I used to play here with the gardener's son when I was little. He locked me in once, and when he came to let me out I wasn't there. He was terrified, thought I'd been kidnapped by ghosts. But I'd found the passage that led straight into the house so I came up behind him and made him jump. He wouldn't play with me after that.'

'Weren't you scared in there, all alone?'

'Yes. But I tried not to think of the spiders that might be lurking in the corners. I knew there wasn't anything else to be frightened of. After all, it was only an old coal cellar. This way. And mind, the steps are a bit slimy.'

Mollie followed her down into what appeared to be quite a large cavern, hewn out of the cliff. It was larger than the cellar behind the potting shed and much easier to access discreetly.

'See?' Charlotte said delightedly. 'I said I could help.'

Mollie nodded. She had to admit that what Charlotte had shown her was likely to be quite an asset to the 'owlers'.

They went back up the steps. 'We'll have to tell Richard where the key is hidden,' Mollie said. 'Or aren't you going to lock the door?'

'Yes. I'm locking the door and I'm keeping the key,' Charlotte said, slipping it into her pocket. 'I told you I wanted to help and if they want to use this cellar they'll have to let me.'

'Oh, Charlotte, this is not a game. What these men do is highly dangerous, not to mention illegal. If they're caught they could be put in prison or transported, not to mention hanged. I know you only want to help, but the best way you can do that is to let them have the key to the cellar, keep your mouth firmly shut and forget you ever saw that dratted lantern.'

'No. I'm determined to help so I'm not giving up the key.' With that, Charlotte stalked back to the house.

The tricky business of Charlotte and the key to the cellar occupied Mollie's thoughts for the rest of the day. She couldn't decide whether or not to tell Richard about it because his temper was understandably uncertain on matters to do with smuggling and he was sure to blame her for letting Charlotte find the lantern, however unwittingly. On the other hand, the cellar Charlotte had shown her would make an ideal hiding place. It was quite a problem.

Chapter Nineteen

The problem of Charlotte and her determination to be involved with the 'owlers' preoccupied Mollie to such an extent that it wasn't until she was sitting with the family at dinner that evening that she recalled that somebody had tried to get into her room the previous night.

She had been certain it was Sebastian until she saw him draped over the banister in the throes of a hangover; but now, as she ate her soup, the thought occurred to her that it could have been a burglar. Yet there had been no mention of anything being stolen, or even disturbed, so that was not very likely. And she was certain that none of the menservants were guilty; in any case, they all slept at the far end of the house or over the stables. So it must have been a member of the family.

She glanced round the table. They were all there. Charlotte, her mother and father, Sebastian and Mark. Arthur was serving. She discounted him immediately. He was middle-aged and totally set in his ways as a 'gentleman's gentleman'. Even in the kitchen he was not comfortable talking to any of the female servants, except Cook, of course, so it was hardly likely to have been him. Both Charlotte and her mother would have rung if they had needed anything; they wouldn't go wandering about trying doors, and of course it couldn't have been Sebastian. That left Mark and James. She gazed at Mark; he was engaged in conversation with Charlotte – or rather, Charlotte was flirting with him and he was trying to respond more seriously, clearly hanging on to her every word. Mollie wished Charlotte wouldn't act like that with Mark; she knew that he was in love with her so it was not a very kind way to behave. He must have felt Mollie's eyes on him because he suddenly looked across at her and gave her a brief, friendly smile, somehow reminding her of the day he had said, 'Welcome to no-mans-land' implying that they were two of a kind. It wasn't true, though. Soon he and Charlotte would announce their engagement and that would set him firmly as a family member, where, Mollie suspected, he longed to be.

Then a thought struck her. Supposing Richard had needed to get in touch with her urgently. He knew which was her window, he had seen the light in it often enough and knowing him, he would find his way into the house somehow, even if all the doors were locked. In her relief at finding the probable solution to the identity of the intruder she had completely forgotten that Richard didn't know she had a new room, let alone where it was located, so it couldn't possibly be him.

'I said, can I offer you another slice of beef, Mollie?'

She looked up, startled. In her preoccupation, she realised that this was the second time James had asked her.

'Oh, er – yes, please. It was very tasty,' she said hurriedly.

'Then I'm surprised it took you so long to reply. Hand me your plate.' Then over his shoulder. 'It's all right, Arthur, we can manage perfectly well.'

As she held her plate out for James to take he managed somehow to get his fingers caught up with hers and gave them a cruel nip, his expression never changing. Then, as he took up the carving knife, she noticed that two of his fingers were badly bruised, the nails quite black.

Her stomach gave a sickening lurch, as she realised she needed to look no further for last night's intruder. She was so shocked and disgusted that she had difficulty in forcing down the rest of the meal.

After that Mollie was very careful to lock her door and bar it with the chair every night. Even so, she would often get out of bed as many as three times just to make sure it was secure. She had known from the beginning that James and Beatrice didn't share a bedroom; Beatrice's rooms were opposite Charlotte's whilst James had rooms on the other side of the main staircase. This was where Sebastian and Mark also had their rooms. It was, perhaps, unfortunate that Mollie's new room was the nearest one to the staircase because it enabled the master to try her door without the risk of being seen. This he continued to do, but less and less often, hoping, no doubt, that after a period of time she would be lulled into a sense of security and forget, or not bother to lock her door.

She never did.

The secret of what he was trying to do hung heavy between them. There was nobody Mollie could confide in and so she was on her guard all the time, making sure never to be in a room alone with James, never passing close to him in the corridor.

For his part, what began as no more than sport to James became an obsession when he couldn't achieve his aim. After all, she was a pretty wench and since Charlotte had begun dressing her like a lady she would pass muster in any company. Sometimes he dreamed of tangling his hands in that mane of dark hair and the things he would like to do with that wide, full-lipped mouth brought him out in a sweat. It was as much as he could do, some nights, to restrain himself from battering down her door.

The most difficult time for Mollie was when they were all round the meal table. Sometimes she could feel his eyes on her and she would keep her own eyes firmly on her plate, knowing that if she looked up she would see a mixture of desire and hatred in his eyes, born of frustration. Yet even more than she feared James Grainger's lust after her, which she knew that ultimately she could deal with – as a last resort she would reveal her identity to him, the thought of incest would surely cool his ardour – she dreaded that in his frustration he would find some reason to have her dismissed. She couldn't bear even to think about that.

She made her way along the cliff path one afternoon in early spring. It was half-tide and the pickers were out, their red cloaks splodging the beach with colour, dragging their heavy baskets to where old Sol waited patiently with his donkey. Whatever happened in the future she knew she could never go back to the back-breaking task of picking mine. She turned off the cliff path and went through the little town, bright in the spring sunshine on her way to visit her aunt and uncle. As she walked she reflected that the day she had vowed to eat at the table of James Grainger she could never in her wildest imaginings have anticipated that one day she would actually live at Cliff House, nor the joys and problems it might bring.

She turned into Copperas Lane and the familiar choking, sulphurous stink assailed her nostrils, although the grubby children playing in the dirt in front of the cottages seemed quite immune to it. At the end of the lane black smoke rose from the boiler house, blotting out the sun, and as she got nearer she could hear the sound of shovelling as the copperas beds were being raked over.

Mollie paused as she reached Uncle Sam's cottage. In the yard of the Copperas House rows of casks filled with the processed crystals to be used in dyeing stood by one of the sheds, waiting to be taken by boat to the dyers, either in Colchester or Ipswich, or even to London. By another shed, another batch of casks was stacked, ready to be taken inside and used in the ink-making process. Men hurried about, pulling trolleys, pushing barrows, shovelling coal, some wearing leather aprons and leggings and long leather gauntlets, others simply in their dirty moleskin trousers and

201

shabby jackets, seemingly heedless of the dangerous materials they worked with. The whole place had a grimy, depressed air under the ever-pervading stink.

Mollie was thankful to have escaped living in the shadow of such a place but she was always mindful that it was the industry from the stinking Copperas House that provided the wealth that had built Cliff House and kept its occupants in luxury.

Thoughtfully, she went up the steps into the cottage that had been her home for most of her life. Aunt Rose wasn't very welcoming and she wasn't alone. A thin girl of about seventeen with a spotty face and nondescript-coloured hair tied back with a faded ribbon was busy with a pile of ironing.

'Cissie looks after me now,' Aunt Rose said smugly. 'She's got your room, an' all.'

Cissie gave Mollie a brief, slightly scared smile. 'Mum turned me out when me stepfather had a go at me, Miss,' she explained. 'So Rose said I could come an' live here.'

'She's a good girl,' Rose said. 'Willin'. Which is more'n you ever were. An' look at you now, dressed up to the nines, apein' your betters an' makin' out you're gentry.' She waved a disparaging hand towards Mollie's blue silk dress and darker blue pelisse. 'What you got in that basket?'

Mollie ignored the jibe and emptied the basket Cook had packed for her earlier on to the end of the table. Rose craned her neck. 'Did you bring a pork pie? I like them pork pies you bring.'

'No. There's a piece of ham and some cheese. And half a fruit cake. Shall I put it all in the cupboard?'

Rose sniffed. 'Yes. Pity you never brought pork pie. Thass my favourite. I 'spect you'll be wantin' a cuppa tea while you're here.' She turned to Cissie. 'Pull the kettle forward, dearie.' She jerked her head towards Mollie. 'This one's got too far above herself to make her own tea.'

'I don't mind making the tea,' Mollie said, smiling at the

202

girl. 'You carry on with the ironing, Cissie.' She went to fetch the cups from the dresser.

'They ain't there. Cissie's had a change round,' Rose said, rubbing her knees gleefully. She didn't volunteer where they could be found so Mollie had no choice but to sit down and watch as Cissie juggled various jobs, just as she herself had been forced to do in the past. The only difference was that Rose, who seemed to have grown fatter than ever and had now lost most of her teeth, looked on Cissie with affection.

Mollie spent a difficult afternoon waiting for Uncle Sam to come home, whilst her aunt carried on a conversation with Cissie and ignored her. Cissie kept darting her sympathetic looks and tried to include her in the conversation where she could.

'My mum remarried six months ago,' she said at one point. 'He's younger'n her. I never much liked 'im.'

'Have you got brothers and sisters?' Mollie asked.

'She did hev a brother but he ran away to sea,' Rose said, torn between not wanting to talk to Mollie and not wanting to be left out of the conversation.

'Mum's hevin' a baby now,' Cissie said. 'But I shan't go back to look after 'er, not if she beg me on bended knee. Not after what that animal tried . . . ' She thumped the iron down on Uncle Sam's shirt. 'Well, I shan't go back, so there.'

'Don't you worry, my lovey. Your Rose'll look after you, never fear,' Rose crooned in a tone Mollie had never, ever heard before. Then she turned to Mollie and her tone changed as she snapped, 'Hevn't you got to get back?'

'Not yet. This is my afternoon off, Aunt Rose. You know Uncle Sam will be disappointed if I don't wait to see him,' she replied quietly.

'You could go over to the works and find 'im.'

'No, he wouldn't like me to do that.' Mollie lifted her head. 'But I'll go and sit on the step outside if my presence offends you.'

Rose grunted. 'No, you can't do that. He might see.' She gave a sigh. 'I s'pose you'd better lay a place for 'er at the table, Cissie. He won't like it if she don't stay to tea.'

Uncle Sam was as pleased to see her as ever. She took a kettle of hot water out to the wash house when he got home so that she could talk to him as he stripped to the waist to wash off the day's grime.

'Aunt Rose seems very taken with your young lodger,' Mollie said, wondering how Uncle Sam viewed the situation.

'Yes. She seem a nice enough little girl. An' willin' to be at Rose's beck an' call.' As he spoke he was scrubbing his face and his bald head with a soapy flannel in a vigorous circular fashion. 'But I reckon Rose'll be disappointed if she thinks Cissie and Richard . . . ' He reached for the towel.

Mollie handed it to him. 'She thinks Richard might marry Cissie?' She raised her eyebrows.

'Thass what Rose 'ud like. Then she wouldn't lose Richard and she'd hev Cissie under her thumb for all time.'

'And what does Richard have to say about that?'

'Not a word. Keeps his own counsel. Mind you, he's not home all that much.' He finished drying his face and looked at Mollie. 'Everything all right with you, my girl?'

She nodded. There was nothing wrong at Cliff House that she needed to worry Uncle Sam with. 'I don't think Aunt Rose likes me coming here now, though. She hasn't been very welcoming today.' She smiled at him. 'Not that I come to see her. I come to see you, Uncle.'

He nodded, soaping scrawny, sinewy arms. 'She's right taken up with Cissie these days,' he admitted. 'I reckon the best thing will be for me to take a walk sometimes on a Sunday afternoon. Then I might drop across you if you happen to be out walkin' too, chance times.'

She dropped a kiss on his still damp forehead. 'I reckon we can arrange something, Uncle. I wouldn't like to lose touch with you. I could always send a message by Mark.'

He nodded again. 'Yes, I'm sure Mr Mark would always let me know.'

She watched as he tipped the dirty water into the yard. The way her beloved uncle lived was a far cry from her own luxurious life. And the differing ways they had both referred to Mark only served to point this up even further. 'I don't think I'll stay to tea, Uncle. I don't really feel welcome today.'

He squeezed her arm. 'I understand, dearie.'

'I'll just collect my basket.' She smiled wickedly as a sudden thought struck her. 'If I don't visit Aunt Rose will miss the goodies I bring, won't she.'

He chuckled. 'Well, she'll only hev herself to blame for that.'

When Mollie told her she wasn't staying Aunt Rose merely said, 'You mighta said that earlier, then Cissie needn't hev laid your place.' She raised her voice. 'Don't forget to bring the ham out, Cissie. Now she's brought it we might as well eat it.'

Mollie kissed Uncle Sam and went to the door where she nearly collided with Richard, just coming in.

'Ah, I'm glad you're here, Mollie-O,' he said, giving her a hug that had a distinct smell of the Copperas House. 'I wanted to see you.'

'Well, you'll have to walk along the road with me then, because I'm just on my way home.'

'*Home*, she says,' Aunt Rose mimicked.

Mollie turned. 'Well, I can hardly call this my home now, can I?' she said with a trace of bitterness. 'I'm not even made welcome when I visit.'

'You'll always be welcome as far as I'm concerned, Mollie,' Uncle Sam said quietly at her elbow.

She kissed him again. 'I know that, Uncle.'

'What was all that about?' Richard asked as they walked up the lane.

He listened, kicking a stone along the road, as she told him of the afternoon's events.

'My mother is turning into a right old misery,' he said when she had finished. 'The only person she's got any time for these days is young Cissie. Mind you, I feel sorry for the kid . . .'

'No more than that?' Mollie looked up at him as she spoke.

'What do you mean?' He looked puzzled.

'Nothing.' She took a deep breath. 'Richard, I'm glad I've got the chance to talk to you because I've got a confession to make.'

He stopped and stared down at her. 'Oh, Moll! You're not up the spout!' The dismay on his face made her laugh out loud.

'No,' she said, 'I'm not, as you so elegantly put it, up the spout.' She grinned. 'I'd hardly come to you if I was now, would I?'

'No, I s'pose not. Unless you wanted me to put in a word for you with Joe Trayler, of course.'

'Oh, Richard!'

He had the grace to look sheepish. 'Well, what is it then?' he asked.

'It's about the lantern.'

'Yes? Did you get the message from young Sid this mornin'?'

'No. I haven't seen him.'

'Good thing I've seen you, then, because there's a job on tonight. Light it tonight. The Revenue Cutter is in for repair so we don't need to worry about that and the Ridin' Officer will be busy further down the coast. While they're outa the way we've got a lot o' stuff to shift . . .'

'Richard,' her voice cut across his words, 'Charlotte knows about the lantern. I've got a different room now. I don't sleep in the attic any more. She came up there when I was finishing clearing it and she found the lantern on the window sill. I tried to fob her off but she guessed what it was there for.'

He stopped and turned to her, a stricken look on his face.

206

'Christ! Now what are we gonna do!'

'It's all right, Dick.' She laid her hand on his arm. 'Charlotte won't say anything, I promise you.'

'Are you sure?'

'Cross my heart.'

'Thass all right, then.' He frowned. 'But how will you manage to light the lantern if you're in a different room? Can you put it in your new window? But they won't see it if you're not up in the attic, will they. Oh, Christ, thass a teaser, that is.'

'Will you stop talking for a minute and listen to me, Dick,' she said impatiently. 'I'll still put the lantern up, don't worry. That's not what the trouble is.' She paused. 'The trouble is, Charlotte wants to help.'

He stared at her uncomprehendingly. 'Help? What d'you mean, help?'

'She wants to help ... with what you do.' For some reason she couldn't bring herself to say the word smuggling.

He frowned. 'What does she think she can do, for goodness sake?'

'Oh, she could help you, all right. She showed me a place where you could hide as much as you liked.'

'Where? Could you show me?'

'It's a huge cellar in the shrubbery at Cliff House. But she's got the key and she won't give it up.'

'Can't you get it off her? Take it while she's asleep?'

'No. She won't let it out of her sight in case I do just that. She's determined to be involved.'

Richard rubbed his chin thoughtfully. 'I s'pose that might not be such a bad idea,' he said slowly. 'After all, nobody would ever suspect two women, would they?'

Mollie's heart sank. This was not at all the reaction she had expected from Richard and unlike Charlotte she had no desire at all to be caught up in his smuggling activities.

They had reached the path along the top of the cliff now; Richard picked a blade of grass and began to chew it thoughtfully, gazing out to sea. After a while he said, 'Well, you can come, jest this once. I don't s'pose she'll wanta do it any more after that.'

'I don't want to do it at all,' Mollie said fervently. 'But if Charlotte comes I won't have any choice, will I.'

'You'll be all right, Moll.' He gave her a hug. 'Jest you make sure that lantern's in place, then be at the top of the cliff steps at two o'clock. There's no moon tonight, but all the same you'd better wear dark clothes, keep close to the bushes and don't talk! And tell Charlotte she must do as she's told without question. You, too, Moll.'

'Me? I'll be too petrified to talk,' Mollie said. Already her mouth felt dry.

He gave her another squeeze. 'It'll be fine, Moll. We've got this running like clockwork. And with a couple of extra hands it'll all be done in a shake of a lamb's tail. You'll see.'

Mollie gave him a wintry smile. Richard was always an optimist.

Chapter Twenty

'Oh, for goodness sake, stop worrying,' Charlotte admonished as Mollie paced anxiously up and down the room after telling her there was to be a 'drop' that night. 'It's going to be exciting.'

That was not the word Mollie would have used and it was with shaking hands that she lit the lantern and left it in the attic window. She shared none of Charlotte's expectations; all she could see was the possibility that things would go wrong.

'Supposing someone heard us come downstairs,' Mollie said as they were putting their boots on in the boot room. 'They'd want to know what we were doing, wandering about the house at dead of night.'

'But they didn't, did they?' Charlotte said, tying the strings of her cloak under her chin. 'And if they had all we had to say was that we were going to the kitchen for a drink.'

'They'd hardly believe that. I can't remember the last time you were in the kitchen,' Mollie remarked tartly.

They let themselves out of the boot-room door and keeping to the shelter of the shrubbery made their way to the cliff steps. It was a little over half tide and they could hear the faint sound of muffled oars under the slap of the waves. They waited for what seemed an age and then Charlotte gripped Mollie's hand as they sensed rather than heard someone coming up the steps. Before long the shadowy figure of Richard appeared with a brandy keg on his shoulder.

'Good. You're here,' he whispered. 'Where now?'

'This way.' Charlotte led the way silently to the door in the shrubbery and unlocked it. In the pitch darkness she went down the steps and lit the lantern she had left there. It gave just enough light for Richard to see his way.

'Go back and show Joe and Fred the way,' Richard said over his shoulder to Mollie. 'They'll be at the top of the cliff by now.'

Mollie went as quickly as she could in the darkness back to the cliff steps. Her heart was thumping uncomfortably and she would have given a great deal to be back in her nice warm bed – a bed she was pessimistic enough to wonder if she would ever see again.

Then there was no further time for thought because Joe Trayler and the man called Fred were just coming up the cliff steps with a keg each on their shoulders.

'Ah, here's my gal,' Joe whispered to Fred. 'Dick said she was gonna give us a hand. 'Ullo, sweetheart.'

'I'm *not* your sweetheart,' Mollie hissed, fear making her aggressive.

'Thass all right. I'm a patient man. You'll come to your senses in the end.'

Mollie turned away from him and noticed that there were two kegs already waiting at the top of the cliff. 'Why don't you let me roll one of those,' she said, trying not to let her teeth chatter. 'It would save a bit of time.' Anything to get the job done quickly, away from Joe Trayler's company and back to the safety of her room.

She found it a bit difficult, rolling a heavy brandy keg quietly through the undergrowth and she could hear the footsteps of the two men lumbering along behind her, cracking twigs and rustling leaves in an alarmingly loud fashion. But when they reached the cellar Richard saw how useful the two girls could be and quickly worked out a scheme whereby the men carried the goods up the steps to the top of the cliff and Mollie and Charlotte ferried them the rest of the way. If they couldn't manage the cellar steps they were to leave them at the top for Richard or Joe to stow when they arrived.

It worked well. In less than an hour everything was stored safely in the cellar. There were kegs of brandy, genever and wine; several bales of silk and lace; boxes of cigars and tobacco – and tea, which the girls didn't have to handle at all because the packets of tea had been had been brought across the German Sea stuffed down the specially made waistcoat and breeches of a man known as Andy, who, when he was divested of his extra clothing, turned out to be not nearly as fat as he at first appeared.

'Good haul tonight, lads,' Richard said happily. He turned to Charlotte. 'We'll fetch it all away tomorrow night,' he promised. 'Thass too late to do any more tonight.'

'Will you need us?' Charlotte asked eagerly.

'No. Your work is done for this trip,' Richard said, grinning at her enthusiasm. 'And I must say thass all gone like clockwork. We shall be callin' on you two gals again, don't you worry.'

Mollie's heart sank but Charlotte clapped her hands. 'Oh, good.' Then a thought struck her. 'Why don't you take the stuff away in the pony and trap, Richard? You could probably do the lot in one trip,' she suggested. 'I'll make sure Bridie's hooves are muffled and as long as you get her back before daylight nobody will be any the wiser.'

Richard's grin widened. 'Ah, you're behind the times, Missy,' he said. 'Hadn't you noticed your groom's a bit reluctant to get the pony harnessed up some mornin's?'

Charlotte frowned. 'Well, now you come to speak of it . . .'

He tapped the side of his nose. 'Thass because he knows she's tired 'cause she's been workin' all night.'

'Oh.' She looked quite crestfallen.

With the night's work done, and a tot of best brandy inside them, the owlers crept away, one by one, Joe Trayler unsuccessfully trying to steal a kiss from Mollie before he left to row back to his father's fishing boat. Richard stayed behind while Charlotte locked the door.

'I shall need that termorrer,' he said when she put it in her pocket.

'I know. I'll come and unlock it for you,' she insisted.

'Don't be a silly gal. Give me the key. We shan't need you termorrer and if you cut up rusty we shan't never call on you again.' He held out his hand. 'Please yerself.'

'Oh, very well.' She dragged the key out of her pocket and gave it to him.

'Thass a good gal.' He put it in his pocket, then he carefully covered all their tracks with dead leaves. 'Off you go, now, both of you,' he said when he had finished. 'Thass bin a good night's work.' He gave Mollie a quick peck on the cheek and did the same to Charlotte.

The two girls crept back to their beds, where Charlotte fell asleep immediately, a smile on her face. But Mollie lay staring up into the darkness for a long time, going over the night's events. Then, just as she was dropping off to sleep she remembered that the lantern was still alight and she had to drag herself out of bed and creep up to the attic to blow it out.

Both girls slept late in the morning.

When Mollie finally entered the breakfast room, Sebastian was the only person left there. He was still immersed in a week-old copy of *The Times*, which the father of one of his richer friends bought every day and which was then handed round to all and sundry. To his annoyance, Sebastian was often the last to receive it and he often tried to persuade his own father to buy it, but without success. He looked up as she walked in.

'Good morning, Mollie.' He smiled at her. Then his smile turned to a frown. 'You're looking a little pale, my dear. Are you feeling quite well?' He put the newspaper

212

down and got up to hold a chair out for her. 'What can I get you? Kippers? Kidney? Scrambled eggs?'

'No, just toast and marmalade, thank you,' she said. In truth her head ached because she had had so little sleep and she wasn't really hungry at all. It didn't help her temper that Charlotte still slept dreamlessly on. She looked round the table strewn with the remains of breakfast. 'Oh, dear, is it that late? Where is everybody?'

He began ticking off on his fingers. 'Mama's with Cook, discussing whatever it is they discuss; Father is in his study, and Mark, of course, has gone to the Works. I assume my beloved sister is still in her room?'

'That's right.' Mollie stifled a yawn. It wouldn't be prudent to admit she was still sleeping. She frowned. 'If Mark has gone to the Copperas House what are you doing here? Aren't you supposed to be there as well? Sir?' she added as an afterthought.

'Don't call me Sir,' he said irritably. Then his good humour returned and he smiled at her. 'And I haven't gone to the Works because I was waiting to see you, Mollie.'

'Oh.' She looked up from taking a bite of toast. 'Why did you want to see me?'

He gave a sigh. 'Because I *always* want to see you, Mollie. Haven't you noticed, I look out for you at every opportunity?'

She shook her head. 'No. Not really.' Although, if she was honest, she had registered that he often seemed to be around and she had wondered why he spent so much time at home instead of at work, which prompted her to say, 'Shouldn't you be going? You'll be late.'

'I'm not going in today. I have to ride over to Ipswich later on, to sort out some business about a barrel of ink that went astray. I can't imagine how it happened. I was sure I put in the order for it.' He began to empty his pockets. 'Oh, Lucifer take it! The damn thing's here. I must have forgotten to put it in!'

'You'd better go and grovel to somebody, then,' Mollie

213

said, watching him stuff the miscellany of papers back into his pocket. 'And I should make sure there's nothing else important lurking there, if I were you.'

'It's your fault, Mollie,' he said, giving one or two of the papers a cursory glance.

'Me? How can it be my fault?' she asked indignantly.

He looked up. 'Because I can't get you out of my mind, that's why. I think about you day and night. You're first in my thoughts when I wake in the morning and the last before I go to sleep at night.' He reached over and took her hand. 'I love you, Mollie,' he said more gently. 'It's not some passing fancy. I love you and I want to marry you. More than anything in the world I want to make you my wife.' He got up from his chair and went down on one knee beside her. 'I know the breakfast room, with all the detritus of kipper bones and kedgeree is hardly the time or place to say this – we should be in some beautiful moonlit garden – but, Mollie, will you do me the great honour of marrying me? I promise I will love and cherish you to the end of my life.'

She stared at him. There was no doubting his utter sincerity. 'Sebastian, I'm truly sorry but I can't possibly marry you,' she said, quietly.

'Why not, for heaven's sake? Give me one good reason.' He sat back on his heels. 'Ah, I know what it is. You think you don't love me enough. Well, that love will grow. I know it will. In any case, I have enough for both of us.' He knelt up again and gave the hand he still held a little shake. 'I'm prepared to take a chance on that.'

She drew her hand away. 'It's not just that, Seb,' she said, shaking her head.

'What is it, then? If you're worried about my parents objecting – which I'm sure they wouldn't, I can always get round them – we'll elope.' He got up and drew his chair close to hers. 'That might be fun, Mollie. We could steal away at dead of night and go to Gretna Green . . .'

'No!'

He sat back, offended. 'Don't say it like that! I've asked

you to marry me, for God's sake, not to take part in some highway robbery!'

She put her head in her hands and began to cry, quietly. 'I'm sorry, Seb, I didn't mean it to sound like that, but even if I loved you the way you would like I still couldn't marry you. I'm sorry.'

'You might at least have the courtesy to give me your reasons, Mollie,' he said stiffly.

'I'm sorry, I can't marry you,' she said again, shaking her head. 'It simply isn't possible. That's all I have to say.'

He got to his feet. 'I really can't see why not, so I shall just keep asking you until I wear you down,' he said. 'I'm not a patient man, Mollie, but I'm prepared to wait for you until – well, until you come to your senses.' He gave a crooked smile. 'I'm not a bad catch, you know. There are a good many young ladies who'd be only too happy ...'

'Oh, Seb, then why don't you marry one of them,' she said desperately.

He looked down at her, the smile gone. 'Because I happen to be in love with you,' he said. With that, he turned and left the room.

She put her head in her hands. Life seemed to be just one complication after another without any glimmer of a solution. Yet, even with all the problems it had brought, she couldn't find it in her heart to regret coming to live at Cliff House. She loved the house, she loved and valued her friendship with Charlotte, she loved having nice clothes. More than anything, she loved the way of life – the memory of her time spent picking mine and living in the shadow of the stinking Copperas House, was like another, hellish existence. She had been so very lucky, because girls with her background didn't get this kind of chance.

Now she was going to have to throw it all away because Sebastian, the son of the house, had fallen in love with her and wanted to marry her. And since she could never tell him the real reason why this could never be the only thing to do was to leave Cliff House and go.

But go where? Whatever Uncle Sam might say, Aunt Rose had made it quite plain that she was no longer welcome at the cottage in Copperas Lane. In fact, Cissie had been given her old room. Not that she wanted to go back there; the very thought of it made her shudder. Yet even her distaste for her old home was tinged with a sense of disloyalty because she loved Uncle Sam and he had always been so good to her. She stared out of the window. Life was sometimes so complicated it was difficult to know which way to turn.

Charlotte wandered into the breakfast room, yawning and clutching a quilted wrap round her. 'I've just woken up. You weren't there and you haven't laid out my clothes for the day,' she said petulantly.

Mollie got to her feet and squared her shoulders. 'I'm sorry. I was sitting here day dreaming and I forgot the time,' she said, making her voice brisk. 'Go back upstairs and I'll bring you your morning chocolate. I shan't be long.' In truth she was glad to put her thoughts of the past hour to one side and to busy herself with the trivia of Charlotte's daily life.

'What were you thinking about downstairs that made you look so miserable?' Charlotte asked when Mollie came in to her room with two cups of chocolate, one for Charlotte and one for herself. 'Surely you weren't thinking about our adventure last night? It was exciting, wasn't it, and Richard made us feel we were being really useful. He's nice, isn't he, your cousin Richard. I like him. I hope it won't be too long before he asks us to help again.' She took several sips of her chocolate. 'He'll have to ask us, otherwise I shan't let him keep the key to the cellar,' she said smugly.

Mollie didn't answer. She knew her cousin well enough to know there would have been a second key cut from the first and safely in his possession by now.

Charlotte looked up, frowning. 'You're very quiet, Mollie. Is there something wrong? You can tell me, you know, I'm your friend.'

You're also my half-sister – the thought stabbed through Mollie's mind. What would you say if I told you that? She finished her chocolate and got to her feet. 'I'm tired, that's all,' she said.

'Yes, it was ages before I could sleep,' Charlotte said, handing Mollie her cup and getting out of bed.

'It wasn't that long,' Mollie remarked. 'You were sound asleep when I remembered the lantern and went up to the attic to put it out.'

'Oh, heavens!' Charlotte clapped her hands over her mouth. 'I clean forgot the lantern.'

'Good thing I didn't, then.' Mollie began pulling clothes out of the chest. 'Come on, get dressed. Your mother will start thinking you're ill again if you don't soon get some clothes on.'

Charlotte came and stood beside Mollie and put her arms round her. 'I really don't know what I would do without you, Mollie,' she said and when Mollie turned to look at her there were tears in her eyes. 'I've never had a friend like you before. Never. Seb's my brother but I don't feel nearly as close to him as I do to you.'

Mollie leaned over and kissed her. 'Do you know, that's the nicest thing anybody's ever said to me, Charlotte,' she said. 'I'll never forget it.'

Lying in bed that night, after spending a companionable day with Charlotte buying ribbons from the shop in the High Street and visiting one of Charlotte's friends, Mollie's mind returned to the problem of Sebastian's proposal. She couldn't accept it even if she wanted to, which she didn't, because he was not the man she loved. But neither could she tell him the true reason why marriage between them was impossible. So the honourable thing to do would be to leave Cliff House, to go away where nobody could find her. But where could she go, with hardly any money? She wished now she had been more careful with the money she had earned and not wasted it all on ribbons and silly hats.

And what could she do? She wasn't clever enough to become a governess and it was unlikely Beatrice would give her a reference if she left giving no good reason.

She could marry Joe Trayler. She examined the prospect. He would give her a home and more children than she could cope with or they could afford. In ten years she would be an old woman, living with a man she didn't even like. She made a face up into the darkness. The best that could be said about marrying Joe Trayler was that, as a last resort, it would at least keep her off the streets.

Suddenly, she sat bolt upright in bed. She had been thinking only of herself and what she was going to do, but what about Charlotte? Impetuous, excitable Charlotte. Now that she had been let into the secrets of the owlers' activities she was desperate to be even more involved. Without someone – and there was no-one else who could do it but Mollie herself – to put a curb on her enthusiasm she could get herself into all sorts of scrapes. Worse, she could land the men in trouble, too. A little thing like forgetting to blow out the lantern could have had quite far-reaching results and Charlotte hadn't given it a second's thought. With nobody at hand to keep a check on her Charlotte could only be yet another danger to the men who were already risking their lives to bring in the contraband.

She slid back down into her bed and pulled the covers up under her chin. There was no solution that she could see. She couldn't stay at Cliff House, seeing Sebastian every day and being pestered for an answer she couldn't give him, but neither could she go away and risk Charlotte's impetuous nature putting the owlers – and herself – in danger of imprisonment, transportation or even the gallows, with her misplaced insistence on being a part of their activities.

But if she couldn't stay at Cliff House yet couldn't leave it, what was she to do? And who in the world could she go to for advice?

Chapter Twenty-one

Mollie found it increasingly difficult to go about her everyday activities, listening to Charlotte's chatter, sewing fresh trimmings on hats and dresses, helping her to choose which of her many pairs of shoes she should wear, advising whether the blue muslin or the pink would look best, when always at the back of her mind was the nagging question of her future.

She tried to avoid Sebastian as far as she could, and when this was not possible she made sure she was never alone with him. Mealtimes were difficult because she would often feel his eyes resting on her and even his most innocent-sounding remark was, she knew, loaded with hidden meaning.

Wearily leaving the table after a meal she had hardly touched one evening, the thought crossed her mind yet again that the fulfilling of her reckless desire to sit at James Grainger's table had brought her none of the satisfaction she had expected and a great deal of heartache that she could never have foreseen.

'Is everything all right with you, Mollie?' Mark caught up with her as she hurried along the corridor to avoid Sebastian.

She stopped and turned to him with a brief smile. 'I'm a little tired, that's all, thank you, Mark.'

'I think it must be rather more than that, Mollie. You ate

very little last night and even less tonight,' he said and there was concern in his eyes.

'Oh, dear. And I thought I was managing to be discreet,' she said, her smile widening. 'I didn't think anyone would notice.'

'I notice most things about you,' he said enigmatically.

She nodded, her smile fading. 'I suppose my uncle asked you to keep an eye on me to make sure I'm behaving properly,' she said with a sigh. Her mouth twisted wryly. 'I hope your reports don't give him cause for concern.'

His face darkened. 'I am not your uncle's spy, Mollie. He never suggested that I should be and if he had I should have declined.' He made to move off, clearly offended.

She quickly put out her hand to detain him. 'I'm sorry, Mark. I shouldn't have said that. It was quite wrong of me.'

He paused and turned back to her. 'The only thing your uncle asked of me was that I should tell him if you were unhappy,' he said quietly. 'I haven't told him that you are, although I rather think something is troubling you.' His deep-set hazel eyes regarded her thoughtfully. 'Be that as it may, I have a message from him. He has asked me to tell you that on Sunday afternoon he will wait at the gap where Old Sol stands with his horse and cart in the hope that you can get away for an hour. Do you think you will be able to manage that? Or is Charlotte too demanding?'

Mollie smiled ruefully. 'She does seem to want my company most of the time, but perhaps I can slip away while she's having her rest.'

'That won't give you much more than half an hour.' He stroked his chin. 'Perhaps I can arrange a walk with Charlotte myself, after her rest. That will give you a little more time with your uncle. He seemed very anxious to see you.'

'Oh, dear. I hope there's nothing wrong.'

He looked down at her, a half smile on his face. 'I think the only thing wrong is that he hasn't seen you for some

220

time and he misses you. I can understand that. Come to think of it, I haven't seen you in Copperas Lane recently.'

'No, I don't go there any more. Last time I visited my aunt, she made it quite plain that I'm no longer welcome in her house.' She gave a shrug. 'Not that Aunt Rose was ever very pleased to give me house room.'

'So that's why your uncle has arranged to meet you at the gap.'

She nodded.

'Well, don't concern yourself about Charlotte. I'm sure I can keep her amused for an hour or two.'

For some reason Mollie felt less grateful for this than she should have done.

Sunday dawned warm and sunny, with the promise of a hot day to come. Mollie dressed carefully to go and meet Uncle Sam, wearing a green and silver striped taffeta dress and a shady, wide-brimmed green hat with a crown decorated with silver flowers. She pinched her cheeks until they hurt in an effort to put some colour in them.

'You look very smart. I shall wear my pink silk when I go for a walk with Mark,' Charlotte said, reclining on her bed for her afternoon rest. 'Did I tell you Mark was taking me for a walk, later?'

'Yes,' Mollie said shortly. 'I've already laid out your dress and parasol. Make sure you use it; it will be hot later on.'

'Shall you be gone long?'

'I dare say I shall be back before you and Mark.'

'You don't sound very good tempered, Mollie.'

Mollie forced a smile. 'I'm perfectly good tempered,' she answered, knowing it was a lie. 'I'm looking forward to seeing my uncle.' That much was the truth.

Uncle Sam was waiting for her. In spite of the hot day he was dressed in his Sunday suit and hat and his boots were well polished. She smiled as she remembered that

Uncle Sam always kept his boots well polished, even for work. He doffed his hat to give her a welcoming kiss and she noticed with sadness that his cravat, very neatly tied, had a greyish tinge to it. She had always been very particular to make sure Uncle Sam's linen was a good colour when she was responsible for it, difficult though it had been in the filthy atmosphere they lived in, and he had appreciated this.

'I've missed seein' you, my girl,' he said, his eyes bright with affection. He put his head on one side. 'You're lookin' a bit peaky, though.'

'No, I'm not.' She put her hand through his arm. 'It's just that you haven't seen me lately. Look, Cook has packed some things for you to take home.' She held up the basket she was carrying. 'There's a bit of cheese, a few eggs, a slice of pork pie and some currant buns. That should please Aunt Rose.'

'Aye, the sight of food always pleases Rose these days.'

Mollie shot him a glance but his face was impassive, so she put her arm through his and said, 'Now, where shall we go? Shall we walk up to the old church?'

'What there is left of it.' He pointed to what was little more than a heap of masonry teetering on the edge of the cliff further along the coast. 'Another great chunk of wall fell in the sea the other day and there wasn't even a storm, jest an ordinary high tide. Soon the lot'll be gone.'

'Well, then we'd better go and take a last look before it disappears completely.'

Sam took the basket from her and they walked together past the sand dunes and up the slope where the cliff rose from the gap, walking along the cliff path in the opposite direction from the naze. It was a beautiful day. The sun was high in the sky but there was enough breeze to take the fierceness out of its heat and the gulls that screamed and wheeled around them showed a brilliant white against the blue sky. Below them the sea was sprinkled with pinpoints of reflected sunlight in the shallows of the quietly receding

222

tide. A lacy frill of froth and bunches of seaweed on the sand marked the high-tide line.

They walked in silence for a while, Sam chewing his moustache, Mollie trying to think of a way to ask him what she should do about Sebastian's proposal that wouldn't result in him insisting that she leave Cliff House. But before she could decide what to say he stopped chewing and spoke first.

'Your Aunt Rose ain't so good, Mollie. She can't get up the stairs now, with her legs bein' so bad, so she hev to sleep on the couch in the livin' room.'

'Has the doctor seen her?'

'The likes of us don't hev no truck with doctors, you oughta know that, Mollie. Anyways, what could he do? Fact is, her legs is too weak to hold up her body an' thass an end to it.'

'And the less she moves the fatter she gets,' Mollie remarked.

'Thass about it.' He nodded, heaving a sigh.

'Is Cissie still there?'

He nodded again. 'I can't say I like the gal but she's a comfort to Rose so I put up with 'er. She's a bit slap-dash. Not like you, my girl.' He squeezed her hand as it rested in the crook of his arm.

Mollie licked her lips. She could see the way opening up that would take her out of her own dilemma but it was not a path she was at all anxious to take. Nevertheless, love for Uncle Sam forced her to offer. 'Do you think I should come back and look after Aunt Rose?' she asked tentatively.

They walked on side by side for several minutes before he answered. During those brief moments Mollie's heart sank lower and lower. She would have to do it if Uncle Sam asked her but she wasn't sure she could stomach the thought of going back to the tiny, cramped cottage in stinking Copperas Lane to care for an aunt who hated her. Not after the luxurious life she had become used to.

'No,' he said at last, his voice firm and she couldn't help

a sigh of relief escaping. 'You've bettered yerself; you're a lady now and you've got a good life. You're still my Mollie underneath, I know, but you can't come back to Copperas Lane. Not now, not never. You wouldn't fit in; you're a cut above the likes of us now an' there's folks 'ud wouldn't let you forget it, so it wouldn't do. You wouldn't be happy.' He laid his hand on her arm. 'More'n anything else I want you to be happy, my girl.'

Her eyes filled with tears. 'But if you need me, Uncle ...'

'We can manage. Cissie tries her best and since Richard moved out ...'

'Richard's gone? Where to?'

'He's got hisself a room in a house off the High Street. Tell you the truth I think 'e got fed up with 'is mother keep tryin' to throw Cissie at 'im. 'E won't hev no truck with the likes of her, an' not to blame 'im, neither. She can be a lazy little slut at times.' It was not often that Uncle Sam spoke ill of anybody.

'Well, if there's anything I can do, Uncle, you've only got to say,' she said. Even as she spoke she realised the total inadequacy of her words.

'I know, dearie, and thass a comfort.' He pointed. 'Look the tide's well down now. We could walk along the sand where thass a bit shaded from the sun and see how much of the old church we can still reckernise. There's an easy way down here.' He pointed to her feet. 'Ah, no, you'll spoil them pretty shoes if we do that.'

'Then I'll take them off.' As she spoke she slipped her feet out of her shoes and bent to pick them up. Then, with the sure-footedness from her childhood that had never left her she made her way down the cliff in her stockinged feet, with Sam just behind her.

They walked along till they reached the great lumps of masonry that had fallen from the church, some of them now half buried in the sand.

Sam stood looking down at them, shaking his head.

'They can't even hold weddin's in the church porch like they used to,' he said sadly. 'Thass too dangerous.'

'It's sad to see it all falling into the sea,' Mollie said, sitting down on a lump of stone that had once been part of the chancel arch.

He sat down beside her. 'They say you can hear the church bell ringin' under the sea on a stormy night, but I ain't never known anyone who's heard it for theirselves,' he said, taking out his pipe and tamping down the tobacco.

'It's a bit like the tales of coffins being washed up when the graveyard collapsed, I reckon,' she said with a smile.

'Oh, no. Thass the truth. I've seen that with me own eyes,' he said, looking at her through a haze of smoke. 'I've seen the coffins stickin' outa the cliff, there, too.' He jerked his head toward the cliff face. 'Thass a sad sight. Some poor heart they thought they'd laid to 'is last rest all stuck out there an' nothin' anybody can do to stop 'im topplin' into the sea an' bein' all smashed up.'

They sat quietly together for several minutes, Mollie with her hands in her lap, Sam puffing on his pipe, contented just to be with her. Then he said, 'There's a farmhouse over yonder on the brink of goin', too.' He jabbed his pipe at the cliff, shaking his head. 'You can't stop the sea, Mollie. Thass too powerful for man to control, an' thass a fact.' He stood up and gazed up at the cliff, where the last few stones of the church teetered on the edge. 'One o' these days, you mark my words, the sea'll eat into all this cliff. Folks won't believe there was ever a church there.'

'I wonder if Cliff House is safe,' Mollie said anxiously.

He patted her hand. 'I reckon thass safe for a good few years yet,' he said with a smile. 'You don't need to worry your pretty little head over that.'

They began to walk back the way they had come. 'I ain't so sure about the Copperas House, though,' he said thoughtfully.

225

Mollie looked at him in surprise. 'But that's nowhere near the cliff.'

'True. But the tide still comes up round the back there.'

She laughed. 'Oh, Uncle, it would take an enormous tide to wash that lot away!'

'Aye. It would, wouldn't it.' But he wasn't laughing.

They parted company at the gap and Sam went home with the basket of goodies. Mollie watched the small, proud, upright figure in his well-brushed but shabby Sunday suit until he was out of sight, then made her way back to Cliff House. As she walked she thought over the fact that she hadn't asked his advice over Sebastian's proposal and it was with regret that she realised that it was not a thing she would ever be able to discuss with him. Close as they still were, there was nevertheless a widening gap between them. Sam's life was centred round his work at the Copperas House; he asked nothing more than to be able to see his days out working there as boilerman. James Grainger and Sebastian his son, Mark Hamilton, his nephew, were all his masters; he regarded it as no more than his Christian duty to doff his cap to them and do their bidding. But Mollie lived with the Graingers, under the same roof, sharing the same board. She had seen both James and Sebastian roaring drunk; she had also seen how Beatrice could get the better of her husband without even raising her voice. At first she had felt she had a foot in both camps – Copperas Lane and Cliff House – but now she realised that her life in Copperas Lane was behind her and there was no looking back.

When she got back to the house Charlotte was not in a very good mood.

'What's the matter?' Mollie asked. 'Didn't you have a pleasant walk with Mark?'

'No. He made me walk much too far and wasn't a bit sympathetic when I said I had a blister on my heel.' She held it out for inspection.

'I can't see a blister,' Mollie said, perversely glad at

Charlotte's dissatisfaction with Mark.

'No, well, it's gone down now,' she said, rubbing it. 'He's not good at looking for fossils, either.' She didn't even ask if Mollie had enjoyed her afternoon.

If she had Mollie wasn't sure what she would have replied. In truth, the walk with Uncle Sam had left her quite depressed.

A week later she still didn't know what to do about Sebastian. His attitude towards her seemed to be changing in an undefinable way. On the few occasions when she couldn't avoid his presence he seemed to treat her in quite a proprietorial manner, which she found disconcerting. She realised that before long she would have to do something to end this cat and mouse game. Only it wasn't a game. Far from it. And she didn't know what to do to end it.

After tossing and turning for what seemed hours, having gone to bed early pleading a headache to Charlotte after several almost sleepless nights, Mollie slipped out of bed and, putting on a wrap, went down to the kitchen for some warm milk, in the hope that this would soothe her into sleep.

To her surprise Mark was there, sitting at the table, an empty dinner plate at his elbow and a ledger in front of him. He looked up and smiled as she entered.

'A kindred soul come to burn the midnight oil?' he asked. 'I find this is a good time to work, when the rest of the household is in bed and everywhere is quiet.'

'Then I won't disturb you,' she said quickly. 'I only came to warm some milk because I couldn't sleep.' She busied herself with a small saucepan, trying to make as little noise as she could. When the milk was warm she poured it into a mug and went to the door.

'Why don't you sit here and drink it?' he asked, rubbing his eyes. 'I could do with a bit of company. These figures are beginning to dance in front of my eyes.'

'Then maybe you should do the same as me,' she held

227

up her mug. 'I'll warm some for you, if you like.'

He nodded. 'Thank you, I should like that, provided you do as I suggested and sit here with me while we drink it.'

He pushed the ledger to one side and put his elbows on the table, running his fingers through his cropped hair. 'It's difficult to make the figures balance when more is being taken out than is coming in,' he said with a sigh. 'Uncle James doesn't seem to realise that the Copperas House can't keep solvent and pay off his gambling debts at the same time.' He gave a rueful grin. 'It wouldn't be so bad if he won occasionally at these cockfights he's so keen on.'

'Cockfights?' She turned from the stove, frowning.

'Yes. Cockfights, cards, he'll gamble on how far a flea can jump if there's nothing else to put his money on,' he said wearily. He looked up at her as she placed a mug at his elbow and sat down opposite him. 'But that's my worry, not yours.' He regarded her thoughtfully. 'What *is* your worry, Mollie? I know something's troubling you because you're not eating properly and now I find you're not sleeping, either.' He put his head on one side. 'I don't want to pry, but would it help to talk about it?'

She stared down at the skin forming on the milk in the mug. She desperately needed to talk to somebody and there was nobody else that she could think of. She looked up and nodded, her hands round her mug, her shoulders hunched. 'I was going to tell Uncle Sam when I saw him last week,' she said, her voice hardly above a whisper. 'But he's got quite enough worries of his own. And in any case, I realised I couldn't tell him ... '

He frowned. 'Mollie, you're not ...? What I mean is, you're not in any trouble ...?'

She looked up at him uncomprehendingly. Then her face cleared and the ghost of a smile crossed her face. 'Well, I suppose I am in trouble, but not the kind you're thinking of, Mark. I'm not pregnant, if that's what you're thinking.'

He flushed. 'I'm sorry, Mollie. I shouldn't have...'

She waved his apology aside. 'It was understandable, I

228

suppose.' She smiled at him. Suddenly, of all the people she knew, she realised that Mark was the one person who might understand her dilemma. She took a deep breath. 'But my problem is not that I'm pregnant, Mark. My problem is that Sebastian wants to marry me.'

His expression changed and she sensed a sudden hostility. 'I don't see that as a problem,' he said coolly. 'I hope you'll be very happy together.' He stood up, his milk only half finished. 'Now, I'll bid you goodnight.'

Chapter Twenty-two

Mollie got to her feet. 'No, wait, Mark. You don't understand,' she said desperately, almost unconsciously holding out her hands as if in supplication.

'I think I do, Mollie.' He paused with his hand on the door knob. 'Sebastian wants to marry you. Well, congratulations. Isn't that what you've always hoped for?' He raised his eyebrows, his expression cool.

She stared at him as her hands fell to her sides. If he had slapped her face she couldn't have been more surprised. 'Is that what you think of me? That I'm a conniving, out-for-all-I-can-get schemer? Is that what you really think of me, Mark?' she asked, her voice quivering with a mixture of astonishment and rage.

'No, of course I don't think that, Mollie,' he said quickly. 'It's just that – well, it's quite plain that Sebastian ... and I thought you ...' he broke off. 'I'm sorry, Mollie. I honestly didn't mean to offend you. Please forgive me.'

She sat down and rested her head on her hand. 'Oh, Mark, you've got it all so wrong,' she said wearily. 'I was going to tell you. I thought you'd understand. I so desperately need to talk to somebody and I thought you would listen.' She closed her eyes briefly, then pulled herself together, straightened up and lifted her chin. 'Clearly, I made a mistake and picked the wrong person,' she said, making her voice bright and talking a little too fast. 'But never mind, I'm sure I shall manage to sort something out for myself. Now, I won't keep you from your bed any longer. I know you're very tired. Goodnight, Mark.' She got to her feet and took the two mugs over to the sink and filled them with water.

When she turned back into the room, hoping he would have gone, she saw that he was seated at the table again. He gave her a lopsided, rueful smile. 'I've said I'm sorry, Mollie, and I meant it. I seem to have got it all wrong, but I truly didn't mean to offend or hurt you. Now, shall we start again?'

She stood looking at him, shaking her head. 'I don't know ... Is there any point?' she asked wearily.

He got up and held a chair for her. 'Please sit down. I promise I won't interrupt or jump to conclusions. I've done that twice in the course of the last half hour and both times I've been wrong. So, tell me, what's troubling you? What would be so terrible about marrying Sebastian?'

She sat down heavily opposite to him. 'In the first place, I don't love him. He's not at all the kind of man I would want as a husband,' she said slowly. 'But I could never marry him even if he was.' She raised her eyes to his and her voice dropped to little more than a whisper. 'You see, he's my *brother*.'

'*What?*' He half rose in his chair, then fell back. 'What did you say? Sebastian is your brother?'

She nodded. 'Well, my half-brother.'

'Your half-brother? But how? I mean ... ' He ran his fingers through his hair as he often did when he was perplexed.

'My mother was a servant here and James, Sebastian's father ... ' She spread her hands. 'It's the old, old story of the master seducing, raping, call it what you will, a girl who had no choice but to comply.'

He digested her words for several minutes, then he

231

looked up at her, frowning. 'Are you quite sure about this? I mean, how can you possibly be certain?'

'My mother was Uncle Sam's youngest and favourite sister. She went to him for help when she was turned out of Cliff House. She died soon after I was born but not before she'd told Uncle Sam the whole story of what had happened. Uncle Sam and Aunt Rose took me in and brought me up. I always knew I wasn't their child, Aunt Rose made sure of that, but it wasn't until I was seventeen that I knew the whole story.' Her mouth twisted bitterly. 'When Uncle Sam told me how James Grainger had used my mother and then blamed her pregnancy on one of the stable lads – the poor innocent lad was sent packing, too, by the way – I vowed that one day I would sit at James Grainger's table, in my rightful place as his daughter. He might not know it, but I would and that would be enough. It would vindicate my mother. Or so I thought.' She sighed. 'You know how it was that I came to live here?'

He nodded. 'Yes. I remember you coming.'

'Meeting Charlotte the way I did was as if Fate was playing into my hands. As if I was meant to come.' She stared out at the blackness beyond the window. 'And I've been so happy here. I've grown really fond of Charlotte. She often says we're more like sisters – little does she know! And I've come to really enjoy my life here.' Her voice dropped to a whisper. 'It's like living in a fairy tale compared with what I'd always been used to, picking mine day after day and living in the shadow of that stinking Copperas House.' She sniffed. 'And now the worst possible thing has happened, something I'd never, ever considered and I don't know what to do. I can't stay here because I could never tell Sebastian why I can't marry him. And I can't go back to Copperas Lane. Apart from the fact that Aunt Rose hates me I couldn't bear to go back there. I've practically no money ...' Her voice tailed off.

He was silent for several minutes. Then he said, 'Are

you quite sure there's no mistake and that James Grainger is your father?'

'Oh, yes. Uncle Sam would never have said it if he wasn't quite certain his sister Mary had been telling him the truth when she told him her story. It's not something he would have passed on to me if he had been in the slightest doubt.'

He frowned. 'Please don't think I'm questioning your word, but I find it strange that with this knowledge your uncle continued to work at the Copperas House,' he said slowly. 'Working for the man responsible for his sister's death.'

'That's exactly what I said to Uncle Sam,' she replied. 'But, as he pointed out to me, where could he have gone if he'd left? As boilerman the cottage went with the job; he simply couldn't afford to lose the roof over his head, especially with a wife and two children to care for. In any case, he'd never told Aunt Rose the full story, so she wouldn't have understood. No, he had no choice but to stay, much as he hated the idea.'

Mark nodded. 'Ah, yes, put like that I can understand his feelings.'

'So, there you are, Mark,' she said wearily. 'Now you know why I can't eat and can't sleep. I can't stay here but I've nowhere else to go. In any case, what reason for leaving could I give Charlotte, when she knows how happy I am? I turn it over and over in my mind but I still don't know what to do.' She put her elbows on the table and rested her head in her hands, the picture of dejection.

He was silent for such a long time that she began to think he had slipped quietly away, leaving her to deal with the problem as best she might. She didn't blame him. After all, what advice could he offer?

'I think you should tell Uncle James the truth and let him deal with Sebastian.' The fact that he had spoken surprised her almost as much as the words he uttered and her head shot up.

233

'I couldn't possibly do that!' she said, staring at him, aghast.

'Why not?'

'He'd sack me on the spot!'

He smiled. 'On what grounds? Because you're claiming he's your natural father? Come now, Mollie, even if he knows it's true he's hardly going to admit it, is he? After all, how would he face Aunt Beatrice with the news that the result of his relationship with a servant had turned up after twenty-odd years?' He shook his head and went on thoughtfully, 'No, the worst thing he might accuse you of is lying and even then he would have to explain to all and sundry what he's accusing you of lying about. Think of the complications *that* might bring. Especially as you're telling the truth.'

'You believe me, then.'

'Oh, yes, Mollie. I believe you. I know Sam Barnes well enough to know he's one of the most honest men I have ever met. He won't have told you something he didn't believe to be true.'

Her shoulders sagged. 'Thank God for that.'

He got to his feet and for a brief moment rested his hand on her shoulder. 'So you'll speak to Uncle James?'

'I'll think about it.' Her face clouded. 'I would hate to do anything that would hurt Mrs Grainger. And if she found out ...'

'I think you're safe enough there. Don't you think Uncle James feels the same? Don't worry, I'm sure he'll think of some way to discourage Sebastian's ...'

'Infatuation.'

'I rather think it might be something a bit more than that, Mollie,' he said gently. 'Nevertheless, I'm sure he'll manage to put a stop to any idea Seb has of marrying you without revealing the real reason for his objection.'

'Perhaps I should just go away,' she said with a sigh. 'It would be far less complicated.'

'Where would you go?'

234

She sighed again. 'I really don't know.'

'Of course, you could always ...'

She looked up. 'Yes?'

He turned away before she could see the expression in his eyes. 'Nothing.' His voice became businesslike. 'I think you must talk to Uncle James.'

Over the next weeks Mollie's feelings see-sawed as she considered Mark's advice. When she got up in the morning she was sure that he was right and that the only thing to do was to reveal her identity and leave the rest to James. But by the evening, as the family gathered round the meal table, with James at the head, looking stern and unyielding, she couldn't imagine ever bringing herself to get as far as knocking at his study door, let alone confessing that she was his natural daughter. And watching Beatrice at the other end of the table, her kind face open and vulnerable, she knew she could never do anything that might risk the harmony of the family she had grown so fond of.

But Sebastian was becoming more and more persistent. Even Charlotte began to remark on his attentions.

'Why do you want to come and look for fossils with us this afternoon, Seb?' she asked, as he lounged in the armchair beside the fire that had been lit in her room against the late summer's chill. 'I know it's a bright day, but it's quite chilly; not at all the kind of day that would normally tempt you down to the beach. In any case, shouldn't you be at work? As Father often says, businesses don't run themselves. Not that he lets copperas get in the way of his pleasures, I've noticed.'

Sebastian stretched his feet out to the blaze. 'I have to ride in to Colchester tomorrow to see a man about the mordant for his dye works, which will take me the whole day. Therefore I think I can claim an hour or two for myself today. And what better way to spend it than with you two charming ladies, learning about some of the strange things that can be dug out of the cliff?' He looked from Charlotte, sitting at her dressing table, to Mollie, who was folding clothes and putting them in the press, hoping for their approval.

'I don't understand. Why are you suddenly so interested?' Charlotte turned and gave him a quizzical look. 'You've never shown the slightest curiosity in my collection before.'

'Well, I've thought about it and it occurs to me to wonder how some of the odd things you collect actually find their way into the cliff.' He frowned. 'Didn't you say you found teeth halfway up? I mean to say, what animal would shed its teeth halfway up a cliff!'

'Oh, listen to this, Mollie. My brother is using his brain!' Charlotte mocked. 'Keep quite still, Sebastian, and Mollie will fetch you a wet cloth to cool your brow.'

'Don't be ridiculous.' Sebastian stood up immediately, offended. 'However, I'm sure I don't want to impose my company on you if it isn't wanted.' He turned to Mollie. 'Since my sister doesn't want my company perhaps you'll be willing to take a walk with me, Mollie,' he said, smiling at her.

She finished what she was doing and closed the press. 'Charlotte has already decided what she would like us to do today,' she said quietly.

'Then perhaps some other time?'

'No, I don't think so.' She went out quietly and closed the door. It was really becoming too much. Not only did Sebastian constantly try to attract her attention at the meal table, now he was seeking her out in Charlotte's room. Somehow she would have to put a stop to it, but the easiest way, simply to walk out of Cliff House and never come back, was also the most difficult even to contemplate. Miserably, she went back to her own room and busied herself doing unnecessary things until she was sure Sebastian would have gone, then she picked up a jacket and matching bonnet and went back to Charlotte.

'Aren't you ready?' she asked, fastening her bonnet

236

under her chin. 'The sun will be gone if we don't go soon.'

Charlotte looked up from the chair Sebastian had been sitting in less than half an hour ago. She looked like the cat that had stolen the cream. 'Sebastian has told me, Mollie,' she said happily.

Mollie frowned. 'Told you what?'

'Oh, don't be coy! He's told me he's asked you to marry him.' Her smile broadened into a beam. 'I think it's wonderful, Mollie. I'm so glad.' She got to her feet and went over to Mollie and gave her a hug. 'We'll be proper sisters when you're married. Oh, won't that be wonderful?'

Gently, Mollie broke away from Charlotte. 'No, Charlotte, it won't be wonderful because I'm not going to marry Sebastian,' she said firmly.

Charlotte sat down again with a bump. 'You're not going to marry him? But why not? It would be absolutely perfect if you two were wed.' Her face was a picture of incredulity. 'Don't you like him?'

'I like him well enough,' Mollie said with a shrug. 'But not enough to want to marry him.'

'Mollie, this is a chance in a lifetime for you,' Charlotte said sternly. 'Don't you realise? Don't you remember where you've come from?'

'Oh, I never forget where I've come from, Charlotte,' Mollie said, keeping her voice neutral. 'And I never forget your kindness in rescuing me and turning me into somebody that I would never have been if it hadn't been for you.'

Charlotte jumped up and put her arms round Mollie again. 'Oh, dear Mollie, I'm sorry. I shouldn't have said that. I never meant to hurt you.'

'You haven't hurt me,' Mollie lied. 'Only reminded me of something I hadn't forgotten.'

'I have hurt you.' Charlotte's eyes filled with tears. 'It's just that I was so happy to think you were going to marry Sebastian and now you tell me you're not.' She took Mollie's hands, which were icy cold, and gave them a little

237

shake. 'Why won't you marry him, Mollie? I'm sure you would grow to love him, in time. A lot of girls don't love their husbands when they marry but they grow fond of them.'

'I can't marry Sebastian, Charlotte. That's all I have to say. I'm sorry to disappoint you but I could never, ever marry him.' Mollie detached herself from Charlotte's hold and went over to the window.

'I can't see why not,' Charlotte said with a flounce.

'Then you must take my word for it.' Mollie turned to look at her. 'And if you love me you won't speak of it again.'

'Have you told Sebastian you won't marry him?'

'Yes. But it's quite obvious he didn't listen or he would never have told you he had proposed.'

'So what will you do?'

Mollie sat down and rubbed her hand across her brow. 'If he persists I suppose I shall have no choice but to leave here,' she said sadly.

'Oh, no. You can't do that. I won't let you,' Charlotte went over and gave her a shake. She crouched down beside Mollie. 'Would it be so terrible to marry my brother?' she asked gently.

Mollie looked down at her, her face bleak. 'Worse than you could ever imagine,' she said.

'That's an awful thing to say!'

'I mean no disrespect to Sebastian, I assure you.'

Charlotte straightened up, frowning. 'I really don't understand you, Mollie.'

'Then shall we forget this conversation and go down to the beach? If we leave it much longer the tide will be too high.'

They went down to the beach and poked about at the bottom of the cliff in a desultory manner for half an hour and then went back to the house. They didn't speak of Sebastian again but his shadow seemed to hang between them, together with the unanswered question of his rejected

238

proposal, whatever they did, whatever they spoke of. There was a rift opening up between them and Mollie was powerless to do the one thing that would close it.

Mark managed to speak to her just before dinner that night.

'Have you spoken to Uncle James yet, Mollie?' he whispered.

She shook her head. 'There hasn't been an opportunity,' she said lamely.

He gave her arm a little shake. 'You *must*. You can't keep putting it off.'

'I know.'

The next day Sebastian rode into Colchester. James went out hunting in the morning and came back flushed with success. Not only had he been instrumental in running the fox to ground but he had won a sizable wager into the bargain. He ordered bread and cheese and ale to be brought to his study and announced that he was not to be disturbed.

Mollie was on tenterhooks. The house was quiet, Charlotte was having her rest and Beatrice was out visiting friends. Now, when James was in a genial mood, would be the perfect time to confront him.

She smoothed her hair and adjusted her cap, made sure the lace at her wrists and neck was crisp and that her dress was neat, then, with a last glance in the long mirror in her room that satisfied her that she looked far more composed than she felt she went downstairs to confront James in his study.

She could hear the voices before she reached the foot of the stairs; then Arthur brushed past her, followed by James himself. As she watched, her hand on the newel post, Arthur flung open the front door and two men came in carrying between them a gate that had been taken off its hinges. Lying on the gate and looking as pale as death was Sebastian.

'Out of the way, girl,' James shouted, indicating to the men to carry their burden straight upstairs.

'Fetch hot water. And send Perkins for the doctor,' Arthur ordered over his shoulder as he brushed past her and followed his master up the stairs. 'Tell him Mr Sebastian has been thrown from his horse.'

Shocked, Mollie hurried along to the kitchen to deliver her message. Perkins was there, enjoying a quiet mug of tea, which he gulped down, burning his throat, as he listened to what little she could tell him of the accident.

'I hope his back's not broke,' Cook said gloomily. 'You say they brought 'im 'ome on a gate? What did 'e look like?'

'He was very pale and his eyes were closed. That's all I can tell you,' Mollie said, careful not to embroider her story.

''E could be dead,' Kitty said, her eyes like saucers.

'Don't speckalate,' Cook said sternly. 'Jest you make haste and get upstairs with that hot water. An' you be quick an' get along to fetch the doctor, Alf.'

'I'm jest orf,' Perkins said, getting to his feet and dabbing at his moustache with a large red handkerchief.

'Do you think we should fetch the mistress? She's gone to see her friend Mrs Bristowe,' Ellis said anxiously to nobody in particular.

'Best wait an' see what the damage is,' Cook advised. 'Don't need to trouble her unnecessary.'

'He looked quite bad,' Mollie said. 'I think he was unconscious.'

Ellis got to her feet. 'I think I'd better send Sid with a message. She'd never forgive me if ... God forbid ... if, well, anything happened.'

Mollie went slowly back upstairs. If anything happened ... if Sebastian died, were the words Ellis couldn't bring herself to utter. Suddenly, the thought flashed though her mind, crushed even before it was properly formed, that if Sebastian died the problem of refusing his proposal would be solved.

Chapter Twenty-three

For a whole week Sebastian lay in his bed, barely conscious, with an ugly gash on his head. Doctors came and went and the household tiptoed around, voices barely above a whisper, hoping for the best but fearing the worst. But as the days wore on and he at last began to sit up and take notice of his surroundings, it became apparent that his injuries were less serious than had at first been feared. Everyone heaved a sigh of relief.

It had been a simple matter to discover what had happened, even before he was able to speak for himself. He had clearly taken a detour on his journey back from Colchester to give his hunter, Jason, a gallop. What was not clear was whether Jason had caught his foot in a rabbit hole or whether he had refused the hedge he had been put to. Either way, the horse had fallen, breaking his leg and had had to be shot where he lay. Sebastian himself had been thrown clear but he had fallen awkwardly, cracking his head on the trunk of an old, gnarled oak tree.

What only the doctor knew immediately, James and Arthur soon realised, and the farm hands that rescued him had suspected, was that at the time of the accident Sebastian was blind drunk. But of course, nobody mentioned this.

Beatrice bustled in and out of the sick room with motherly concern, making sure he had everything he could possibly need. Sometimes she would take her sewing and sit with him. This, she quickly discovered, was more of an irritation than a comfort to him so she stopped doing that and contented herself with a brief daily visit.

'He's very bad tempered,' she confided to Charlotte and Mollie as they all sat together in the parlour one rainy afternoon. 'I don't know what to do to please him.'

'Just leave him be, Mama,' Charlotte said cheerfully. 'No doubt he'll regain his good humour when one or two of his cronies decide to pay him a visit.'

'He's asked after you once or twice, Mollie,' Beatrice said, regarding her thoughtfully. 'Suggested that perhaps you might like to pay him a visit.' She frowned. 'I'm not sure that it would be a very good idea.' It was quite clear what she feared he might have in mind. 'He's not very strong yet ...'

Mollie shook her head. 'I don't think it would be at all a good idea, Mrs Grainger,' she said firmly.

'Oh, go on, Mollie.' Charlotte winked at her and gave her a nudge. 'Humour a sick man. I'm sure it would cheer him up no end.'

'Another time, perhaps.' Mollie got to her feet. 'Please excuse me, I have things to do in my room.'

She escaped, went upstairs and sat on the window seat in her room, looking out over the grey expanse of sea. She had always been fascinated to observe the changing colours and moods of the sea and how the water sometimes took on the colour of the sky. On a day like today, whilst the clouds were low and full of rain it had been flat and the colour of lead. As the rain ceased and the clouds lifted and thinned, as they were beginning to do now, the sea was lightening in colour and the grey turning to a dull, gently heaving green.

She was glad to note that it was still relatively calm following the rain, with no more than a slight swell, with a few white horses towards the horizon, because earlier in the day Sid, the gardener's boy, had sought her out and whispered with a wink, 'There'll be movement ternight, Mollie.

242

Dick sends 'is love.' Mollie had received the news keeping her expression blank, irritated that Sid quite plainly knew exactly what he was talking about – his father had obviously taken him into his confidence – so it was pointless to pretend ignorance. The only thing to do was to thank him with a brief nod and send her love in return. That way, Richard would know she had received the message safely. Her dilemma now was whether or not to tell Charlotte what was in the offing. The two girls had 'helped' with two more landings since Charlotte had first revealed the cellar in the shrubbery and everything had gone smoothly both times, but Charlotte was becoming reckless, her excitement overruling her caution and Mollie was fearful that their luck wouldn't hold.

She rested her head against the cold window pane. Sometimes, carrying the burden of her complicity in Richard's unlawful exercises, plus the ever-present worry of Sebastian's proposal, she felt the weight of the world rested on her shoulders.

Charlotte came into the room without knocking and went over to the window seat, where she sat down with a flounce of skirts. 'It's no use, you'll have to marry Seb,' she said, grinning at Mollie. 'I've just looked in on him. He's pining. Obviously, he's dying of love for you.'

'Don't be stupid.' Mollie's voice was unusually sharp. 'Of course he isn't pining. He'll be as right as rain in a couple of days. The tumble he took from his horse shook him up, that's all. Has anyone told him Jason had to be shot?'

'Yes. I think Papa's told him. He was in there with him for quite a long time yesterday.'

'Well, he's pining for his horse, then.' Mollie turned away from her and stared out of the window. 'The sea's quite calm,' she said, changing the subject.

Charlotte followed her gaze. 'A calm sea, not too much moon. A good night for a drop,' she remarked. She glanced at Mollie. 'Have you had a message?'

243

Mollie didn't reply but remained staring out over the sea.

'Ah. You have. You have had a message. You've got to put the lantern up, haven't you.' Excitedly, Charlotte caught her arm.

Mollie shook her off. 'Yes, I have. Now, be quiet, will you. This isn't a game.'

'I know that,' Charlotte said crossly. 'Why do you think I'm so anxious to help Richard stow the stuff safely? He said last time we're getting so proficient that the job was done in half the time because we lent a hand.'

'It took you long enough to lock the cellar when we'd finished.' It was Mollie's turn to be cross now. 'I'd been up to the attic and put out the light before you came back in.'

'It doesn't do for us to come back in together,' Charlotte said and Mollie noticed the faint pink glow in her cheeks.

'Charlotte, you're not . . . ' she began, remembering her escapades with Captain Pilkington..

'Not what?' Her face was the picture of innocence. 'I only stay to help Richard cover our tracks and make sure the door is properly bolted and locked. Nothing more than that. What time will it be tonight?'

Mollie sighed. It was no use trying to discourage Charlotte so she didn't try. She did swift calculations in her head. 'Tide's at two. About midnight, I reckon.'

'Good. I'll be ready.' She looked Mollie up and down. 'What about you? Are you coming? You don't have to if you don't want to.'

Mollie nodded. 'Of course I shall come. I can't let you go without me,' she said, but there was reluctance in her voice.

In the event the drop went very smoothly. Joe Trayler carried the goods to the foot of the cliff whilst his father looked after the dinghy, then Richard and Andy carried them up the steps to where the two girls waited to transport them to the safety of the cellar. When everything was safely ashore Joe and his father rowed back to their smack and sailed round to Mersea island, where they would land their catch the next morning and no questions asked.

After they had gone Richard and Andy sat in the cellar with the two girls, surrounded by the night's haul, with a warming tot of contraband rum in mugs that Charlotte had thoughtfully provided.

Mollie put her mug back on the shelf. The rum had sent a warm glow right down to the tips of her toes and fingers and given her a sense of calm and well-being. It occurred to her that she could have done with the rum before, rather than after the night's activities. She knew now the meaning of the words 'Dutch courage'.

'We should go back now, Charlotte,' she urged. 'There's nothing more we can do here.'

'Thass right. You go an' get your beauty sleep, both of you. We shall need you to keep a lookout next week some-time,' Richard said.

'Oh, good. When?' Mollie could see Charlotte's eyes sparkling even in the dim light of the candle stuck on top of a box.

'Thass jest it. We ain't sure. Thass why we've got to keep a lookout,' Andy said.

'So you won't need the lamp put in the window,' Mollie said, relieved.

'No. I don't reckon so,' Richard said, scratching his stubbly beard. 'The stuff's comin' in on a different boat next time. Joe's dad reckons he's gettin' a bit long in the tooth for the job so we've had to find another way to bring it over an' we ain't got it up an' runnin' properly yet. That ain't to say we won't need the light but we ain't sure. I'll hev to let you know when we've got it sorted out.' He grinned. 'Thass the trouble with these Dutchmen, they don't speak the King's English.'

'We'll wait to hear from you, then,' Charlotte said, excitedly. She caught Richard's arm. 'You will involve us, won't you, Dick?'

245

He put his hand over hers, a gesture not lost on Mollie. 'Oh, yes, we shall involve you, darlin', never fear. An' if you get a wheeze about where the Ridin' Officer is patrollin' you best let us know. He's gettin' a bit slippy, these days. Never know where he's gonna turn up next.'

'Well, you'd better make sure you know where he is or we'll all end up in gaol,' Charlotte said with a laugh, not taking him seriously.

'Oh, come on. I'm tired. We've been here long enough tonight,' Mollie said irritably.

'You go on. I'll be along in a minute. Dick and I have got to cover our tracks.' Charlotte gave her a push.

Mollie was too tired to argue. She stumbled up the cellar steps and crept back to her bed. Her last thought as she gratefully cuddled the hot brick she had had the foresight to place there earlier was that Charlotte was old enough to look after herself.

'I nearly got caught last night,' Charlotte said gleefully when Mollie took in her chocolate the next morning. 'I was just coming up the stairs when Arthur came out of Seb's room.'

'What did you do?' Mollie turned away and drew back the curtains. She was constantly annoyed at the way Charlotte treated Richard's dangerous smuggling activities as no more than an exciting adventure. She wouldn't think it was so funny if they got caught. And neither would her parents.

'I slipped behind the curtain in the alcove at the top of the stairs. I'm sure he didn't see me because the only light was from his candle and anyway he's as blind as a bat without his spectacles.' She laughed delightedly. 'He went down the stairs *swearing,* Mollie. Something about so-and-so people getting him up in the middle of the so-and-so night to fetch hot so-and-so toddies. And he looked so funny in his nightcap and dressing gown and without his spectacles. I'm sure I shall never be able to keep a straight face when he's all dignified in his smart breeches and waistcoat and stiff collar.'

'Don't be so unkind,' Mollie snapped.

'Well, don't be so starchy, then,' Charlotte snapped back. 'I don't know what's the matter with you, Mollie. You go around with a face as long as a wet week all the time, these days. You're just no fun any longer.'

'Then perhaps you'd rather find somebody else to run around after you.' Mollie threw the dress she had just taken out of the press down on to the bed and went to the door.

Charlotte scrambled out of bed and ran over to her. 'Oh, Mollie, I didn't mean it,' she cried, flinging her arms round her. 'Of course I don't want anybody else. I want you.' She held her at arm's length. 'It's just that ... ' She peered at her closely. 'Are you ill, Mollie? Is there something you aren't telling me?' She led her over to the window seat. 'You're my best friend, you know. I've never forgotten what you did for me over that dreadful business with that soldier ... what was his name? Captain Pilkington – I can't remember his Christian name – Arnold! That's right. Oh, I was a stupid little goose, wasn't I, to be so taken in by him, and you were so sensible. God knows what I'd have done without you. Now, if only you'll tell me what's troubling you I'm sure I can help.'

Mollie chewed her lip, near to tears. It would be so comforting to lay her head on Charlotte's shoulder and reveal her true identity. But something – perhaps it was Charlotte's overexuberant personality, her child-like conviction that everything would come right if that was what she wanted – held her back. It was salutary that she had had difficulty in even remembering the name of the man who had seduced her and nearly ruined her life; what would have happened if Mollie hadn't come to the rescue didn't bear thinking about.

She gave a sigh. 'It worries me very much that you seem to regard what we do to help Richard as a game,' she said slowly. 'Have you considered, *really* considered, what

247

would happen if we were caught by the Revenue men?'

'We won't get caught, Mollie.' Charlotte said, smiling encouragingly. 'Just think about it. How long has Richard been doing this? Years and years. And he's never been caught yet. You should have confidence in your cousin, Mollie. He knows what he's doing.' She shrugged. 'Anyway, look at the coastline. All those creeks and inlets and wide expanses of marshland are a gift to owlers. Who would think, when it's so easy to land goods almost anywhere on remote, flat, marshland, where they can be easily carried away, that anyone would be fool enough to bring them in on our beach, where everything has got to be hauled twenty or thirty feet up the cliff and then somehow taken through the town. It wouldn't make sense, would it? That's why the Riding Officers concentrate on the marshes and don't come this way.'

'Dick's luck won't hold for ever,' Mollie warned. She stared out of the window. 'I hate him being an owler, I always have,' she said vehemently. 'I'm so afraid.' She turned bleak eyes on Charlotte. 'Ever since I've known about it I've had sleepless nights wondering which I consider the worst, him being put in prison, or sent to the gallows, or being transported to Australia so we never see him again. Which would you prefer?'

Charlotte got up and began to walk about the room. 'You shouldn't talk like that, Mollie. You shouldn't even think those thoughts.'

'And what about if we were caught, you and me? The gallows? Transportation? Prison?'

'Oh, don't! Don't!' Charlotte put her hands over her ears. 'I don't want to hear any more.' She swung round. 'I'll ask Dick not to take any more risks. He'll listen to me, I'm sure he will.' She smiled winningly at Mollie. 'There. Does that please you?'

Mollie managed a wan smile in return. 'You can try. And it would please me if you succeeded.'

'There, then.' Imagining she had resolved Mollie's

worries Charlotte rubbed her hands together. 'Now, what shall we do today, Mollie?' Her face fell. 'Oh, drat. I promised Seb I would go and play cribbage with him this afternoon. Never mind, you can come too, Mollie. Three people can play cribbage, can't they?'

'I don't know. I've never played cribbage. In any case, I don't feel like cards. I think I'll go for a walk while you're with him. The fresh air will do me good.'

'Have you got a headache?' Charlotte was immediately concerned.

'Yes, I have. Perhaps the fresh air will help to clear it.'

'You see? I knew you weren't feeling well.' Charlotte put her arms round her. 'Dear Mollie. You see, we're so close I know when you're not well even when you try to keep it from me. Very well, you take a walk whilst I play cribbage with my bad-tempered brother. At least I shan't have to put up with his stuffy sick room – he's coming down to the parlour.'

'He's better, then?' Mollie asked.

'Oh, yes. He's perfectly all right. Just likes to have people running around and making a fuss of him.' Charlotte put her head on one side. 'I'm sure he'll improve enormously when he sees you, Mollie.'

'Don't say that!' Mollie said, through gritted teeth.

Charlotte frowned. 'What is it, Mollie? Why are you so set against Sebastian? He really loves you, you know. I'll grant you he's a bit wild at times but I'm sure he'll settle down when you're married.'

'We're not going to be married, Charlotte,' Mollie said wearily. 'I've told you that a thousand times.'

'Why do you find him so repulsive?'

'I don't find him repulsive. I know he'll make somebody a good husband. But it won't – it can't be me.'

'Why not, for goodness sake? Surely ...' Charlotte bit her lip. Now was not the time to remind her yet again where she had come from.

'Because ...' Mollie hesitated. It would be so comfort-

249

ing to be able to tell the truth. But then the consequences of revealing that truth flashed through her mind. It would not only split the family she had come to love but it would mean she would have to leave Cliff House. 'Because I can't,' she said lamely.

Charlotte studied her, frowning. 'I think there's something you're not telling me, Mollie.' A look of alarm crossed her face. 'Is it something you know about Seb? Something he hasn't told us? Oh, Mollie, he hasn't got some village girl into trouble and married her to keep her family quiet so you can't marry him because it would be bigamy?'

Mollie pealed with laughter, the tension broken. 'Oh, Charley, you've been reading too many penny romances. No, I assure you it's nothing like that.' She took Charlotte's hand. 'Can't you just accept that it would be quite wrong for me to marry your brother, dear?'

'Don't you love him, just a little bit?'

'I like him very much. But I shall never marry him.'

'Is there somebody else, Mollie? Are you in love with somebody else?' Charlotte persisted. 'Someone I don't even know?'

Mollie smiled, a rather sad smile. How could she admit to Charlotte that she was more than half in love with the man Charlotte herself was destined to marry? The man whose devotion Charlotte took for granted and treated so casually.

'No, Charlotte,' she replied. 'I don't have some secret life, if that's what you're thinking. I'm not in love with somebody you don't even know.' Her tone became business-like. 'Now, for goodness sake, get dressed. Half the morning's gone already and look at you, you're still in your nightgown.'

Chapter Twenty-four

It was not a particularly pleasant afternoon for a walk. A chill breeze was blowing off the sea, sending clouds scudding across the sky and there was a hint of rain in the air. But Mollie had begun to feel stifled in the house; she needed to let the air fan her cheeks and ruffle her hair. But more than anything, she needed to be by herself. Grateful for the pelisse she had only put on as an afterthought, even though the summer was not yet finished, she set off for the naze.

To her right the sea was a dirty brown as it crashed over the shallows and churned up the sandy, muddy bottom. There was still an hour or so to go before full tide so the waves were not yet lashing the cliff face; instead they flung a mess of frothy detritus, seaweed, shingle, lumps of wood, bits of old fishing nets, on to the beach, most of which was dragged back by the undertow, only to be flung again, a little higher up on the next wave.

There would be good pickings after this tide, Mollie thought, gazing down at the restless water; there would be plenty of stones, as some called them, washed up from the sea bed or out of the cliff. A couple more hours and the women would all be out there, bent double over their baskets, anxious to pick their share of copperas before the threatening rain fell in earnest and soaked them to the skin. She turned and continued on her way, offering up a quick prayer of thankfulness that she no longer had to pick mine every day. She realised with surprise that it was not much more than two years since she had been part of that life, out with her basket every tide. It seemed like a lifetime.

She walked on towards the tall, landmark tower. It was not used so much now as it was no longer thought necessary for the soldiers to keep a constant watch, waiting for an invasion by the French; an invasion that was considered less and less likely. The windows were barred and shuttered but there still remained the bench by the door where the soldiers used to sit in the sun, polishing their boots or – more often – playing cards. Mollie went over and sat down, leaning her back against the warm bricks; turning her face to the sun she closed her eyes.

It was just what she needed, quiet and peaceful, with only the sounds of the seagulls screaming over the water and the rhythmic thrashing of the waves on the shore, a sound she had always found to be calming, ever since the days when Richard used to take her to the beach as a small child to pick mine with him and she had been proud to have her own little basket to fill. She sighed. Why was it that her mind kept going back to the days when she picked mine on the beach? Was it fear that those days were about to return?

She plucked at a stray thread on her pelisse, a part of her mind registering that it needed a stitch, trying to find a way out of the terrible dilemma she was in without going back to her old life, a life in which she would be completely on her own, because Aunt Rose would never have her back, even if she wanted to return to Copperas Lane, which she most emphatically did not.

She could always marry Sebastian, of course, the thought came to her unbidden. If she didn't speak of it nobody would ever know their true relationship. Except Uncle Sam, who she loved best in the world and could never bring herself to deceive, and Mark, who she could so easily love just as much. And she would know. She would know she was committing a mortal sin. And for a man she didn't even like much. No, whatever the consequences, she couldn't ever agree to marry Sebastian.

The only alternative was to marry Joe Trayler. He was a good man, and would be glad to marry her. She had no doubt he would make her a home as comfortable as his means allowed. But would it be fair to him? She forced herself to face the fact that living at Cliff House had made her ambitious for better things; a life above her proper station. Yet was this such a bad thing, she asked herself desperately? Was it so terrible to want a better life?

The tide had turned before she got up from the bench, stiff and cold, and began to make her way back to Cliff House. She was no nearer a solution to her problem than before.

The house was warm and welcoming, the carpets thick, the lamps bright, as if to taunt her, 'Make the most of it, you won't be here much longer.'

She took her boots off in the boot room and then went up to her room, the spacious, comfortable room she had grown to feel so at home in. She sat on the window seat, gazing out at the sea, quite content with her own company. She glanced at the little clock on the mantelpiece; she had been away too long, Charlotte would be wondering where she was. She went over to the mirror and gave her hair a quick flick with the comb to tidy it and went to report to her. On her way downstairs again, the smooth feel of the banister under her hand, she met Mark on his way up. Her heart gave its customary leap at the sight of him.

'You're home early tonight,' she said in surprise.

He nodded. 'I've brought the books home with me.' He smiled. 'It's quieter here. And more comfortable.'

'I can believe that. Less smelly, too.' She said, smiling back at him. She made to carry on down the stairs, then stopped and turned back. 'Have you seen Uncle Sam lately? Is he well? I don't see very much of him these days. I miss him.'

'No, I know. He misses you, too.' He held her gaze. 'He sends you his love,' he said quietly.

'Will you give him mine in return?' she said, equally quietly.

'I will.' He hesitated and for a split second Mollie had the wild feeling that they hadn't been talking about Uncle Sam at all. Then he said, his voice quite matter-of-fact, 'Have you spoken to Uncle James yet, Mollie?'

She shook her head. 'No, I haven't.'

'You must, you know,' he said urgently.

'I know. I was going to. In fact, I was on my way to see him just as they brought Sebastian home after his accident ...' she spread her hands. 'I'm afraid I haven't found the courage since.'

'But you must do this, Mollie. You know that, don't you.' He gave her arm a little shake. 'You can't allow Sebastian to go on thinking ...'

She nodded. 'Yes. I know,' she interrupted, unwilling to let him say the words. She turned away. 'It's just that ... well, everything will change. I shall have to ...' She bit her lip. 'Everything will change. And I don't want it to,' she added miserably.

'I understand,' he said, taking her hand and giving it a squeeze.

She pulled it away and hurried on down the stairs lest he should see that she was on the verge of tears. She knew that it was only pity that prompted him to be kind to her, but pity was the last thing she wanted from him.

She reached the parlour door and took a deep breath before she opened it, ready to smile and greet Charlotte and Sebastian and ask after their cribbage afternoon. But, to her consternation Charlotte was not there, the cribbage board had been put away and Sebastian was alone.

'Oh, I'm sorry. I was looking for Charlotte. I thought she would be here,' she said, preparing to leave again.

'No, don't go, Mollie.' He held out his hand, smiling. 'It's been such a long time and I've been longing to see

254

you. Come and sit down.' He patted the settee beside him.

She ignored his invitation and sat on the edge of a chair opposite. 'You're looking much better,' she said, for want of something to say. In fact, he looked very pale and there was a jagged scar on his temple.

He gave a quirky smile. 'I don't know how you can say that, since you didn't visit me when I was sick,' he said. 'I hoped you would, Mollie. I was longing to see you. And now you're here. Why won't you come and sit by my side?'

'I'm quite comfortable here, thank you,' she said primly.

'It's all right, Mollie. You can relax,' he said and she sensed the suppressed excitement in his tone. 'I've spoken to my father and he's quite willing for us to marry.' He got up from his seat and went over to her and pulled her to her feet. 'You see? All your worries were for nothing. We needn't hide our love any longer. We can announce our engagement right away.'

He bent to kiss her but she twisted away. 'No!' she said, shielding her mouth with the back of her hand. 'I told you I couldn't – wouldn't marry you, Sebastian.'

He took a step back, shocked at her vehemence. 'But I thought it was because you were afraid my parents would object.'

She shook her head. 'I never said that.'

'I know. But that was the reason.' His eyes searched her face. 'Wasn't it?'

She shook her head. 'No, it wasn't. I told you, I don't love you ... in that way,' she said, not meeting his eyes.

He moved to take her in his arms again. 'I've told you, darling, I have enough love for both of us. You'll learn to love me in time, Mollie. I know you will.'

She shook her head again. 'It isn't possible,' she said.

'But why? I don't understand you. Why isn't it possible?' he frowned.

She went to the door. 'I must speak to your father,' she said, a hint of desperation in her voice. 'Is he at home?'

255

He nodded. 'In his study, I think.' He was too surprised at her change of tone to argue further.

James's study was a somewhat sombre room which overlooked the garden. The furniture was heavy and dark, and there were thick velvet curtains at the window that blocked out a good deal of the light. A permanent, all-pervading smell of stale tobacco smoke clung to furniture and hangings alike. As Sebastian had predicted, he was there now. He was sitting at his desk, which was strewn with papers of no importance at all, staring at nothing in particular and had hardly moved, except to light another cigar, for almost an hour. He was thinking about his son and the woman he insisted he wanted to marry. Mollie was a comely enough wench; in truth, he had fancied her himself when she first sat at his table and to his shame had tried several times to get into her room. But then he had realised his folly – Beatrice wouldn't stand for yet another servant being dismissed in disgrace; it had already happened two or three times in the past – so he had thanked God nobody knew and found himself a willing little widow in Kirby. As he had long ago impressed upon his son, it was always advisable to play away from home.

He dragged his mind back to the question in hand. The girl, Mollie. He chewed on his cigar thoughtfully; it was true she was only of common stock from Copperas Lane, indeed, hadn't she spent half her life picking mine with the other poor women? A rough, swearing, blaspheming rabble if ever there was one, he imagined. Yet there was no sign of this in her bearing; she was well spoken and quiet and her table manners were impeccable. He shifted uncomfortably in his chair as he recalled the number of times his own careless behaviour at table had caused a raised eyebrow from his wife.

But what of his business acquaintances? His friends? Not that he had many close friends. His shooting, hunting and gambling cronies? Would he be a laughing stock among them when they heard that he had agreed to his

256

son marrying his daughter's maid? Well, companion, as Charlotte insisted she be known these days. He scratched his whiskers. Sebastian had hinted that if he didn't get his way over this he would enlist in the Army. That was what had decided the matter because it would surely break his mother's heart if her only son went to war. And the war would hot up again, there was no doubt about that. In fact, he hoped it wouldn't be too long in coming because they needed the revenue from the gunpowder produced at the Copperas House. If he was honest his gambling debts were getting a bit out of hand. Throwing good money after bad in order to recoup some of his losses simply hadn't worked.

He cut another cigar and lit it. There was always something to worry about.

There was a knock at the door.

'Come in!' he called impatiently, glowering at the door. He didn't like being disturbed in his study.

He was still glowering as Mollie slipped inside and closed the door behind her. Seeing his thunderous expression it took all her courage not to turn and run, but she took a deep breath to steady herself and with a lift of her chin said quietly, 'I had to come and see you Mr Grainger because I have something of the utmost importance to say.'

'Hmph,' he said unhelpfully.

'It concerns the fact that Sebastian wishes to marry me.'

He leaned his elbows on the desk. 'Has he got you in the family way? Because if he has I'm willing to pay you handsomely to ...'

'No! I am not expecting his child!' Her eyes blazed with fury. 'And I might remind you that it is Sebastian who wishes to marry me, not the other way round.'

He sat back in his chair again and picked his teeth. 'All right, then. I've told him I won't raise any objections. What more do you want?'

'I want nothing except to tell you that it cannot be. We cannot be married.' She found she was twisting the lace apron she was wearing round her hands and she forced herself to stop and to smooth it down over her gown.

'I don't see why not. You'll never get a better offer, a woman in your position.' To his surprise he found he was affronted at her rejection of his son.

She made a dismissive gesture with her hand. 'Be that as it may. We still cannot be married.'

'Oh, and why not, may I ask?'

'Because I am his half-sister. We share the same father.' Mollie watched as James's expression turned from incredulity to fury.

He got to his feet so abruptly that his chair toppled over backwards. 'How dare you come in here and make such an accusation!' he shouted, his face turning a dull purple. 'How dare you claim to be my ... my ...'

'Your daughter,' Mollie said quietly. 'My mother was Mary Barnes, maid to your wife some twenty years or so ago. She was dismissed for becoming pregnant. By you. A stable lad was accused and dismissed, too, although of course he had nothing to do with it.'

'It's a lie. A cock and bull ...' He checked himself at the unfortunate phrase. 'A pack of lies. I suppose your mother cooked up the yarn.'

'My mother died soon after I was born,' Mollie said quietly. 'My birth killed her.'

'Hmph. Well, these things happen.' He glared at her. 'It had nothing to do with me.'

'I think it did, Mr Grainger. My mother told her brother, my Uncle Sam, what happened to her, how you went to her room, night after night and took advantage of her until she became pregnant, then you had her thrown out. When she died Uncle Sam gave me a home. He told me my history when I was old enough to understand and I believe him, just as he believed his sister.'

'You're lying. I don't remember a Mary Barnes ever working here.'

'I come from a God-fearing family, Mr Grainger. We

258

think it a sin to lie,' Mollie said, keeping her voice low. 'But I can believe you didn't know my mother's name. I doubt you know the names of half the servants who have worked here.'

'Get out!'

She went to the door. 'Very well. But will you tell Sebastian that it is not possible for us to be married because we are related?'

'I shall tell him no such thing. It's all a pack of lies. But I shall tell him he would be a fool to even think of it.'

'That won't do any good, Mr Grainger. He is quite determined to make me his wife.' She came back into the room. 'But if you refuse to tell him the one thing that would dissuade him, will you be happy for him – for us – to marry and commit the sin of incest?'

He recoiled as if she had struck him. Then he recovered himself. 'I think you'd better leave this house,' he said coldly. 'I shall see to it that you are given a substantial sum of money to assist you in finding another position.'

'I don't want your money, Mr Grainger,' she said sadly. 'But I can see I have no choice but to leave, although I have been very happy here with Charlotte and I think she will miss me.' Her mouth twisted wryly. 'She often says we are more like sisters than mistress and maid but I have never told her that we are indeed ... '

'That's enough!' he barked.

She smiled. Looking at this red-faced, lying, blustering man she felt that she was the one in control of the situation. She took a deep breath. 'When I was told my mother's story, I swore that one day I would sit at my father's table,' she said, keeping her voice low. 'I didn't know how I would achieve this but I felt that if only I could do that it would in some way vindicate my mother for the harm he did her.' She lifted her head. 'I have sat at your table many times now, Mr Grainger, and I hope my mother is looking down from heaven and smiling to think I am in my rightful place, even if I am the only

259

one to know it. I shall go now. Goodbye ... father.'

She saw him wince at her last word as she went out and quietly closed the door behind her.

Chapter Twenty-five

'Why didn't you tell me yourself? Why did I have to find it out from my father?' Sebastian's face was a mask of rage as he confronted Mollie.

'You shouldn't be here, you know, you shouldn't come to my room,' Mollie said nervously as he slammed the door and stood with his back to it.

'To the devil with that! Answer me, Mollie, why didn't you tell me yourself?' He glared at her. Then his expression softened and he took a step towards her. 'Oh, Mollie, did you really think it would make any difference to the way I feel about you?'

She backed away, amazed at his attitude. 'But of course it makes a difference, Seb,' she said desperately. 'We're brother and sister, well, half-brother and sister. We have the same blood in our veins.'

He shrugged. 'Oh, come on! How can we be sure of that? Your mother could ...'

She sprang at him and for a moment he thought she would strike him. 'Don't you *dare* imply that my mother was ... was a loose woman,' she hissed, through gritted teeth.

He held his hand up to shield himself. 'I wasn't. I didn't mean ... of course I didn't mean that,' he said weakly. 'But sometimes, well, sometimes mistakes are made.' He smiled winningly. 'And if you're willing to take that risk,

Mollie, I am. I'd risk anything to make you my wife, you should know that.' He held out his hands to her. 'I'm crazy about you.'

'You don't mean that,' she said, horrified. 'You *can't* ...'

He looked slightly uncomfortable. 'Well, to tell you the truth, my father didn't seem to take your claim too seriously,' he said with a shrug. 'After all, what proof have you got? None at all. Only what your uncle – what's his name? – Sam – says your mother told him before she died.' He spread his hands. 'Well, I mean to say ... she could have told him anything, couldn't she? She'd hardly be likely to admit being dismissed after a tumble in the hay with a stable boy. In fact, father and I had a bit of a laugh over it in the end.'

Her expression had changed from incredulity to fury as he spoke. Now, she stepped forward and delivered a stinging blow to his cheek. 'How dare you! How dare you doubt my uncle! I'd take his word before I'd believe your father any day,' she spat. 'I know Uncle Sam spoke the truth. I know I'm your half-sister, God help me.' She turned away. 'And don't think I wouldn't give worlds for that not to be true,' she said bitterly.

He took a step towards her. 'So you do love me, Mollie,' he said eagerly, trying to take her in his arms. 'I knew you did. Well, we needn't let this thing stand in our way. We'll simply go away where nobody knows us. We can still make a life together. Why? What's the matter?' he asked in surprise as she twisted away from him.

'You! You're what's the matter,' she cried. 'You would be prepared to risk committing *incest* just to get your own way! My God, you disgust me!'

'Yes. I'd do anything,' he flung back at her. 'If it's true. Which I very much doubt.'

Almost beside herself with fury, she picked up a book and threw it at him, hitting him on the shoulder. 'Get out of my room.'

He picked up the book, smoothed the pages and handed

it back to her. 'Do you realise what you're asking, Mollie?' he said quietly.

'I'm not asking anything. I'm telling you to get out of my room.' She snatched the book from him. 'Now, please go.'

'If you send me away now I shall go right away,' he said, looking at her intently. 'I'm warning you, I shall go straight to the garrison in Colchester and enlist in the Army.'

She gave a weary sigh and turned away. 'It's no good you trying moral blackmail on me, Sebastian, because I really don't care where you go or what you do,' she said. 'I don't care if I never see you again. In fact, I think I'd prefer it that way.'

'You don't mean that?' He shook his head, unable to believe what he was hearing.

She lifted her chin. 'Oh, yes, Sebastian, indeed I do mean it. I'm like my mother and my uncle, I never lie.'

'You may wish you'd never said that,' he predicted, 'when it's too late.'

She walked over to the window and stood with her back to him, looking out at the sea, a green, gently heaving carpet of waves stretching as far as the eye could see. 'Goodbye, Sebastian,' she said.

She didn't move until she heard the door click and knew that he had gone, then she went over and sat down on her bed. She found that she was shaking, her teeth were chattering and she felt deathly cold. She pulled the eiderdown off the bed and wrapped herself in it, rocking back and forth. She had never loved Sebastian, never really liked him if the truth were told; he was too much like his father, but now she hated him with a viciousness she hadn't believed herself capable of.

She didn't know how long she had been sitting there when the door opened and Charlotte came in.

'I didn't want to disturb you; I thought I heard Sebastian's voice.' She looked round the room, then back at Mollie, her face a picture of shock and admiration as she nodded towards the bed. 'Oh, Mollie, you haven't . . . you and Seb haven't . . . '

Mollie gave a brief glance in the same direction. 'Indeed, we have not,' she said wearily. 'Quite the contrary, in fact.'

'What do you mean?' Charlotte asked, puzzled.

'I've told him I can't . . . that I won't marry him.'

'But I thought you were in love. I thought it was what you wanted.' Charlotte sat down with a thump beside her on the bed, the corners of her mouth turned down in disappointment. 'I was so looking forward to you marrying him so that we would be sisters, real sisters, at last. What's gone wrong, Mollie?'

'I've never said I was in love with Sebastian, Charley. If you think back you'll realise that,' Mollie said, shaking her head. 'Anyway, I could never marry him and I told him so.'

'Was he very upset?' Tears were brimming in Charlotte's blue eyes.

Mollie nodded. 'He was a bit. He threatened to go and join the Army if I wouldn't marry him.'

'That's blackmail.'

'That's what I told him.'

'Well, I wouldn't worry about it. He's not likely to do anything as melodramatic as enlisting; he's much too fond of his creature comforts.' Charlotte dashed the tears away. 'All the same, it would have been nice . . . ' Her voice trailed off, then she brightened. 'But at least it means things won't change so you'll still be here with me.'

'If I stay,' Mollie warned.

'What do you mean, if you stay? Of course you'll stay. You're my companion. You can't leave unless I dismiss you and I shall never do that because you're also my best friend.' She planted a kiss on Mollie's cheek.

Mollie smiled wanly and said nothing. How could she tell Charlotte that it would be impossible for her to stay once the truth was out, that her father had been taking his

264

pleasure with a servant when she was still a babe in arms? And that she, Mollie, was the result of his dallying? She gave herself a mental shake in an effort to put the whole episode out of her mind and got to her feet.

'Come on,' she said, 'we'd better get you dressed for dinner. What are you going to wear? Your blue silk?'

Charlotte put her head on one side. 'No, I was thinking the blue silk would look well on you, Mollie. You look as if you need cheering up a bit. I'll wear the green, I think.'

In spite of the blue silk dress Charlotte had insisted she should wear, Mollie went down to dinner that evening feeling more than a little apprehensive. She had considered asking for her meal to be sent up to her room but decided that this would be a cowardly way out. Better to face whatever there was to be faced and be done with it since this was possibly the last meal she would take at the Graingers' table.

James and Sebastian were both late into the dining room. As Mollie sat waiting for them with Beatrice, Charlotte and Mark, who for once was home early, she realised that Mark was the only one present who knew her true identity. Neither Beatrice nor Charlotte had any inkling of the bombshell that was about to be dropped on them. Or was it? If James intended to persist in his denial that he had fathered her perhaps he would decide that there was nothing more to be said on the matter. But even if nothing was said tonight things couldn't go on as they were because the truth would always lie there between them, like a dangerous black bog that always had to be carefully skirted round.

Then there was Sebastian. What of him? How could she ever face him again? She crumbled a piece of bread in her fingers, letting the conversation wash over her as she tried to think what to do.

Nobody seemed to notice.

Mark and Charlotte, who was at her most flirtatious, were having an animated conversation about dogs and Beatrice was gently worrying over the fact that the soup would spoil if the men didn't soon make an appearance when James suddenly burst in, waving a letter.

'I've just found this! The young puppy! He's done it; he's left to join the Army! Well, he won't get far. I've sent Perkins to saddle up Boxer and go after him.' He threw himself down in his chair, breathing heavily.

For several minutes there was a stunned silence in the room. Beatrice took out a lace handkerchief and dabbed her eyes, her face working. Then, with an effort she composed herself and rang the bell. When Tilda appeared, she said quietly, 'You can bring in the soup, Tilda. Oh, and will you ask Bragg to go to the stables and prevent Perkins from leaving, please? And if he's already gone then he must go after him and fetch him back.' She gave Tilda a brief nod. 'That will be all, thank you, Tilda.' She turned and looked at her husband. 'If Sebastian is bent on joining the Army I see no reason to prevent him, James. Perhaps it will make a man of him, which nothing else seems to have done so far in his life.'

James's jaw dropped. 'You can't mean that, Madam!' he roared. 'Have you forgotten Sebastian is our only son? You can't be willing to let him go ... to send him off as ... as cannon fodder.'

'If I know our son he will avoid going anywhere near any fighting,' Beatrice said with a sigh.

'That is not the *point,* Madam.' James banged his fist down on the table. 'I have a business to run. I can't allow him to go running off to God knows where ...'

'He hasn't run off to God knows where, James, don't be so melodramatic,' she snapped, her suppressed grief at her only son's departure making her sharp. 'He's either gone to the garrison at Harwich or the one at Colchester. Didn't he say in his letter? No? Well, no doubt we shall find out which in due course. Now,' as the soup tureen was placed in front of her, 'if you will say Grace we can rather belatedly begin the meal. Ah, mushroom soup,' she said in a tone of forced brightness. 'My favourite.'

The meal continued in an uncomfortable silence. From time to time James glared at his wife. 'You have no idea what you are allowing the boy to ...'

'Eat your meal and stop fretting, James,' she interrupted. 'You'll give yourself dyspepsia.'

'But he's the *heir*. I can't risk his life on some god-forsaken battlefield, woman!'

Beatrice put down her napkin on the table. 'James. Sebastian has no interest whatever in the Copperas House, you know that as well as I do. Better, in fact, since you must know how many times Mark covers up his misdeeds. I think the best thing you can do is to give him your blessing and buy him a commission. It is to be hoped that the Army will make a man of him. And that's the last I wish to hear on the subject.' She rang the bell. 'Thank you, Tilda, you can clear the dishes and bring in the pudding.' She turned to Mollie, her eyebrows raised. 'Are you not well, my dear? You haven't eaten your vegetables.'

'I'm not really hungry tonight. I've got rather a headache,' Mollie said apologetically. In truth she felt sick. Sick because she knew that it was her fault that Sebastian had carried out his threat and gone to join the Army; and sick to think that his father would know it. She couldn't bring herself to lift her head to look at him, fearful of what she might see.

But she couldn't close her ears.

'I know perfectly well what's wrong with her,' James barked. 'She's upset now because she knows it's all her fault. She was fool enough to turn down his proposal of marriage, so in a fit of pique he's gone off to enlist. Mind you, he must have been out of his mind, wanting to marry a servant in the first place. It's just not the done thing.' He glared at Mollie. 'And as for you, I don't know how you had the effrontery to refuse his offer; you'll never get a better one, a woman in your position.'

Mollie's head shot up and she found herself staring at James in astonishment. His expression was blank and she realised that as far as he was concerned the conversation in his study might never have taken place.

'Is this true, Mollie?' Beatrice asked, looking at her intently.

Mollie pulled herself together and nodded. 'Yes, I told Sebastian I couldn't marry him,' she whispered.

'Then there is nothing more to be said.' She stood up. 'Come along, Charlotte, Mollie, we'll go into the drawing room and leave the men to their port.' She walked the length of the table, pausing by her husband's chair. 'I'm sure there is no need to worry about Sebastian, James,' she remarked with a twist of her lip. 'He is too much his father's son to risk exposing himself to any danger.'

A little later, seated by the fire in the drawing room with the tea tray in front of her and the two girls seated opposite, Beatrice said thoughtfully, 'I wonder if I was a little hard on your father, Charlotte. He sees no wrong in Sebastian, you know. But, much as I hate to admit it, the boy has a weak streak. A spell in the Army will do him no harm at all.' She sighed. 'Will you pour the tea, dear? I confess I feel a little shaken by what's happened and Mollie looks positively ill.' She leaned over and patted Mollie's hand. 'Don't worry, my dear, I'm sure James didn't mean what he said. He was a little overwrought. You were quite right to turn Sebastian down if you didn't feel it was right to marry him.'

Mollie glanced at her sharply, slightly surprised at her turn of phrase, but her expression was bland, with no hint of any hidden meaning.

'I think perhaps I should go away,' she said miserably. 'I seem to have caused a great deal of trouble.' She shook her head. 'I never expected ... never wanted Sebastian to fall in love with me, really I didn't.' She covered her face with her hands and wept.

'Of course you didn't, my dear,' Beatrice said. 'And if I know my son, he'll get over it as soon as he claps eyes on another pretty face.'

'Well, anyway, you can't go away,' Charlotte said firmly. 'I can't do without you, Mollie.'

Mollie raised a tear-stained face. 'I don't think your father will allow me to stay, not after what's happened.'

'The female servants are no concern of James,' Beatrice said, equally firmly. Her face softened. 'Not, of course, that we think of you as a servant, Mollie, dear. And I agree with Charlotte, we can't do without you. You've become almost as much a member of the family as Mark. So let's have no more talk of you leaving us. In any case, where would you go?'

The same question echoed round and round in Mollie's brain for most of the night. The thought of going back to Copperas Lane filled her with dread, although she knew Uncle Sam would welcome her. But to go back to that tiny cottage, perpetually shrouded in a filthy sulphurous cloud – an atmosphere she had never even noticed until she left it – knowing that Aunt Rose didn't want her and would make her life a misery, was out of the question. Neither could she face the prospect of marriage to Joe Trayler.

In the morning she got up early and dressed, her head aching from lack of sleep, and realised that all she had established was what she didn't want to do, the things she couldn't face. It was no help in deciding her future.

As summer slipped into autumn and autumn into winter things more or less returned to normal. Mollie accompanied Charlotte to the haberdashers, helped her to trim bonnets, sorted and labelled fossils and tidied up after her. This was no mean feat, since Charlotte was the untidiest person she had ever known. They talked and giggled together, just as they had always done, tried out new hair styles and studied the latest fashion catalogues.

But Mollie knew that eventually it must all come to an end. Almost every evening, when James came into the dining room and took his place at the head of the table, he

269

would stare mournfully at the empty chair that had been Sebastian's, shaking his head, then he would turn a malevolent gaze on Mollie.

'My God, are you still here?' he would sneer, as if he couldn't believe his eyes.

'Of course Mollie is still here. This is where she lives,' his wife would answer smoothly.

'This is where my son lives, but he's not here,' James invariably replied.

'Have you heard from him?' Beatrice asked one evening.

'Yes. He's at Salisbury. He's got his commission.'

'You might have shown me his letter.'

'I didn't think you would be interested.'

'I am his mother. Of course I'm interested.'

And so it went on. Mollie could see the rift deepening between James and Beatrice and this only increased her sense of guilt.

One morning, after yet another sleepless night she got up early and splashed her face with cold water, then put on a warm cloak and went down to the beach. The tide was out and the pickers in their red cloaks were mere red splodges in the distance so she had a wide expanse of beach to herself. It was cold; so cold that the ridges of sand were rimed with frost and shards of ice lay at the water's edge. As she walked briskly along towards the naze, her hands warm in her rabbit-skin muff, the wind brought tears to her eyes and roses to her cheeks. But she hardly noticed the cold. Her thoughts were too taken up with her future. In spite of the fact that Beatrice and Charlotte both insisted she should stay at Cliff House she didn't, in all conscience, see how she could. Her secret appeared safe at the moment; she realised now that whatever happened James was never going to admit the truth; but he could and did make life difficult for her at every opportunity because she was a perpetual thorn in his flesh, reminding him of things he would prefer to forget. Things he thought had been well buried in the past. Moreover, if – when Sebastian came

270

back, having made his point, the whole thing would start all over again.

She paused and gazed out to sea. If only life were as uncomplicated as the sea. The tide came in and went out, ruled by the moon, whatever else happened. Sometimes it was calm, sometimes rough; that was like life.

'Oh, thank goodness you've slowed down. I thought I was never going to catch up with you.'

Mollie turned and saw Mark hurrying along the beach towards her.

Chapter Twenty-six

Mollie watched as Mark approached. He was warmly clad against the icy north wind in a long overcoat with an astrakhan collar and with a long black scarf wound round his neck. He was walking so fast that he had to hold on to his hat so the wind didn't blow it away.

'My goodness, you walk at quite a pace,' he remarked breathlessly as he reached her. 'I thought I should never catch you up. Are you making for somewhere in particular?'

'Only to the point and back,' she said, nodding towards it. She smiled slightly. 'Where else could I be going on this beach?'

He followed her gaze along the bleak coastline, where gulls swooped and wheeled noisily, adding to the sense of desolation. 'Um. Yes, I see what you mean. Well, would you object to me walking along with you?'

'No, of course I wouldn't. But I'm not sure that I'm very good company.'

'I'll take my chance on that.' They walked in silence for a few minutes, then he said, 'In fact, I have a message for you. I came home too late to give it to you last night.'

She stopped and turned to him anxiously. 'Oh?'

'It's no cause for worry. It's just that your uncle says it's a long time since he saw you and can you meet him on Sunday afternoon?'

272

Her face cleared. 'Yes, I'll be glad to,' she said warmly. 'Would you tell him I'll see him at the gap at two o'clock?'

He nodded. 'Yes, of course.' He gave her a sideways glance. 'I know it's not my business, Mollie, but do you intend to tell him what's been happening at Cliff House?'

'I don't know. I don't know what to do. I don't want to worry him, he's got enough worries of his own, but ...' She gave a sigh. 'I reckon he was afraid something like this might happen; that's why he didn't want me to come here. But now it has perhaps he'll know what I should do.'

He was silent for some time, then he said, 'If you don't want to worry your uncle, would it help to talk to me, Mollie? I don't want to pry, but I believe I'm the only person in the family privileged to know your history, so if it would help ...'

'I think it might,' she said slowly. 'It would be good to talk it over with someone. If nothing else, perhaps it will help me to make up my mind what I should do. At the moment my head seems to be going round in circles.'

'I seem to remember some time ago I counselled you to reveal your identity to Uncle James,' he remarked. 'I still think that might be the best course, Mollie.'

She turned to him in surprise. 'Oh, didn't you realise?' She stopped in her tracks and stared at him. Then she shook her head. 'No, of course you couldn't know.' She began to walk again. 'I plucked up courage and did that, Mark, but he refused to believe me. He simply would not admit that I might be his daughter. In fact, he cast the gravest aspersions on my mother's morals, which, as you can imagine, I found deeply offensive.' She turned away so that he shouldn't see the tears in her eyes.

'Oh, Mollie. I am so sorry.' Savagely, he kicked a stone towards the water. 'But I suppose I should have known it was no more than might have been expected,' he said bitterly. 'My Uncle James has few scruples when it comes to lying his way out of trouble.' He gave a sigh. 'And of course you have no concrete proof. How could you have?'

'No. But I have my uncle's word and that's enough for me.'

'And rightly so.' He stopped and turned to look at her. 'I have great respect for Sam Barnes. Like you, I would stake my life on his integrity.'

She bowed her head. 'Thank you for that, Mark.' She looked up, tears glistening in her eyes. 'But I'm afraid it doesn't solve my problem. I still don't know what to do, Mark. Charlotte won't hear of me leaving Cliff House, and neither will Beatrice, but my presence clearly offends James now. I dread sitting at the same meal table.' She gave a small mirthless laugh. 'Ironic, isn't it, when you think that my one ambition was to sit at his table, in my rightful place, even though he wouldn't know it. Now, he does know it's my rightful place, even though he won't admit it, and I wish I wasn't there.' She shook her head. 'But I can't keep asking for my meals to be sent up to me. In any case, that would be a cowardly way out.'

'And you're no coward, Mollie,' he said quietly. 'So what are you saying? That you wish to leave Cliff House?'

'Oh, I don't *wish* to, but what else can I do? James pretends that he wants me out of the house because he says I've driven Sebastian away, but of course that's not the real reason. And when Sebastian comes home things will be even more difficult.'

He shrugged. '*If* he comes home. From what I can gather he's having the time of his life in the Army. Now he's escaped I can't see him wanting to come back and run his father's ailing business.'

She shot him a look. 'Is it really ailing?'

Another shrug. 'It wouldn't be if my uncle didn't gamble away half the profits. But ... speak of the devil ... there he goes, look.'

'Where?' She looked about her.

He pointed to a spot way beyond the red-clad pickers to where a lone horseman was galloping at breakneck speed along the beach towards the ruins of the old church.

274

'He's taken to doing that since Seb left. Relieves his feelings, I suppose. Or his conscience,' he added thoughtfully.

'And it's all my fault.' She took her hand out of her muff and rubbed the tears away, then replaced it. 'Oh, I know I must leave; I can't put it off much longer. But where can I go? What can I do? I've no money to speak of ...' Her voice trailed off. 'I should have saved my wages instead of spending them on fripperies, but I didn't think ...' She gave an involuntary shiver as a sudden gust of wind blew its icy breath on her face.

He took her arm and led her into the shelter of the cliff. 'I'm sure I could lend you some money, Mollie, if that's your only problem,' he said gently.

'It's not just that,' she answered miserably. 'I would need to find work. And what can I do? I spent a good part of my life picking mine, but I couldn't go back to that. I just *couldn't.*'

'No, of course you couldn't,' he agreed quickly. 'That's quite out of the question.'

'And I couldn't take up a post as governess because I'm not educated. I couldn't even read till Charlotte taught me.'

He gave her arm a little shake. 'Stop thinking about what you can't do and concentrate on what you can. Now, what are you good at?'

She frowned, then her face cleared. 'I always kept my aunt's house clean. Perhaps I could find a post in service if Mrs Grainger would give me a reference.'

'I was thinking along different lines, Mollie. You can sew, can't you?'

'Oh, yes. I've always been good with my needle.'

'Well, how about offering your services as a seamstress?'

She frowned. 'Do you think I could?'

'It's hardly for me to judge,' he said with a smile. 'I'm certainly no expert on ladies' fashions. But you seem to do quite a lot of sewing for Charlotte; she's always preening about the way you've altered things, taken bits off this or

275

put bits on that, whatever it is ladies do with their dresses. She seems to think quite highly of your efforts.'

She laughed in spite of herself at his clumsy attempts at describing changes in fashion. 'I suppose you're right. At least it's something I've had plenty of practice in doing.' Her mind began to race ahead. 'But who would want me? And where would I live? I'd have to find a room somewhere. And it couldn't be in Nazecliffe.'

'No, no, that's much too close. You'd have Charlotte dragging you back to Cliff House the minute she found out where you lived. Colchester would be better. It's quite a nice place, about fifteen miles away. Or there's Ipswich. I'm sure there would be plenty of people wanting your services in either of those places once they knew.'

She nodded, biting her lip.

'I could look out for a room for you, if you like,' he said gently.

'That would be kind. I've never been to Colchester. Or Ipswich.'

'Well, I sometimes have to go and visit the dyers in the course of my work. Colchester is quite a pleasant little town. Very old, of course. There's a huge castle on the hill, built by the Normans, I believe. And there's a very good market. Ipswich is very old, too.' He smiled at her encouragingly. 'But you're not here for a history lesson. Look, I'll see what I can find for you, but I warn you, it may take a while.'

'Thank you,' she said in a small voice.

'And don't worry, I will lend you whatever money you need to get you started,' he added.

'Thank you,' she said again. 'I shall pay you back as soon as I can.'

He waved her remark aside. 'You needn't worry about that. I shall know where you are, so I shall be able to keep track of you.'

She nodded. For some reason, instead of being happy that her future was being decided she found herself getting

276

more and more depressed. 'We should be getting back,' she said dully. 'Thank you for your help, Mark.'

He hesitated, looking at her intently. 'You're quite sure this is what you want, Mollie?'

She shrugged. 'I don't really have any choice, do I?'

'I suppose not.'

They walked back in silence, each busy with their own thoughts. Mollie was not sure whether she was feeling increasingly miserable because the wheels were being put in motion for her to leave Cliff House, or because it was Mark who was so willing to help her to get away. Perhaps he would be glad to see her leave. In any event, he was determined to keep track of her until he got his money back. But after that ... She stole a quick look at him, but his expression was set, giving nothing away.

As they neared Cliff House he took out his pocket watch and glanced at it.

'I hope I haven't made you late for work,' she said anxiously, feeling an even stronger sense of rejection.

'What? Oh, no, I was glad of a breath of fresh air. The atmosphere in that place stifles me at times. And it's getting worse.' He held the gate open for her and laid his hand on her arm as she went through. 'Don't worry, Mollie. I promise I'll find you a nice room in Colchester. And I shan't abandon you. I shall keep an eye on you to make sure you're all right.' He smiled at her. 'Now, come on, let's see if there's any breakfast left. I don't know about you, but I'm starving.'

'Yes, I believe I am quite hungry,' she replied, anxious that he shouldn't know how apprehensive she was about the future.

The following Sunday she told Charlotte she was going to see her Uncle Sam.

Charlotte eyed her suspiciously. 'I hope you're not think-ing of going back to live with him, Mollie,' she warned. 'I know you're feeling a little unsettled, now that Seb's gone, but you'll get used to the idea.' She was still deluding herself that Mollie was in love with her brother. 'Anyway, he'll be back,' she said cheerfully. 'When he judges his absence has made your heart grow fonder.'

Mollie smiled in spite of herself. 'No, I'm not thinking of going back to live in Copperas Lane, Charley,' she said firmly. 'And if you'd ever been there you'd never have suggested that I might be. It's a dreadful place.' She looked round Charlotte's very feminine, expensively furnished room. 'You've never been there so you could never imagine what it's like, Charley, the hell-hole that has paid for all this,' she said, shaking her head. 'And my Uncle Sam not only works there but lives right next door to it.' She gave a shudder. 'Oh, no, I could never go back there to live.'

'That's good, because in any case, I wouldn't let you,' Charlotte said happily. She put her head on one side. 'I'll always want you with me, Mollie. You know that, don't you? Even when Mark and I are married.'

'And when will that be?' Mollie asked, making her voice light although her heart was heavy.

She laughed, a delighted little giggle. 'Oh, not for ages yet. I'm not ready to settle down to domestic life yet. Mark knows that. He's quite happy to wait.' She became serious. 'I suppose I *do* love him, Mollie,' she said with a frown. 'He's been part of our family for such a long time and it's been assumed that we shall marry for so long that sometimes I wonder if I really do. Well, of course I do love him, I think he's a darling, but I sometimes wonder if I'm really *in love* with him. Is that something different?'

'Quite different, I should say,' Mollie said. 'I should have thought you would realise that. After all, you thought you were in love with Captain Pilkington, didn't you?'

'Oh, yes, so I did. I'd quite forgotten.' She gave a toss of her head. 'But that was merely infatuation. Nothing serious.'

No, but it could have been if I hadn't helped you out,

278

Mollie thought privately, but she wisely didn't pursue the matter.

'Have you heard from Richard lately?' Charlotte asked, suddenly changing the subject. 'It's quite a long time since there was a drop.'

'No, I haven't, for which I'm profoundly glad,' Mollie said fervently. 'Winter time is hardly the time for that kind of business.'

'I would have thought it exactly the right time,' Charlotte said. 'After all, the Riding Officer is less likely to be around when it's raining and blowing a gale. He'll be holed up in his little snug drinking confiscated liquor.'

'Well, maybe Dick hasn't been able to fix things up with the people on the other side,' Mollie said, being deliberately vague.

'I do miss ... I do miss ... um, the excitement,' Charlotte said on a wistful note.

'Well, I don't!' Mollie was quite firm on that.

But as she made her way along the cliff path to meet Uncle Sam the following Sunday, Mollie recalled her conversation with Charlotte. It was yet another thing to worry about. In her anxiety over her own future she had quite overlooked the business with Richard. She had always been afraid that if she wasn't there to keep a curb on Charlotte there was no telling what she might do that would endanger both Richard and his cronies, not to mention threatening her own safety. Mollie wondered briefly if she should confide in Mark, and ask him to watch out for Charlotte, but soon decided against this. There were more than enough people involved as it was. She sighed. There was really nothing she could do. Richard and Joe Trayler and Charlotte and Andy and anybody else concerned must take their chance. She had worries enough to contend with.

'Hullo, dearie. You're lookin' a bit peaky today.'

She had been so busy with her own thoughts that she had come upon Uncle Sam without even noticing him. She gave him a wide smile. 'Oh, Uncle. I didn't realise you were there,' she said, kissing his whiskery cheek and getting a whiff redolent of rotten eggs that no amount of washing could erase from those who worked at the Copperas House.

'Penny for 'em?' he asked, giving her a searching look. 'You were so far away in yer thoughts thass no wonder you didn't see me.'

'Oh, nothing much.' She gave herself a mental shake and linked her arm with his. 'Where shall we walk to? It's too cold to stand about for long and you've got no overcoat.'

'I've got me muffler. Thass all I need to keep the cold out.'

'Are you sure? The wind is coming from the east. I shouldn't be surprised if we get some snow before long.'

'Nah.' He lifted his head and sniffed the air. 'That'll rain afore mornin'. I can smell it in the air. Come on, we'll walk to the old church and you can see where the last of it fell over the cliff in the gales we had a week or two back.'

They walked along to where the cliff had finally given way and the last of the old church had toppled down onto the beach.

'Good thing, really,' Uncle Sam said. 'The youngsters used to come and play in the church even though they'd bin warned that worn't safe. Thass a mercy none of 'em ever had a accident. Coulda bin killed.' He stared down at the heap of stones and masonry being lapped by the waves. 'Thass safe enough now, though. They can clamber about on them stones without comin' to too much harm.'

Mollie followed his gaze. 'I can remember lying in bed and listening to the bell tolling when I was a little girl,' she said thoughtfully. 'That church had been on top of the cliff for hundreds of years and now it's no more than a heap of stones. In a few years time nobody will even remember that there was once a church here. Sad, isn't it?'

'Thass life, dearie. In a few years time nobody'll remember you an' me, neither. 'Cept through our children an' our children's children.' He gave her a sideways glance. 'An'

280

talkin' o' children, I s'pose you hevn't found yerself a nice young man? I should like to see you settled, Mollie.'

'Not yet, Uncle.' She linked her arm with his as they turned to go back the way they had come. 'How is Aunt Rose?' she asked, anxious to steer the conversation on to safer ground. 'And Cissie? Is she still living with you?'

'Ah, I was comin' to that,' Sam said, giving his moustache a quick stroke. 'Yer aunt ain't so well, these days. We can't move 'er off the sofa she's got so fat.' He gave a sniff. 'Tell you the truth, I don't think she'll be with us much longer.'

'Oh, I'm sorry to hear that.' It was true because Mollie knew that in spite of everything Uncle Sam was fond of his wife. 'Does Cissie look after her?'

He nodded. 'Yes. That gal has really turned up trumps. Nothin' is too much trouble for 'er. She's turned into a good little cook, an' since I had a go at 'er an' asked 'er if she couldn't keep the place a bit more ship-shape she's smartened everywhere up a treat.' He stopped and turned to Mollie. 'I s'pose you wouldn't like to come an' give yer aunt a look? I think she'd be glad to see yer.'

Mollie frowned. 'Are you sure, Uncle? I've always felt she preferred my room to my company. I know she was glad enough when I moved out.'

'She ain't like that now,' he assured her. 'Come on. Cissie'll make us a nice cuppa tea, then I'll walk back a way with yer. I'd like it if you'd do that.'

'Yes, all right, Uncle.' She smiled at him. 'You know I'd do anything for you.'

Even risk the kind of welcome she knew she could expect from Aunt Rose.

Chapter Twenty-seven

Mollie walked back to Copperas Lane with Uncle Sam. They only passed one or two people in the High Street because all the shops were closed, it being Sunday. Only at Mrs Barr's corner shop, which was open all day every day and which took the tokens earned by the pickers, was there any activity. As they turned into Copperas Lane and went past the cottages Mollie felt very conscious of her smart warm blue cloak with its fur collar, matching fur muff and her soft leather boots. Though everything she was wearing had once belonged to Charlotte it was all very good quality and a far cry from the threadbare skirts, the faded red cloaks and the heavy boots of the mine pickers; just the same as she herself had worn in the past. In another life.

'You'll notice a difference,' Uncle Sam said as they walked down the lane to the cottage that she had once called home. 'You might recall young Cissie was a bit slovenly when she first come to live with us. Rose didn't seem to bother but I didn't like it an' I said to 'er, "Cissie," I said, "If you're gonna live 'ere then you've gotta keep the place ship-shape, like my Mollie used to. I'll tell you what I want done an' I shall expect you to do it."' He nodded to himself. 'I told her, straight, if she was gonna live with us she'd gotta earn 'er keep. She soon learned.' He nodded again. 'Mind you, I was never harsh with 'er, but I let 'er

282

see that I wasn't hevin' no nonsense. She ain't all that bright – not like you, dearie – but provided I keep a eye on 'er she can sweep an' clean as good as the next one. An' she think the world of my Rose.'

By this time they had reached the cottage. Mollie had to suppress a cough as the stink of the Copperas House caught in her throat, but Uncle Sam didn't notice it; he'd lived with it for too many years.

They went up the steps and into the house.

'I've brought yer a visitor, Rosie,' he said, going over and kissing his wife. 'Mollie's come to see us.' He turned to Cissie, sitting by the fire with a basket of mending. 'Pull the kettle forward, Cissie, an' let's hev a cuppa tea.'

Cissie, a plain, slip of a girl with a childlike eagerness to please Sam, jumped to her feet and did as he asked, then busied herself getting down cups and saucers from the dresser and putting them on a tray.

Mollie went over to the sofa where her aunt lay, propped up with pillows. She was, as Uncle Sam had said, fatter than ever and her face was the colour of putty.

She put out a pudgy hand to Mollie. 'Thass nice to see yer, Mollie,' she whispered, her breath coming in short gasps. 'I'm glad you've come. I ain't well, as you can see, but Cissie here is good to me. She's a good gal, Cissie. Jest like you usta be.' She closed her eyes, exhausted by that speech.

Shocked at her aunt's appearance and taking her last words for the nearest Rose would ever get to an apology for the way she had treated her, Mollie looked across at Uncle Sam, but he was standing by the fire, waiting for the kettle to boil, rubbing his hands against the cold and didn't seem unduly troubled. She turned back to Aunt Rose.

'Is there anything you'd like? Anything I can get for you, Aunt?' she asked.

Rose licked her lips. 'I'd like a bit o' that ham you used to bring home sometimes, girl. That was rare tasty. I could quite fancy a bit o' that.'

283

'I'll make sure you have some, Aunt,' Mollie promised, patting her swollen hand.

Cissie poured the tea and offered Mollie a griddle cake as the three of them sat round the table, Uncle Sam and Mollie near the fire and Cissie – who was clearly a little nervous in Mollie's presence, regarding her, in her smart clothes, as something akin to gentry – next to Rose in case she needed anything. But Rose had fallen asleep and was snoring gently.

As she drank her tea and ate the cake Cissie had made – which was very good; Uncle Sam had been quite right in saying she was a good cook – Mollie could see that Uncle Sam had trained her well; the room was bright and clean, the table scrubbed and the china on the dresser sparkling. Aunt Rose was covered with a clean patchwork quilt and her sheet and pillowcases were crisp and white – no mean feat, living in the shadow of the Copperas House.

When she finally got up to leave Mollie knew she had no need to worry about her aunt and uncle. Cissie clearly idolised both of them and after Aunt Rose's death, which surely would not be long in coming, she would continue to care for Uncle Sam. Just as Uncle Sam would look after Cissie and shield her from the rigours of life.

'I'll walk back a little way with you,' Uncle Sam said. 'Thass beginnin' to get dark. I don't like the idea of you goin' along that cliff path on your own.'

Mollie didn't argue. She knew it was no use, so she dropped a kiss on her sleeping aunt's forehead – something she would never have been encouraged, nor have wished to do in the past – and followed her uncle down the steps to the lane.

He nodded towards the black buildings of the Copperas House as they passed them. 'I must check the fires when I get back,' he remarked, as much to himself as to Mollie. 'Sid Pearce is s'posed to be lookin' after the furnace this weekend but I like to drop by an' make sure he's keepin' the fire stoked up. There's a lotta money tied up in the stuff

284

in that boiler. If the temperature ain't kept right the liquor won't crystallise properly when it's run out into the coolers.'

She followed his gaze. The yard was well swept and tidy; two wheelbarrows and several coal shovels stood by the coal stack next to the boiler house and barrels, labelled with splashes of different coloured paint to indicate their destination, were lined up outside the drying sheds. Further away, towards the quayside, were the long beds where the copperas stones gathered from the beach were stored to weather. Over the whole place was the familiar sulphurous, rotten-egg stench, which she hardly used to notice but now caught in her throat and made her choke.

Uncle Sam took her arm. 'Come on, dearie. You don't want to loiter 'ere. Time you was gettin' back where you belong.'

She didn't answer. How could she tell him that she no longer knew where she really belonged? She knew she should tell him that she would soon be moving away from Cliff House but he would inevitably ask why and how could she speak to him of her reasons? And particularly of the aspersions James Grainger had cast on her mother? In any event, now was not the time. Uncle Sam was talking about his wife, of the young girl he had married, not the bloated invalid Mollie had seen that afternoon. Mollie understood that it was his way of coming to terms with the loss he knew he would soon suffer and she listened quietly and let him talk, setting aside for the moment her own problems.

When they reached Cliff House he paused. 'I shan't expect you to come, when – ' he gulped '– when anything happen,' he said euphemistically. 'There'll be plenty people around to see after me an' Cissie.'

'I'll come if you want me, Uncle. You know that,' she replied.

'Aye, I know it. But I reckon it's best this way.'

He kissed her goodbye and she found her cheeks were wet, but whether from his tears or her own she couldn't tell.

*

Just over two weeks later Richard brought news of Aunt Rose's death.

Mollie and Charlotte, both wrapped in cashmere shawls against the draughts, were sitting in the library by a huge fire, reading. Outside, the rain, encouraged by a stiff March wind, lashed the windows, and the noise of the sea hurling itself against the cliff could be heard even through the closed casements.

There was a brief knock on the door and Tilda came in and announced, with more than a trace of disapproval, that Miss Mollie's cousin Richard had come to see her.

Charlotte immediately sat up in her chair, her face alight with anticipation.

Mollie got up and laid a hand on her shoulder as she passed her. 'I think I know why he's here,' she said, quietly. 'I told you my aunt was very ill, didn't I, Charley?'

'Ah, yes.' Charlotte sank back into her chair. 'Where is he, Tilda?'

'I'm afraid he's in the boot room, Miss. He wouldn't come into the hall, nor the kitchen, he said he was too drippin' wet. So the boot room was the only other place I could think of. He was ready to stay outside in the rain, but I knew that wouldn't be right.'

'You did quite right, Tilda,' Mollie said. 'He'll be perfectly happy in the boot room. I'll go down and see him. I shan't be long, Charley.'

'Ask him when ...' Charlotte checked herself and began again. 'Ask him if he would like a cup of tea.'

Richard was, in fact, drinking tea out of a thick kitchen mug when Mollie reached him. His sou'wester lay on the bench beside him and he had unbuttoned his oilskins. He was still wearing his heavy leather sea boots.

She went over and kissed his wet face. 'I know why you've come, Dick,' she said quietly. 'She's gone?'

He nodded. 'Ten days ago. In 'er sleep. It took eight of us to carry the coffin to the graveyard. Well, you know

286

what a weight she was. Dad said not to tell you till it was all over.' He spread his hands. 'He said there was nothin' you could do an' there was plenty o' women to do the honours when us men got back from the burial.' He looked up and smiled. 'She enjoyed a bit o' that ham you sent down for 'er. That was almost the last thing she et. The rest of it did for the funeral so that was put to good use.'

Mollie nodded. 'I'm glad I was able to do that for her. It ... well, it sort of made things right between us.'

'I know what you mean.' He took a draught of tea. 'You didn't hev a very good childhood, Moll, did you. She was a bit of an old bitch to you.'

'Ssh. You mustn't speak ill of the dead,' Mollie said quickly. 'Is Uncle Sam all right?'

'Yes. I think he's quite glad to know she's at rest. An' Cissie's there. She'll see after 'im. She's a good kid.'

Mollie put her head on one side. 'Good enough to marry?' she asked with a smile.

'Good God, no!' He looked quite horrified.

'That's what your mum hoped.'

'Maybe she did. But I'd want a wife with a bit more about 'er than Cissie's got. Oh, she's good hearted enough, but she ain't exactly ... ' he gave a shrug, making his oilskins crackle. 'Well, you know what I mean.'

'Yes, I know what you mean. I was only teasing. But it's time you settled down, Dick.'

He drained his mug and stood up. 'I can't do that. I got too much to do. I got plans, Mollie.' He tapped the side of his nose. 'Which brings me to the other reason I've come today.'

'Oh, yes?' Mollie eyed him suspiciously.

'The lantern ... '

'Dick! Not in this weather! You must be barmy!'

'This wind will've blown itself out by termorrer night an' that'll take the rain with it. And thass the night we plan to bring a big lot o' stuff ashore. Thass taken a long time to get it set up with them on the other side but thass all in

place now an' the first run is all set for termorrer night.'
He leaned down towards her. 'We've set up a decoy at
Mersea so the Ridin' Officer *and* the Revenue Cutter will
be there all ready to nab a fishin' boat they've got wind of.
On'y they'll find thass as clean as a whistle. Meantime,
while they're dancin' around there, we'll run our stuff up
the beach an' into the cellar an' nobody any the wiser.'

'So if it's all set up you don't need the lantern lit,' Mollie
said, relieved.

'Yes, we do. They need to know nothin's gone wrong.'

She gave a sigh. 'I don't like it, Dick,' she said, shaking
her head. 'One of these days ... '

'I've told you afore, you don't hev to like it. Jest do it.'
He gave her a hug, making her shawl and her green
woollen dress wet from his oilskins. 'For old times sake.'

She hugged him back, then pushed him away. 'You think
you can twist me round your little finger, Dick Barnes.'

He grinned. 'Well, can't I?'

'Tell Uncle Sam I'll come and see him soon,' she said,
ignoring his last remark.

He rammed on his sou'wester and went happily off into
the rain and Mollie went back upstairs to Charlotte.

'You're all wet,' was Charlotte's first remark. 'Have you
been out in this rain?'

Mollie brushed her dress. 'No, of course not. But
Richard gave me a hug and his oilskins were wet.'

'What did he want?' Charlotte gave an excited wriggle.
'Is there to be another drop?'

'In the first place he came to tell me that my aunt has
died.' She sat down and stared into the fire. 'I hadn't
realised quite how fond Uncle Sam was of her. I'd never
even seen him kiss her until the last time I went to see
them. He'll miss her now she's gone.'

'Yes, I expect he will.' Charlotte tried not to sound
impatient. She raised her eyebrows. 'Was there anything
else?' she asked nonchalantly.

Mollie turned her gaze on Charlotte and smiled a little at

her transparency. 'As a matter of fact there was.'

'Yes?' She gave another little wriggle and a toss of her fair curls. 'Well, come on, don't keep me in suspense.'

'Tomorrow night,' Mollie said with a sigh. 'It's to be tomorrow night. I've got to put up the lantern because there's going to be a big drop.'

Charlotte clapped her hands excitedly. 'So they've managed to arrange it?'

'Seems like it,' Mollie said. 'I only hope the weather will be a bit better than it is today. Richard says it will. He's full of weather lore so I suppose he knows.'

'I'll make sure there's a good supply of candles down in the cellar. I can get to it from the wine cellar so I shan't need to go outside.'

Mollie frowned. 'Through the wine cellar?'

'Yes, I told you ages ago, don't you remember? I found a passage, well, more of a tunnel really, when I was little and used to play with the gardener's son.'

'Well, you'll have to watch out for Arthur.'

'I'm not stupid,' Charlotte said scathingly. Then her mood changed and she brightened up. 'Ah, yes, I nearly forgot. The Barratts are coming to dinner tonight. Now, what shall I wear?'

The rest of the afternoon was taken up with looking over Charlotte's wardrobe and deciding what she and Mollie should wear.

'I believe their son is coming with them,' Charlotte said. 'How would you fancy being married to the heir of a dye works, Mollie?

Mollie laughed. 'I wouldn't fancy it at all. Have you ever been near a dye works? It smells almost as bad as the Copperas House. In any case, I'm sure the Barratts are looking for somebody with a fortune for their son and heir, so you'd better watch out yourself.'

'Oh, I'm already spoken for,' Charlotte said carelessly.

'But your engagement hasn't yet been announced. Why is that?' Mollie forced herself to sound casual. In truth

289

Charlotte didn't behave in the least like a woman in love. Mollie suspected that her marriage to Mark, when it eventually took place, would be rather a matter of expediency on her father's part than any romantic feeling on Charlotte's.

The other girl gave a shrug. 'Plenty of time for that,' she said. She held a peach-coloured silk up against her. 'What about this for tonight? And you can wear your lilac satin. It looks well with your dark hair.'

Mollie frowned. 'Do you not think I should wear black? My aunt has just died, remember.'

'Oh, dear, yes. I suppose you should. Oh, that's a pity, especially as you were not at all close to her.'

'All the same, it's a mark of respect. It's what Uncle Sam would want.'

'You haven't got a black dress.'

'No. Well, never mind, I won't come down tonight. I'll have my dinner in my room.'

'Oh, no, you can't do that.' Charlotte pinched her lip. 'You could wear my grey skirt, it's quite dark. And perhaps mama has got a black blouse. I'll go and see.'

'It doesn't matter, Charley. I really don't mind ...'

But Charlotte had gone, running along the corridor to find her mother. Five minutes later she came back, her mother behind her, carrying a black satin blouse.

'My dear, I didn't know.' Beatrice kissed her sympathetically. 'I'm so sorry. Are you very upset? Would you prefer to take your meal in your room?'

'I was never close to my aunt,' Mollie said honestly. 'In fact, she died a fortnight ago but I didn't know till my cousin came and told me this afternoon.'

'Then there's no reason why you shouldn't come down tonight.' Beatrice was quite definite on the subject. 'But I think you would be right to wear black as a mark of respect.' She looked at the dark grey skirt lying on the bed. 'Yes, with this blouse of mine you will look quite suitable.' She smiled as she saw Mollie eyeing her ample figure. 'Oh,

290

this blouse has been in my wardrobe since I was slim enough to wear it. I'm sure it will fit you, dear, but it will need an iron running over it.'

Mollie felt very drab beside Charlotte, at her animated best in her peach silk, flirting shamelessly throughout the meal with Duncan Barratt, Alfred Barratt's son. Duncan was a suave, smooth-talking young man, quite up to parrying Charlotte's coy thrusts. Afterwards, he insisted on turning the pages for her as she played the piano and much giggling and dropping of music ensued.

Mollie felt quite sorry for Mark and went over and sat beside him.

'Charlotte plays well,' she remarked. 'I wish I had her talent for music.'

'She sings well, too, when she can be persuaded,' he said, glancing over towards where she was searching through the music Canterbury, with Duncan kneeling at her feet. 'Perhaps Duncan Barratt will exercise his charms in that direction.'

Mollie wondered if he was jealous at the way his future wife was behaving. As far as she could tell he seemed quite relaxed and his last remark had been without any trace of sarcasm that she could detect. She stole a look at him and was disconcerted to find his eyes resting thoughtfully on her. She blushed. 'Perhaps Charlotte would sing if you asked her to,' she said.

He shook his head. 'I don't think so. In any case, I wouldn't dream of asking her.'

'She's looking particularly pretty tonight.'

'Mm. Peaches and cream.' He smiled at Mollie. 'Black is more elegant, if I may say so, although I appreciate the reason you're wearing it. My condolences, Mollie, at the death of your aunt.'

'Thank you, Mark.' She frowned. 'I suspect you knew about it before I did. Why didn't you tell me?'

'Because your uncle asked me not to.' He laid his hand

over hers and then quickly removed it. 'You must understand, Mollie, you live in a different world now. If you had gone to your aunt's funeral the people from Copperas Lane, the people she knew and lived among, would have been uncomfortable, intimidated, I might almost say. It would have inhibited the women who waited while the men went to the burial and the atmosphere after the burial would have been less relaxed. Do you understand?'

She nodded. 'Yes, I think so.'

'Your uncle knew this. That's why he asked me not to say anything to you. He's very wise, your Uncle Sam.'

She nodded. Suddenly, her eyes filled with tears; not tears of grief for Aunt Rose, but tears of sorrow for brave, upright Uncle Sam, who had lost the woman he loved.

Chapter Twenty-eight

Charlotte was keyed up with excitement. Her eyes sparkled and she chattered incessantly, grasshoppering from one thing to another until Mollie's mind was in a turmoil.

'Can't you be quiet for just five minutes, Charley?' Mollie threw down the hairbrush she had been using on Charlotte's curls and put her fingers to her temples.

Charlotte's eyes widened in surprise as she stared at Mollie's reflection in the mirror of her dressing table. 'What's the matter, Molls, have you got a headache?'

'No, I haven't, but it's no thanks to you. Do you realise you've been talking non-stop ever since you woke up? You didn't even stop when you ate your breakfast. Whatever's the matter with you?'

'Nothing's the matter,' she said nonchalantly. Then, unable to contain herself, she hunched her shoulders in delight, 'Well, it's just that I'm looking forward to tonight.' She clapped her hands. 'It's going to be so exciting!'

'Oh, Charley. You regard it all as some kind of game, don't you,' Mollie said, shaking her head in exasperation. 'Can't you get it into your thick head that we could all end up in prison, or at the end of a rope for what we do?' She shook her head again. 'Yes, of course you do, I've drummed it into you enough times.'

'Don't be so anxious, Mollie,' Charlotte said with an affectionate smile. 'If the Riding Officer were to come by as we were in the middle of getting the stuff ashore I would take him to one side and say, "Why, Mr Doe, what are you doing, out on such a cold night. Let me take you into the house and make you a hot toddy." You know he finds me irresistible.'

'But what if he were to question what *you* were doing, out on the cliff in the dark on such a cold night,' Mollie asked drily.

'I'd say I was looking for my little dog.'

'But you haven't got a dog.'

Charlotte leaned forward and examined a minute spot on her chin. 'No, but he doesn't know that, does he?'

Mollie picked up the hairbrush again. 'Oh, you're incorrigible.'

Charlotte laughed. 'Mollie! Where did you learn such a long word? And what does it mean?'

'I learned it from a book and I think it means there's no arguing with you, the mood you're in. Now, let me pin up your hair. You have to go visiting with your mama today.'

'Oh, drat it, so I do.'

After Charlotte had gone out with her mother Mollie went up to the attic to make sure the lantern was trimmed ready to light when darkness fell. She had left it on the windowsill in her old room and although there was no reason to think the room had been touched since she left it she felt that she needed to check that the lantern hadn't been moved. She realised that it was all part of her unease at being caught up in her cousin's unlawful dealings, but she couldn't help herself. She was filled with such foreboding that it came as no surprise when she reached the door to find that it was locked.

Her heart began to thump wildly. She'd had a feeling that something would go wrong; now what was she going to do? If she couldn't put up the light the whole plan would fail and Richard would blame her. She tried the door again, rattling the door knob. She couldn't imagine why her old room should have been locked and she looked round in desperation to see if there was anything she could use to force open the door. But there was nothing but a narrow, empty corridor.

Then she remembered that the room next to her old room had been used as a junk room where all the old discarded furniture from the rest of the house was stored. Perhaps she would be able to find a key in there that could be made to fit. If that door wasn't locked, too.

Fortunately, it wasn't.

She stepped inside and gazed round. It was full of discarded furniture, some of it broken; old washstands, chairs, desks from the schoolroom, a large doll's house that Charlotte had long outgrown and a fort, complete with soldiers, that had presumably belonged to Sebastian. There were several trunks and packing cases against the wall, on which boxes of books were stacked. Everything was covered in a thick layer of dust.

'What are you doing here? You've no call to come up here. These are the *servants'* quarters.' It was Ellis and her tone was icy with sarcasm.

Mollie spun round. She hadn't heard Ellis approaching. 'Oh, you made me jump,' she said, putting her hand to her heart. She smiled at Ellis and said the first thing that came into her head. 'I came up to see if I could find a little jewel box Miss Charlotte had as a child. She thought it might make a present for Cook's little granddaughter.' She gave a shrug. 'But it doesn't matter.' She turned to leave the room, then she frowned and said, keeping her voice casual, 'My old room seems to be locked, Ellis. Do you know where the key is?'

'Why do you need to go in there? All your things are downstairs now.' Ellis was still hostile.

'I've lost a small brooch and I can't think where else it might be.'

'All the rooms not in use are locked. You'll find the key on the ledge above the lintel.' She nodded towards the place.

295

'Ah, thank you,' Mollie said, feeling along the ledge and finding it. She turned and smiled at Ellis. 'I've looked everywhere downstairs and I shouldn't like to lose my brooch because my uncle gave it to me. This is the last place I can think of where it might be, although I swept the room well before I left it.'

'Perhaps you'll find it under the bed, then,' Ellis said slyly, and went on her way down the stairs.

Mollie unlocked the door. Inside, she closed it and leaned back against it, closing her eyes. She found she was trembling.

She sat down on the uncovered bed springs and leaned against the rolled-up mattress to collect her thoughts. She hadn't bargained on being accosted by Ellis; on the other hand she would never have found the key to her room if she hadn't arrived so perhaps it was for the best. Almost absentmindedly, she unpinned Uncle Sam's brooch from the underside of her collar and re-pinned it on the front. She smiled to herself. At least she would be able to claim she had found what she was looking for if Ellis were to ask, even if it did imply she hadn't swept under the bed. She put her head in her hands. She hated all this underhand business, although Charlotte seemed to thrive on it. The trouble was, there seemed no end to it. If tonight's drop worked well Richard would organise more and then more. Mollie stared up at the window. It was said that you could get used to anything but she didn't think she would ever get used to being involved in owling.

She pulled herself together. Make sure the lantern was ready to light, then put it out of mind for a few hours, she told herself. She climbed on the chair, cleaned all the dust from the lantern, made sure the candle wick was trimmed and left the tinderbox beside it. Then she brushed down her skirt, made sure the brooch was in place and went out, locking the door and leaving the key above the lintel.

*

Charlotte was highly amused when Mollie told her what had happened while she was out. Nevertheless, when it was time for Mollie to go up and light the lantern she agreed to go along to her mother's room to make sure Ellis was fully occupied, helping Beatrice to dress for the evening meal.

'I don't think my nerves would stand another meeting like that with Ellis,' Mollie said fervently. 'And I'm running out of excuses to be up in the attics. Oh, and don't forget to be disappointed that I couldn't find the little jewel box you had as a child to give to Cook's granddaughter, if Ellis asks.'

'I don't remember having a little jewel box as a child,' Charlotte said, frowning.

Mollie gave an exasperated sigh. 'Oh, don't be so awkward. Just pretend you did.'

Once the lantern was alight it was simply a case of behaving normally until the household had retired for the night. Mollie was so apprehensive that she had difficulty in swallowing her meal and knocked over a carafe of water in her agitation but Charlotte had no such inhibitions and managed two helpings of jam roly-poly.

Afterwards, she played the piano a little before yawning and feigning tiredness.

'You've had too many late nights,' her mother said, indulgently. 'An early night will do you good. I think I shall retire early, too, since your father has gone out and Mark, it appears, hasn't yet returned from work.'

The two girls escaped to Charlotte's room.

Charlotte immediately went over to the window and pulled the curtain aside. 'Richard was right. The rain has stopped and the wind has dropped. In fact, it's a pleasant, calm evening.' She looked at her little enamelled clock on the mantelpiece. 'Oh, look at that, we've got hours to wait.' She paced up and down the room impatiently. Then she said, 'Let's play chess. It'll help to pass the time.' She dragged the little chess table over to the fire and sat down.

Mollie sat down opposite. She knew she would be beaten; Charlotte was a much better player at the best of times and tonight she had difficulty in keeping her mind on the game. They played three games which Charlotte won easily so they turned to backgammon and the same thing happened.

'You're just not concentrating,' Charlotte pouted.

'No, I'm too tired. I think we should both rest for a couple of hours or so. We've got a long night ahead of us,' Mollie said, rubbing her eyes.

'Oh, I'm far too excited to sleep. But you go to your room. I'll call you when it's time,' Charlotte said happily, waving her away.

In fact, it was Mollie who couldn't sleep. After cat-napping till one o'clock she got up, dressed and went through to Charlotte, who was snoring gently, dead to the world.

For some reason this irritated Mollie.

'Come on, it's time to go,' she said, shaking her by the shoulder more roughly than she would normally have done.

'Oh, fancy that! I must have dropped off!' Charlotte's eyes shot open as she sat up and swung her legs over the bed to step into the dark skirt Mollie was holding for her. Then they both donned their warm, dark cloaks and slipped out of the room and down the back stairs, carrying their boots. The house was in darkness; the curtains were drawn at the windows and every last candle had been extinguished so they had to feel their way, Charlotte leading and Mollie following.

'We'll go through the wine cellar,' Charlotte whispered, catching Mollie's hand. 'This way.'

Mollie opened her mouth to protest, but Charlotte was dragging her along in pitch darkness, down the kitchen corridor, past the butler's pantry to the door at the end. Here there were steps leading down to the wine cellar and Charlotte lit the lamp Arthur kept at the top of the stairs to light his way to James's store of wines and spirits. Through the whitewashed cellar, where the walls were lined with racks of bottles and casks to a small door in the corner, half-hidden behind empty wine crates. They stopped and put on their boots, then Charlotte took a key from her pocket, unlocked the door and led the way through.

Reluctantly, Mollie followed Charlotte along a low tunnel, where there was barely room for them to stand upright, for what seemed a very long way.

'We shall come out halfway down the cliff and fall to our death,' Mollie hissed.

'Don't be silly. Of course we shan't. I know what I'm doing. Look, here we are.' Charlotte held her candle high as the tunnel opened out into the familiar cellar used by Richard and his cronies to store their contraband.

'Oh.' Mollie looked round, surprised to find where she was. 'Oh, thank heaven for that!' She sank down on to an old packing case.

'You haven't got time to sit there,' Charlotte said, pulling her to her feet. 'We need to go and see what's going on. The men may be waiting for our help.'

'They used to manage very well without us,' Mollie grumbled.

'Well, they don't need to now.' Charlotte unlocked the door and they stepped outside into the fresh night air and scrambled through the undergrowth.

'It's still very soggy underfoot,' she warned. 'Be careful where you put your feet.' She clutched Mollie's arm and pointed. 'Oh, look, I saw a pinprick of light out on the horizon. Did you see it, Mollie? There, it's gone now. I reckon it was a signal. But it seemed a long way out and the men will have to row out to fetch the stuff.'

'It always looks further out in the darkness,' Mollie said, a trifle irritably, her feeling of unease undiminished. 'It probably isn't that far.'

'Oh, I wonder where the men are,' she said eagerly. 'I can't hear any sound of oars. Do you think they've got anything ashore yet?'

'How would I know?' Mollie's irritation was now increased by wet branches brushing her face and getting caught up in her hair.

'Come on, Molls, don't lag.' Charlotte caught her hand. 'We'd better go to the steps. There may be some things already waiting.'

Charlotte hurried across the lawn, the wet grass squelching under her boots, pulling Mollie along behind her. There was nothing at the top of the steps so they made their way further along the cliff top where there was a better view of the beach.

'Ah, I think I can see some people moving about down there against the pale sand, now my eyes are getting used to the darkness,' Charlotte whispered after a few minutes.

'Yes, it looks as if there are three or four of them, but I can't see their boat. I expect they left it tied up under the lea of the cliff,' Mollie said. 'Drat it. That means we're too early. It'll be an hour or more before anything comes ashore. But I was sure Dick said be here by two o'clock.'

'Perhaps we should go down to the beach and let them know we're here,' Charlotte suggested.

'No, we would only get in the way. Better we stay up here,' Mollie said. 'Or go back to the cellar.'

'No, we might miss something.'

Mollie knew it was useless to argue, so they walked up and down on the cliff top for a while to keep warm, pausing every now and then to see if there was any movement from below, when all of a sudden Charlotte lurched against Mollie.

'Whoops. I think I must be a bit dizzy. I thought I felt the ground move,' she said with a nervous little laugh.

'That's all we need, for you to start being ill,' Mollie replied unsympathetically. She steadied her. 'Are you all right now?'

'Yes, I think so. No, wait a minute, there it goes again.' She clutched at Mollie. 'Whatever's the matter with me!'

'It's not just you, I felt it too! Oh, my God, I think it's the cliff moving!' Mollie grabbed her and they began to run away from the cliff edge, jumping across a split in the ground that was beginning to open up. There was a noise of earth and stones rattling and then a thud as a huge chunk of cliff broke off behind them, right where they had been standing, and slithered down to the beach.

'Heavens, that was a near thing!' Charlotte said breathlessly, a sob catching in her throat, as they leaned against each other in relief.

'We mustn't stay here. It's not safe. More of it could go at any minute.' Mollie began to pull her away.

'But we can't just leave! What about Richard? What about the men down there on the beach?'

'Oh, Lord! You're right! They could be buried! But how can we get to them?'

'The steps.'

'They've probably collapsed. There's no telling how far along the cliff has gone.'

'Well, it's the only way down. Oh God I wish there was a moon.'

'Careful,' Mollie warned. 'Test each step before you put your weight on it and keep away from the edge. The steps can't be far now. Oh, this bit seems pretty solid, thank goodness.'

'And I can just see the outline of the railing where the steps are so it looks as if they've held.'

They reached the steps and very gingerly made their way down to the beach. They could see the shadowy figures of two men moving about near the landslide.

'Richard?' Charlotte and Mollie called, both at the same time.

As they got closer they could see that the men were scrabbling furiously at the landslip of earth and stones. Mollie recognised Joe Trayler.

'Oh, it's you, darlin',' he said breathlessly when he saw Mollie. 'Well, now you're here you can make yourself useful. Hold the lantern high so we can see what we're doin'.'

'Is Richard buried under there?' Mollie was so choked with fear that she could hardly get the words out. 'He is, isn't he. I can hear him swearing.'

'Ah, now we can see better. Aye, there 'e is, over there! Looks like 'e's half buried. Thank God 'e's still breathin'.'

'Yes, I bloody well am still breathin'. But I won't be if you don't soon get me outa here,' came Richard's furious reply. 'My bloody leg's killin' me. I think the soddin' boat fell on it.'

'Orl right, mate, don't get yer dander up. We'll fetch you out as quick as we can.'

'You'd better be quick, before more of the cliff goes,' Charlotte said anxiously, trying to climb over and reach Richard.

'We'll do a lot better if you keep outa the way, missy,' Andy said sharply. 'What you can do if you wanta make yerself useful is take that other lantern and swing it back an' forth, reg'lar like, so them out there in the big boat'll know ternight's drop is orf.' He beckoned to Mollie. 'Thass it, girl, over here. Hold yours high.'

It seemed an age, during which several times the ominous sound of pebbles and gravel sliding could be heard from further along the cliff, before Richard was freed and dragged to safety on the sand.

He lay there panting and groaning as Joe and Andy squatted beside him and Charlotte and Mollie looked on.

'Thass 'is leg, look.' Joe pointed to Richard's torn and bloody trouser leg. 'Musta got it caught on the edge of the boat. 'E'd jest gone to fetch it from where we'd left it under the cliff when the bloody cliff collapsed on 'im. We'll hev to get 'im somewhere where we can hev a good look at it. God knows where. Looks pretty bad to me.'

'If you can carry him up the cliff steps we can put him in the cellar where we store the goods,' Charlotte said decisively. 'Nobody will ever find him there. He'll be quite safe and Mollie and I can look after him. Come along. Hurry up.'

Joe looked questioningly at Mollie.

She nodded. 'It'll be all right. We'll make him comfortable. But can you carry him?'

'Reckon so. If not me an' Andy'll manage between us.'

'You'll have to be quiet. We don't want to wake the whole house,' Charlotte warned.

Joe gave her a scathing look in the darkness. 'We're owlers, Missy. Bein' quiet's second nature to us. Now, give us a hand, Andy.' The two men bent over Richard. 'Come on, me old shiner. Up you come.' With one quick movement the practically unconscious Richard was lifted up off the beach and over Joe's shoulder. 'Right, Andy. You steady 'im as we go.'

Charlotte led the way up the steps, miraculously still not affected by the landslide, and keeping to the shadow of the shrubbery, with Joe Trayler behind her, carrying Richard as if he weighed no more than a pound of sugar. Andy followed next, supporting Richard's head, and Mollie brought up the rear, the whole party moving like ghosts through the undergrowth.

They reached the cellar and Joe laid Richard down very gently on a pile of sacks. He had regained consciousness and was beginning to moan.

He turned to Charlotte. 'What now, Missy? Who'll see after 'im, now?'

Charlotte looked at him, her eyebrows raised in surprise that he should have even asked. 'Why, me, of course. Who else?' she said briskly. She turned to Mollie. 'You'll help me, won't you, Mollie.'

Mollie nodded, staring down into the white face of her cousin. She'd had a feeling all along that the night would end in disaster, but she hadn't envisaged anything like this.

Chapter Twenty-nine

Andy took out a large knife he used for gutting fish and began to cut away Richard's trouser leg.

'Go to the kitchen and get warm water to bathe it,' Charlotte commanded Mollie. 'Oh, and some rag.' She sat down on the floor and took Richard's head in her lap. 'There, that's more comfortable, isn't it,' she said, stroking his head, as if to a child.

The rest of the night passed in a haze for Mollie. She forgot how many times she was forced to crawl back along the tunnel, first to fetch water and rag, then for more rag to bind the cleaned leg, which was not, as they had at first feared, broken, although it was badly lacerated, and then for the pork pie that was left over from supper, and some bread and cheese. And all the time sick with worry over Richard, not knowing quite how badly he was hurt, nor what was to happen to him.

After some argument, it was decided that Joe should be the one to stay with Richard for what was left of the night and Andy was sent home. Richard was made as comfortable as possible on a heap of sacks and covered with a blanket that Mollie had fetched from her own bed. Joe had to make shift sitting on up-ended brandy casks with his back against the wall.

'I've slept in worse places,' he told the girls when they expressed concern. 'An' it won't do for me to sleep too deep. I gotta keep a eye on me mate, there.'

'I don't like leaving him,' Mollie said anxiously. 'He's my cousin; I ought to look after him.'

'You go an' get your beauty sleep. I'll see he don't come to no harm,' Joe said with a yawn. 'I'll give 'im another drop o' brandy if he gets restless. That'll keep 'im quiet. He'll be all right till mornin'.'

There was nothing more they could do so the two girls staggered back along the tunnel to the wine cellar and up to their rooms, surprised to find that the first blue streaks of dawn were already appearing on the horizon.

'I could have stayed with him,' Charlotte muttered crossly. 'I wanted to stay with him.'

'You know that wasn't possible,' Mollie replied, equally crossly. 'He'll be perfectly all right with Joe. In any case, if anyone should have stayed with him it was me, since I'm his cousin. But, look at you, a bath is what you need more than anything. You're filthy. But you won't get one tonight. I'm not lugging hot water up from the kitchen at this hour. There's cold water in the ewer; you'll have to make do with that.'

Charlotte looked at her. 'You're a fine one to talk. Your face and hands are black.'

They both turned to the mirror and burst out laughing at the grimy images that confronted them.

Mollie held out her hands. 'I'm not surprised, I was crawling about half the night in that filthy tunnel,' she said, looking down at them. She shook her head. 'I'm never going to do this again, Charlotte,' she said seriously. 'Not ever. Not even for Richard. This was the last time. I've had enough.'

'You might not have to,' Charlotte replied enigmatically.

'What do you mean by that?'

'I mean you might not have to. Don't forget to put out the lantern before you go to bed.'

'Oh, drat it.' Mollie left Charlotte and hurried up to the attic to attend to the lantern. Next door, she could hear

Kitty moving about in her room, already preparing to go down and get the fires alight at the beginning of the new day. She hurried back to her room, where she gave her face and hands a perfunctory wash in cold water, then tumbled into bed and fell asleep immediately.

The next three days were a nightmare. Richard became feverish and couldn't be moved, so Joe couldn't leave him. Joe was proving a real friend, doing everything possible to make him comfortable, feeding him small amounts of soup, changing the bandages on his leg and even bathing his brow.

To Mollie's surprise, it was Charlotte who offered to slip through the undergrowth to the cellar during the day, or crawl through the tunnel to reach it at night to take the men food and drink. At least twice a day she visited them, smuggling Richard delicacies to try and tempt him to eat, or a pillow for his head.

'You don't need to, come, Mollie,' she said. 'It won't be so noticeable if only one of us goes.'

Mollie could see the wisdom in this because there was great excitement and much to-ing and fro-ing when the cliff fall was discovered, mixed with mild consternation at the way the garden of Cliff House was being eroded.

James went and examined his shrinking land with Bragg, the gardener.

'You'll just have to put up another fence across where the end of the lawn is now,' Bragg,' he said. He eyed up the land and pointed with his crop. 'Oh, it's still got a good long way to go before the house is in any danger.'

He strode off, calling for Perkins to saddle his horse.

Bragg looked after him shaking his head. 'A good long way to go, he says,' he remarked to Sid, who was with him, 'But my granddad, who was gardener here years ago, used to tell of a big orchard with all manner o' fruit tress in it beyond this lawn. Well, there's no sign or any fruit trees now and in years to come I don't reckon there'll be any sign o' Cliff House, neither.'

306

'Can't anything be done to stop it, Mr Bragg?' Sid asked.

'No, boy. There's no stoppin' the sea eatin' into the cliff. Look what happened to the church up the other end, there. Nobody couldn't stop that topplin' over when the cliff fell down. An' nobody'll be able to stop it this end, neither.' He ruffled Sid's carroty hair. 'But I don't s'pose it'll be in my lifetime. Nor yours.'

Sid grinned up at him. 'So does that mean the master is right? We don't hev to worry yet?'

'Reckon so,' Bragg agreed reluctantly.

It was after nearly a week, when the excitement of the cliff fall had died down, that Cook began to be suspicious at the way food that had been left on the slab was mysteriously disappearing.

'I b'lieve we've got a thief in our midst,' she said portentously to Arthur one morning when Mollie was there making Charlotte's hot chocolate. 'I left a platter of cold roast beef, all sliced up, on the slab in the larder. And what do I find when I go there today? Only two slices and a sliver o' fat. So where's it gone, thass what I want to know.' She glared round the kitchen, her arms akimbo. '*And* best part of a fresh-baked loaf. An' don't tell me the mice've bin at it, neither. This is not the work o' mice.'

'Rats?' asked Arthur, helpfully.

She looked at him scathingly. 'Two-legged ones. Else we've got the fattest rats this side o' Ipswich. There was a pork pie yesterday, an' a great lump o' cheese the day before, an' the milk is gone almost afore it's in the jug.' She folded her arms. 'I pride myself nobody gets up from my table hungry so I dunno why anyone should want to steal food. In any case, they'd only hev to ask if they wanted more.' She shook her head. 'I don't understand it. I don't understand it at all.'

'We shall have to keep a watch,' Arthur said, nodding importantly.

'Indeed we shall, Arthur.' Her eyes narrowed. 'Mind you, I hev my suspicions.'

Mollie escaped with the hot chocolate and went up to Charlotte.

'Cook's on the warpath,' she said, giving Charlotte her drink. 'She's missed all that food you've stolen from the kitchen.'

'I didn't steal it,' Charlotte said petulantly.

'Well, I don't know what you'd call it, then. You didn't ask and you're not intending to give it back.' Worry was giving a sharp edge to Mollie's voice. 'I told you not to take too much, but you wouldn't listen.'

'Well, there are two hungry men to feed,' Charlotte said defensively. She frowned. 'Well, one, really. Richard's not eating much.' She took several sips of chocolate. 'I'm a bit worried about him, Mollie. He's still very feverish and Joe says his leg looks bad.'

'I'll go and see him. Perhaps we can get him to Uncle Sam's,' Mollie said. She was annoyed with Charlotte for not letting her do anything to help the men in the cellar.

'No.' Charlotte shook her head slowly. 'He's too ill to be moved that far.' She looked up. 'I've been thinking about it all night. I'm going to have him brought up to Seb's old room.'

Mollie gaped. 'You can't do that! Everybody will know what's been going on! And what if Sebastian should come home?'

'Seb's not going to come home. Not now he's escaped. He's enjoying life far too much in the Army.' Charlotte drained her chocolate and handed the cup impatiently to Mollie. She got out of bed and began to throw her clothes on, not waiting for Mollie to help. 'I can see now, I should have done it before and not left it until Richard was so ill. He didn't even know me last night.' She waved Mollie away. 'You go and make up the bed. And make sure there's a hot brick in it. But first, send Perkins for Dr Marshall. I'll go and tell Joe to bring Dick indoors.'

'But your mother ...'

'I'll take care of her. Don't *fuss,* Mollie, just do as I ask if you don't want to lose your cousin.' Charlotte was already halfway out of the door.

Mollie went and did as she had been asked, her mind racing ahead. James Grainger was certain to call in the Riding Officer when he found out who Richard was. And he was sure to find out; it would be impossible to smuggle a sick man into the house and up the stairs without the whole household knowing. She could just imagine his glee at turning Richard in, once he'd found out that he was her cousin. That is, if Richard lived long enough to be turned in. From what Charlotte had said and the fact that she was bringing him into the house, he must be very ill. Perhaps dying. She couldn't bear even to think of that so she put all her mind to tucking in blankets and smoothing sheets.

'What are you doing in Sebastian's room, Mollie?'

She shot round. A frowning Beatrice was standing in the doorway wearing a green morning gown, a shawl thrown carelessly round her shoulders.

'Charlotte asked me to come and put a hot brick in the bed, ma'am. She's ...'

'Out of the way, please, Mama.' Charlotte called from the corridor. 'We're bringing a sick man up the stairs.'

Beatrice's jaw dropped and she looked from Mollie to her daughter, hurrying towards her. 'Sebastian?' she asked anxiously. 'What's wrong with my boy? Why didn't someone tell me he'd come home.'

'No, it isn't Sebastian, Mama. It's Richard. This way,' she called over her shoulder to Joe, who was carrying Richard on his back with the same ease as he had carried him up the cliff steps.

'What? I don't understand. Who is this Richard? You can't bring him in here! He's filthy!' Nevertheless, Beatrice was too surprised to do other than stand aside to let Joe into the room so that he could lay his burden carefully on the bed.

309

'Did you find him a nightshirt? He'll need a nightshirt, Mollie. And hot water. He'll need to be bathed after a week in that cellar.' All the time Charlotte was helping Joe to ease off his jacket.

'I think you should leave his friend, whoever he is, to finish undressing him, Charlotte,' Beatrice said distastefully, finding her voice at last. 'It's no task for a lady. Come with me. I think you owe me an explanation for all this.'

While this was going on, Mollie had run down to the kitchen for hot water. She hurried back with the large copper jug, followed by Dr Marshall and almost ran into James, just coming out of his bedroom.

'What the hell's going on? What's all the hullabaloo? Marshall? What are you doing here, man? Has somebody died?'

'This way, Dr Marshall,' Mollie said over her shoulder, and to James, 'No, Sir, nobody's died.' But they soon will, she said under her breath, most likely at the end of a rope. Because she knew that if James Grainger didn't turn Richard and Joe over to the authorities, Dr Marshall surely would.

'I'll see you later, Marshall,' James said and stalked off to his breakfast.

Dr Marshall was in the room with Joe for a long while. Together they cleaned Richard up and then the doctor attended to the wounded leg.

Mollie hovered outside the door in case she was needed, pacing up and down and twisting her apron into a rag in her anxiety.

After over an hour the doctor emerged. 'The young man is your cousin, I believe, Miss,' he said, giving her an appraising look.

'Yes, Sir, he is,' she said, forgetting her new status and bobbing him a curtsey. 'Is he ...? Will he ...?'

'He'll live. But mainly thanks to his companion in there. He's nursed him well. Your intended, I believe?' He quirked an eyebrow at her.

310

Her jaw dropped. 'Joe? My ...? No, indeed he is not, Sir.'

'No? Well, you could do worse. And you've good reason to be grateful to him.' He marched off down the stairs.

Mollie went into the room where Richard lay. He was asleep, his face almost the same colour as the pillow on which his head rested.

Joe was tidying the room. He looked tired and grimy. 'Doctor said we was on'y jest in time. Another day an' he'd hev bin a gonner,' he said wearily. 'I did what I could for 'im, but that cellar was no place for a sick man.'

'I know. Thank you for what you did, Joe,' she said. She laid her hand briefly over Richard's as it rested on the counterpane. 'I wanted to have him taken to Uncle Sam's but Charlotte refused. She wouldn't even let me visit him ... I don't know why.'

He grinned at her. 'Don't you? Then you must be blind, girl.'

'What do you mean?'

'I mean Charlotte an' Richard. Like that.' He held up his hand, the first two fingers twisted together. 'She's bin like a mother hen fussin' over 'im. "You won't let 'im die, Joe. You mustn't let 'im die. I can't live 'ithout 'im, Joe." All the time, every day, thass what she's bin sayin'.'

Mollie sat down on the chair with a bump, her eyes wide, her head shaking from side to side. 'I never realised ... I never even gave it a thought ... but now you come to speak of it, yes, there were times.' She looked up at Joe. 'Now what?'

He rubbed his stubbly chin. 'I need a wash an' shave.'

'All right. I'll go and fetch you some hot water.' She got to her feet. 'And there are clothes in the wardrobe there that will probably fit you, too. I'm sure Seb won't mind you borrowing them.'

'Seb, is it? I thought you was *my* girl.'

'I'm not anybody's girl, Joe,' she said firmly. She looked at him and at her cousin, still asleep. 'It may have saved Dick's life, bringing him here,' she said with a sigh, 'but what now? How are you going to explain what you were doing when the accident happened? And why you were in that cellar. You could both end up ...'

'Sh, my lovely.' Joe put his finger to his lips. 'You don't need to worry your pretty little head over us. We shan't take no harm. You'll see.'

'What are you going to do, then?'

He grinned at her. 'I got a little job to do. Then, when you've fetched me some water I'm gonna spruce meself up so you won't be able to resist me.'

'Oh!' She flounced out of the room and down to the kitchen.

Henry Marshall was enjoying the first brandy of the day with James in his study.

'He'll live?' James asked casually, examining the tip of his cigar.

'Oh, yes, he'll live, but it was touch and go. His friend had done a good job on him. It wasn't his fault it went bad.' Henry filled his pipe from James's tobacco jar and tamped it down. Then he picked up a spill and lit it from the fire. When he'd got it going to his satisfaction he remarked, 'You know who they are?'

James nodded. 'Yes, I do. Deuced awkward.'

Henry gave a shrug. 'Will you turn them in, or shall I?'

James swirled the brandy in his glass. 'I'll do it.' He watched the amber liquid settle. After a while, he said, 'I never liked that Charles Doe, y'know. Bit too full of himself.' He looked up. 'I don't see why we should do his job for him, do you? He's the Riding Officer, so it's up to him to catch the owlers; that's what he's paid for. Why should we hand them to him on a plate?' He picked up the decanter and held it up so that the light shone through the brandy. 'After all, it's hardly to our advantage to turn them in. A drop more, my friend?' he asked with a wink.

'Thank you.' Henry held out his glass. 'This is a fine

brandy, James.' He took a savouring gulp. 'And I've got some very good claret at home that you might like to try, some time.' He tapped the side of his nose. 'I'm inclined to agree with you over all this, James.' He puffed on his pipe for several minutes. 'You've got to hand it to these owlers. They're brave men and they do provide a valuable service to the community, on the quiet.' He finished his brandy and got up to go. 'I'll drop by again tomorrow and see how the patient is.'

James went to the door with him. As Henry swung himself up onto his horse he had the satisfaction of seeing a large bulge under the saddle blanket and felt the hard wood of a brandy keg at his back. Oh, yes, he decided, it would be very foolish to turn the owlers over to the authorities. A case of cutting off one's nose to spite one's face.

He lifted his hand in farewell. 'Call me if I'm needed, James,' he called. 'There'll be no charge.' He patted the bulge behind him and rode off.

Whilst James and Henry Marshall were drinking illicit brandy and deciding on the fate of its providers in James's study, Beatrice was impatiently questioning Charlotte in the morning room.

'But who *are* these men?' she asked for the third time, having been too agitated to listen when Charlotte told her the answer the previous times.

'The sick man is Mollie's cousin, Richard,' Charlotte explained patiently. 'The other man is Joe, his friend.'

'But what are they doing in my house? And more to the point, what is that man doing in Sebastian's bed?'

'Richard is in Sebastian's bed because he hurt his leg very badly when the cliff fell the other night.'

'But that was a week ago.'

'I know. Joe has been looking after him.'

Beatrice put her head in her hands. 'I really don't understand ...'

'Never mind, Mama.' Charlotte went over and laid a

hand on her mother's shoulder. 'It doesn't matter.'

'But they are strange men. In my house. They could murder us in our beds.' Beatrice turned a tear-stained face to her daughter.

'They're not that strange, Mama. I told you, Richard is Mollie's cousin and Joe is his friend.' She smiled encouragingly. 'Surely you don't begrudge Mollie's cousin a bed in our house now he's injured?'

'I suppose not,' Beatrice said doubtfully. She gave a shudder. 'But from what I saw of them they could be criminals, or smugglers ...'

'Oh, really, Mama,' Charlotte said with a laugh, adjusting her mother's collar, made out of a piece of Mollie's Brussels lace. 'Can I get you a glass of Madeira, to calm your nerves?'

'Yes, I think that would be very nice, dear,' Beatrice said faintly. 'And then I think I shall go to my room.' She didn't add 'and lock the door', but that was exactly what she was intending to do.

314

Chapter Thirty

Charlotte escaped from her mother and went back to Richard.

He was awake and propped up in bed, looking much better and drinking soup from a mug. Mollie was sitting at the foot of the bed. There was no sign of Joe.

''E's gone home to let 'is mum an' dad see he's safe,' Richard volunteered when Charlotte asked. 'Although Andy said he'd go an' tell them he hadn't come to no harm when the cliff fell. I dunno what Andy told me dad, though. He couldn't exactly say I hadn't come to no harm, could he?'

'I'll go and see Uncle Sam and tell him what's happened,' Mollie said. She smiled, shaking her head. 'Do you know, I really couldn't believe it was Joe when I saw him all dressed up in Sebastian's clothes. I'd never seen him look so smart. He's quite handsome when he's had a shave and brushed his hair.'

'Yeh, he scrubs up well.' He put his thumb up. 'There y'are, girl. I've always told you Joe's the man for you, but you wouldn't listen.' He finished his soup and gave the mug to Charlotte. 'They'd make a good pair, Mollie an' Joe, don't you reckon, darlin'?'

'Oh, yes. It would be absolutely perfect because then the four of us could set up house together,' Charlotte said, her eyes sparkling.

'I dunno about that, sweetheart,' Richard said, managing

to pull her to him so that he could get his arm round her. 'I want you all to meself. They'll hev to fend for themselves. Mind you, they could come an' help out in the pub now and again.'

'Before you decide my future, let me tell you I'm not intending to set up home with *anybody*, least of all Joe Trayler,' Mollie said sharply, annoyed that her future was being mapped out for her in such an arbitrary manner. Then Richard's last words registered and she looked from him to Charlotte and back again. 'Pub? What pub?'

'Oh, hasn't he told you? Dick's bought a pub in Colchester,' Charlotte said excitedly. She took his free hand in hers. 'And that's where we're going to live after we're married.'

'It's at the Hythe. Not too far from the river,' Richard added.

'It's called The Jolly Sailor. And there's a passageway ...'

He gave her a little shake. 'Now, now, don't give away our secrets, darlin'.'

Mollie could hardly believe her ears. She hadn't realised things had progressed this far between them and she was filled with misgivings.

'I shouldn't make too many plans, if I were you,' she advised. 'Your parents have probably got a different husband in mind for you, Charley.' She turned to her cousin. 'And much as I love you, Dick, I hardly think you're the kind of man James Grainger is going to allow his daughter to marry.'

'Oh, I shall get round Papa. He always gives in to me,' Charlotte said airily, with a toss of her head.

Mollie got to her feet, suddenly tired of listening to their pie-in-the-sky ideas that hadn't a hope of coming to fruition. 'I'll go and see Uncle Sam and tell him what's happened to you, Richard. He should be home from work by the time I get there.'

'Oh, no, Mollie, you can't possibly go. We need you here as chaperone. Mama would be horrified if she thought

316

I was alone here with Richard,' Charlotte said anxiously.

'Oh, leave the door open and sit over the other side of the room, then she'll have no cause to complain,' Mollie said, waving her arm vaguely. As far as she could see that was the least of their worries.

She put on a warm cloak and boots to walk the mile or so to Copperas Lane. She walked briskly because the light was already beginning to fade into a raw, frosty evening. By the time she arrived in Copperas Lane Uncle Sam was just coming out of the gates of the Copperas House.

His face lit up when he saw her. 'Jest a minute, my girl,' he said after their first greeting, 'Mr Mark is still in his office. I'll tell 'im you're here. He's always said he's on'y too happy to walk you home.'

'Oh, there's no need for that, Uncle,' she protested.

'That'll be pitch dark in half an hour so I don't want you walkin' home alone,' he said. 'I'll be happier if you've got company on that lonely ole cliff road. You go on in. Cissie's there. She'll make you a cuppa tea.'

Secretly pleased at her uncle's insistence on alerting Mark to her presence, Mollie went up the steps and into the house. What she saw there pleased her even more. Everywhere was neat and tidy and Cissie had a kettle of hot water on the stove ready for Sam to clean himself up in the wash house as soon as he got home. The table was laid ready for his meal, which was the succulent stew bubbling on the other side of the stove and Cissie herself looked happy and healthy; she had put on a little weight and it suited her. She was wearing a spotless white apron over a grey skirt and blouse and her hair was tied back with a black ribbon.

She dipped a curtsey when she saw Mollie. 'Oh, Uncle Sam *will* be pleased to see you, Miss,' she said, with a wide smile. 'He's often talkin' about you.' Then the smile died and she said, uncertainly, 'He said I was to call him Uncle Sam. I hope you don't mind, Miss.'

317

'Of course I don't mind, Cissie. I'm only too glad he's got you to look after him. And I can see you do that very well.' Mollie unwrapped the pork pie Cook had given her. 'You can put this on the slab for another day. Mmm, that stew smells delicious.'

'Will you hev a drop, Miss?' Cissie asked shyly.

'Yes, please, I'd love some,' Mollie said, smiling at her and pulling up a chair to the table. 'And, by the way, there's no need for you to curtsey to me, Cissie. I was brought up in this house, remember, and picked mine for most of my life.'

She spent a pleasant hour with Uncle Sam and Cissie, during which she told them about Richard's accident and the ensuing events at Cliff House.

'Thass about time he gave that business up,' Sam said, clamping his gums on to his pipe. 'One o' these days he'll get caught by the Ridin' Officer an' that'll be the end of him.'

'I agree with you, Uncle, and that's what I keep telling him. But I think perhaps he does intend to give it up, soon. He told me today he's bought a pub in Colchester.'

Sam nodded. 'Yes, he said as much to me last week. P'raps that'll settle him down. Let's hope so, anyway. One good thing about his night malarkies is that he ain't short of a copper. He's made hisself a tidy little nest egg over the years, 'cause he ain't one to spend a penny if a ha'penny will do.'

'Did he also tell you he's planning to get married?'

Sam looked at her over his pipe, which he was having trouble getting to draw. 'Married? Richard? No, he never said nothin' to me about getting' married. Who to?'

'Charlotte Grainger.'

He stared at her for a minute, then began to chuckle. 'Oh, my dear life, whatever next!' he said, giving up his pipe for lost and mopping his moustache with a large red handkerchief. 'Well, stands to reason that'll never come to

318

anything; he must be daft to think it might! The Master won't never agree to her marryin' one of his workmen, will he. He'll want her to marry somebody who's got enough money to prop up his business. Thass what he's relyin' on, if you ask me.' His voice dropped. 'There's too many accidents down there these days.' He jerked his thumb in the direction of the Copperas House. 'An' thass all due to the fact that things ain't looked after like they oughta be. Pipes leak acid, hoists snap, troughs rot, an' all because they've bin patched and bodged up instead of bein' renewed. Why, on'y today, the stagin' round the ink vat collapsed because it was rotten an' should have bin replaced ages ago.'

'Oh, dear. Was anyone hurt?' Mollie asked, full of concern.

He nodded. 'Yes, it was a bad business. Harry Jakes fell and hurt his back. Don't know how bad he is yet. Mr Mark said he was goin' to go an' give him a look before he goes home. Mind you, it would've bin a lot worse if Harry had fell in the vat instead of slippin' down the side. Thass common knowledge that if you fall in the ink you're dead within forty-eight hours an' there's nothin' anyone can do about it. Thass why men don't much like workin' in the ink shed. Not that it's any more dangerous than the rest o' the jobs, not if you're careful an' the equipment is sound. But thass enough of that. Cissie, pour me another cuppa tea and another helpin' o' that stew. More stew for you, Mollie?'

'No thank you, but what I had was delicious. You're a good cook, Cissie.'

'Aye, she's a good girl,' Sam said contentedly. 'She looks after me a treat.' He looked at the clock. 'I reckon Mr Mark'll be about ready to leave, Mollie. He said it would be about this time.'

'Oh, then I'd better be off. I wouldn't want to keep him waiting.' She put on her cloak, kissed her uncle and went out into the night.

Mark was already waiting for her at the gate and they fell into step as they walked up Copperas Lane and out on to the High Street, where the oil-lit shop windows cast a yellow light on the road. But once they were out on the cliff path the darkness was complete, the sky over the sea like black velvet speckled with pin-prick stars. The only sounds were of their shoes, ringing on the frost-hard path and the sound of the sea, slapping quietly as it receded from the shore.

'Thank you for waiting for me, Mark,' Mollie said, for some reason suddenly feeling a little shy in his presence.

'Believe me, it's my pleasure,' he replied. 'I told you before, I'm always happy to walk you back from your uncle's house. And tonight, I'm glad of some company.'

'You mean because of the accident? Uncle told me about the staging collapsing.'

Mollie sensed that Mark was glad to talk about it.

'I've been to see Harry,' he said. 'It may not be quite as bad as we feared. He can feel his legs and move his toes a little so it may be that his back is not broken but just badly bruised. That's what Dr Marshall says, anyway.'

'Oh, they called the doctor in?' Mollie was surprised. There wasn't usually money to spare for doctor's bills in Copperas Lane.

'I called the doctor,' Mark corrected. 'I thought we owed Harry that much. After all, he fell because the staging was rotten, not because he was being careless.'

'Yes, Uncle Sam was saying things don't get repaired as they should.'

'He's right.' Mark gave a sigh. 'I've been battling over this for years. I really can't understand how my uncle can have such little interest in a business that was started by his great-grandfather.'

'His great-grandfather? Goodness, surely it's his duty to look after it and build on what is already there. After all, he has children of his own to hand it on to.'

'Perhaps that's why he cares so little about it,' he said thoughtfully. 'After all, Sebastian has never shown any inclination to take it over. I think he was glad to escape into

320

the Army, to tell you the truth. And of course, Charlotte, being a woman, could hardly be expected to take it on.'

'No, but if she married the right person, maybe her husband would be happy to run it,' Mollie said, reluctantly, knowing that this was exactly what Mark was being groomed for.

'Maybe.' His tone gave nothing away.

They walked in silence for several minutes, the only sound in the darkness the regular, relentless, swish of the waves. 'You would think he'd be proud of his family's achievements and be anxious to carry them on,' Mollie said.

'Yes, you'd think so. But I can tell you he isn't.' There was bitterness in Mark's tone. 'All he thinks about is how much he can milk the business for so that he can keep up with his gambling cronies. He takes out money that should be ploughed back into repairs and new equipment. And I'm sure you've noticed that Aunt Beatrice has to run the household on little more than a shoestring.' He paused for a moment, then went on, 'I do what I can to keep things going, but since there's not so much cloth-making in the district now, the dyers are buying less from us, and my uncle does nothing to encourage trade with them. In truth, it's mainly the materials for gunpowder we supply for the war with France that's providing us with the money to pay the wage bill at the moment. If things go on as they are and James Grainger continues to gamble the profits away it's difficult to see what will happen in the future.'

Mollie said nothing. There was little she could helpfully say about the Copperas House and Mark seemed so worried and dejected that this didn't seem the right time for him to learn about Charlotte's madcap idea of marrying Richard. In any case, like Uncle Sam said, it would probably come to nothing. But Richard's presence in Sebastian's old room couldn't be hidden from him. And he would think it strange if she didn't mention it.

321

'You remember the collapse of the cliff last week?' she said carefully.

'Yes, it was quite a fall, wasn't it,' he agreed, glad at the change of subject.

'There hadn't been particularly high tides battering the foot of the cliff, so I don't know why it should have happened like that,' she said.

'I think it was probably due to all the rain we'd had in the previous days,' he said thoughtfully. 'You see, these cliffs are made of clay, not rock – that's why we get the copperas from them – so if they get too waterlogged from the springs deep inside them they become unstable and break away.' She felt rather than saw him shrug. 'That's my theory, anyway.'

'I hadn't thought of that,' she said. Then she added, 'My cousin Richard was down on the beach right underneath the cliff where it collapsed. He hurt his leg quite badly.'

'Oh, I'm sorry to hear that. But he was lucky not to be buried alive, I should think. I wondered why he hasn't been at work and your uncle didn't say.'

'Uncle didn't know. And I suppose he might have been buried if his friend, Joe Trayler, hadn't been there to dig him out and look after him. But his injury was quite bad, so Charlotte suggested Joe should bring him into the house. He's in Sebastian's room now.'

'In Sebastian's room? Good grief! What did Aunt B. think of that? Not much, I guess.'

'No, she was convinced that we'd all be murdered in our beds. I think she thought they were pirates or something.'

'Owlers, more likely,' he said quietly, then more loudly, 'Poor fellow. I'll go along and see him before I go to bed. How long will he be staying?'

'I don't know. Until he's able to walk, I suppose. Or until Mr Grainger throws him out.'

'Oh, I'll be surprised if Uncle James does that,' he said enigmatically.

Frowning, she twisted round, trying to see his expression. She recalled that he had mentioned 'owlers' and hadn't shown any surprise that Richard had been on the beach in the middle of the night, but she could only see his profile, faint against the pale water and she stumbled on the uneven ground.

'Careful,' he said, taking her arm to steady her.

Neither of them spoke again, but he was still holding her arm when they reached Cliff House and she had made no attempt to free it.

Richard stayed in Sebastian's room for a week. At the end of that time, with the aid of crutches, he was able to walk downstairs to the kitchen for his meals and to walk short distances outside.

'Your cousin will be going home soon, I take it?' Beatrice asked Mollie one morning. 'I think he is sufficiently recovered to leave now.' She frowned and leaned towards Mollie. 'I think Charlotte is paying him rather too much attention, to tell you the truth, Mollie. Not that I have anything against your cousin, my dear,' she added hastily, 'but, well, you do understand what I mean ...'

Mollie smiled a somewhat sickly smile and went to find Richard.

He was in the boot room with Charlotte. They sprang apart when Mollie entered.

'I think it's time you went home, Dick,' she said, preferring not to notice that Charlotte was blushing and fiddling with her bodice. 'Mrs Grainger is beginning to think you're outstaying your welcome.'

'Nonsense,' Charlotte said briskly. 'We're going to be married. There's no question of Richard outstaying his welcome.' She took his hand.

'I don't think your mother is aware of this,' Mollie said. 'From what she was saying to me ...'

'I'm going to tell her this morning. In fact –' Charlotte turned, with a flounce of skirts '– I'll go and tell her, right

323

this minute. I'm sure she'll be delighted.' She blew Richard a kiss and went off to find her mother.

'I still think you'd do well to pack your bag, Dick,' Mollie said dryly. 'I'll come and help you if you like.'

It was fortunate that Beatrice was in her room when Charlotte gave her the news, because Charlotte had to burn feathers under her nose to bring her round.

'Did I hear you aright, Charlotte? You want to *marry* that ruffian who's been staying – against my better judgement, I might add – in Sebastian's room?' Beatrice said faintly as she staggered to her chaise longue.

'That's right, Mama. And he's not a ruffian, he's Mollie's cousin, as you very well know.' She lifted her chin. 'I'm in love with Richard, Mama, and we intend to be married as soon as he is well enough.'

'Oh, no! That can never be!' Beatrice promptly fainted again and had to be revived with more burning feathers and a liberal glass of Madeira, followed by a second, which she drank with rather unwise haste.

'I can't believe I'm hearing this,' she said when she'd finished it, handing Charlotte her glass for yet more. 'Firsht, my houshe is filled with ruff-ruff-ruffians and then I find you have this hare-brained notion of marrying one of them. Have you quite laken teave of your senses, Charlotte?' She shook her head and frowned a little as she realised that in spite of her efforts to be firm and unyielding, her words weren't coming out quite as she intended. 'In any case, you hardly know the man. He's only been here a week,' she continued slowly, forming her words with care.

Charlotte didn't refill the glass but put it down out of her mother's reach. 'Oh, I've known him much longer than a week, Mama.'

Beatrice reared up, jerking her head forward like an angry turkey. 'How long? Where?'

Charlotte thought carefully. She could hardly tell her

324

mother she had got to know Richard through aiding him to smuggle goods. 'I've told you, he's Mollie's cousin. That's how we became acquainted.' She hurried on, before her mother could say anything further, 'But I think you're being a little unfair, Mama. When you know Richard better, I'm sure you'll like him.'

'I don't intend to know him better,' Beatrice said with more than a hint of petulance.

'Oh, come now, Mama. How can you say that? After all, you've become very fond of Mollie, haven't you?'

'Mollie's different,' Beatrice said, still making sure to form her words carefully. 'I regard Mollie as one of the family.'

'Well, soon you'll be able to regard Richard in the same way.' Charlotte beamed at her.

'Never!' Beatrice passed her hand across her forehead, searching her fuddled mind for what she knew would be the deciding factor, if she could only think what it was. It had been a mistake to drink two glasses of Madeira so quickly, she realised that now, but she had needed more than a few feathers burned under her nose to revive her from the shock Charlotte had given her.

For once, she wished James were here – she normally preferred her room to his company – but in this situation perhaps he would know what to do. Ah, yes, that was it. That was the deciding factor.

'It's quite out of the question. Your father will never allow it!' she said triumphantly. She waved Charlotte away, having successfully dealt with the matter. 'Now, I don't wish to hear another word. I must lie down. Listening to all this nonsense has given me a headache.'

Chapter Thirty-one

Later that day, Beatrice was pacing up and down the length of the morning room, her purple skirts swishing at every turn, after summoning James, who would have preferred to be out riding. He stood by the window, his attention divided between the bright, cold sunshine of early spring outside and the dark storm of his wife's temper inside.

Each time she reached him she said, 'It's not to be supported, James. There can be no question of this marriage. He must leave this house immediately.' She put her fingers to her temples. She still had a raging headache, which wasn't improving her mood.

'I agree with you, my dear. I'll speak to him,' James said for the fourth time, his voice uncharacteristically mild. 'Of course, the marriage is out of the question.'

Beatrice stopped in her stride and glared at him as his words finally penetrated. It wasn't often that he agreed with her and she was immediately suspicious of his motives. 'Charlotte is quite determined, you realise that?'

'Charlotte will do as she's told or her allowance will be stopped. Now, sit down, my dear. Getting yourself into such a pet will only bring on one of your heads.'

'I've already *got* one of my heads, James.' Nevertheless, she sat down by the fire. 'Oh, what's to be done?'

He came and stood on the hearthrug with his back to the fire, lifting his coat tails to get the maximum warmth where

326

it mattered. 'As I said, I shall speak to the young man. I think he is sufficiently recovered to go back to wherever he has come from ...'

'Under some slimy stone, if you ask me,' Beatrice said cruelly.

' ... wherever he has come from,' he continued as if she hadn't spoken. 'This idea of marrying him is probably all in Charlotte's mind and the poor unsuspecting young man has no idea of it.' He had heard tales of some well-to-do women who liked a tumble with the stable lad or gardener, the rougher the better, and wondered if his daughter might harbour the same desires. He knew the feeling himself; kitchen maids, milk maids ... he felt the familiar hot sensation that had nothing to do with the warmth from the fire and dragged his attention back to his wife, which immediately dowsed it.

'She knows very well that she is to marry Mark,' he said briskly. 'He will be a very suitable husband for her; he's steady and hard-working and knows the business inside out. And she's fond of him, I know that.'

'But is he fond of her, James?' Beatrice asked.

'Of course he is. Who wouldn't be? A pretty gel like Charlotte.' He shrugged. 'In any case, she'll inherit the business, so he'd be a fool not to want her, after all the work he's put into it.'

Beatrice nodded. She could see the wisdom of James's words and a marriage between her nephew and Charlotte was a dream she had cherished ever since he came to Cliff House. Having never spoken of it to her husband she hadn't realised that he had similar plans for their daughter. Sometimes she almost felt a flash of the old affection for James.

'Nevertheless, I think you must make it plain to this young man – Richard, or whatever his name is – that you won't tolerate any idea of marriage between him and Charlotte,' Beatrice said firmly.

James looked out of the window again at the sunshine.

'I've told you, my dear, I shall speak to him.' With that he managed to make his escape.

In the event, James found the young man quite reasonable.

After a pleasant day in the saddle and a good dinner James summoned Richard to his study and even offered him a glass of the brandy that some weeks ago had found its way to the wine cellar via the owlers' courtesy and the tunnel.

'Your health, Sir,' Richard said, holding the glass up so that the lamp shone through the golden liquid. 'Nice drop o' brandy.'

James nodded. 'I always appreciate a good brandy.'

'Well, there's plenty more where that came from.' Richard swirled the illicit liquid in his glass and watched it settle. He knew exactly why he had been allowed to make himself comfortable in the deep leather armchair by the fire in James Grainger's study.

James, sitting in an identical chair on the opposite side of the fire, cleared his throat. 'There's something I have to say to you, Barnes.' He cleared his throat again, slightly nervous at broaching what could be a rather tricky situation. 'It's like this. Whilst I appreciate what you ...' he held up his glass. 'Indeed, I'm very grateful ... you understand my meaning?'

'Oh, yes, Sir, I understand,' Richard said with a grin. He knew the old bugger didn't want to jeopardise his supply of smuggled drink. 'I don't reckon you need to worry about that.'

'Good.' James nodded several times. 'But what I have to say is ... about my daughter.' He took a generous gulp of brandy to boost his confidence and went on with a rush, 'You must understand that I really couldn't countenance you marrying her. I'm sorry, Barnes, but it wouldn't be at all a suitable match. I mean to say, you're nothing more than a labourer in my Copperas House, for God's sake. You surely can't expect to marry into my family.'

328

Richard drained his glass and put it down where James would find it easy to refill. 'It wouldn't be easy, I grant you,' he said, watching the liquid flow into the glass. 'But Charlotte and me ...'

James waved his arm dismissively. 'A passing fancy, I assure you. Charlotte is infatuated and you're flattered by her attention.'

'I don't think it's quite as simple as that, Sir,' Richard said, letting his gaze rove round the study at the heavy furnishings and the prints.

James followed his gaze, then got up from his chair with a sigh, went over to his desk and pulled out his cheque book. 'How much?'

'How much is it worth to you, Sir?' Taking his time, Richard drained his glass and got to his feet to pick up the cheque James had written, raising his eyebrows at the size of it.

'Thank you, Sir. I'll pack my bag an' be off first thing termorrer,' he said, picking up the stick he still used and limping to the door.

'I'm glad to find you're such a reasonable man, Barnes.' James refilled his own glass, relieved the confrontation had gone so smoothly.

As soon as Beatrice found out what had passed between James and Richard – and James lost no time in telling her – she made it her business to make sure her daughter was left in no doubt that her lover had been bought off.

'So much for his undying love,' she finished complacently.

Charlotte sat for several minutes, saying nothing, her hands clenched in her lap. Then she got to her feet.

'Well, you've got what you wanted, Mama. I hope you're satisfied,' she said bitterly.

'As time goes on you'll be glad things have turned out this way, Charlotte, dear.' Beatrice said. She was surprised that Charlotte had taken the news so calmly. She'd been prepared for hysterics.

'Perhaps.' Charlotte got to her feet, her shoulders drooping. 'I think I shall go to my room, if you don't mind, Mama.'

'Yes, that's probably the best thing,' Beatrice said sympathetically. 'Mollie will bring you some chocolate, won't you, Mollie?'

'Yes, of course.' Mollie had been sitting quietly, listening to the conversation. She was disappointed in Richard. She never thought he would have allowed himself to be bribed in that way.

She went down to the kitchen. Richard was there, finishing off a large helping of plum pie.

'So you'll be off in the morning,' she said as she stood at the stove making the chocolate.

'Thass right. Me leg's a lot better now.'

'And I can see there's nothing wrong with your appetite,' she said tartly.

He shrugged. 'Well, I gotta stoke up. No tellin' where me next meal is comin' from, is there?' He gave her a wink, which she ignored.

'It won't be from here, that's for certain.'

'How's Charley taken the news?' he asked, spitting out a pip.

'Very quietly. She's gone to her room. I reckon she can't believe you'd do such a thing to her. And neither can I. I'm disappointed in you, Dick.' She took the chocolate and went to the door.

'You'll get over it,' he said cheerfully.

'I only hope Charlotte will, too,' she replied and went upstairs to Charlotte's room.

Charlotte was already in bed. 'Do you want to talk?' Mollie asked as she handed her the drink.

Charlotte shook her head. She was rather pale and her hand shook as she took the cup. 'No, I'll drink this and then I'll try and go to sleep,' she said in a small voice.

'Are you quite sure?' Mollie asked, studying her, surprised she wasn't in a frenzy of screaming and shouting as she usually was when things didn't go her way.

330

'I'm weary, that's all.' Charlotte finished her drink and handed the cup back to Mollie.

'Well, if you need anything you've only got to ring the bell,' Mollie said. In truth, she herself was tired after the emotion of the day's events.

'Thank you, Mollie. Thank you for everything.' Charlotte slid down under the covers and closed her eyes.

Mollie went to her room. As she lay in her warm, soft bed in the darkness she didn't know whether she was more surprised that Richard, who had seemed genuinely to care for Charlotte, had been prepared to give her up so easily in return for a cheque from James; or whether Charlotte's reaction had surprised her more. She certainly hadn't expected her to take it so calmly.

Yet perhaps it wasn't so out of character. Less than two years after her torrid affair with Captain Pilkington Charlotte couldn't even remember his name. Yet if Mollie hadn't intervened it could have ended in complete disaster. Maybe it was not in Charlotte's nature to care very deeply for anybody.

Or maybe her true, lasting affection was for Mark and anything else was no more than passing fancy. Mollie could understand that; what she couldn't imagine was how love for Mark could ever leave room for passing fancies.

The next morning, after a surprisingly deep and dreamless sleep, Mollie was up early. She went first along to Sebastian's room to make her peace with Richard. Whatever had happened last night he was still her cousin and she was fond of him; she didn't want him to leave thinking she was still angry with him.

But the room was empty. Every stick of Richard's belongings had gone and the room was as neat as a new pin.

She went down to the kitchen to make Charlotte's morning chocolate and to ask Tilda what time he had left.

'I dunno. I haven't seen him. Ask Kitty. She's always first up,' Tilda said.

Kitty hadn't seen him, either. 'But I was a bit late up, today; it bein' so cold and I could have bin in the morning room, clatterin' about doing the fires when he left,' she said.

'Never mind. Perhaps I'll see him when I go to visit Uncle Sam. He often turns up there.'

'He must've gone off in a bit of a huff,' Tilda remarked. 'He never even stopped to say goodbye to any of us. I'd have thought he would, because we've had some good old laughs with him at mealtimes down here in the kitchen.'

Mollie made the chocolate and took it up to Charlotte. She'd been in a strange mood last night; numb might best describe her. But now she had had all night for the news to sink in and Mollie prepared herself for a tantrum. Of course, she, Mollie would be blamed. In the absence of Richard to vent her spleen on, his cousin would be the next best thing. She took a deep breath to prepare herself and pushed open the door.

Charlotte was not there. The bed was rumpled; the wardrobe doors were swinging open, drawers had garments hanging out of them and there were discarded clothes all over the floor. Mollie picked up a shoe and stood with it in her hand, staring at the chaos, her mouth hanging open.

Where was she? Had she gone for an early ride to clear her head? She stepped over petticoats and shifts to look in the wardrobe. Yes, the dark-green riding habit had gone, so that must be the answer.

Then, out of the corner of her eye she saw a scrap of paper, tucked in the mirror frame on the dressing table. She pulled it out, unfolded it and began to read.

Dearest Mollie,
Please don't be angry with me, but I really love Richard and he loves me. Papa won't let us be married so we're eloping. When we're married, which will be as soon as we can find a clergyman, we shall return home to The Jolly Sailor (I like that, home to the Jolly

Sailor). I do hope you'll come and see us there.

*You can tell Papa that Richard has torn up the
cheque. He says I'm worth a good deal more than two
hundred pounds to him and anyway he doesn't need
Papa's money because he's got plenty of his own.
(I daresay the cheque would have bounced, anyway.)*

*Tell Papa it's no use trying to fetch me back; by the
time you read this we shall probably be married and
even if we're not I expect I shall be pregnant.*

Thank you for everything, Mollie.

I'm glad we shall be related.

Love, Charlotte.

Mollie sat down on the bed with a bump and read the letter
through twice more. Then she closed her eyes. Of course.
She should have realised what was afoot. Last night's
callous behaviour was totally unlike Richard; she had
thought that at the time. And she had been equally surprised
at Charlotte's mute acceptance of her fate. Now it was clear
that they had already made plans to elope, so James's
refusal to allow them to marry was irrelevant.

She turned the letter over in her hand and a smile spread
across her face. She wished them luck. Oh, yes. She
wished them all the luck in the world. She tucked the letter
under Charlotte's pillow and set about tidying the room.

The news would keep for an hour or two.

She took her time and was still sorting and putting things
away over an hour later when Beatrice came into the room.
She was wearing a paisley shawl over a pale-blue morning
gown and she had dark circles under her eyes.

'I've hardly slept a wink so I've come along to see how
Charlotte . . . ' She stopped, staring round the room. 'What's
this? Where is she? Has she wrecked the room in her temper?
Oh, dear, I thought she took the news a little too calmly last
night.'

Mollie took the letter from under the pillow and handed

it to her. She read it through twice, shaking her head.

'Why am I not surprised?' she asked wearily. She walked over to the chair by the window and sat down, the letter still in her hand. She looked up at Mollie. 'What's this Jolly Sailor she talks about?' she asked, frowning.

'It's a pub my cousin Richard's bought in Colchester.'

'He's *bought* a public house?'

Mollie nodded. 'Richard isn't short of money, Ma'am. In fact, I believe he's quite a rich man.'

'But I thought he was only a labourer at my husband's Copperas House.'

Mollie pursed her lips. 'He's got other interests, Ma'am.'

Beatrice digested this. Then she said, 'Do you think they really are in love?'

Mollie chewed her lip for a few seconds. Then she said, 'Yes, I believe they are. I think they're what you might call kindred spirits because they've both got the same spirit of adventure. And I know Richard well enough to know that he'll care for Charlotte and look after her.' She nodded. 'Their relationship might be a bit stormy at times but I reckon they'll be very happy together.'

Beatrice smiled at her. 'Then what more can a mother ask?' Her smile faded. 'Of course, my husband may not be quite so accepting of the situation.' She looked up at Mollie. 'I think you'd better come with me, Mollie. I fear I may need a bit of moral support when I show him this.' She glanced down at the letter again and Mollie noticed that there was a faint smile playing round her lips.

James had not slept well. Congratulating himself on the way he had handled the young puppy who had the effrontery to think he could marry Charlotte, he had drunk rather more brandy than he should have. The result was a head the size of a barn.

He cringed when Beatrice burst into his study, waving a letter. He needed peace and quiet, not a nagging wife.

But when he read the letter, all his fury boiled over and he turned his wrath not on Beatrice, but on Mollie, standing just behind her.

'This is all your fault!' he raged. 'If you hadn't come into my house Charlotte would never have met this cousin of yours and all this would never have happened. I blame you entirely, Miss.'

'James!' Beatrice was horrified. 'How can you say such a thing!'

He banged his fist on his desk. 'Because it's true. God damn her. Not only has she driven my son away by her refusal to marry him – a marriage that, God knows, I only agreed to because I thought it would make a man of Sebastian – but now my only daughter has gone off with *her* relative.' He stormed across the room and jabbed his finger in Mollie's direction. 'If *she* hadn't come into my house none of this would ever have happened. This ... this *creature* has cost me both my children!'

Mollie, standing behind and a little to one side of Beatrice, just inside the study door, bowed her head. Everything James said was true. None of it would ever have happened if she hadn't made that vow to sit at his table; a vow she could never have dreamed would have such far-reaching results.

Beatrice turned and to Mollie's surprise, laid her arm round her shoulders.

'I think you're forgetting two things, James,' she said quietly. 'The first is that you've never taken any interest in either Sebastian or Charlotte, except when it suited you. They grew up in this house hardly knowing who you were. It's true, you hoped Sebastian would take an interest in your business, but only so that you didn't need to. In the event, he proved to be too much like you to care about anything but hunting and gambling. And as for Charlotte, it was only when you realised that she had become a very pretty young woman that you saw her potential to marry a rich man and keep you out of penury.'

'Have you quite finished, Madam?' James, barked, his face purple with rage.

Beatrice lifted her chin. 'No, James. I said there were two things you had forgotten. The second one is that you have three children, not two.' She drew Mollie forward. 'Please remember that this girl is also your daughter.'

'No! This bitch is no get of mine! I want her out of my house and out of my life. Now, get out. Both of you!' He went over and flung open the door.

'Come along, Mollie.' Holding her head high, Beatrice took Mollie's hand and led her from the room. As she reached the door she stopped. 'You know it's true, James, however much you try to deny it,' she said quietly.

'Bah!' He slammed the door, barely giving them time to get through it. Then he strode over to his desk and snatched up Charlotte's letter, read it through again, tore it in half and threw it into the fire. He watched it burn, then, with an ugly expression on his face he rang the bell and called for his horse to be saddled, flung himself out of the house and galloped off towards the town.

Chapter Thirty-two

Beatrice stalked back along the corridor to her room.

Mollie followed in a daze, her head spinning from the morning's events, taking a little running step to catch up with her as she strode on ahead. How could she possibly have known? Who could have told her that she was James's illegitimate daughter? James would never have done so. Sebastian? No, he hadn't believed it was true. So who could it have been?

They reached Beatrice's room.

'Come in and shut the door, Mollie,' Beatrice ordered. She flopped down on the chaise longue and began to massage her temples. 'Ring the bell, would you, dear, and ask Tilda to bring us some tea ... no, wait a minute, perhaps coffee would be more in order.'

'I'll go ...' Mollie started towards the door.

'No, no.' Beatrice shook her head irritably, 'I said ring for Tilda. You don't look as if your legs would carry you as far as the kitchen. In any case, I want you here, with me.'

Mollie did as she asked, then went over and sat down in the chair Beatrice indicated, suddenly realising that her legs were indeed quite shaky. Beatrice leaned back on her cushions with her eyes closed and was silent for quite a long time. 'I expect you're wondering how I knew?' she said, opening her eyes at last.

337

Mollie nodded, licking her lips.

She smiled gently. 'My dear, I've always known, ever since the day I first saw you.' She looked up as Tilda entered with the coffee. 'That's right, put it down there. Did you bring two cups? Good. That will be all, thank you, Tilda. Mollie will pour.'

Mollie poured the coffee, keeping her hands steady with difficulty. 'But how could you have known?' she whispered as she added cream and put a cup on the little table beside Beatrice. 'And if you knew, why did you let me come here?'

'Ah, just how I like it.' Beatrice took several sips of coffee before she answered. Then she said, 'The first time I saw you, Mollie, you reminded me of somebody, but I couldn't think who. Then, when you told me your history, I knew who it was you reminded me of – a young girl called Mary, who had been my maid until she disgraced herself by becoming pregnant.'

'It wasn't . . . ' Mollie began hotly.

Beatrice held up her hand to silence her. 'I know it wasn't her fault, Mollie. But be that as it may, when I thought about it I realised that you were just about the right age to be the child she would have borne and the more I looked at you the more I could see the likeness, especially round the eyes. Hers were an unusual brown, just like yours.' She shook her head. 'Oh, no, there's never been any doubt in my mind that you were Mary's child. But I chose my words badly when I implied it was her own fault. Of course it wasn't. If anybody was to blame it was me. It was *my* fault.'

'How could that be?' Mollie asked with a frown. 'I don't understand.'

'No, of course you don't,' Beatrice said, turning her head away, and there was bitterness in her voice. 'You don't know what it's like to be married to a man whose habits are on a par with a rutting stag. I put up with it until Charlotte was born, then, having done my duty and

338

provided James with the two children he needed, I closed my bedroom door to him.' She gave a shrug. 'I was well aware that he would find his pleasures elsewhere, if, indeed, he wasn't already doing so, but I didn't care, so long as he left me alone.' She took several more sips of her coffee. 'What I hadn't realised was that he had begun to use Mary, my own maid.' She paused. 'I never discovered whether he took her to spite me or because she was such an attractive girl; I suspect it was a little of both. At any rate, the inevitable happened, she became pregnant. Somebody had to be blamed – not the master of the house, of course, that would never do – so some poor little stable lad took the rap and both he and Mary were sacked. That was the last I heard of either of them, until you appeared, Mollie.' She smiled at her. 'Mary was a lovely girl, and you're very like her, did you know that?' She didn't wait for an answer, but went on, 'except that she was fair, whilst you are dark.' She sighed. 'I was really very fond of her and I always felt guilty at the way she had been treated and the fact that I had never tried to find her and help her. When you came on the scene it was almost as if you had been sent. At last I could assuage my guilt, by giving Mary's daughter – and I was pretty sure that you were Mary's daughter – the good life that had been denied to Mary.' She gave a twisted little smile. 'I can't deny that I also felt a perverse sense of satisfaction in bringing James's illegitimate child to live in the house right under his nose,' she added honestly. She put out her hand. 'But what I hadn't expected was that I would grow to love you almost as much as I love my own daughter, Mollie. You're a great comfort and strength to me and I want you by my side, especially now that Charlotte has had the courage to go with the man she loves.'

Mollie's eyes filled with tears. 'Thank you for saying that, Mrs ...'

'I think we're close enough for you to call me Beatrice, now,' Beatrice interrupted with a smile.

Mollie nodded. 'Thank you, for those kind words,

Beatrice, and truly I should like nothing better than to stay here with you. But how can I? You heard what your husband said. He wants me out of his house and out of his life.' A tear rolled slowly down her cheek and glistened there.

'I shall speak to him.' Beatrice's mouth set in a hard line.

'I don't think that will do any good,' Mollie said sadly. 'He may be my natural father but he hates me and I fear nothing you can say or do will change that.' She turned her head away and gazed out of the window at the sea, a heaving, grey-flecked mass stretching as far as the eye could see. 'It was wrong of me to come here in the first place,' she said quietly, 'I can see that now. But it would be even more wrong for me to stay, now that Charlotte has gone.'

Beatrice nodded, reluctantly realising the wisdom of Mollie's words. 'So what will you do, child? Where will you go?' she asked, her voice tinged with anxiety.

She gave a shrug. 'I don't know. I could marry Joe Trayler, I suppose. He's not the man I would have chosen but ...' She was quiet for a moment, then she said, 'Or I could set myself up as a seamstress somewhere, Colchester, or Ipswich perhaps.'

Beatrice sat up. 'Yes, that might be a very good idea,' she said slowly. 'You're very good with your needle and I dare say I could help a little by recommending you to my friends. I'm afraid I can't do much for you financially, though; money is very tight nowadays.' She put out her hand. 'But having said that, please don't think I want you to go, Mollie. Perhaps when all this has blown over we'll be able to work something out so that you can stay here.' Now it was Beatrice's turn to dab her eyes. 'In any case, I shall speak to James, because I really don't know how I can manage without you, my dear, especially now that Charlotte has gone.'

Mollie left her and went back to Charlotte's room to

finish putting things away. Over the past hour the enormity of what Charlotte and Richard had done had been eclipsed for her by Beatrice's revelations, but as she finished clearing up the room and sat down on the bed to think about it she realised that with Charlotte gone there really was no longer any place for her here at Cliff House, in spite of what Beatrice said. She squared her shoulders. Surely she could make a living as a seamstress; after all she had had plenty of practice, making over Charlotte's dresses. She wondered if Mark had yet found her lodgings in Colchester as he had promised; surely it shouldn't be too difficult to find a room.

Then, thinking of Mark, she realised that he didn't even know of Charlotte's elopement with Richard; he would have left to go to the Copperas House before her note had been discovered. With a sigh she fell back and rested her head on Charlotte's pillow. Here was yet another complication. How on earth would Mark take the news that the woman he had been in love with for years had gone off with somebody else? Mollie's cousin, Richard, at that. She rolled her head on the pillow. It was all such a terrible mess and she could see that she was the cause of most of it.

When the bell went for dinner – a fairly new innovation by James – after a day that had passed in something of a daze for Mollie, she sat down at her dressing table and tidied her hair. The reflection that stared back at her was pale, with dark smudges under brown eyes that looked too big for such a pinched face. She leaned her head on her hand; she looked just as she felt, quite washed out. It was no use, she simply couldn't face a meal with the family tonight. By this time Mark would have been told of Charlotte's elopement and like James, he would blame her for it. She could perhaps bear that but what she couldn't face was to see his grief-stricken face at the loss of the woman he loved. Nor could she face James's accusing, malevolent stare.

She threw herself down on her bed and closed her eyes.

341

Tomorrow she would leave, quietly and without fuss. Perhaps Uncle Sam would take her in for a few days, just until she could decide what to do with her life. But she wouldn't stay with him long; she had disrupted too many lives with her presence to risk upsetting his.

A knock at the door disturbed her train of thought.

It was Tilda.

'The missus says dinner's waitin' and are you comin' down.' Her eyes widened. 'My God, you look terrible, Mollie. Can I get you a powder or suthin'?'

'No. I'm all right, thanks, Tilda. But I'm not hungry. Make my apologies to B ... the missus, will you, there's a dear.'

'All right.' Tilda came over and patted her hand. 'I 'spect you're upset about Miss Charlotte goin' off like that. That was a rare do, wasn't it! Do you reckon she'll ever come back?'

Mollie gave a shrug. 'She might. She won't be living too far away so she'll probably come to see her mother sometimes.'

Tilda put her head on one side. 'Thass really upset you, hasn't it, Mollie. Never mind. I'll bring you up some soup. It's leek an' potato, Cook's special. You'll like that, won't you? An' I'll tell the missus you're too upset to come down.'

Mollie nodded. 'Thanks, Tilda.'

The soup was very good. When she had eaten it she packed a bag, selecting what she would take very carefully because she didn't want James to accuse her of stealing Charlotte's belongings, even though she wouldn't be there to hear him. When she had finished she undressed and slipped for the last time into the comfortable bed in her own pretty room.

After a miserable, mostly sleepless night she rose early and put on her favourite green velvet dress. After stripping the bed and making sure the room was perfectly clean and tidy she put on her thick pelisse, picked up her bag and left, sadly closing the door on what had been a very happy episode in her life. Then she went quietly down the back stairs and let herself out through the boot room, not losing sight of the fact that this was the way Charlotte had taken her in the very first time she had visited Cliff House.

It was bitterly cold, and a stiff east wind was blowing. After a moment's thought she decided that it would be more sheltered to walk back along the beach rather than take the cliff path, which was exposed to full extent of the wind's buffeting. She skirted the place where the cliff had collapsed on that fateful night, almost burying Richard, and made her way over to the cliff steps. She noticed that already in places sea lavender was beginning to sprout on fallen lumps of clay.

As she descended the steps she could hear the pounding of the waves on the shore and she saw that the tide was coming in fast. But there was still a fairly wide stretch of sand between the cliff and the sea so she set off at a good pace.

A wintry sunrise threw a shaft of light over the grey, heaving sea. An omen of good things to come, Mollie told herself, pulling back her shoulders and holding her head high as she marched on, her bag, with all she owned in it, clutched firmly in her hand.

Suddenly, above the noise of the sea she heard a voice shouting, 'For heaven sake don't walk so fast! This is not the first time I've had to run to catch up with you!'

She swung round and to her amazement saw Mark racing along the beach towards her, hatless and with his coat flying open.

'Where in heavens name do you think you're going?' he asked breathlessly when he caught up with her.

She stared at him. He was unshaven, his cravat bands were hanging loose and the flannel waistcoat he wore to work was only half buttoned.

He followed her gaze. 'I'm sorry,' he said with a trace

343

of impatience, 'but I looked out of my window as I was dressing and saw you slipping out of the boot room, so I didn't have time . . . ' He ran his fingers through his tousled hair. 'Where do you think you're going, in God's name, Mollie?'

She gave a slight shrug. 'Does it matter?'

'Of course it matters.' He gave her arm a shake.

She detached herself and began to walk again. 'If you must know, I'm going away because I seem to have done nothing but harm since I arrived at Cliff House,' she said in a flat voice. 'Sebastian has gone; that was my fault, because I wouldn't, *couldn't* marry him; now Charlotte has gone, too, and that was my fault because if she hadn't met my cousin Richard she wouldn't have run off with him, breaking your heart and upsetting all her father's plans. As I see it, the best thing – the *only* thing I can do is to leave before I cause any more trouble.'

'You're quite wrong, you know,' he answered, keeping pace with her, his hands deep in his pockets. 'All right, I agree Sebastian went off in high dudgeon because you wouldn't marry him. But, believe me, he'd been looking for an excuse to get away from his father, from the copperas business and everything to do with it, for a long time. You provided him with something really dramatic, allowing him to pretend he was leaving because of his unrequited love for you.'

'But he wanted to marry me,' she protested. 'He would have done *anything*. Even when I told him I was his half-sister he still wouldn't take no for an answer.'

'I'm not suggesting he wasn't in love with you at the time, Mollie,' he said more gently. 'But I know Sebastian of old. He only wants what he can't have. And the more he can't have it the more he wants it.' He paused. 'I've had a couple of letters from him since he left and I can assure you he's having the time of his life in the Army. His father bought him a commission – which I might add, he could ill afford to do – and he's living it up in Salisbury, nowhere

344

near any line of battle. He's not short of female company, either, from what he's told me.' He turned to her with a wry smile. 'So you could say you did him a good turn, Mollie; you gave him a wonderful excuse to get away from the life he hated.'

They walked on in silence for a bit as she digested this. Then she said, 'But what about you and Charlotte?'

He frowned. 'What about me and Charlotte?' he repeated ungrammatically.

'Well, if it hadn't been for me she would never have met my cousin Richard and she would have married you, I'm sure she would . . . ' her voice trailed off.

He stopped in his tracks, forcing her to do the same. 'Is that honestly what you think?' he asked.

'What?'

'That Charlotte and I had planned to marry.'

'Why, yes.' She looked up at him in surprise. 'Charlotte told me . . . '

He returned her gaze, his jaw set. 'What exactly did Charlotte tell you, Mollie?'

She turned away from him, looking towards the sea, absently noticing how the flotsam from the pounding waves was gradually inching up over the sand as the tide rose. 'She told me that you were in love with her,' she whispered, embarrassed at having to admit that they had discussed his innermost feelings. 'She said you'd been in love with her for a long time and she supposed that eventually you would be married.'

He made a sound that was something between a snort and a laugh. 'I think my esteemed cousin was rather deluding herself on that score,' he said. 'I can't imagine where she got the idea from that I might be in love with her, except, of course, that she thinks she's irresistible to every young man she meets. But I can assure you that Charlotte is not at all the kind of wife I would choose, so please don't feel guilty on that score. Your cousin Richard is more than welcome to her, as far as I'm concerned, Mollie.'

Mollie gaped. 'Do you really mean that?'

'Oh, I do, indeed,' he said firmly. 'I wish them luck. I hope they'll be very happy together.'

'I feel sure they will be,' she said, still reeling from surprise at his reaction. 'They're two of a kind; adventurous, impetuous and ...'

'...with total disregard for anything but their own wishes,' Mark finished for her, dismissing the subject. His voice softened. 'But what about you, Mollie? Having got all that out of the way, why must you run away like this?' There was genuine concern in his voice.

'How can I stay when James hates me so much?' she asked desperately. 'I know Beatrice doesn't want me to leave but James will never forgive me for being the reason both his children left home. And even worse than that, he'll never forgive me for bringing his past back to confront him, reminding him how he raped my mother.' She paused. 'No, I can't stay, you must see that.'

'So?'

'I think Joe Trayler would quite like me to marry him,' she said quietly.

'Do you love him?'

She shook her head. 'No. But at least I'd have a roof over my head.'

'That's no reason. You can't marry a man you don't love simply to get a roof over your head,' he said furiously.

'Plenty of women do,' she replied. She turned to face him, suddenly angry at his tone. 'Anyway, you don't seem to have done very well in finding me a room in Colchester so that I can set myself up as a seamstress.'

He sighed and kicked at a pebble before they began to walk again. 'No, that's true,' he said quietly. 'To tell you the truth I haven't looked very hard.'

'But I thought you were trying to find me somewhere to live. I've been waiting for you to tell me ...'

'I haven't looked for a room for you because I didn't want you to leave Cliff House,' he interrupted.

346

'I don't understand,' she said, frowning. She stared ahead, suddenly realising that they had walked much further along the beach than she had realised. They were well past the gap to the town and were approaching the ruins of the old church, which had fallen off the cliff and were now partly submerged in the sand. 'We've come too far,' she said inconsequentially. 'We're well past the gap. We should turn back.'

'We've come too far to turn back,' he said, wilfully misinterpreting her words and turning her to face him. 'There's something I have to tell you,' he said, keeping his hands on her shoulders. 'I love you, Mollie. I think I've loved you almost from the first time I saw you, even though I've always known you don't care for me. But the truth is, I didn't try to find you a room in Colchester because I couldn't bear the thought of you leaving Cliff House, where I could see you almost every day.' He dropped his hands to his sides. 'So, if you're prepared to marry that man, what's his name? Joe Trayler, just to get a roof over your head, you might as well marry me. At least there would be love on my side, if not on yours.' He put his hand up and impatiently brushed a lock of hair away from his forehead.

Smiling, she put her hand up to his face. 'Oh, Mark, of course I'll marry you, if you'll have me. And not just to get a roof over my head, either. There's love on my side, too, and has been for a long time, even though I tried to fight it because I thought you were promised to Charlotte.'

He bent his head to kiss her, then pulled back and rubbed his chin. 'I'm sorry,' he murmured, 'I didn't have time to shave.'

She pulled him down to her again. 'Don't be silly. As if it mattered ...'

Some time later, still enfolded in his arms, she looked up at him. 'We can't continue to live at Cliff House, can we,' she said. 'James would never ...'

He kissed her again. 'No, of course not. We'll find somewhere, sweetheart.' He rested his rough, unshaven

347

chin on her hair. 'And I may have to look for other work, too.'

She leaned back in his arms. 'You would do that? For me?'

He grinned at her. 'Why not? I'm standing here up to my ankles in ice-cold water because I can't bear to let go of you, so what's a small problem like finding another job?'

They both looked down at the tide, swirling round their feet and burst out laughing as they hugged each other again.

Then they turned as they heard the sound of pounding hooves on the sand.

'Oh, it's only Uncle James, out for his morning gallop on the beach,' Mark said, still holding her close. 'He's done that ever since Sebastian left. Well, he can be the first to hear our news.' He waved to James as he approached, then his expression changed. 'Good Lord, look at the speed he's travelling! He doesn't usually go at that rate. Something must be wrong.' He watched his uncle's approach for a few seconds, then shouted, 'My God, he's coming straight for us!' As he spoke he picked Mollie up bodily and leapt over several large lumps of stonework from the old church to get out of his way.

Even as he did so, James, his face contorted with naked hatred, tried to swing his horse round to take a run at them but the horse, momentarily unbalanced, either stumbled or slid on a piece of wet seaweed. James tried to keep his seat but somehow lost his hold and was thrown to the ground, landing heavily on his back, half in and half out of the water.

Chapter Thirty-three

For a moment Mollie and Mark stood, frozen to the spot, hardly able to believe what they had just witnessed. Then Mark came to his senses and raced across to where his uncle lay, partly in the water and knelt down beside him.

Mollie followed. 'Is he . . . ? Will he . . . ?'

'He's still alive,' Mark said, getting to his feet. 'But he's barely conscious so he can't help himself. And the tide's still on the make.'

'Can we move him?'

Mark shook his head. 'The trouble is, we don't know if he's broken anything so we could make matters worse if we try.'

'But we can't just leave him where he is. Can't we drag him up the beach a bit?'

Mark put his hands under James' arms and tried to pull him further out of the water. 'No, he's much to heavy for us to move. But wait a minute, Boxer might do it . . . ' He straightened up and glanced round. The horse was already well off into the distance, kicking up sand as he galloped along the beach on his way back to the safety of his stable. 'Oh, damn the stupid horse, racing off like that!' he muttered under his breath.

'You'll never catch him. It'll be quicker if you run for help, Mark. I'll stay here with James and make sure his head stays above the water,' Mollie said. 'Any other time the pickers would be on the beach and we could have sent one of the children for help, but it's the wrong state of the tide for them to be out and there's not another soul in sight.'

Mark started up the beach, then turned back, looking anxiously from Mollie to James and back again. 'He was trying to kill you, Mollie. He was galloping straight for you. I'm not sure that I should leave you with him.'

'If he'd killed me he would have killed you, too, Mark.' She gave him a little push. 'But now's not the time to worry about that. You go for help. Look at him, what harm could he possibly do me? He's barely conscious.'

Mark took a last look at his uncle before he ran off up the beach, taking long, athletic strides. 'I'll be as quick as I can,' he called over his shoulder.

Mollie watched him until he reached the gap and then turned her attention to James. He was lying on his side with his legs and half his body in the water, his chest and his head resting on sand that would soon be submerged. His hat had fallen off and with it his wig, revealing a scalp that was bald except for a few wispy strands of grey hair. He looked vulnerable and old, very different from the bombastic, arrogant man she was used to seeing strutting about the house. As she watched, a wave, higher than the rest, lapped round his head and then drained back.

If help didn't soon arrive he would be totally submerged and it would be too late to do anything for him.

She went and crouched down beside him, shivering as the cold lapped round her legs. She put her knee behind him to try and roll him a little further up the beach but he was a big man and now that he was partially waterlogged he was even heavier than before. He opened his eyes when he felt her efforts. 'You'll never shift me,' he muttered through chattering teeth.

Relieved that he was conscious she said breathlessly, 'Mark has gone for help. If you could try to push with your elbows, together we might just be able to get you a bit further up the beach.'

With much grunting and groaning he tried to move but even their combined efforts were fruitless. By the time they had finished the useless struggle most of his body was submerged. Only his head and shoulders were clear of the water and soon they would be covered, too.

He looked up at her, an expression of loathing on his face. 'You're enjoying this, aren't you,' he said, his whole body shivering with a mixture of cold and fear. 'You'll enjoy watching me drown.'

'I'm not going to let you drown,' she replied. She sat down in the icy water and eased his head onto her lap. 'Since I can't move you, this will give us a bit more time and Mark should be back with help soon.'

'Why should you care whether I live or die?' he muttered, his eyes closed.

'I don't know, except that you're my father, so it's my duty to do what I can for you.'

'That's what *you* say.'

'You can't deny it's true. Can you feel your feet and legs?'

'No, they're too bloody cold.'

'Are you in pain?'

'I don't know. I told you, I'm too bloody cold to feel anything. Bah! I got a mouthful of water, then. Lift me up higher.'

She knelt and pushed her knees under his shoulders so that she could hitch his head a bit higher as the tide continued to rise.

'You might as well know I intended to kill you,' he said. 'You've been nothing but a thorn in my flesh ever since the day you first came to my house and when I saw you on the beach I saw my chance to run you down. But the bloody horse threw me.' He took several panting breaths. 'So, now it's your turn. You've got your chance to kill me. Nobody would blame you. All you have to do is get up and walk away.'

351

'I can't do that. You're my father,' she repeated, shivering as much as he was from the cold. 'It's my duty to do what I can for you.'

'Well, even if you save me from drowning you needn't think I shall welcome you as a long-lost child when this is over,' he said with as much bitterness as he could muster. 'I shall never acknowledge you as mine.'

'Maybe not, but you know in your heart that I am your child however much you deny it. I know it, too and so does your wife.' She shifted her position slightly to ease her back, surprised that a man's head should be so heavy.

'That's right, let me drop. Now you know I shall never acknowledge you as mine you don't need to bother about me any more. You can let me drown,' he said, his voice heavy with sarcasm.

'I shall not let you drown,' she said. 'I am your daughter. I owe my beginning to you, however careless and cruel your part in it was; now you will owe your life to me, however much you loathe me and hate the thought of it. Oh, no, father, never fear, call it my revenge if you like, but I shall not let you drown.'

He closed his eyes at that and they remained in silence, with the cold sea gradually, insidiously creeping higher and higher until it was as much as Mollie could do to hold his head above the water.

It seemed like hours, but in fact it was less than twenty minutes before Mark returned on a horse he had borrowed. Behind him were men bringing a makeshift stretcher to carry James back to Cliff House. He was blue with cold and slipping in and out of consciousness as they lifted him carefully on to it and carried him along the beach to the gap where a cart was waiting to carry him to Cliff House.

Mark helped Mollie to her feet but by that time she was so numb and stiff after being in the icy water that she couldn't stand. She doubted she would ever be warm again, even when he took off his coat and wrapped her in it, then

352

lifted her on to the horse and got up behind her.

'We'll soon have you home and tucked up in a warm bed, my love,' he said, holding her close so that she would get some warmth from him.

'James?' she murmured through chattering teeth.

'Oh, don't worry about him. The old reprobate is so pickled in alcohol that the whisky in his veins will have kept him from freezing,' Mark replied with uncharacteristic lack of sympathy. 'It's you I'm concerned for, my darling.' He laid his lips against her hair and held her even closer.

Mollie vaguely remembered people running as she was carried up the stairs in Mark's arms, then the pain of her extremities tingling back to life in a warm bath before sinking into the soft comfort of her bed, the bed she had never thought to sleep in again. She slept and felt a slight sense of annoyance when vague figures she didn't recognise – everything was vague, nothing was real – woke her to feed her warm drinks. Once she thought she saw Dr Marshall, another time she saw Uncle Sam sitting beside her bed, but when she put out her hand he wasn't there. Then she thought Mark was there, holding her hand and she smiled at him and fell into a deep, happy sleep, dreaming that he'd told her he loved her.

When she woke she was reluctant to let the dream go, but she heard a noise in the room and her eyes flew open, breaking the spell. Only the spell wasn't broken, because Mark was indeed sitting beside her, holding her hand and with such an anxious expression on his face that she put her other hand out.

'You've shaved, Mark,' she whispered, smiling a little but wondering why it should be so important.

He put her hand to his lips. 'Oh, thank God, you've come back to us, Mollie,' he murmured. 'I ... we were so worried about you.'

'Were you?' She frowned. 'Why? Where have I been? Oh, yes, I remember, I was very cold, even colder than

353

when I used to pick mine on the beach. But I'm warm now.' She gave a little wriggle. 'And this bed is so very comfortable. Mark?'

'Yes, my darling?'

'I think I should like some of Cook's delicious broth. I'm very hungry.' She looked up at him. 'What did you call me?'

'I called you my darling, because you are, my very precious darling.' He got up to ring the bell, pausing only to drop a kiss on her forehead. 'And even more precious because I was so afraid we were going to lose you. You've eaten nothing for nearly a week. You had us all really worried.'

'A week? It doesn't seem that long.'

'That's because Dr Marshall gave you something to make you sleep. You were totally exhausted from the events of the past few days, Mollie, even without nearly freezing in that icy water. I guess it was your tough early life that saved you.'

She tried to think, to understand his words but she couldn't make the effort. Instead, she was content for Tilda to come in with extra pillows and for Beatrice, looking rather pale and with red-rimmed eyes, to bring her a swansdown wrap to put round her shoulders.

'Dear Mollie,' she said, her eyes brimming with tears. 'You're awake at last. Are you feeling better?'

'A little tired, that's all.' Mollie frowned. 'And ... not quite sure what's happened to me. Why do I feel so tired?'

Beatrice squeezed her hand. 'Ah, here's your broth. We'll talk later.'

Mark came in with a tray.

'You shouldn't be waiting on me, Mark,' she said, still rather puzzled.

'I'm not only waiting on you, I'm going to feed you to make sure you eat every last drop,' he said, winking conspiratorially at Beatrice.

He sat down and began to spoon the broth for her.

354

'Tell me what happened,' she said between mouthfuls. 'Why am I here? Why do I feel so weak? And why are you here, looking after me, Mark?'

'I'm here because you've promised to marry me,' he said. 'Don't you remember? And I'm looking after you because I refused to let anyone else do it.'

Her face broke into a delighted smile. 'And I thought it was just a dream. That's why I didn't want to wake up.'

'It's no dream, sweetheart,' he leaned over and kissed her. 'It's real.'

'Yes, I remember now. I was leaving and you came after me and told me you loved me.' She put out her hand and touched his face. 'You hadn't shaved, I remember that. Oh, I was so happy, Mark. I'd loved you for such a long time.' She smiled at him, then her smile faded as her memory returned. 'Then James came.' Her eyes widened. 'He was trying to kill me, Mark, he told me so.'

Mark nodded. 'He might have killed us both if we hadn't reached the ruins of the old church. That's what saved us, being among the heaps of stone and rubble, because Boxer stumbled, or slid on a piece of seaweed; whatever it was it threw James and he landed in the water. But you didn't let him drown, even so.'

'No. I held his head up so he could breathe. Heads are very heavy, Mark. I hadn't realised how heavy a human head could be.' She took another spoonful of broth. 'Oh, it was so cold; so dreadfully, dreadfully cold,' she said with a shiver. She went on, 'I knew he hated me, but I think he hated me even more because I refused to let him drown. He told me he would never acknowledge me as his daughter, but he can't deny it's true. I know he knows it's true and that's enough for me.' She leaned back on her pillows. 'Of course, he won't let me stay here, but that doesn't matter, does it, Mark? We'll have our own house soon. It doesn't have to be very big, just as long as we're together.' She put out her hand and he took it. 'But what about your work?

355

What about the Copperas House? Will you have to leave it when we marry, Mark?'

'No, I don't think so.' He hesitated. 'There's something you don't yet know, Mollie,' he said.

She sat up. 'Your work? James is turning you out of the Copperas House? Oh, Mark!'

He shook his head. 'No, sweetheart. Not that.'

'Then what?'

'It's Uncle James. He didn't survive. Being thrown from his horse and then the time he spent in the icy water was all too much for his heart. He was dead by the time they got him home.'

'So all my efforts were in vain,' she said sadly, leaning back on her pillows again.

'No. You did what you could. And James knew that.'

'I didn't exactly make my peace with him,' she said wryly. 'He died still hating me.'

'Only because you refused to treat him as he tried to treat you.' Mark got up and kissed her. 'Now I think you should sleep again, sweetheart. That is, if I haven't given you rather too much to think about.'

She smiled. 'I shall sleep because I shall only think about you, my love.' Even as she spoke her eyes were closing.

Three days later James Grainger was buried. The funeral was attended by his son, Sebastian, looking very smart in his officer's uniform, his son-in-law, Richard Barnes, his wife's nephew, Mark Hamilton, and Dr Marshall as well as his solicitor and a few business acquaintances. The scene at the graveside was one of duty rather than grief.

At Cliff House, dutifully following the burial service in the prayer book, were the women of the household, suitably clad in sombre black, Beatrice and Charlotte, and at Beatrice's request Mollie.

Returning from the funeral, Charles Bennet, James's solicitor, read the will.

'It's a new will,' he began, clearing his throat. 'My

356

client came to me only the day before he died and insisted that it should be drawn up and signed then and there.' He coughed discreetly. 'He was not in a mood to be dissuaded ... er, not, of course, that it's my business to persuade or dissuade ...'

'Oh, never mind all that,' Sebastian said impatiently. 'Cut out the formalities and read the will. I need to get back to my regiment.' He had coarsened, and Mollie noticed with some amusement that in spite of his fervent protestations of undying love and his declaration that he was only joining the Army because he couldn't live without her, he had hardly spared her so much as a glance ever since he had returned to Cliff House.

The solicitor cleared his throat again and proceeded to convey James Grainger's wishes to his family. They were fairly straightforward. He left Cliff House and everything in it to his wife, Beatrice.

'That's fair enough,' Sebastian said, nodding magnanimously. 'In any case, *I* don't want it.'

'May I go on?' Charles Bennet looked at Sebastian over the top of his gold-rimmed specatacles. Sebastian nodded, so he continued, 'To my wife's nephew, Mark Hamilton, I leave the Copperas House and everything appertaining to its upkeep, since he is the only person to have shown any interest in it.' There was a sharp intake of breath from Sebastian but the solicitor ignored it and went on, 'To my children, Sebastian and Charlotte, I leave nothing at all, since they have been nothing but a disappointment to me. Sebastian persistently refused to have anything to do with the business that should rightly have been his inheritance, choosing instead to join the Army and Charlotte has disgraced herself by eloping with a man of what I will only call questionable morals.' He looked up again. 'My client was not in a mood to be argued with when he gave me his instructions,' he said apologetically. 'These were his exact words and his express wishes.'

357

'Good, because I didn't want the damn business. I think we should sell it,' Sebastian said.

'I'm afraid that isn't up to you, sir,' the solicitor said in his dry, bookish voice. 'The business now belongs to your cousin, Mr Mark Hamilton. It's his decision whether to keep it or sell it.'

'The devil it is!' Sebastian muttered.

The solicitor ignored him and turned to Charlotte. 'I'm afraid the same thing applies to you, my dear. You have no say at all in what happens to your father's business.'

Charlotte linked her fingers through Richard's and gave Mr Bennet a winning smile. 'It's perfectly all right, Mr Bennet. I'm quite contented with my father's wishes since I already have all I could possibly want. We don't need anything more, do we, Dick?' she looked lovingly up at her husband.

He grinned down at her. 'No, we do all right with the pub an' that,' he replied enigmatically.

Mollie shot him a glance. She rather thought she knew what 'an' that' meant – a continuation of his owling activities, with his wife's all-too-willing assistance. He winked at her, proving her right.

'Sebastian went off in high dudgeon because he'd been cut out of his father's will,' Beatrice said thoughtfully, as she sat by the fire with Mark and Mollie after everybody had left. 'I don't think he realised that the Copperas House is something of a poisoned chalice, isn't it, Mark? From what I understand it isn't exactly thriving, and hasn't been for some years.'

Mark smiled. 'Only because there has been more taken out than put in.'

Beatrice nodded. 'My husband was an incurable gambler.' She took a deep breath. 'Well, that's all over now. Perhaps you'll be able to make it pay.'

'I think I shall, in time. But first, there are repairs and improvements to be made.' He leaned forward in his chair,

358

rubbing his hands together. 'Oh, I can see a great future, once we get the business back on its feet.'

Beatrice turned to Mollie. 'I hope you and Mark won't think of leaving Cliff House when you are married, my dear. There is plenty of room for you to have your own wing and it would be a great comfort to me to know that you were here.'

'Thank you, Beatrice.' Mollie, curled up at Mark's side, looked up at him. 'I think we should like that very much, wouldn't we, Mark?'

Beatrice watched them for several minutes, then a smile spread across her face. 'I'm sure when my husband left Mark the Copperas House he had no notion that he planned to marry you, Mollie. I suppose in a way you might call it poetic justice.'

Mark dropped a kiss on the top of Mollie's head. 'Yes, I suppose you could call it that. And where better for us to bring up our children than in the house that your great-great-grandfather built, my love.'

Mollie looked blank. 'My great-great-grandfather?'

'Of course.' Beatrice clapped her hands delightedly. 'You belong here, Mollie. Don't you see? This really is your rightful place.'